"Some 50 million Americans share a belief that these are the last days. Contemporary life and its myriad contradictions exhibit all the signs and symbols that herald the end of the world."

—"Waiting for Armageddon"
The New York Times Book Review

The Blood of the Lamb

"Fascinating. Monteleone's prose is a notch or two more sophisticated than that of Tom Clancy. He keeps the action moving and incorporates a little sex and a lot of violence. [*The Blood of the Lamb* is] hard to stop reading

—*The Star-Democrat*
Easton, Maryland

"Monteleone gives the idea of genetic cloning a new twist in this apocalyptic thriller set in the final days of the 20th century. A riveting story about evil done in the purported service of good."

—*The Birmingham News*, Birmingham, Alabama;
The Sunday Record, Hackensack, New Jersey;
The Sun, Lowell Massachusetts

"A real page-turner."

—*Booklist*

"A swirling, satisfying read of moral proportions that will grip the reader's attention until the very end. It reverberates with subjects in today's news, and is a chilling prediction of things to come. In short, I found it probing and dead-on accurate, a page-turner too entertaining and too frightening to put down."

—Ken Eulo
author of *The House of Caine*

"Thomas F. Monteleone is a powerful writer and in *The Blood of the Lamb* he has produced a powerful, disturbing, and ultimately wonderful book. It should be on everybody's must-read list this year."

—Warren Murphy
author of *Grandmaster*

"A multi-viewpoint thriller with Vatican assassins and secret motives and cloak and dagger galore, *The Blood of the Lamb* is a good page turner.

—*The Midwest Book Review*

"You've probably been wondering what would happen if they cloned Jesus. I certainly have.

"[In *The Blood of the Lamb*] Mr. Monteleone skewers the Catholic Church and American televangelists with equal cynicism, portraying each as manipulative and unprincipled."

—*The Atlanta Journal-Constitution*
Atlanta, Georgia

THE BLOOD OF THE LAMB

THOMAS F. MONTELEONE

TOR

A TOM DOHERTY ASSOCIATES BOOK
NEW YORK

This is a work of fiction. All the characters and events portrayed in this book are fictitious, and any resemblance to real people or events is purely coincidental.

THE BLOOD OF THE LAMB

Copyright © 1992 by Thomas F. Monteleone

Cover art by Dave Fishman

A Tor Book
Published by Tom Doherty Associates, Inc.
175 Fifth Avenue
New York, N.Y. 10010

Tor ® is a registered trademark of Tom Doherty Associates, Inc.

ISBN: 0-812-52222-2
Library of Congress Catalog Card Number: 92-3604

First edition: July 1992
First mass market printing: April 1993

Printed in the United States of America

0 9 8 7 6 5 4 3 2 1

This one is for
the memory of
Mario Martin Monteleone,
my father,
who gave me the power
to dream.
Thanks, Dad. I'll always love you.

"And I say unto thee, thou art Peter, and upon this rock I will build my church; and the gates of hell shall not prevail against it."

—Matthew 16:18

BOOK ONE

"And the word was made flesh, and dwelt among us, and we beheld his glory, the glory as of the only begotten of the Father."

—John 1:14

PROLOGUE

Rome, Italy—Ponti
August 8, 1967

In the five years he had been working for Father Francesco, Amerigo Ponti had been requested to do many strange and secretive tasks.

But nothing had resembled this latest assignment.

First, the old Jesuit had obtained special passes so that Amerigo could work at the Pontifical Academy of Sciences—a small miracle when one considered the immense web of Vatican bureaucracy. But in a more amazing display of power and influence, Father Francesco had given him the extra-special photo-ID badge which proclaimed Amerigo Ponti to be a member of the Pope's *Commissione Straordinaria*.

The Special Commission.

Everyone in Rome had been wondering about the Commission. What made it so "special"? Where were the men who comprised its ranks? The rumor mill, which normally ground loud and long in the Holy City, remained curiously quiet. The true nature of the Special Commission was locked in a vault of total secrecy. The Commission was getting ready to begin its work—whatever that might be—this very morning in the lower levels of a building of the Academy of Sciences.

And an intense young Jesuit, Amerigo Ponti, had been handed a skeleton key! He would know everything about the mysterious Commission. Amerigo was struck once again by

just how powerful and influential Father Francesco was—
especially for someone not yet forty. Did he have a direct line
to the Pope himself?

Incredible!

It was eight o'clock on a bright summer morning. Amerigo
walked through the Vatican gardens, heading east with a firm
athletic stride, entering the Academy through the employees'
entrance. A guard sitting by a turnstile idly glanced at
Amerigo's workpass and waved him on. The tall, handsome
young man was merely one of many workers funneling
through the checkpoint.

His instructions from Father Francesco were simple: enter
the building using your Academy pass and take the elevators
to the basement installation, where another set of turnstiles
would admit only members of the *Commissione*. Show the
guardia there your photo-ID and proceed to the nearest washroom. Inside, in private, open the envelope containing your
final directions.

Simple, he thought. Amerigo patted his breast pocket,
where he'd tucked Francesco's envelope. As he waited for the
elevator, other government workers gathered around him.
None of them could possibly suspect he was on a secret mission for the Society of Jesus! Just the thought made Amerigo
proud. Only five years out of seminary school, and already he
was one of the Society's most trusted soldiers.

The elevator doors opened and he stepped inside with a
handful of men all wearing the plastic-coated badges that
identified them as Commission members. Amerigo tried to
appear calm, disinterested, but his heart had begun racing.
"This is the most important assignment of your life," Father
Francesco had told him. "You must not fail."

And he would not, thought Amerigo. He *could* not.

The doors eased open and everyone filed out, quietly
queueing up for review by two uniformed guards. The line
moved slowly as each Commission member's photo was
scrutinized and name checked against a list on a clipboard.
Amerigo had never seen Vatican security guards take their

jobs so seriously. When his turn came, his heart was beating so fast, he feared the guards would hear it.

The security man reached out, held his badge at an angle to cut down the glare, his gaze shifting from the photo to Amerigo's face, then back down to the badge photo.

"Ponti," the guard said as he checked off a name on the clipboard. *"Bene. Avenzate, presto."*

Nodding as nonchalantly as possible, Amerigo pushed through the stile and headed down the main corridor. Commission workers surged around him. Everyone seemed very familiar with the vast warren of hallways which comprised this lower level of the Academy—a part never seen by the tourists. Amerigo walked straight ahead, firmly and with confidence, as though he too knew what he was about. Inwardly, he grew ever more frantic as he searched for a washroom. Every door along the hallway bore a number followed by a single letter. Was there some code he had not been told?

No, thank God. To his right he spied a door plainly labeled LAVATOIO. Selecting the stall farthest from the door, Amerigo quickly pulled the heavy, manila-stock envelope from his pocket. It was small but sturdy, the sort of envelope that might contain someone's weekly salary. Breaking the wax seal marked with Father Francesco's own signet ring, Amerigo looked inside to find a single typed sheet of paper and a key taped at its bottom.

My God! he thought repeatedly as he read his orders. Unbelievable!

And yet, he *must* believe . . . accept, and obey.

He employed his Jesuit training to remain as calm as possible, accepting his instructions as work in the service of God. After memorizing every word and removing the key, Amerigo dropped the paper into the toilet, where it dissolved immediately upon touching the water.

Leaving the lavatory, he slipped into the main corridor and walked to the designated area. No one took any special notice of him as he sought out Room 009-C. When he found it, he openly produced the key from his pocket and slipped it into the lock. Only if it did not work would he look foolish. Holding his breath, he turned the key.

The tumblers gave way; Amerigo sighed involuntarily as he pushed open the door, stepped through, and closed it quickly behind him. The room had been outfitted as a miniature laboratory, full of chemical glassware and rack-mounted electronics he could not identify. In the center of the room, on a large table, lay a large laminar-flow cabinet. Its triple-paned glass panels and micron-machined edges made it perfectly airtight. Through the glass he saw the object of his mission.

Santa Sindone! thought Amerigo. He made the sign of the cross and approached the table.

He worked quickly and efficiently, and was gone within fifteen minutes.

Later that evening, Amerigo sat at the bar of a discotheque in the heart of the tourist district. He sipped a Coke and tried to look as though he belonged. The music was loud, colored lights flashed in all directions, and the women in their miniskirts and long, straight hair looked more provocative than ever. He felt uncomfortable even sitting in a place like this. The smoke, the noise, and the alcohol were all combining to make him feel ill. This was no place for a soldier of Christ.

He could not believe Father Francesco had chosen a disco as a meeting place.

"Ah, Amerigo," said a familiar voice at his back. "It is good to see you."

Turning on his stool, Amerigo Ponti was surprised at the sight of Father Francesco, towering over him. The priest wore a baggy, double-breasted suit, a white shirt, and a dark tie. Amerigo had never seen Francesco dressed in anything but his clerical collar and vestments. It was startling to see him in street clothes. Francesco was a tall, thin man in his thirties—so young to be so powerful. His cheeks were sallow and gaunt, and his cold blue eyes gave his face a distinctly vulpine aspect. The Jesuit's military brush-cut hair made him look very unstylish despite the suit and tie.

"Good evening, Father. You look . . . different."

The priest smiled briefly, grimly. "You have it?"

Amerigo nodded. "Yes, Father."

"There were no problems? You were not noticed?"

"It was easy! Just as you promised. There was not the slightest suspicion, I assure you." Amerigo was proud to report his success.

Father Francesco nodded. "Good. Good." The bartender drifted by, but the Jesuit sent him away with a practiced wave of the hand.

Amerigo sipped his cola, staring at his boss expectantly.

"Well?" asked Father Francesco.

"Well what, Father?"

"Aren't you going to give it to me?" The priest's voice was hard, cold; his gaze, merciless.

Amerigo felt immediately foolish. Digging into his jacket pocket, he handed a glass vial to his boss.

The Jesuit slipped the container into the breast pocket of his suit without even glancing at it. "You followed the procedures exactly?"

"Of course, Father."

"And you are certain you obtained what I required?"

"I would stake my life on it," said Amerigo.

The priest smiled again, ever so slightly. "Yes, of course." He paused and looked about the club. "Very good, Amerigo. As usual, you have performed well. Come, let us leave this ugly place."

Happy, Amerigo slid from his stool and followed the lean priest to the street. A black Mercedes sedan was waiting at the curb. As Father Francesco opened the back door he motioned to Amerigo. "Come, son. Tonight you can ride with me."

Feelings of pride and honor washed over Amerigo as he climbed into the back seat. His superior was truly pleased with his work! Father Francesco moved into the front passenger seat, next to his driver. Amerigo settled into the plush leather of the rear seat, suddenly noticing another person in the car—a mustachioed man wearing a black suit and Roman collar.

"Amerigo Ponti, this is my friend, Father Masseria."

"Good evening, Father," said Amerigo, smiling at the priest.

"Good-bye, my son," said Masseria.

Amerigo was confused. The Mercedes accelerated away from the curb and he was pushed deeper into his seat. Father Masseria reached into his outer jacket and suddenly there was a 9mm Beretta in his hand, pointed at a space between the young man's eyes.

"Father, I don't underst—"

There was a soft *pffit!* as the gun discharged through its silencer, sending a single slug into the center of Amerigo Ponti's skull. He was dead before the back of his head slammed against the car window.

"*Presto,*" said Father Francesco to his driver. "The docks. We'll dispose of him there."

The driver nodded, accelerating around the nearest corner.

ONE

Brooklyn, New York—Carenza
August 15, 1998

Father Peter Carenza had gotten up early to take a walk through the neighborhood of Bay Ridge while the temperature was still moderate. He was not a lover of hot weather, especially the high-humidity days that marked August in New York City.

As usual, he stopped at Curtis's corner grocery for the *Daily News*. Strangers who spotted the young man dressed in a T-shirt and jogging shorts would never suspect he was a priest. Peter's lean, athletic body was made for playing left field or shooting three-pointers from the top of the key. Only his regular parishioners recognized him as a *padre*.

"Good morning, Father!" said Henry Curtis, a short, stocky man with a carefully trimmed beard, who looked a lot like later portraits of Henry VIII. "I wanted to thank you for helping my wife yesterday."

Peter smiled. "Henry, it was nothing, really."

"Maybe not to you," said the grocer. "But the one day I gotta drive into Jersey . . . that's the day my little Jeanine falls down and cuts her knee! Sixteen stitches they put in her!"

"How's she feeling this morning?" asked Peter as he bent down by the cash register to pull a newspaper from the stack.

"She's gonna be fine. Because you drove her to the hospital so fast, Father. I don't mind tellin' you—you're the best thing that ever happened to this neighborhood."

Peter could feel himself blushing. "Well, thank you, Henry. But I was just doing my job . . ."

Curtis nodded, smiled. "Maybe so, but we can still tell you how much we appreciate you, right?"

Peter chuckled softly, embarrassed, but pleased to know that he had been accepted so readily by the members of the neighborhood, as well as the parish. He did honestly love helping and working with people, and believed that was the most important part of being a parish priest. Father Sobieski warned him not to spread himself too thin, but Peter thrived on the extra projects he'd taken on at Saint Sebastian's.

His parish, just north of the Verrazano Bridge, was a mixed bag of nationalities, ages, colors and incomes, and he liked it that way. The parishioners had accepted him quickly and seemed to trust him. They often commented on his lean, handsome features and his naturally resonant speaking voice. Many times his pastor told him that he was a born leader in the Church, and that he would have a very satisfying vocation within the Archdiocese of New York.

Tucking the paper under one arm, Peter left the grocery and crossed Fourth Avenue to begin his job. He had about fifteen minutes to get down to the ball fields at Dyker Beach Park where he coached the CYO's Pony League baseball team.

The sun was heating up the dusty field when he arrived, but he put the boys through a heavy workout anyway. His team was in first place in the East division and he didn't want to lose any steam with the playoffs coming up next week.

Two hours later, Peter jogged back to the rectory, caught a quick shower and some lunch, and settled back to watch the Yankee game before preparing the Saturday evening Mass.

Ever since the rules had been changed, allowing the requirement for mandatory weekly Mass attendance to be satisfied on Saturday evening as well as by the regular Sunday Masses, the parishioners of Bay Ridge had gradually become more accustomed to the new latitude. In the beginning, the more traditional, and usually older, Catholics continued their Sunday rituals, apparently believing the Saturday Mass somehow not quite acceptable.

To counteract this, Pastor Sobieski began scheduling all Saturday evening Masses with Father Carenza, whose magnetic personality and popular sermons began drawing more and more attendees to the Saturday evening service. Even though Peter didn't want to feel proud or boastful, he knew the move had been a huge success. He couldn't help but notice how the old stone church was filled to standing room on Saturdays. And a lot of the attendees could still be seen on Sunday mornings, unable to break old habits, but so eager to hear Father Carenza speak, that they'd begun going to Mass twice each weekend. Peter knew it was a quiet testament to his popularity in the parish. He never talked about it, tried not to dwell on it, but it was fact, just the same.

Of course, he had mentioned the changes to his friend Dan Ellington, a Jesuit who taught English and Comp Lit at Fordham. Jesuits, acknowledged Peter with a wry smile, were more at home with boastfulness.

And so, that evening, he stood before his congregation, reading the day's Gospel, a passage from Luke, preparing to speak on the theme of friendship. Though he'd showered again before dressing, he was beginning to sweat heavily under the thick linen and wool vestments. Outside, the air was steaming up as the heat of the day radiated from the city's concrete and stone. Brooklyn in late summer was like a tropical rain forest—without the rain and without the forest. The oppressive heat and humidity created a stifling, ovenlike atmosphere. To make things worse, Father Sobieski had announced over breakfast that morning, that the air conditioning in the church had broken down. Although the repair crew would do the best they could, the unit probably would not be fixed until Monday because of that most favorite of excuses—they needed a special part. Peter knew his audience was uncomfortable, yet they all sat watching him expectantly.

Peter never prepared his sermons ahead of time, unlike his colleagues at St. Sebastian's. Even Father Sobieski, who'd been preaching to his flock for almost forty years, still sat down near the end of the week to pen notes and phrases to be issued from the pulpit. Peter had always felt that speaking from notes was somehow counterfeit. He preferred a more spontaneous approach, making his sermons more casual, like unrehearsed conversation. In his earliest days in the seminary's preparatory school, studying Elocution, Debating, and Independent Thinking, he had discovered a natural talent for extemporaneous speaking. He loved it and his audiences seemed to love him for it.

Sometimes, when he was speaking to his parish, he felt like an entertainer, like a stand-up comedian who was ad-libbing his way through the performance of his life. It was a heady, exhilarating experience, like walking a tightrope without a net. It was working right on the edge of his abilities, on the precipice of his next thought. Most of the time, he had no idea what his next words might be, yet the words were always there.

Today was no different. He addressed the sea of faces about the virtues of friendship, of love in its purest sense. He incorporated the myth of Damon and Pythias, the epic adventure of Roland and Oliver, and the legendary bond of Arthur and Lancelot into his sermon, so that it seemed less a preachy lecture than a wonderful narrative. Weaving various mythic and literary elements throughout his message created a marvelously rich tapestry for his audience—a story full of compassion and love and human understanding. When he closed with the words of the Lord about there being "no greater love than that of the man who would lay down his life for his friend," he sensed an undercurrent in the crowd, a just-barely-suppressed urge in them to stand up, en masse, in spontaneous applause.

Peter had moved them with his words, with his resonant, modulated voice. He had transfixed them, every one of them, with his special gift. As he stood there, basking in that briefest of moments in which he could actually feel the power he held over them, he knew he enjoyed it. If this was pride, if it was a sin to feel this way, he could not help himself. Later he would ask God for forgiveness.

After serving Holy Communion, he completed the Mass and stood by the door for the time-honored tradition of shaking hands with his parishioners. Many of them queued up to say a word or two instead of just rushing home. It was another small but obvious indication of his popularity at Saint Sebastian's. As the line finally thinned out, an attractive woman approached him, gently shook his hand, then held on.

"Excuse me, Father Carenza," said Margaret Murphy. He knew her from her attendance at the elementary school PTA meetings. Something about the way she wore her yellow and white cotton dress, the way she applied her cosmetics, imparted to her a very sad, very helpless aspect. Or perhaps it was her eyes that gave her away—she looked disheartened, even fearful, like a small bird that had fallen from its nest.

"I was wondering," she continued, "if I could have a small talk with you . . ."

He looked at his watch automatically. He hoped it didn't seem rude. "Right now?"

"I don't want to impose, Father, but if you have a few minutes . . .? I just don't have the time during the week, and it's so important . . ."

He could not ignore the subtle note of pain in her voice. Though he wanted to go back to the rectory, kick up his feet, drink a cold beer, and just suspend his thinking for a few hours with a movie on Cinemax, he knew his first obligation was to this woman who sought his help.

"It's no problem, Mrs. Murphy," Peter said. "Why don't you meet me over at the rectory? Just give me a few minutes to change out of my vestments."

A small smile, weak and fragile, illuminated her face. "Oh, thank you, Father Carenza. I'll be waiting for you there. Thank you."

Time passed quickly as he sat with Mrs. Murphy in the first-floor study. It was a small room, lined with bookcases.

Several soft-bulb lamps and two well-padded chairs in front
of the desk in the corner made it a comfortable room. It was
a good place to conduct one-on-one counseling sessions with
parishioners, and Peter did not think he intimidated Mrs.
Murphy as he relaxed behind the desk and listened, without
comment, to her tale.

It was a not-uncommon domestic scenario: hard-working
blue-collar husband; overburdened wife trying to keep a clean
house, supervise four children, and still be the passionate
whore in bed. The demands of modern living were often
more than many couples could bear, and Peter knew people
sought release from the pressure in most of the standard
ways.

Rod Murphy had selected a neighborhood bar as his ally
against all the hassles in his world, and was spending more
and more of his free time pounding Budweiser at the hard-
wood. He was a big man who worked as a journeyman elec-
trician for a contractor. His drinking wasn't a problem on the
job yet, but it was sending fault-lines through the foundation
of his marriage, and Margaret was getting very scared. She
told a teary story of late-night arguments fueled by an
unstaunched flow of alcohol.

Peter had listened to semi-hysterical parishioners many
times as they cried out under the impossible weight of their
lives. In almost every instance, he found it best to remain as
silent as possible while they uncapped the lid of their emotions and pain. Only after the demons were revealed could he
successfully deal with them.

After almost an hour, Mrs. Murphy's tale was exhausted.
Peter looked at her lean face, now puffy and red about her
eyes, and reached across the table to her. She let him grasp
her hands like a child might seek the comfort of a parent.

"Oh, Father, I'm sorry. I'm so embarrassed. I had no idea
I would get like this."

He smiled softly, shook his head easily. "Like what? Margaret, please realize that you're just letting yourself be human. We all feel pain, just as we feel joy—that's what sets us
apart from the rest of God's creatures."

Peter tried to imbue his mellow voice with a semi-hypnotic suggestion that everything was going to be fine. Almost instantly the lines of tension in Margaret Murphy's face softened and began to vanish. Although Peter, an orphan raised by the Church, was admittedly not an expert in the dynamics of families, he possessed a keen sense of understanding of the human psyche. And it was not as if he'd never had any affairs of the heart. His interest and involvements with young women before he answered his calling to God had been educational as well as enjoyable. Peter had not grown up in a bubble of parochial glass.

His compassion was an intuitive ability. Coupled with his knack of saying precisely the right thing to a troubled soul, it made him an extremely successful counselor.

He spoke calmly and without the austere tones of a lecture. By asking subtle questions, exercising the gentle, probing skills of a veteran therapist, Peter was able to slowly lead Mrs. Murphy toward her own particular conclusions. If allowed to discover for herself insights into her complex problems, he knew, she would be more willing to attempt solutions. It's always easier to act on your own beliefs than what others try to force upon you.

"Father Carenza, I don't know how to thank you," said Mrs. Murphy when she stood up to leave.

"You already have," he said.

"So much wisdom for someone so young. It's hard to believe." She looked at him with glistening, doe's eyes. It was a gaze that combined the elements of respectful child, infatuated girl, and lustful woman. Peter sensed this conflux of emotions emanating from the woman and was confused by the feelings stirred within himself.

He blinked, then looked away for a moment and broke the mini-spell which had formed between them. Margaret Murphy must have sensed it too, because she also blinked before flushing slightly and raising a delicate finger to her temple.

"Please stay in touch, Margaret," Peter said. "And remember that you're welcome here anytime."

"I will, Father. You don't know how much better you've

made me feel. I think I understand what's going wrong, and I think I can see some ways to make it better."

"Good. Good," said Peter as he glided out from behind the desk and escorted her to the door.

After he'd watched her walk slowly down the shrubbery-lined path to the sidewalk, Peter closed the front door slowly. He was feeling good about himself, aglow with the knowledge that he'd helped another person desperately in need. Turning into the main hall, he headed for the kitchen. Despite the gradual setting of the sun, it was still muggy and hot, and a cold beer sounded very good just about then.

When he opened the refrigerator and found nothing but a few cans of Diet Pepsi, he could only shake his head and smile. Wasn't that always the way? How many times had he looked in the Frigidaire for something else, reaching around six or seven bottles of Beck's Dark or Michelob, ignoring them?

But now, tonight, nothing but a cold, dark beer was going to do it for him. Checking his watch, he saw he still had enough time to run up to the deli on 90th Street and get a six-pack before the nine o'clock movie started. Peter quickly changed into shorts, T-shirt, and his high-topped Reeboks, and headed for the store.

Shadows along the side streets grew longer and deeper as he walked toward the main intersection at Fourth Avenue. With no large pockets in his shorts, Peter carried his keys and several ten-dollar bills in a small, zippered waist-pouch. Summer sounds of rock music, crying babies, and blaring televisions poured forth from open windows. The heavy rectangles of air conditioners droned and sweated into the streets. Everything blended together in a pleasant mix, a vital, living neighborhood. Peter ran a hand through his dark brown hair, pushing the damp strands away from his eyes. So damned humid. That beer was going to taste good—no question.

He'd just passed a narrow alley when he heard the voice at his back. "Okay, hold it right there, you yuppie-muthahfuckah . . ." Nasal, whiny, young. Peter kept on walking, pretending not to have heard anything.

Suddenly, long bony fingers were digging into his left shoulder. A vicious tug spun him around so quickly, he almost lost his balance.

"Hey, you deaf or sumpin'?! I'm talkin'-a *you*, asshole!"

In the half light of the fast-approaching dusk, Peter came face-to-face with a black boy of perhaps sixteen. He wore a bandanna around his head like a samurai warrior. A gold tooth accented his inappropriate smile. A scraggly green tank top revealed the muscles of his power-forward torso; the knees were ripped out of his jeans. The oven-glazed look in his eyes suggested a mind racing out of control on some kind of drug.

Slowly the boy raised his right hand and pointed a small-caliber gun at Peter's face. "Back up, man," he said. "This way . . ."

He indicated that Peter slip into the alley, into the narrow shadows and the smells of garbage baking in plastic trash bags.

"What do you want?" asked Peter as he complied, carefully moving off the main sidewalk, feeling the alley wall against his back.

"Now give it up, chump . . ." the kid said, still smiling. He was twitchy, jittery. All his movements were sharp and tight. He looked unstable as all hell.

Peter felt his heart begin to pump harder than he'd thought possible. Even in the gathering darkness he could see the gun clearly, and though it had a small-bore barrel, its muzzle seemed as wide as a well and twice as black. It was like staring into a bottomless pit, a place where, once you fell in, only death survived.

Reaching into his waist-pouch, Peter produced the keys and the two bills. "That's all I've got, man," he said softly. "Here, take it. You're welcome to it . . ."

With feline quickness the boy moved, snatching the money from Peter in an eyeflash. The gun bobbed and weaved in the kid's hand but was still pointed at Peter. He wanted to do something—jump, roll, run—anything, but he was rooted to the sidewalk. He felt paralyzed and helpless. It was a terrifying feeling with which his normally analytical mind could not cope.

"Hey, man, what the fuck is this!" The boy's smile flowed into an angry scowl. "Twenny bucks?! That ain' shit, man! Where's the rest of your money?"

"I'm sorry, but that's all I have. Honest."

"Bullshit! You gots money in your shoe, man. Take off them shoes."

"Please, really," said Peter. "I really don't. Why don't you just—"

"Take 'em off, you asshole!" The kid almost screamed out the words.

Peter slowly began unlacing his high-tops. Couldn't anybody hear this clown? Couldn't anybody see what was happening?

"Okay, dump 'em out!" said his attacker once he'd taken off both white leather shoes.

"There's nothing in them," said Peter. "Look . . ."

"Goddammit! Take off you fuckin' socks! *That's* where you got it!"

Peter pulled off the white cotton gym-socks, trying to keep an eye on the obviously very frustrated boy. His plan was not going well and he was confused and angry. When he saw no extra cash concealed in the socks, his whole body went rigid with rage.

"You just fuckin' wiff me, man. I'm gonna shoot your chump-ass!"

Pressing himself against the wall, Peter felt the heat of its rough brick through his T-shirt. "Please," he said. "Look, take the money, please . . ."

The boy scowled and raised the gun, his arm rigidly outstretched. "Man, *fuck* you! You *dead!*"

Peter heard a voice cry out, uttering a single, piercing syllable—*"No!"* In a timeless instant, he realized it was his voice, shrieking into the darkness, surrendering to some atavistic impulse. He heard the sound as though in a vast tunnel, and the rolling echo of his scream was as terrifying as the empty eye of the gun.

He saw the ropy muscles tensing in the boy's thick forearm, and powerful fingers. In another instant, the gun's trigger would click back and the hammer would trip.

Instinctively, he raised his hands to his face.

A brilliant flash of light, like the furious blue explosion of a high-voltage discharge, filled the alley. Like a photograph, the image of the boy's face—blue-black flesh shiny with sweat, eyes swollen with a primeval fear—sizzled and popped in Peter's mind.

The gun dropped from the boy's charred hand, clattering to the asphalt. The air was charged with the foul scent of ozone and seared flesh. What had, moments before, been a human being was now a smoking column of greasy charcoal.

Stunned, Peter watched the thing totter slowly from side to side before falling forward at his feet.

His lungs filled with the heavy stench of burned fat; he gagged. Backing away from the burned lump, Peter tried to rationalize what he'd seen.

Lightning.

The mugger had been struck by lightning.

But the bolt had come from Peter Carenza's hands . . .

TWO

Rome, Italy—Sister Etienne
August 15, 1998

It was a typically warm, summer morning in the cloistered Convent of the Sisters of Poor Clares. After a meager breakfast, the nuns were allowed a half hour of private meditation in the convent gardens. Sister Etienne, a slender, healthy woman of almost fifty, exited the dining hall and crossed under the Roman stone arch that marked the entrance to the central atrium of the convent.

The very large quadrangle was formed by the walls of four separate buildings. It overflowed with shady oaks and dogwoods in late blossom. The garden was crisscrossed with many brick-laden paths, all lined by mulched flower and shrubbery beds. The dusty smell of boxwood and pachysandra commingled with the sweet scent of begonias, snapdragons, and honeysuckle. Sister Etienne loved this garden and felt especially at peace during her morning walks through its summery greenery.

Glory be to God, she thought, as she passed beneath a thick-bowed oak. That poem by the American, Kilmer, was perfectly true. She had lived in the Convent almost all of her life, had left it only twice since coming to the Sisters of Poor Clares at the age of twelve, but Sister Etienne knew that no other part of the world could be as beautiful as the convent garden. She had been born Angelina Pettinaro, daughter of a Calabrian fisherman who had been too poor to provide for his seven children after his wife died of cancer. To make things easier, her older brother joined the Italian National Guard and Angelina entered the sisterhood.

Since she'd always been a deeply spiritual girl, she found the life of a nun much to her liking. She preferred the convent's order and discipline to the uncharted chaos of the modern world, and she absolutely loved the almost perfect opportunity to serve her Lord God in any fashion He deemed. Sister Etienne believed she had demonstrated her absolute loyalty to the Church and her faith in the wishes of God many times in her life—especially when Abbess Victorianna had selected her to work with Father Francesco and Cardinal Lareggia.

The Abbess had always been so proud of her! Etienne once overheard her superior speaking to a group of visitors; the Abbess had singled Etienne out as one of the most devout members of the entire Order.

Now, now, she thought. You're woolgathering again! This time is supposed to be spent in meditation and private prayer.

To waste it upon prideful thoughts was sinful at least. Etienne paused before a bed of roses, lifting a soft yellow bud from amidst thorny stems and leaves. Unexpectedly, the flower broke loose, as if it had been waiting to fall into her hand. Holding it up to the soft, morning light, she could see the bud's intricate structure through its translucent petals. The beauty of a rose held all the proof she needed to verify the miraculous power and majesty of the Lord. Etienne often used such examples from nature to inspire her private devotions and prayers.

Staring into the depths of the rose, trying to follow the convolutions of each whorled petal, she perceived a new complexity in its design. It was like staring into the center of a figure-ground illustration, a deliberately conceived pattern of optical illusion. The image swam before her eyes as though trying to change into something else. She felt a wave of nausea crash over her in the next instant, a sensation of hideous sickness worse than she'd ever thought possible. Something burned and clawed at the inside of her stomach; her skull felt as though it were expanding, like a balloon about to rupture. She felt herself falling but the pain of the impact was far away, detached, as though it belonged to someone else.

What was happening to her?

She tried to stand up straight, but disequilibrium kept her pinned to the ground, weaving on her knees. A low keening sounded deep within her skull, growing louder, changing into a dull buzz—a hypnotic sound that blotted out all other sensation. Etienne stared trancelike into the depths of the rose. The buzzing reached a new height—nothing existed in the world other than the rose and the buzzing in her head. Surely the bones of her skull would soon fracture, exploding like a grenade and spraying the gray-white mucus of her brain everywhere. Etienne waited for the image to become real.

Suddenly her nostrils burned with the sweet, acrid pungency of the grave. A dark, roiling stench, it was the smell of the end of all things, of decay and corruption, of consummate foulness. It was the stuff of dread and repulsion and all that was, or ever could be, *evil*. She felt a chasm opening under her soul as the fetor became a windstorm in the darkness below her. The rose and the garden and the rest of the world rushed away in all directions with dizzying speed. Etienne floated in the stark nothingness at the end of time.

She wanted to scream but it was impossible. Paralyzed and helpless, she slowly twisted and writhed under the foul breath of pure malevolence. Convinced she had gone mad, or worse, had perished from a sudden stroke or coronary, and, despite her faith, had been thrust into the deepest pit of hell, Etienne finally surrendered her soul, in desperation opening herself to God.

And the Vision came to her.

Gathering itself, taking substance, the pieces of the image came together like the video of a shattering stained-glass window played in slow-motion and reverse. Etienne watched the horror unfold like the blossom of the blackest rose . . .

THREE

Brooklyn, New York—Sobieski
August 15, 1998

Father Sobieski had never seen Father Carenza look so upset.

Stan Sobieski had seen the vacant, terrified look in more than one priest's eyes—the look of a cleric who suddenly lost his faith—but his instincts told him this wasn't the problem at hand. After more than forty years in the priesthood, you sensed such things . . . and he'd been told to watch this priest carefully.

Carenza had come to Sobieski's room wanting to talk, but

had said nothing yet. Stan looked at him as he sat fidgeting in front of his desk. The young priest looked away nervously. There was no denying how handsome he was. His rugged good looks certainly didn't hurt his popularity with the parishioners. They all loved his easy, engaging smile—a smile conspicuously absent right now.

"Let me start with a question," said the young priest. "Have you ever . . . I mean, have you ever heard . . . of a priest, well, actually *killing* someone?"

"What?!" Sobieski had been trained to expect anything, but he couldn't conceal his surprise. "Good Lord, Peter, what're you talking about?"

Peter Carenza looked down at his hands; he held them palms-up, as though seeing them for the first time, the way an infant slowly becomes aware of itself. "It was self-defense, I think."

Sobieski looked at the young man until he finally raised his head, and eye contact was reestablished. "Peter, are you trying to tell me that you . . . you killed a man?"

"I . . . I think so." Father Carenza again looked at his hands, slowly buried his face in them.

My God! This was crazy, thought Sobieski.

"Do you want to make a confession, Father?" Sobieski tried to sound calm and professional, but the quaver in his voice betrayed him.

Peter shook his head slowly. "No. No confession."

"Well, what then? I'm listening . . ."

Carenza paused, looked out the window, then back at him. "Maybe I'm going about this wrong. Let me start over."

Sobieski watched him swallow with difficulty. There was a patina of sweat on his forehead. Such a dear man. It was hard to see him twist and suffer so.

"Before you do," said Sobieski, "would you like a small taste of something? I've got some brandy in my cabinet . . ."

Father Carenza looked at him, nodded. "Yes, I think I could use a drink. Thank you, Father."

Sobieski moved from behind the desk to the small oak cabinet next to his television. From within it, he produced a decanter and two snifters. Pouring expertly, he proffered one of the crystal goblets to the young priest, kept the second for himself.

Father Carenza sipped from his glass tentatively, allowing the dark, amber liquid to scorch a path down his throat. He repeated the maneuver, then looked Sobieski in the eye.

Stan smiled benignly. "Peter, let's stop beating around the bush, all right?"

"Father, I'm sorry," interrupted Carenza. "But you have to believe me when I tell you . . . this is crazier than *any*thing you've ever heard."

Stan leaned forward, studying Carenza. He was very agitated, fearful, losing control. Sobieski spoke as calmly as possible. "It can't be as bad as all that."

"Can't be as bad . . .?" Peter shook his head. "I don't know . . . I'm sorry, Father—but you're going to think I've lost my mind."

Sobieski tried to smile, did a half-assed job of it. "No, I won't. Trust me, Peter. But for God's sake, would you please tell me what happened?" Sobieski drained the rest of his brandy. Its spreading warmth seemed to give him strength. Alcohol was becoming more of a need for him than he cared to admit.

Father Carenza drew in a breath, exhaled slowly. "All right, then, listen . . ."

Haltingly, Father Carenza recounted his walk to the deli, the mugger, and . . . the disaster.

When he'd finished, he looked spent, exhausted, overwhelmed. His breath came in short gasps.

Sobieski wasn't sure if it was the alcohol or his training or something else, but he felt oddly numb.

"You say it was like a . . . a blue fire?"

Peter nodded.

"Lightning? Could he have been struck by lightning? They say lightning can do funny things . . ."

Peter frowned, shook his head. "Do 'they say' it can jump from your hands?"

Sobieski felt foolish, looked away from his charge. There

was no doubt that the younger priest believed what he was saying. Judging from his apparent emotional state, a hoax was out of the question.

"Tell me, Peter, is the ... *body* still there?"

Father Carenza massaged his temples slowly, keeping his eyes tightly shut. "I don't know. I guess it is. I kind of panicked. I just ran back here as fast as I could. I had to talk to somebody right away."

"Perhaps we should go back ..." said Sobieski.

Peter looked up at him sharply. "You mean back to the alley?"

"Yes."

"God, I don't know if I can."

"It might be best," Sobieski said. Actually it was probably the only way he could verify what happened. He had no great desire to see the poor bastard, but it was necessary. His superiors would ask for proof.

"What was it, Father Sobieski? If that was a miracle, it's the strangest one I ever heard of."

Stan Sobieski was not certain if there was an answer to that question. He felt inadequate, unable to ease Carenza's despair, and hated himself for lapsing into homilies when the man needed trenchant psychological insight and honest support.

He felt compelled to say something, anything. "Father, we have no way of understanding the ways of God. But if He has chosen you to witness or perform a miracle, even if it's something we might find distasteful or even horrible, then you must simply bear up and accept what God asks of you. It is a responsibility to the Lord, and if necessary you must carry it, like a cruel cross, for the rest of your days."

The young priest looked up at him, pausing for a moment. "But why?"

"Peter, if this really happened—"

"What do you mean 'if'?! You still don't believe me, do you?"

Carenza pushed back his chair, stood up and turned to leave.

"Father, where're you going?"

"You wanted to see proof, didn't you? All right then, let's go. Right now!"

Peter none-too-gently tugged Sobieski from his chair. Well, he'd told Carenza to put up or shut up.

God help me, Sobieski thought. God help us all.

FOUR

Brooklyn, New York—Windsor
August 15, 1998

How did that old song go?

Another Saturday night and I ain't got nobody, I got some money cuz I just got paid . . .

Well, at least the first part was right. Working weekends was such a locked-in part of her job, Marion Windsor *never* got much time off for a regular old Friday or Saturday night date. As far as the money went, it seemed like she was always scrimping for lunch money by the end of the pay period. Even though her television journalist's job paid pretty damned well, she had a lot of expenses because, more than anything else, she was single and living in Manhattan.

Marion smiled to herself as she drove toward the Bay Ridge precinct house on Fourth Avenue. At thirty years old, she knew, she was reaching the age where the timing of certain career moves was critical. Every local TV reporter wanted to "go national" on one of the networks or cable channels. Since early in the decade cable news's profile had risen. It still wasn't as glamorous as the networks, but national exposure was national exposure.

And, even if Marion didn't want to admit it, as a woman

on the Tube, she had to "give good camera." Old ideas died hard, and despite the prevalence of female reporters and anchorwomen, damned few had any wrinkles or flaws. Of course the men could still be gray, bald, liver-spotted, or dewlapped.

It wasn't fair, but that's the way the game was played.

All humility aside, Marion knew she was a good-looking woman, and if network slots were assigned purely on looks, she figured she'd have as good a chance as anybody. Her taste in clothes was neither trendy nor flashy, but she wasn't a frump. She could be comfortable in a pair of jeans or a suit from Saks. Her auburn hair and sea-green eyes warmed up any television monitor and the alto timbre of her voice carried just the right blend of wonder and expertise. Since getting the job at WPIX five years ago, she'd become popular with the viewers and had steadily built a reputation among her colleagues as a thorough investigator. Her bosses soon realized they were wasting intelligence and resourcefulness by sending her out to cover the Boat Show at Madison Square Garden or the St. Patrick's Day parade.

Oddly, Marion discovered she had a knack for getting past the smooth surface of a story. She could pry the lid off a news piece the way you'd open up an old watch to see how it worked. Her big break came when she got the chance to check out a scam involving city purchasing agents and bogus vendors. Her initial story led to a week-long special assignment that unveiled corruption in other shadowy corners of city government. The story was nominated for several awards, and though she didn't win, Marion knew she'd "made her bones" in the industry. She was a Member of the Club, and people took her seriously.

Her beat was Brooklyn. Gradually she'd focused in on the crime stories that bubbled out of that borough, and she soon became a regular face in the crowds at all the Brooklyn precinct houses. Using her intelligence and natural charm, she established contacts and confidants at most of the stations. She had a reputation for being a fair and honest reporter, so a lot of the cops weren't afraid to tell her things she needed to give her stories the depth and reality that made them so distinctive.

Damn, I'm good, she thought as she parked her Mazda RX-7 in the back lot of the 72nd Precinct station. Smiling to herself, she gathered up her mini-camcorder and adjusted the sound levels on her body-mike before going in the back door, looking for Corporal Binderman.

"Marion!" came a familiar voice.

Elbowing her way through the lobby which was, as usual for a Saturday night, filled with every type you could think of, she worked her way to the dispatch desk. Freddie Binderman, all two hundred fifty pounds of him, sat before his radio consoles, smiling expectantly.

"Hi, Freddie, what've you got for me?"

Freddie moved a large McDonald's vanilla shake to the far corner of his desk in a half-assed attempt to hide it. "Gee, Marion, you sure do look nice tonight . . ."

"Why thank you," she said, trying to mask her impatience. Twenty minutes ago, he'd called her with a tip on what might be an interesting story. He wouldn't give her any details— other than that it was "pretty weird"—and by now her curiosity was raging.

Freddie's unflagging infatuation with her only complicated the situation. Several times he'd actually worked up enough courage to ask her out, and once she'd accepted a lunch date, back in early spring. It had been a mistake. Freddie had taken it as a sign she wanted to get involved with him romantically, and she'd had a hell of time getting out of the situation without ruining the professional side of the relationship.

Freddie continued to just stare at her while the noise and color of the precinct whirled around them. This was no good; she had a job to do.

"Uh, Freddie . . . what's going on out there?"

He grinned self-consciously. "Sorry, Marion. Here . . ." He handed her a piece of paper with an address on it. "Came in just before I called ya. A kid said he saw a jogger gettin' mugged, and the guy got hit by lightnin'."

"What? *Who* got hit by lightning?" She glanced at the address—it would be easy to find.

"The mugger. Our blue-n-white's on the way now. I heard 'em on the radio, callin' for a meat wagon." Freddie took a pull off the double straws in his vanilla shake. "The guy must be a real crispy critter from what the kid said . . ."

Marion grimaced, nodded. "Freddie, your descriptive powers are stunning."

"Really? Do you really mean it, Marion?"

"Corporal, you're incredible, you know that?" She smiled and waved good-bye. "I'll let you know how it turns out."

"You kiddin'? Hey? I'll be watchin' y' on the news tonight. I'll see for myself."

Quickly she jumped into her Mazda and cut through the back streets to the scene of the incident. She'd already lost a lot of time, and she hoped she hadn't missed all the action. Turning the final corner, she eased her RX-7 up to the nearest curb and jumped out. Apparently the ambulance hadn't arrived yet—a good sign as far as she was concerned. A rim of spectators defined the entrance to the alley, and as soon as some of them recognized her and her equipment, they began forming a path for her.

When she reached the innermost circle, she saw a patrolman kneeling by an odd-looking, blackened lump. He was covering it with a blanket. The other cop was kneeling, talking to a Latino boy of perhaps ten or eleven. Adjusting the gain on the directional mike, Marion keyed on the mini-camcorder and listened to the interrogation through her headphones. The reception wasn't the best, but she could still hear every word.

". . . and I was just cutting through the alley, honest, Officer."

"All right, kid. Right. Just tell me what you saw, okay."

"It was getting dark. I heard a guy screaming and yelling, so I stopped an' turned around to run."

"Why?"

"The guy sounded real angry, man. You know—mean and shit."

The cop nodded. "Oh yeah, right. Mean and shit. Okay, so what happened? What did you see? You said you saw it happen."

"I did! I did see it! I was hiding behind those trash cans—right back there.

"He was holding a gun on this guy, this guy in gym shorts. The dude with the gun, everybody in the neighborhood called him Venus, man. I don't know his real name. Anyway, he was all 'based-up, man, I could tell."

The officer nodded, wrote down a few words on his notepad.

"Then what happened?"

"Venus said he'd shoot him if he didn't give him his money, and the guy didn't have any, see, so I knew he was going to get shot." The boy paused to rub his nose nervously. "I never saw somebody get shot before . . ."

"C'mon, kid, out with it. Did you see anything or not?"

"I saw it, man. Venus sticks the gun in the other guy's face! All of a sudden I see lightning bolts! They come out of his hands and *zap*! that crazy mother is gone, man . . ."

The boy seemed to be staring through the brick wall of the alley, as though witnessing the scene all over again. Something about the way he talked compelled Marion to believe him. Marion talked to people all the time in her business. You got to know when they were lying and when they weren't.

This kid was telling the truth—at least as he knew it.

"Lightning bolts, huh?" The cop closed his notebook, shook his head and smiled. "Yeah, right, kid . . ."

"Hey, man, it's the truth!"

The cop stood and looked at his partner. "We ain't gonna get anything else. I'm gettin' fairy tales here . . ."

The other cop nodded, frowned knowingly. "Where the hell's that ambulance? Good thing this guy doesn't really need it."

The boy tugged at the officer's sleeve. "Ain't no fairy tale, man. That dude stood there kinda smokin' for a second or two, and then he fell over. Pieces breakin' off and shit. Just like you guys found him. I swear."

"Sure, kid. I'll put it in my report . . ."

Marion's pulse started to jump as she heard the wail of the ambulance as it wheeled around the corner. Doors opened, slammed shut as paramedics rushed into the alley.

"Jesus Christ, what's *that*?" asked the first one to peek under the blanket.

"That's the victim," said the first cop. "Hit by lightning, I figure."

The paramedic, a young red-haired kid of maybe twenty-two, shook his head. "I don't know, Jack. I seen lightning victims, and none of 'em ever looked like that."

The officer shrugged and lifted his cap to absently scratch his scalp. It was like a signal to clear the area; the paramedics began to gingerly wrap up the remains, and the officers started dispersing the crowd, which had been, Marion noticed, uncharacteristically silent.

"Okay, show's over, folks," said the cop who'd been interrogating the boy.

"Aren't you going to ask him what happened to the mugging victim?" asked Marion.

The cop, whose silver badge announced his last name as Jaskulski, looked at her, suddenly recognizing her. "Miz Windsor, how ya doin'?"

"Well, aren't you?" she persisted.

Jaskulski grinned lopsidedly, then flashed a glance at her mini-camcorder. "Hey, look, I don't tell you how to do your job."

Marion turned off her equipment. "All right, Officer. Off the record: what do you think happened here?"

He shrugged. "Search me. That's the truth."

"Do you think there *was* a mugging victim?"

"Look, I don't know. But I can tell you one thing, Miz Windsor—if there was, he sure as hell didn't have any lightnin' bolts comin' outta his hands."

The paramedics eased past them, carrying the lump of charcoal on their collapsible gurney. Marion could not ignore the still-heavy scent of seared flesh.

"Well, I gotta get back to work," said Jaskulski. "It was nice meetin' ya, Miz Windsor. I catch you whenever I can."

"Thank you," she said absently, switching her equipment back on just in time to track the gurney being loaded into the rear of the ambulance. Beyond the vehicle, just coming into the picture, were two priests in long black cassocks and white Roman collars. One looked to be in his late sixties; the other was broad-shouldered, young, and handsome.

"You're a little late for the last rites, Fathers," said the ambulance driver as he climbed into the cab.

"Wait!" said the younger priest, the one with thick dark hair and penetrating dark eyes. He looked somewhat distraught. Despite his occupation, Marion found herself extremely attracted to him. Hormones . . .

The paramedic in the shotgun seat looked back. "Yeah, Father, what can we do for you?"

"Someone called us," said the young priest. "For extreme unction. Can you give us just a minute with the victim?"

The paramedics exchanged what-the-hell glances and the driver jumped out to reopen the rear doors. "Okay, Father, but you ain't gonna like this one . . ."

Lifting the sheet, the younger priest appeared to be displaying the remains to his older colleague. They exchanged a few words, but Marion was too distant to hear; she wondered if her directional mike was getting anything coherent. After a moment, the younger priest muttered a few words of prayer and made the sign of the cross over what had once been a human being. The entire scene hadn't taken more than a minute or two to play out, but she could not help but notice how utterly shaken the older priest now appeared to be.

Something very unusual was going on, Marion thought.

The paramedics closed their vehicle and drove off. The two priests stood and watched it disappear around the corner, then walked off into the dusky shadows. Strange. Very strange.

Turning around, Marion was surprised to see the witness, the Latino boy, still standing in the alleyway. His dark bangs hung almost in his eyes, which were large and round, almost too large for his narrow little face. He was looking at Marion with a combination of suspicion and admiration.

"Hi," she said, letting her mini-camcorder roll.

"I seen you on the television," the boy said.

"What's your name?" Marion smiled, took a few steps closer to him. The autofocus on her camera whirred softly, capturing a nice image of the waif's face.

"Esteban."

"That's a pretty name," she said, pausing for a moment, then: "Did you really see what you told that policeman?"

Esteban nodded.

"What happened to the man who did it? The man who made the lightning?"

"He got scared. He ran away."

"Oh, I see." Marion reached up to stop tape.

"But he came back," Esteban continued.

"What? What do you mean? He was *here*? When?" Her pulse was jumping again. Marion had learned to trust her instincts, her somatic senses. Her body was telling her she might be on to something.

"Just before the ambulance left. I saw him right back there." Esteban pointed to the curb behind her.

"There wasn't anybody there except those two priests," she said, trying to fit all the pieces together in her mind.

"That was him," said the boy. "The priest. The young one."

"Are you sure?"

"Oh yeah," said Esteban. "He had different clothes on, but it was him. The dude stuck that gun in his face and *zap*!"

"Zap?" she asked cautiously.

Esteban smiled. "Yeah, the padre puts up his hands and Venus is one crispy critter . . ."

FIVE

Brooklyn, New York—Carenza
August 16, 1998

Peter spent the next day trying to go about his routine duties, trying not to think about the killing.

Impossible.

Saying morning Mass, shopping at the neighborhood grocery, chairing the monthly Cub Scout meeting, watching a ballgame . . . no matter what he tried to do, thoughts of the killing intruded.

He wished he could reach Daniel . . .

Father Sobieski had referred to the job of a priest as sometimes a cruel cross to bear. Peter shook his head slowly. How correct his pastor had been . . . Peter was going nuts. And Sobieski was acting strange, too. Ever since Peter had taken him to the ambulance, the old priest had shied away from him, and he wasn't making any effort to help him through this whole crazy mess. This morning, Sobieski had informed everyone in the rectory he was taking the day off to visit a sister in New Haven who had been taken suddenly to the hospital.

The only person with whom Peter had shared everything seemed to be deserting him.

Peter couldn't sleep or eat, couldn't listen to others' conversations; he had no patience with anything or anyone. He could not even pray without being driven to distraction by the images repeating in his mind's eye. His colleagues and parishioners noticed the changes in him immediately, and it pained him greatly to see the surprise and shock in their faces. What was the matter with their mild-mannered, kindly parish priest?

If only he could tell them . . .

Clearly, things could not continue like this; he needed to talk to Daniel Ellington as soon as possible. He'd repeatedly called his best friend, who taught English Lit at Fordham, but Dan hadn't been in his apartment and the department receptionist said he had a heavy class schedule.

Peter could talk to Dan about anything; and Dan would help. Peter was having an increasingly difficult time trying to pray—something that had always been an integral and comforting part of his life. He was growing more and more terrified that this horrible incident would irrevocably distance him from his God and his charges—the people of Saint Sebastian parish.

In this way lies madness, he thought. The worst thing he could do at this point would be to doubt his own resolves of faith or the power and wisdom of God.

Reaching for the phone, Peter decided to try to get through again. Dan would probably be in a summer-school class, but he would try his office anyway. Peter flipped through his Rolodex until he found the number he could never seem to remember, then punched it in.

You have reached the Department of English . . . said the recording of a slightly nasal female voice. *Regular office hours are from eight* AM *until four* PM *Monday through Fridays throughout the summer session. Hours will be extended during fall semester registration during the week of—*

Peter hung up the phone. He'd forgotten it was Sunday and Daniel would be anywhere but locked up in his cave-like office cubicle.

Peter dialed his friend's residence number and waited through a series of rings.

Then: "Hello, this is Father Ellington . . ."

"Hello, Dan, it's Peter."

Ellington's tone immediately brightened. "Peter, how're you doing? It's been a while."

"You know how it is," Peter said, trying to chuckle audibly. "You can always say you're busy and it covers a multitude of sins."

Daniel Ellington agreed and they continued to exchange small talk for a minute or two. The men had met and become very close while studying in the seminary and, after both had been ordained, had remained in touch through sporadic correspondence. Peter had accepted his assignment at Saint Sebastian's while Daniel spent the next few years gaining his Ph.D. with the Jesuits and eventually securing a professorship at Fordham University. Peter had been surprised and pleased to learn that his close friend had ended up in New York, but in the year since Daniel's arrival, he and Peter had managed only several afternoons together. Both had busy schedules and commitments, and free time was scarce.

Peter had always liked Daniel because he was a no-bullshit kind of guy. You always got a straight answer from Daniel because he was insufferably honest. You knew where you stood with him and his opinions were always sincere. He was an intelligent, deep-thinking, sensitive type with an abiding love of books. Peter had always felt he would have made a great writer, had he not chosen the priesthood.

"So what's the occasion?" asked Daniel, obviously tiring of the ritual pleasantries. "Don't tell me you're trying to talk me into another one of those baseball games . . ."

Peter smiled. Daniel had always sneered at organized sports as a means of keeping the working classes' minds off the real issues of the world.

"No, no ballgame this time, I need your help, Dan."

"Is it anything serious?" Immediately Daniel sounded concerned and solicitous.

"I would say so, yes . . ." Peter paused for a moment. "Something happened to me, Dan. Something strange and terrible, and I need to talk about it."

"You know you can tell me anything, Peter—you don't need to be so mysterious about it."

Peter cleared his throat, continued. "I wish I could tell you more, but I can't. Not over the phone."

"The phone? Have you started moonlighting for the CIA or something?"

Peter tried to laugh, failed miserably. "No, nothing like that. I'd just feel better if I talked to you in person."

"You're not in any trouble, are you?" Daniel persisted.

"Would that be spiritually or physically?" asked Peter, trying to make light of the question.

"Either one, damn it! Come on, Peter, you sound pretty weird, so don't be so surprised that it's worrying me. Let's cut the bullshit, okay?"

Peter smiled in spite of the tension twisting inside him. "Spoken like a true Jesuit, Daniel."

"We don't forsake our brains for the Church." Peter could almost hear his friend shrug. Daniel had often told him that he believed a new order was coming in the Church, and that sooner or later some of the more medieval beliefs and traditions would be blown away. So far, the winds of change blowing from the Vatican had been weak indeed.

"So when do you want to see me?" asked Daniel. "My guess would be as soon as possible, right?"

"I was hoping you'd say something like that. What's your schedule?"

Daniel exhaled audibly. "I was going to drop off some exams at my office. Why don't you just head over now, and I'll meet you there."

"Sounds good. See you soon."

"Hey," said Daniel, "whatever it is, everything's going to be all right."

"I hope so . . . I really do." He paused, drew in a breath. "Thanks, Dan. I mean that. Bye."

Feeling better, Peter hung up the phone. It was good to know that he could depend on Daniel for friendship and guidance—even if the latter was of a radical mien.

". . . and no, it's not hard to believe," said Dan. "If you said it happened, then I accept that it happened. Now, where do we go from here? Isn't that the next question?"

Peter looked at his friend, who was sitting behind his paper-covered desk with his feet up on the edge. He was stocky, but not overly so. He had longish, golden-blond hair and he'd always looked like a California surfer. Leaning well back in his swivel chair, Dan looked totally relaxed, despite learning his friend had just killed a man. The office was small, lined with sloppy bookcases, and shaded by heavy brown drapes. The space was cramped, but warm and comfortable. He liked the baronial clutter of the room very much. It was like—

Dan cleared his throat. "Hey, Carenza . . . you listening?"

"Oh, I'm sorry," said Peter. "I was just thinking . . . daydreaming, really. It keeps me from going nuts."

"I was hoping that by letting it all out you'd feel some relief," Dan said, frowning. He sat upright, dropping his feet to the floor.

"Well, I do, but it's not just that I . . . I killed a man, Dan . . . it's *how* I killed him!"

"I know, I know . . ."

"No, you don't. You can't possibly know what it's like to have this force come out of you and . . . and do what it did. The news said it was a freak lightning accident, but I know better." He looked up at his friend. "Dan, what's going on here? Is this a test of my faith? I thought God stopped doing this sort of thing a long time ago."

"So did I." Dan smiled, shook his head. "Actually, we descendants of Saint Ignatius wonder if he ever did this sort of thing in the first place."

"So tell me: where *do* we go from here?"

Dan lit a cigarette and drew on it slowly. "Well, I think the first step is to do what any Jesuit would do."

"What's that—get drunk?"

"Your sense of humor's coming back. That's a good sign," said Dan. "No, actually, I was thinking of doing some research. You know—check the literature, and see if anything like this has happened before."

Peter brightened a bit. "You think that's a good idea?"

"Sure. It's a start. I'd be very surprised to find you were the first case like this on record."

Peter nodded. Maybe his friend was right. Without really thinking about it, he checked his watch and saw it was getting late. After dinner he had a practice scheduled with his Pony League team. Standing up, he reached out and took Daniel's hand.

"Thank you. For listening."

"Isn't that what they told us in the seminary: 'Be a good listener and you'll be a good priest'?"

"I guess so."

"So give me a few days to check some things out. I'll be finished with my summer school class and then go to the theological library and do some digging around. Can you meet me back here a week from Monday, in the morning?"

"Sounds good. I'll be here. About ten?"

Dan nodded, the friends shook hands again, and Peter left the office, making his way out of the complex of Fordham University buildings, into the streets of the Bronx. Although by no means cool, the blistering heat of the previous week had eased up. Peter had never grown accustomed to the overwhelming humidity that plagued New York during the summers. How much longer till October?

As he stood there, trying to flag down a cab at the intersection of Webster Avenue and Fordham Road, Peter considered what he should do next. His pastor didn't look like he was going to be any help. Thank God he had a friend like Dan Ellington, or Peter might have to book himself an appointment with a psychiatrist. Dan could be trusted with whatever Peter told him.

He was a true friend.

A cab slipped out of the main traffic flow and homed in on his position. Cries of children playing stick-ball punctuated the street sounds of horns and screeching tires. Everything seemed so normal, it was hard to hold on to the reality of what had happened to him. Maybe he was wrong; perhaps he had only imagined the energy coming from his hands.

The cab pulled to a stop in front of him.

Peter climbed inside, giving the rectory's address in Bay Ridge, and the cabbie nodded and punched the accelerator. Peter was seized by the back seat as the big Checker surged into the southbound current on Webster Avenue.

His next thought was dark; no, not freak lightning—just a *freak*.

SIX

Vatican City—Lareggia
August 17, 1998

Deep within the bureaucratic warren of the *Governorato*, the Vatican's largest governmental administration building, lay the unimpressive office of Paolo Cardinal Lareggia, who served on the Curia as the Chief of the Office for Personnel Relations of the Holy See. The name of the Curia implied something impressive and powerful, but Lareggia knew in reality that it was nothing more than a vast civil service administration that blanketed the Vatican with paperwork and bureaucracy. The widespread arms of the Curia embraced every concern of the city—from economic affairs to newspaper publishing to the *Cohors Helvetica*, the Swiss Guard.

Cardinal Lareggia's job was to oversee the lay employees who worked for the bishopric of Rome and see that they were kept happy. This was no small task considering Italy's galloping inflation and the relatively meager wages offered by the Curial payroll masters.

This did not mean, however, that Lareggia lived a likewise spartan existence.

The Cardinal was a large man—a man some would call fat, almost grossly so. The feasts at Lareggia's table had become almost legendary within the Sacred College of Cardinals. He lived well, and why not? At the age of seventy-two he was one of the elder statesmen in that select group of Church leaders. With age came some privileges and some power.

Paolo Lareggia was not above using whatever of both came his way.

His intercom buzzed erratically as he sat behind his desk initialing some requisitions for reshipments of office supplies.

"Yes, what is it?"

"You have a security communication on the scrambler," said the flat voice of his male secretary. "Code name: Bronzini."

The Cardinal grinned to himself. *Bronzini!* What a surprise to hear the code name. It was a name he had spent so many years waiting to hear, the name of a person with a message both wondrous and mysterious. His breath stuck in his chest; he forced himself to swallow and willed his heart to reclaim its regular rhythm. Bronzini . . . at last.

The Cardinal spoke into the voice-activated intercom: "I will see to this myself. Thank you."

Lareggia pushed his bulk away from the desk; the wheels of his chair groaned. He stood with effort and trundled across his office to a sophisticated electronics console. He had shied away from hi-tech equipment as long as possible, but as his position within the Church infrastructure rose and his superiors recognized the need for the Vatican to be conversant in the twenty-first century, he had acquiesced to the demands of keyboards, mice, and terminals.

After a few deft strokes, his personal monitor awaited his logon code and passwords. Then the screen blinked and de-rezzed into the image of an old man with wispy white hair and a long thin face. The man wore the traditional Roman collar and black habit of a parish priest; he could not conceal his surprise as he recognized the red vestments of Lareggia's high-ranking office.

"Ah, excuse me, Cardinal," he said slowly, obviously embarrassed. "I was told to contact 'Paolo' by means of the

Archdiocese scrambler if anything . . . I mean, if I ever found out . . ."

Lareggia waved him off. "I know why you are calling. You are Father Stanislaus Sobieski. You have been instructed to keep a watchful eye upon Peter Carenza."

"Yes, that's right," said the priest, relief easing into his old face.

Lareggia fought to keep his voice under control. Was this the moment? The sign they'd been waiting for? His heart began to jump again beneath the folds of clothing and the flab of his chest. "You have information for me . . . ?"

"Yes, Cardinal."

"Absolutely no one must know you are contacting me."

Sobieski appeared immediately concerned. "What about the staff here at the Archdiocese?"

Lareggia smiled. "Our scramblers are used frequently. Your visit is nothing out of the ordinary—only your message, I expect."

"Oh yes, I think it is."

Paolo drew a breath, steadied himself and exhaled. "So, tell me, Father, do we have a sign?"

Sobieski nodded. In several succinct and obviously rehearsed sentences, the American priest told the story of the mugger and his death by fire.

"From his *hands*?" asked Lareggia in a hushed voice. "My God, I had not expected anything like this . . ."

The Cardinal paused to consider the details of the story. So graphic, so full of demonstrative power! His breathing became more labored, making him more aware of his enormous weight. He did not want the American to detect his growing anxiety, but perhaps there was no hiding it. A cleansing fire. From his hands . . . !

"Tell me," said Lareggia. "How did Carenza react when he told you what had happened to him?"

Sobieski swallowed once before beginning. "Understandably he was stunned. He is still shaken by the experience. He doesn't know how or why it could have happened. Neither do I, but apparently you do."

Paolo sighed as he ignored Sobieski's coy attempt to extract information. "Who would not be stunned by such an experience? How is his health?"

"He appears to be fine, physically. Mentally, I think he's having problems dealing with the fact that he's killed someone, especially in such a spectacular way."

Paolo nodded, steepled his hands in front of his face. There was much to do now. He had to contain himself and remain calm. Everything must be done properly, according to the grand plan.

"What about the local authorities?" asked Paolo. "Did they discover what happened?"

"The police investigated it like any other death, yes, but . . ." The priest almost smiled as he shook his head. "Cardinal Lareggia, this is New York City. People die here all the time, in all kinds of weird and terrible ways. The police did not give this death any special attention, believe me."

Paolo nodded, choosing not to ponder the implications of a city which could ignore something so wondrous. "That is good," he said after another pause.

"What now, Cardinal? Do you have more instructions for me?" asked Sobieski.

"Send him to me. Immediately."

"To you? To the Vatican?" Sobieski could not conceal his surprise.

"Exactly. His place is with us."

"Well, what do I tell him? How do I get him to agree to such a trip?"

Paolo waved his hand in dismissal. "Tell him the Vatican has a special committee which investigates miraculous phenomena. Tell him any damnable thing you wish, Father. Just get him here as soon as possible!"

"Of course, Your Grace."

"I will arrange for funds for the journey to be transferred to Saint Sebastian's accounts—and perhaps something extra to help your community programs. You have done well, Father."

"Thank you, Cardinal. Thank you."

"Good. Transmit the particulars of his arrival via this com-net. Retain your logon and passwords. They will remain valid until I hear from you again."

Father Sobieski stared into his own monitor for a moment. "That is all, then?"

"Yes. *Arrivederci*, Father."

Paolo punched a key and the image wavered for an instant before disappearing. Sobieski was a fine priest who had done well. There was no price tag on such loyalty in this day and age.

No, thought Paolo Lareggia, who had grown up on the docks of Naples as an orphaned street-child, who had learned the savage ways of the world before entering the priesthood. No, loyalty and trust were rare commodities.

Getting up from the console chair with more than a little effort, Paolo steadied himself and cursed his ever-increasing bulk. He lumbered across the office to his window, which overlooked the Via Della Fondamenta and the rear view of Saint Peter's Basilica.

It was a warm day and the humid breath of late summer penetrated the screened-in opening. The daily patterns of life swarmed and circulated through the Vatican as the Cardinal looked down upon the utterly familiar cityscape. Tourists straggled about in small groups and in more organized guided tours; traffic water-bugged in and out of the narrow streets and wide boulevards, skittered across the bridges; pigeons fluttered and brawled to get the best positions on ledges and gargoyles and window-sills.

It was a beautiful city. Paolo Cardinal Lareggia had a difficult time not thinking of it as *his* city. He had long ago given up the city of his birthplace, never mentioning it to anyone, even refusing to allow himself to think about his humble, embarrassing beginnings.

And yet, this day, suddenly wondering if he and the others were doing the proper thing, he found himself drawn back to the long-ago days of his youth . . .

He hadn't been obese back then. At fourteen he was tall and large-boned, almost a head taller than the other boys his age. After escaping from the orphanage three years before, he had carved out an existence on the docks of the city.

It was a filthy place. Disease stalked the wharves and flophouses like a bold wolf. The many rats could often be seen in the shadows, squirming and folding all over each other. Their hardened droppings formed a thick carpet over the planks and gangways. Paolo and another boy lived in an abandoned storage shed. His days were occupied with the hunting and gathering necessary for survival—fruit and dried meats stolen from an unwary vendor's stall, discarded, halfrotted vegetables from ships' crates, and the occasional purse rousted from any stroller foolhardy enough to come too close to the jungle's edge defined by the boundaries of the dock and the residential streets.

There were endless nights of fights and drinking bouts, and women who had whiskey on their breaths and a stench between their legs.

Paolo lived hard, fought hard, and by the time he was sixteen, he had the size and the wisdom of a full-grown man. He thought he was the bravest, the toughest, the most feared, but a deckhand from a Turkish ship who didn't like the swagger of his walk challenged him to a fight to the death. The fight rolled out of the grimy tavern into the streets, which were sluiced with the garbage and the slime of human waste. The battle raged all through the night and into the pink dawn, as Paolo and the Turk clawed and punched and slashed at one another. A great crowd gathered and followed their progress across the dock. Its cheering and goading became a monotonous drone fueled by rum and opium. It was not until he realized that he must indeed kill or be killed that any true fear entered his heart.

Paolo had hurt scores of people, even maimed his share of men who crossed him, but he had never killed a man. And when the moment arrived, when he had snatched the Turk's hidden knife from the man's grip and pressed its curving blade against the side of his enemy's slippery throat, Paolo knew that he could not kill so easily.

When he tried to make his hand move that extra inch, to

puncture the stretch of shining flesh and rip across the veins
and arteries of the neck, it was as though he had become a
piece of stone. In that moment he knew that there was a place
where his mind and body would draw the line. A line he
could not cross.

The Turk lay unconscious beneath his weight, and as the
crowd screamed like ancient Romans for his blood, Paolo
cast the knife into the water, stood, and walked away.

The incident had been witnessed by a priest who ran after
him, befriended him, and found him a room at the Franciscan
Monastery, where he exchanged his labor for warm meals and
a roof over his straw bed. The monastic life agreed with him.
He returned to his schooling and excelled as a student. In the
ensuing years, he was not surprised to receive a calling from
the Lord. His power and cunning and endurance served him
well in the priesthood and he quietly but steadfastly rose
through its ranks from apprentice to pastor and monsignor, to
bishop, and finally, one of its youngest cardinals. Always
tough-minded, but fair, he acquired a reputation for independent thinking that was both an asset and a hindrance, in the ascending hierarchy of the Roman faith.

Paolo Lareggia shook his head as the memory faded. His
hands were slippery with perspiration, trembling slightly from
the crystalline recollection of the fight with the Turk. It had
seemed so damnably real . . .

Why should I have such thoughts now? he wondered, trying to be analytical.

Because the time was almost at hand.

Because he had waited so long and now the time of the
reckoning was so very close. The thought settled into him
like a rock falling into the placid waters of a still pond. The
memories were a humbling experience. They were a part of
his life Paolo had tried to forget, to banish from his present
persona of power and wisdom. But he needed to be humbled.

He knew that God had sent him those memories, so strong
and full of the stench and sweat of his youth, so that he
would not forget that he was only a man. Though he sometimes entertained thoughts of being the grandest theological

architect since Saint Peter himself, Paolo was, after all, only a simple man, with simple beginnings.

It was the plan that was grand. It was the plan that would supersede all other things in the world. That Paolo Lareggia had been the originator of what was to come was of little consequence.

He needed to be reminded that he was but an instrument in the hand of God. Willing. Able. Proud, maybe. But in the end, only an instrument.

Looking up to the blue depths of the afternoon sky, like Constantine, seventeen hundred years before him, Cardinal Lareggia looked for a sign from the Lord. That he saw nothing out of the ordinary did not dissuade him from the sense of righteousness and truth he carried in his heart.

SEVEN

Manhattan, New York—Windsor
August 17, 1998

Marion Windsor didn't know if she had her hands on a Career-Making Story or not, but she was going to check it out just to make sure.

Sitting in WPIX's video editing studio, she kept reviewing her raw footage from the "lightning" story. Although she was no electronic wizard, she'd learned to use some of the digital equipment that made videotape such a facile medium. She could slow down the action, she could zoom in on a particular face, analyze a voice, and she could play/rewind/playback anything she wanted as many times as she wanted.

Marion pushed a strand of reddish-brown hair out of her eyes as she leaned over the Sony console. Her camcorder had captured a truly grim image. By stopping the tape and zooming up, Marion was able to get a surprisingly clean blow-up of what had once been a human being. It was really just a blackened torso with a smaller charred lump on the top. The arms had been burned off and the head was recognizable as such only because the lips and cheeks had been burned away to reveal yellow-white teeth in a horrific smile.

She pushed up the gain on the audio track.

I seen lightning victims, and none of 'em ever looked like that.

She pressed a key and listened to the voice of the red-haired paramedic several more times.

Could it be that this wasn't a struck-by-lightning after all? Could what the kid had said be closer to the truth?

She fast-forwarded to her exchange with Esteban. Slowing down the tape, she studied the kid's face, looking for that gleam in the eye, that ever-so-slight facial tic which sometimes gave away the deliberate liar, the person who was talking just to get his mug on the evening news. Esteban's face was an open book. It told a simple story of awe, respect, and fear. Marion saw no lies in the boy.

She replayed the tape several more times, marking the time-code for possible cuts and compilations in case she wanted to assemble a video fill for her narration. The material she had wasn't a story yet, but her experience and training were working on autopilot. The first time she realized this, she realized she was a true professional.

She paused at her last shot of the two priests, the old, wispy-haired guy and the one who was simply too handsome to be a priest. They leaned over the gurney and the younger one raised the sheet. Marion studied their faces. The old guy's registered the expected horror and revulsion, but the younger one was totally different. His face was hard and cold, as though he already knew what he was going to see. He looked at the older priest, said something, then looked back at the victim for a moment before making the sign of the cross over the remains and beginning a prayer.

Marion absently bit her lower lip as she rewound in

slo-mo, pausing right before the young priest spoke. From the quality of the raw sound of the playback it was obvious the directional mike had been operating at the outer limits of its abilities. There was noise on the tape, but it was dicey as to whether or not there were actual words. Marion had seen the edit-techs use the computer to enhance aural as well as visual images. With the right software and a simple mixing board, if you knew what you were doing, you could make an interview conducted in a factory sound like it happened in a studio.

Marion wasn't that good, but she'd learned a few things by watching and asking questions. The techs loved to talk about their toys. It was funny how men never outgrew their need for toys; as they grew older they just traded up for more flashy, sophisticated ones.

She smiled as she keyed up the enhancement program and ran the piece of tape with the priest's words across the analyzer head. Rewind. Playback. The words were louder, clearer, but still not intelligible. She ran the enhanced sounds through again, and again, until finally: *"See, Father . . . I told you. Look at him."*

Marion leaned back in her chair, staring at the frozen image of the young priest turned toward his older colleague. Something weird was going on here. The priest was connected to the incident. Marion's pulse started jumping as she sensed the possibility of uncovering some kind of mystery. There was a story here, goddammit, and one way or another, she was going to get into the heart of it. It shouldn't be too hard to identify the priests. Most likely they were from the neighborhood, and a little digging would take care of it. But first, she had something else to do.

After making dupes of everything, she pulled her tapes, powered-down the equipment, and left the studio. Walking to the subway, a single thought passed through her mind: *time for a visit to the city of the dead.*

She took a cab to County Hospital, and found her way through the corridors to the morgue. She'd met Dr. Fritz

Huber, Brooklyn's Chief Medical Examiner, while doing the story about the Belt Parkway Killer four years earlier. Dr. Huber, an older man, took a kindly interest in her desire to be a good journalist. He'd gone out of his way to teach her the ropes of police procedure and the methods of a city coroner. He coached her on how to get along with some of the more difficult captains and detectives in the borough, and he never asked for anything in return other than her friendship.

Although she didn't often see Huber, she considered him a friend and more. He was the closest thing she'd had to a father since her dad had died just before she left Chapel Hill's School of Journalism.

"Can I help you?" asked the receptionist in the dingy lobby of the old city building. The guy was reading the latest issue of *Survival Weapons and Tactics*; he was thin, angular, and distinctly avian in his movements and appearance. His thick bank-clerk glasses and long, pianist's fingers gave him a delicate aspect, but he spoke with an off-handed, almost surly manner.

"I'm here to see Dr. Huber," said Marion, smiling her best on-camera smile.

"He's busy, lady." Bird-man reached for his magazine, dismissing her.

"I called earlier." This kind of guy pissed her off easily, but she kept her cool. "He's expecting me."

The guy looked up from his pages and grimaced as he tapped a key on his phone console and told another secretary to let Dr. Huber know he had a visitor.

"Who should I say is calling?" he asked with obvious disinterest.

"Marion Windsor, thank you."

A circuit flared momentarily in the dim mass which passed for the man's brain. "Hey, ain't you the chick on the tube? I seen you do the news, right?"

Marion nodded. No smile this time.

"Jeez, that's pretty neat. Nice to meet you."

A door opened to the lobby and Dr. Huber appeared. Not very tall, he was getting almost stout enough to fill a doorway. Although pushing retirement age, he still had a headful of thick pepper-and-salt hair. His eyes were large and bright behind his Ben Franklin glasses, and his smile accented his carefully trimmed beard. There was an unequivocally European aspect to his bearing and appearance.

"Marion!" he said joyfully, approaching her with open, ready-to-hug arms. "Good to see you again!"

"Hello, Fritz. You're looking great. As usual."

"So do you, believe me! Come on. You know the way." He released her, ushered her through the door and down a long, dingy corridor toward his office.

"You're just biased," Marion said absently. The forensic pathology section of the hospital was a shadowy, grim place. The gray-green walls and the dead-brown tiled floors imparted a dungeon-like atmosphere to the hallway. The air carried an insistent chemical smell—a mask of disinfectant and the sting of formaldehyde.

"Is this visit for business or pleasure, my dear?" Fritz Huber asked as they entered his office.

"A little of both," said Marion, "but I have to admit I'm working on a story and I need your help."

"Sure . . . sure!" said Fritz. He moved behind his desk, then leaned back and cracked the window, despite the air conditioning. When he pulled a fat short cigar from his center desk drawer, she understood the action.

"So," said Fritz, snipping off the end of the stogie with a pair of scissors designed for that singular job. "Do you have a good boyfriend yet?"

She shrugged. "I have a boyfriend, but I don't know how good he is. We have our ups and downs, I guess."

"Yes, yes. We all do." He fired up the cigar with an old Zippo, clanked out the lighter's flame, and looked at her through the billowing cloud of smoke. "Now tell me, Marion . . . what brings you here, eh?"

"I'm investigating that struck-by-lightning incident—the night before last in Bay Ridge."

Fritz nodded, puffed again.

"Did you work on it?"

He shrugged. "Nah. Not at first, anyway. Dr. Holstein was assigned to the job, but he called me in during the autopsy."

"That's what I wanted to ask you about, if you don't mind."

"No, of course not." Puff. Puff. Blow.

Marion cleared her throat, thankful he'd opened the window to increase the circulation. She'd never understand why anyone would want to put something as foul as a cigar into his mouth.

"The cause of death wasn't lightning, was it?"

Fritz did not try to conceal his surprise. "How did you know that?"

"Call it a hunch." Marion shrugged. "What did you find out?"

Fritz leaned back in his chair, ran a hand through his hair. "Well, Dr. Holstein got suspicious when he began cutting. You see, a person struck by lightning or by a high-voltage line gets burned. Badly burned. But the cauterization is limited to the integument, the skin. When Dr. Holstein opened up the victim, he found the guy's organs were all cooked from the inside out like he'd been in a microwave oven."

"And that's not the usual pattern for lightning?"

"Not that I've ever seen. Of course lightning's real funny. There's lots of crazy stories about it."

"What did you put down as the official cause of death?"

Fritz grinned around his cigar. "Lightning."

"Why? If you don't think that's what happened?"

"Because I haven't the foggiest idea what else it could be!"

Marion leaned forward, stared at him. "Fritz, aren't you at all curious?"

"Of course I am, but my God, Marion, do you have any idea how many cases I've been curious about in thirty-five years in this business?" He puffed erratically at the cigar. "Hell, I've seen the results of death from everything from machine guns to toothbrushes and everything in between. There've been more than a few that made me wonder what was really going on."

"But . . . ?"

He shrugged. "But you can't follow up on all of them, especially one like this punk. He had a rap sheet you wouldn't believe. Whatever cooked him, I say they picked the right guy!"

"Venus Tyson. I heard he was wanted for murder and armed robbery," said Marion.

". . . and I'll let you in on a little secret," Fritz continued, hardly hearing her. "When you get to be my age, you start thinking more about retirement and pensions than you do about your job. You might not like hearing that, but it's true."

Marion nodded, trying to mask her disappointment. She'd thought Fritz would have been more help.

"Hey, what's the matter? I say something wrong?"

"No, not really. It's just that I have a feeling that this case is more than meets the eye."

"Why's that? He was just a punk."

"No, not the victim," she said quickly. She briefed him on what she'd learned from the young eyewitness and the tape of the priests.

After listening without interruption, Fritz Huber chuckled softly. "Well, you've got a point there. It's not a story you hear every day."

"You think it's silly, don't you?"

"Marion, when you work as a coroner in New York City, you see some pretty 'silly' things." He smiled his most fatherly smile. "If you have any brains, you learn one thing: nothing's really 'silly.' "

"Then you think I should follow it up?"

"Why not? At least you'll get to meet your handsome priest." Fritz chuckled, took another puff on his cigar. "And by the way, if you're talking about Bay Ridge, you might want to start with Saint Sebastian's on Fourth Avenue. My oldest son used to live right near there."

Marion stood up, walked around the desk and hugged Huber before he could move from his chair. "Fritz, you're one of a kind, you know that? Thanks for everything."

"Hey, besides blow a little smoke in your face, what did I do?"

"You gave me what I needed to keep going on this story," she said.

"What's a little information? I just wish I saw more of you than the evening news. When're you going to come over and have dinner with me and Alice?"

"Give me a date and I'll be there. Otherwise we'll never do it, you know that."

"Next Tuesday. Seven o'clock. How's that?"

Marion pulled out her notebook and wrote it down. "All right, it's official. Thank you, again, Fritz."

"Do good work, Marion."

She smiled and kissed him good-bye on the cheek. "I will."

It was *him*.

He stood at the door of Saint Sebastian's rectory staring at her. In an instant of time Marion was able to mentally photograph him. He had the longest lashes, the darkest eyes . . . his features were Mediterranean, yet almost delicate. His thick brown hair was stylishly cut. His shoulders were broad. Handsome was the only word to describe him, although hunk would do in a pinch.

Get a hold on yourself, girl . . . This is a priest, we're talking about here.

"Can I help you?" he asked, as time speeded back up to normal. He wore a pair of casual slacks and an NYU sweatshirt.

"Yes. My name is Marion Windsor," she said. "I'm a journalist for WPIX. I videotaped you at the scene of the lightning accident last evening, and I was wondering if I might talk to you for a few minutes."

She wasn't sure, but he seemed to tense up for a moment before turning on a smile.

"Why, certainly, Ms. Windsor. Please, come in. My name is Father Carenza."

Italian, she thought. Of course. He could be another young Pacino or De Niro with those looks.

He led her down a short hall to a room with a desk and bookcases. She took the opportunity to glance into some of the other rooms on the first floor, noting the tastefully contemporary furnishings, the *de rigueur* crucifixes, portraits of Mary, and pieces of statuary.

Father Carenza seated himself behind the small desk, folded his hands neatly on the blotter, and tried to look relaxed. He failed miserably, and Marion started wondering anew if she was really onto something. She sat down and stared at him. Your move, Father.

"What can I do for you, Ms. Windsor?"

"Father, I saw you administering the last rites to the victim. I was wondering if perhaps you might have known the boy, if there's anything you could tell me about him?"

"—No, I didn't know him. Not at all."

"Then what were you doing at the scene, if I might ask?"

He shifted in his chair, his dark eyes looking at a point on the wall past her head—as though avoiding her.

"I, uh . . . I was out taking a walk with my pastor when we heard about the accident." He looked at her, then quickly away. Father Carenza was not accustomed to telling such boldfaced lies.

She nodded. "I see." Marion paused, produced her mini-camcorder from her bag. "Do you mind if we record this conversation?"

"Actually I'm not sure what Archdiocese policy is on that sort of thing, and Father Sobieski's not here right now . . ."

Marion smiled, folding up the electronic gear. "No problem, Father. But tell me this. A small boy said he saw you getting mugged by the victim earlier in the evening. In that alley. Is that true?"

She watched as he opened his mouth to respond and found that the words would not come. He had seized up for a second, obviously unsure what to say or do. He looked helpless and Marion felt sorry for him. She didn't like harpooning him like this, but she'd learned that direct confrontation was always the best way to get to the heart of a story.

Coughing nervously, Father Carenza suddenly focused a

most penetrating gaze full bore upon her. "Yes, it's true. I'd been there earlier. I escaped . . . and I ran away."

Marion nodded. She was surprised that he admitted it so readily. She wasn't accustomed to city inhabitants being so open, so honest. Perhaps naïveté, or his religious training, made him so different.

"The boy said he saw something else," she said softly. Better to handle this delicately.

The trapped-scared expression returned to his face. "Did he?"

"He said there was a flash of light and the mugger was killed. He said you caused it."

"That's pretty ridiculous, isn't it?" Father Carenza tried to smile.

"I don't know, Father. I've seen so many strange things in my business . . ."

The young priest looked at his watch and stood. "I'm afraid I'm running out of time, Ms. Windsor. I've got to go to a school meeting right after dinner."

"I see."

"I hope I've been some help," he said lamely as he escorted her toward the door.

"Well, yes, you have, Father. I hope my questions didn't disturb you."

"Have you ever been mugged, Ms. Windsor?" He paused by the open front door; their gazes locked for an instant. Marion felt the impact of his look clear down to her toes.

"No, I haven't."

"It's not something you want to remember with much fondness, believe me."

"I'm sure it isn't," she said, sensing his embarrassment. All right. Enough was enough. They shook hands. "Thank you, Father. Thank you very much."

"Good night, Ms. Windsor."

She descended the porch steps to the sidewalk, glancing back at him as he watched her depart. She had a feeling they would be talking again.

EIGHT

Vatican City—Francesco
August 17, 1998

The telephone rang and Father Giovanni Francesco moved to his desk to pick it up.

"Hello . . ." he said in a whisper-quiet voice. "Francesco speaking."

"Good afternoon, Father, it's Victorianna . . ."

Francesco reacted instantly. "Why do you call me here!? I don't want there to be any record of contact between any of us."

The woman cleared her throat. "I'm sorry, 'Vanni, but we have a bit of an emergency."

"What? What are you talking about?"

"It's Etienne," said his colleague of more than thirty years.

Giovanni gritted his teeth. Damn this woman! Getting information out of her was like pulling teeth! "What about Etienne?"

"Well," said the Abbess, "she's . . . she's had a *vision*."

The words struck a resonant chord in him. From his earliest years in the Catholic Church he'd heard the stories about select people, usually very pious individuals, "having a vision." In layman's terms, it meant receiving a special message from God—actually seeing something grand and beatific unfold before your eyes. The Fatima incident was perhaps the most famous, but Giovanni had heard hundreds of others during his seventy-one years.

He reached for a cigarette in his cassock pocket, found

only an empty pack. Damn. "What kind of vision? What did she see?"

"We don't know," said Abbess Victorianna. "We found her in the garden. We thought at first that she was having some kind of seizure. She's in the convent infirmary, but she may have to be moved to a hospital."

"Is she conscious?"

"Just barely. She keeps saying she's seen God and the end of the world."

Giovanni smirked. "Yes, of course. She and a thousand others . . ."

"'Vanni, you forget who we're talking about here." The nun's voice was stern, penetrating.

He sighed audibly. "Very well, I'll come see her. Perhaps she'll tell me something she won't tell anyone else."

"You flatter yourself, Father."

"If not I, then who better?" He smiled into the receiver. "I will also speak to Paolo."

"All right. I will await word from you."

"Within the hour, Sister. Good-bye."

He hung up the phone as an arthritic pain misfired the synapses of his right arm. One of the prices paid for not dying young.

On hearing the word "vision," a knot had formed in the base of Giovanni Francesco's stomach. That knot seemed to be swelling, growing hot. These days, whenever anything out of the ordinary occurred, his ulcer immediately started sending out warning signals. He winced at the incipient pain. Damn, he was finally starting to fall apart.

Giovanni reached for a Turkish cigarette from the gold filigreed box on the desktop, lighted it from a Zippo he'd had since World War II.

It might be a good idea to have Targeno involved in this. He could be trusted. Perhaps he should secretly investigate the nun's story.

Giovanni called his secretary and had him contact Targeno, requesting that the man come to the Jesuit's office as soon as possible.

Slowly drawing on his cigarette, savoring the taste of the special tobaccos, Francesco walked slowly to the window and looked out upon a westering afternoon sun. A warm glow danced upon the red-tiled rooftop of the Ethiopian College beyond the Viale Dell Osservatorio. His office in the *Governorate* was on the west side of the massive building which afforded him a view of the Grotto of Lourdes, the heliport, and part of the Wall of Leo IV. It was the view commonly called the "Vatican's back yard," the part of the city less-known to the tourists and the photographers of postcards.

Giovanni preferred it that way. He exhaled a thin, blue plume against the windowpane as he considered the implications of the latest news.

So the woman had had a vision. He had made light of it to the nun—no sense getting her disturbed. But was it, in fact, a Sign? There had been nothing up to now, even though the three of them had been watching carefully. But now, coupled with the stunning news from Sobieski ... Giovanni smiled, drew in another lungful.

Yes, this was *it*.

He turned from the window, heading for his desk. He was a tall, thin man. His cheeks were sallow, gaunt, and his face had a wolfish aspect. Although past seventy, he still looked vigorous and alert. Many of his colleagues had told him he was too tough to die.

And perhaps they were right.

Officially, he was not a member of the Curia; his title in the catalog of various Vatican commissions was Prefect of Public Welfare, which meant he was employed by the Curia to oversee the day-to-day activities of government agencies ranging from the Bureau for Tourist Information and Safety to the Vatican Fire Department. For the majority of curial staffers, civil servants, and even many of the other cardinals themselves, Giovanni was just another cog on the great Vatican wheel of bureaucracy. He also served as special Papal Liaison to the Society of Jesus.

This meant he was in touch with the inner circle of Vatican power brokers capped by the Pope himself. Over the years

Giovanni had cultivated connections in all the organizations that might someday be of use to him, most notably the *Servizio Segreto Vaticano*, the Vatican Secret Service.

He smiled to himself as he butted out his cigarette in a gold and sterling silver ashtray. The average Catholic on the street, in any city in the world, would probably laugh at the idea of their Church employing an underground police force, much less an espionage unit. But it was true. The SSV trained its members at a six-hundred-year-old Corsican monastery whose monks were experts in the most deadly arts and whose methods of training were more rigorous than the CIA, KGB, M15, or even the Israeli Mossad.

Formed immediately after World War II by Pius XII, the SSV had grown to be an incredibly influential power in world politics. Giovanni had been asked to join back in 1946 because of his extensive experience as a liaison to America's OSS after the Anzio invasion. He smiled as he remembered those heady, adventurous days. The world would blanch if they ever discovered some of the SSV's global maneuverings.

The assassinations of Franco and Brezhnev were two of his personal favorites. Neither the Spaniards, or the Russians had ever suspected a thing. Timing, in Francesco's business, was crucial, and the timing in both instances had been exquisite.

The phone shrilled and he picked it up, automatically reaching for a cigarette, lighting it with the American Zippo that would surely outlast him.

"Yes?"

"I have contacted Targeno, sir."

Giovanni exhaled. "And . . ."

"By chance, he was in the building," said the receptionist, his voice flat and full of discipline.

"Very good." Another pull on the Turkish blend.

"He should be here at any moment."

"Thank you, Spinelli. That will be all. Just send him in when he arrives."

The receptionist hung up, leaving Giovanni to his thoughts once again.

Targeno.

Giovanni was completely ambivalent about the man, feeling toward him both love and hate, admiration and fear. Over the years, Targeno had acquired a reputation of being fiercely dedicated to completing every SSV assignment. Failure had become anathema to him. He succeeded every time out, and he did so with a merciless determination that had become legendary among the ranks of the field agents. Many thought he was insane, but all respected him. Most feared him, but loved to work with him because he was so efficient, so dependable, so clean. He had a nickname which had sprung from these attributes: *Il Chirurgo*—The Surgeon. That Targeno carried a six-inch stiletto, and could use it with the slick speed and confidence of a surgeon, enhanced the image.

Dangerous. Crazy, perhaps. But the best, all the same.

As if on cue, the door to Giovanni's office opened, revealing the stern face of the receptionist. "Excuse me, sir, but he's here . . ."

Before Giovanni could say a word or make a gesture, a tall, broad-shouldered man pushed past the receptionist and into the room, slamming the door behind him. It was a typical entrance for Targeno, who always acted as though there was no time, never enough time, as though he was always on a tight schedule.

"You wanted to see me?" said the agent in a silky baritone that could have belonged to a radio announcer.

"That is correct," said Giovanni. "Sit down, please."

Targeno remained standing before the desk in parade rest. He wore a fashionable black suit, a white silk shirt with french cuffs and silver links, and a maroon tie. His hair was styled in the latest continental cut. Aviator glasses obscured eyes Giovanni knew to be so brown and deep they were almost black. Targeno's face was ageless—he could have been anything from thirty-five to fifty—and he held the pure essence of experience in his eyes. When he concealed those eyes, he became a slick, unidentifiable being. He remained standing.

"I said you could sit down," said Giovanni, taking another drag from his cigarette.

"I would prefer to stand, Father."

Giovanni shrugged. "Suit yourself." Exhale.

"Those things are going to kill you. You know that, don't you?" The baritone voice was so smooth, almost seductive.

"They haven't yet, and it's been fifty-five years," said Giovanni. "And at my age, what difference does it make?"

Targeno stood up straighter. "I was checking on some things down in Data Retrieval, Father. You said you wanted me."

You bastard, thought Giovanni. He was impatient. Impertinent. One of a kind.

"I've often told you the day might come when I would need your skills, your loyalty . . ."

Targeno nodded.

"That day has at last arrived," Giovanni said, moving away from his desk toward the window, purposely turning his back on the agent. It was a tactic he'd found effective in dealing with people from whom he required respect.

"'Vanni, I am very busy," Targeno began.

Francesco whirled, eyes ablaze. "Do you think I don't realize all that? You know I have some influence. Besides, Cardinal Masseria and his precious SSV owe me a few favors."

"I see," said Targeno calmly. "Then what is it you want?"

"There is a nun in the Poor Clares convent infirmary. She's had a vision, and I want her under surveillance. I want her interrogated. Carefully, of course. Let her think you're a doctor. I may see her myself, but you may fare better.

"A nun?" Targeno smirked to himself. "And for this you need someone like me? Father—"

"Yes! I need you!" Giovanni paced back and forth. "I cannot explain everything to you—but your 'techniques' may be useful."

"Is the nun in danger?" Targeno shifted his feet ever so slightly.

"No, not at all." Francesco wondered how much to tell this most trustworthy of men.

"You say she's had a vision?"

"Yes, and it's your job to find out what she saw."

Targeno shrugged. "All right, 'Vanni. I'll finish my business downstairs and go to the convent. You'll clear things with Masseria?"

Giovanni nodded. "Consider it done. Now, please, get going."

Targeno nodded, quietly departed. Giovanni waited till he was alone before phoning the third member of the triumvirate.

"Office for Personal Relations . . ." said a voice.

"This if Father Francesco. I will speak to Cardinal Lareggia, please."

"One moment, Father."

There followed a series of clicks and beeps. The Vatican phone system left much to be desired. Finally another extension began ringing.

"Cardinal Lareggia's office . . ." said a male voice.

He repeated his request. More infernal beeping and clicking.

Finally: "'Vanni, what can I do for you?"

"Paolo," he said, "there is more news."

Quickly he related the little he'd learned from Abbess Victorianna.

Cardinal Paolo Lareggia said, "Do you think this has anything to do with the Carenza incident?"

"Who knows?" said Giovanni. "I'm going right over there to speak with her myself."

"Keep me informed."

Giovanni smiled. "Oh, I will, don't worry. What's the latest from America?"

"He arrives tomorrow."

"Is everything prepared?" Giovanni lighted another cigarette.

"Things progress."

"You know," he said, exhaling, "I sometimes forget exactly what it is we're doing. And then it hits me again. And I'm stunned all over again."

"I know," said Paolo. "I feel like a young man again. Ready to kiss a beautiful woman. Full of excitement."

Giovanni nodded. It had been many years since he'd felt such powerful anticipation.

"I understand," he said softly into the receiver.

"It is a wonderful thing that has happened, yes, Father?"

"Finally," he said. "Good-bye, Paolo. I shall speak to you when I return from the convent."

He hung up the phone and stared absently at the burning end of his cigarette. What in God's name *had* they *really* done?

Anticipation consumed him like an obscene tumor. After all these years, the answer was within his grasp . . .

NINE

Brooklyn, New York—Sobieski
August 23, 1998

"Rome? Why? What for?" asked Father Carenza. The young priest was stunned by his pastor's announcement.

Stan Sobieski looked at Peter, who was pacing in front of Sobieski's desk, running his hands through his dark hair. The young man's whole bearing revealed his struggle through the emotionally devastating incident of the mugger's death; his face reflected the effects of the stress. Lines had gathered around his usually bright eyes, his cheeks seemed a bit gaunt, his lips were cracked and chapped.

"Peter, you have to understand, there are special Papal committees that study phenomena such as yours. The Vatican has always been concerned with miracles."

Peter barked out a nervous laugh. "Miracles! You call what I did miraculous? Stan, for God's sake, I *killed* somebody!"

"It was self-defense," said Sobieski. "You have to remember that. You have to stop punishing yourself."

Carenza continued pacing. "The Vatican! I can't believe they want to see me . . ."

"It's true. You saw the telegram."

"But why did you even tell them? I can't believe this," said Peter. "Things are getting out of hand."

"What I did is required by the Archdiocese. The Church is always interested in any 'supernatural' phenomena, especially any involving the clergy. You know that, Father."

Peter nodded, looked absently out the window. "I guess I'd better go upstairs and pack," he said resignedly.

"I suppose you should, yes," said Sobieski.

Carenza paused and looked back as he reached the door. "I still can't understand what the rush is . . . I mean, it just happened last week."

Sobieski cleared his throat. "Who can say what Rome's thinking might be?"

Peter smiled, a small ironic smile, turned and headed for the stairs. Sobieski watched him go, then returned to his desk. He was thinking about Archbishop Duffy, nine years ago, telling him that a new priest was being assigned to him. Peter Carenza.

He remembered getting the letter of assignment from the Archdiocese explaining that he would be getting a boy fresh from the seminary, then the call from Duffy, and then, before Peter arrived, the surprise visit from a high-ranking Jesuit from the Vatican.

That had been his first meeting with Father Giovanni Francesco, a grim and determined-looking man who had been very comfortable handing out orders. His instructions had been quite clear, if somewhat mysterious. The Vatican wanted Carenza watched closely. Sobieski was to report to Francesco's office once per year, and immediately if he observed any "noteworthy" behavior on the part of the priest. Sobieski was even given access to the Church's security communications equipment at the headquarters of the New York Archdiocese.

Then Peter Carenza had arrived. Sobieski could still remember his incredulity—the young man seemed so ordinary, so normal.

And for nine years, things had been perfectly normal. Boringly so.

Until now.

Sobieski had always wondered at the Vatican's special interest in Carenza, but he never questioned what was asked of him by the bigwigs. If a special Papal committee felt something was necessary, then he would do it. It had been that simple.

But now . . . now that he'd seen the charred body and listened to the priest's story, and especially since he'd seen the glow of excitement behind the eyes of that fat Cardinal, Lareggia, Sobieski would give his eyeteeth to be going back to Rome with Peter.

He sighed and sat back in his desk chair. Knowing Vatican bureaucracy, it was a good bet he'd never hear another word about the whole thing.

TEN

Vatican City—Carenza
August 24, 1998

The flight from JFK was insufferably long. Peter did not like being confined in such a small space, and the conversation of his seat-mate, a sales executive for Burroughs Business Machines, had paled many hours before touchdown at Roma Internazionale. Peter simply didn't care which company's machines controlled the world banking market. He tried sleeping, but the seats in the 747 were just not designed for that. He had never been able to doze off in a sitting position and was therefore doomed to the full impact of a monstrous case of jet lag.

He was met at the airport by a priest named Orlando, who stood by the arrival gate holding a placard labeled CARENZA in black letters. The priest was extremely quiet and reserved, driving almost wordlessly through the streets at high speed. Though Peter's Italian was very rusty after all his years in America, it would get him by, but all his attempts to begin conversation were blunted by Orlando's clipped responses. Peter wondered why he was receiving such brusque treatment if he was supposed to be something of a celebrity to this special committee.

The ride from the airport was a blur of speed and color. It was the first time he'd been back to Italy since childhood, and his memories of the city were dim and episodic. Although this was the country of his birth, he did not feel the strong nationalistic surge he expected. He was probably more of an American than he'd ever stopped to consider . . .

Father Orlando negotiated the black Mercedes sedan through many twisting avenues, avoiding the large tourist-clogged boulevards for more expedient back-streets. Crossing the huge Via della Conciliazione, then jackknifing back through some smaller lanes, the car approached the Vatican from the southeast, skirting Saint Peter's Square. As they neared the Square, the traffic became more congested and the sounds of passionate activity grew loud and boisterous. Thousands of people were descending upon the Vatican this clear, warm morning. Spread out before Peter was a vast, multicolored array of cardinals and bishops in their reds and purples, friars and nuns in more subdued mantles, day workers, government officials, tourists and locals. A never-ending stream of human traffic.

His driver avoided all this by ducking in between the Palace of the Holy Office and the Basilica, heading ever closer to the looming architecture of the *Governorate*. Orlando had told him that he would meet with Paolo Cardinal Lareggia, the Prefect of the Curial Committee on Miraculous Investigations. He wondered what kind of questions the committee would ask. Would they be hostile? Skeptical? Empathic? He hoped they would understand the trauma of his experience and the unshakable knowledge that he'd taken a human life.

After some more sharp turns, the Mercedes emerged on the Via Della Fondamenta. Father Orlando fixed his bearings upon the sprawling Government Palace to the west, homed in upon it and drove the car around the back of the building where a porte cochere and glass double doors awaited them. A valet opened the rear door and guided Peter into the building's lobby—a cavernous room presided over by several members of the Palatine Guard. They wore standard security officer uniforms and were all business. Father Orlando spoke to them curtly; they nodded and issued Peter a pass to be clipped to his jacket lapel.

"This way, please," said the priest, guiding him to a bank of elevators. Hundreds of Vatican employees wove their way through the open space like bees in a hive. Peter entered a car with a crowd of workers and the once-again silent Orlando. They didn't depart until the elevator reached the top floor; then the two men walked down a long hallway to a set of double doors carved from heavy slabs of oak.

Inside, a male receptionist wearing the cassock of a monsignor rose from his desk to greet them. "*Buon giorno*, Father Carenza," he said in neutral, but cordial tones. "The Cardinal has been expecting you. Please wait one moment . . ."

The Monsignor buzzed the inner sanctum of the Cardinal, and Peter listened to an unexpectedly high-pitched voice ask for the "the priest" to be ushered in.

Orlando nodded and pushed through another set of double doors, these decorated with a great deal of gold filigree. Peter followed, unable to ignore the bold opulence of the Vatican hierarchy. Catholic liberals were always screaming about the wealth squandered in Rome while the Latin American countries wallowed in abject poverty. Those golden doors would make a hell of an argument, thought Peter.

"Cardinal Lareggia," said Father Orlando, "this is Father Peter Carenza, from New York."

Peter stared at the Cardinal. The man was seated behind an ornate yet fairly ordered desk. He wore a red cassock with no frills other than a large gold crucifix on a heavy gold neckchain. His face was very round and pale. His bald head and a spectacular set of double chins contributed to his overall moonish aspect. To say the man was fat would be gross understatement.

Cardinal Lareggia was *huge*. Porcine. Corpulent. Obese. Take your pick. Here, thought Peter, was a guy who clearly liked to sit down to the table.

Bracing himself on his desk, Lareggia rolled back his chair and stood up, holding out his hand. His lips were wet and dark, his smile stretched and somewhat forced. "Father Carenza, it is a pleasure to meet you!" He spoke serviceable, though accented, English.

"Thank you, Cardinal."

"Please, have a seat," said Lareggia. Then to Orlando, in Italian: "That will be all, Father. Thank you, and good-bye."

Peter seated himself in the chair facing the large desk, furtively appraising the rich decor of the office. The Cardinal sat, picked up a thick folder of papers, opened it, and began scanning some of the sheets.

"I suppose you're rather baffled by all this, hmmm?" Lareggia's voice seemed too high for a body so large and imposing.

"Well, yes, I guess I am. I didn't even know the Church still investigated . . . ah, miracles, so seriously."

"Oh, yes. We do, Father. We certainly do." He continued to scan through the papers in the file. "Let's see, it says here you were born in Italy, just outside of Rome . . . Interesting. A wonderfully strange coincidence, yes?"

"That's right," said Peter. "My parents were killed in a car crash and I was raised at the Orphanage of Saint Francis of Assisi until I was around eight years old."

Lareggia nodded. ". . . and then you won an Ignatius Loyola scholarship to attend a Jesuit boarding school in America. Very impressive, Father."

"Thank you," said Peter, eyeing the thick file on Lareggia's desk. How had they assembled so much information on him so fast? "It looks like you already know everything about me."

The Cardinal smiled thinly. "We are quite thorough." He coughed gently. "Did you enjoy upstate New York? I hear it is very beautiful."

"The seminary was in the Adirondacks. I loved it."

"Yes, of course. I've never been to America, but I'm told it is a most diverse country." It seemed that Lareggia was playing some oft-rehearsed part. He spoke with no real conviction, like a bad actor. What was going on here?

The phone rang and the Cardinal picked up the receiver. "I told you I wanted no calls," he said, then after a short pause: "Oh, 'Vanni, I didn't know it was you . . . I am sorry." Another pause. "Very well. Later this afternoon will be fine."

Hanging up the phone, Lareggia looked at him. "That was one of the other members of the committee who will be . . . ah, studying your case. Father Giovanni Francesco. It seems he's being delayed this morning with another member of our committee. I'm sorry, Father, but we will have to postpone our first session until this afternoon. Four o'clock."

"That's okay," said Peter, wondering what the rush was. He'd been brought here directly from the airport, and now it seemed they'd planned some kind of immediate interrogation!

Lareggia nodded and closed the folder.

"Excuse me," said Peter, "but I'm still a little confused. Actually, I'm a lot confused."

"What can I help you with, Father?"

"For openers, where am I going to be staying? How long will I be here?"

Lareggia smiled. "You really *have* become an American, haven't you, Father? So direct. Well, we have an apartment for you at the Teutonic College, here in the Vatican. Father Orlando will take you there. You can spend some time freshening up, and perhaps do a little sightseeing.

"Father Orlando will return for you at half past three. When you get here you will be interviewed by the committee.

We are also arranging for you to be examined by our physician. I trust that is acceptable to you?"

"Yes, I think so," said Peter, arranging his questions in his mind. "Do you think you could tell me more about this Curial Committee for Miraculous Investigations?"

Lareggia shrugged. "What is there to tell, really? The Holy Mother Church has always been interested in validating any evidence of the Hand of God in our daily lives. What better way to support the faith than to prove the existence of miracles?"

Peter nodded. What a bunch of self-serving, party-line rhetoric . . . It was obvious the Cardinal wasn't going to tell him anything important. Maybe he ought to just go to his room and let the jet lag overtake him.

He decided to push a step farther.

"One more thing," he said. "Why were you in such a big hurry to see me?"

The Cardinal smiled, this time more genuinely. "Because I was sincerely interested in meeting you, Father Carenza. For some reason, your case fascinates me."

The fat man spoke so openly and with such obvious truthfulness Peter was practically overwhelmed by his sudden candor. It made Peter feel embarrassed. His instincts were telling him something was amiss, but he wasn't even close to figuring it out.

"I see . . ." he said after a pause. "Well, thank you. I guess I should be flattered." He leaned forward. "But I have to tell you, what happened to me was very unpleasant. Horrible, actually."

Lareggia waved his puffy hand in the air in a gesture of dismissal. "Ahhh! There will be plenty of time to discuss things like that."

He buzzed the intercom and called for Father Orlando, who appeared at the double doors almost instantly.

"Yes, Your Grace?"

"Escort Father Carenza to his apartment, please."

"Very well," said the priest.

Lareggia stood up, shook hands with Peter.

"Four o'clock," he said in farewell.

The apartment at the College was decorated in Italian Pro-vincial, which seemed very much like French Provincial ex-cept for the antique white and gold worked into the grain of the furniture. Despite being ornate and formal, the bedroom proved comfortable enough. Peter fell asleep and napped into the early afternoon. When he awoke, he was initially disori-ented, and hungry. Armed with the map and some lire that Orlando had given him, he entered the back streets of Vatican City.

Exiting the building and strolling a bit, he found himself on the Piazza dei Protomartiri. He was facing the southern side of St. Peter's Basilica; to his right lay the Arch of the Bells, which led to the huge Bernini colonnade and St. Peter's Square.

Peter decided to avoid the huge crowds gathering with the squadrons of pigeons in the Square, which was not really a square but an enormous, encapsulated circle. He paused to take in the grandeur of the Basilica, then decided upon a route which would give him a brief but thorough education in Vatican geography. It was probably best to get the sightseeing in while he had the chance. If he had to spend a lot of time with this Curial Committee, he might not get to see much of anything.

And so he walked west, crossing the Via delle Fondamenta, then north along the Viale Del Giardino Quadrato, which bor-ders the maze-like beauty of the Vatican Gardens. He bisected the Viale Vaticano, turned left and followed the winding road as it circumscribed the city. The walk took more than an hour and was a calming experience. There was less traffic on the periphery; the slight elevation of the road afforded Peter a composite view of the Vatican. He was able to pause at will, fix various landmarks in his mind, and slowly orient himself to his new environment. It was a beautifully clear day full of bright contrasts— the blue sky against the white stone of the buildings, dark green cypresses dotting the sandy hills.

Finally coming full circle, he entered Saint Peter's Basilica, amazed by its truly awe-inspiring dimensions. It was undoubtedly the most flamboyant Catholic church in the world. Tagging along with a tour, Peter learned that the Basilica was not the Pope's parish church—that was the little church of Sant' Anna, by the gate of the same name. St. Peter's had started out as a small memorial chapel that Constantine had urged built to honor the first Pope. And somehow, through the ages, it just kept getting bigger—just like the Catholic Church itself.

Peter wandered through the immense Basilica, hushed by the solemnity of the grottoes, uplifted by the soaring vision and power of Michelangelo's Sistine Chapel ceiling and the frescoes of Botticelli, Signorelli and Perugino.

After an al fresco lunch, he kept walking, heading north, into the shadows of the papal palaces, toward the Vatican museums to the east of Stradone Dei Giardini. Time passed quickly. When shifting shadows made him realize how late it had become, he doubled back, wondering if Cardinal Lareggia's gopher, Father Orlando, was out hunting him down. It was well after three-thirty when he cut across St. Peter's Square to return to the Teutonic College.

Like an impatient vulture, Father Orlando waited for him outside the apartment. The man appeared flushed with anger, but still tried to hold his emotions in check, volunteering only that the Cardinal had become alarmed by his absence, and that the committee awaited him.

Turning without another word, the priest led Peter to a black Mercedes that squatted in wait like a sleek, hard-shelled bug. Peter followed his escort slowly, for some reason feeling the first twinges of fear.

ELEVEN

Rome, Italy—Targeno
August 25, 1998

Targeno didn't like taking orders from the Jesuit, but he had no choice, really. He did not obey out of friendship. In his special business, Targeno knew, he could have no real friends, could trust no one—especially priests who believed it was occasionally okay to kill people. But Father Giovanni Francesco was so well-connected in the Vatican infrastructure, Targeno couldn't tell the man to go fuck himself—an act he would love to watch.

No. It was a time to call in a few favors. That was the way it was in politics and espionage. You always owed somebody. Somebody always owed you.

Her name was Sister Etienne. She was a nun of the Convent of Poor Clares in Rome. Her real name was Angelina Pettinaro. She'd been born to some poor *mameluke* in Calabria. No doubt the bastard had been too poor to raise all the kids his stiff cock kept bringing into the world, so he dispatched as many of the girls to convents as his fat wife would most likely let him, thereby easing both his pocketbook and his conscience.

And the Church still carped about birth control . . . !

Targeno shook his head, grimaced to himself as he sat waiting in the convent's reception hall. He looked at his watch; the day was half gone already. *Damn* Francesco!

A door opened at the end of the sparsely decorated room, and a tall, graceful woman in the habit of an abbess entered. She glided toward him with the stylish confidence of a ballet dancer. Although the woman had to be at least sixty years old, she looked attractive. Targeno imagined she must have been a strikingly beautiful woman when she was younger. Why would anyone so full of elegance want to throw it all away in a fucking convent? The world was truly full of twisted people.

"Mr. Targeno," said Abbess Victorianna. "I think you can see Sister Etienne now."

He nodded, followed the willowy woman through a doorway that led to a flight of stairs. He walked softly behind her, emulating her delicate step.

"The doctors cannot find anything physically wrong with her," said the Abbess. "But she has been very upset by her religious experience."

"Upset?" Targeno asked in his most velvety voice. "Is she coherent?"

"It is difficult to say. Father Francesco stopped by earlier and she was not very cooperative."

Targeno stopped at the top of the stairs. "What does that mean? Did she tell him anything or not?"

Victorianna's eyes met his for an instant. A surge of repressed passion passed between them and she looked away sheepishly. She was embarrassed as much by what she sensed in the agent's eyes as the message she was about to deliver.

"When she recognized Giovanni, she became hysterical."

"She does not like him?" Targeno smiled. "Well, at least she shows good taste in men."

"This is no laughing matter," said Victorianna. She turned and continued down the corridor, stopping at a linen closet from which she produced a white cotton physician's coat.

Targeno slipped off his black jacket, traded it for the white coat. "How do I look?" he asked as he shrugged into it. "Another Dr. Schweitzer, no doubt . . ."

Victorianna smiled in spite of the gravity of the situation.

"The infirmary is through these double doors. She's in the first room to the right."

Targeno nodded and pushed through the doors. Entering the nun's room, he was assaulted by the utter whiteness of everything—walls, cabinets, sheets. Sunlight streamed through gauzy curtains and he wished for his dark glasses. The woman lying in the bed stared straight up toward the ceiling, not acknowledging his presence. She had the eyes of a schizophrenic, of someone who looked upon a world not our own. Targeno was surprised by her healthy, youthful aspect. Although he knew her to be in her late forties, her skin was smooth and clear, her dark hair vibrant and full of natural luster.

Another beautiful woman wasting away in the convent.

"And how are we feeling today?" he asked as cheerily as possible, stepping into her field of vision.

She continued to stare upward, saying nothing. Targeno recognized the symptoms of severe shock, and knew he would waste his time with the normal rigors of interrogation. Experience had prepared him for such problems, however, and he reached into his back pocket for what appeared to be a gold cigarette case.

Opening it, he retrieved a small hypodermic needle and a syringe filled with xylothol, a mild hallucinogenic which made sodium pentothal seem like Kool-Aid. So you don't want to talk? he thought to himself, smiling. Well, try this for a little wake-up!

He waited only several minutes, after the injection, before her blue eyes unglazed and she focused upon him.

"Etienne," he said softly. "I am your doctor, and you must tell me what happened to you, so I can make you well."

"No . . ." she said, her voice soft, almost elegant. "Nothing can make me well. I have seen the end of the world."

"Really . . . ? What was it like?"

"It was terrifying." She looked away as though embarrassed. "I cannot tell you."

"Yes. Yes, you can. It is all right to tell me anything."

Turning back, she looked directly into his eyes—suddenly

unnaturally alert. Her features, though calm, were somehow transfigured. "I don't know you," she said. "I will tell you nothing."

"If you want to get well, you must tell me what happened to you . . . what you saw that frightened you so."

"I don't care about getting well," she said forcefully. Targeno had never seen anyone speak so coherently under the influence of xylothol. "And there is only one man I will speak to."

"Who might that be?" Targeno could sense failure, but he pressed on.

"His Holiness. I must see the Holy Father." Etienne rolled over and faced the wall.

This was ridiculous. The woman was laced with enough chemical to get a rhino to sing, yet she handled it like sugar water. He'd never seen anything like this; he'd have to be patient. The drug would eventually prevail.

"Etienne . . . you must talk to me." He touched her shoulder, tried to roll her back to face him.

She looked at him over her shoulder. "Do you believe in God?"

"I . . . I'm not sure," he said honestly. "Why?"

"Because He believes in you."

He chuckled. "I've never heard it put quite like that."

The woman turned away, stared at the ceiling again. Her lips moved slightly, as though she might speak. He decided to wait her out. Despite her resistance to the drug, she was having difficulty fighting a compelling urge to speak.

As Targeno hoped, after a short silence, the nun blurted out a tearful confession: "I have committed a terrible sin against man and God. Now I must suffer for that transgression. Even though I believed I was doing God's will."

"What do you mean?"

"That's what they told me—it was God's will."

"*Who* told you?"

"The Cardinal . . . and the others . . ."

Targeno had no idea what she was talking about. The temptation to ignore her words, dismissing them as the ravings of a religious nut, was tempered by a nagging, instinctive feeling that he'd happened upon something fairly big. He'd felt similar hunches all his life, and many times had survived because he relied upon his instincts rather than pure logic. Perhaps he should pay attention to those feelings now.

"Can you tell me their names?"

Etienne smiled, looked deeply into him. "Why not? Cardinal Lareggia, Father Francesco, and my Abbess, Victorianna. They came to me a long time ago . . . when we were all very young."

"For what?" he asked softly. The xylothol was working well; she spoke more freely.

"They needed my help. Without me, their plans were impossible."

"Are you going to tell me *why* they needed you?"

She giggled like a schoolgirl. "Maybe . . ."

"Does it have anything to do with your 'vision'?"

A chuckle. "Oh yes!"

"Etienne, I am waiting . . ."

". . . and I am deciding. Whether or not to tell you anything."

"You've already told me plenty." He tried an old interrogation trick.

"I have?"

He was always surprised at how often it worked.

"Yes, my dear sister . . . All about the Cardinal and his friends."

"Did I tell you about the doctor?" Hesitancy punctuated her question.

"The doctor . . . ?" Targeno's pulse jumped. He was enjoying this. As each new clue fell from her lips, he became more intrigued. "No, you did not. Can you tell me about him?"

She looked away, batting her long eyelashes.

"They brought him in to . . . to work with me. He was a nice man. Very gentle."

"What was his name? You never mentioned it."

"Didn't I?" She giggled again. "It was Krieger. Dr. Rudolph Krieger."

TWELVE

Vatican City—Krieger
August 25, 1998

So, the time had finally come round, Rudolph thought wearily as he rode in a black Mercedes from Roma Internazionale. All this time, he'd been living quietly in a small village in Switzerland, having all but forgotten the work he'd performed so long ago. No, that was untrue. He would never forget what he'd done. But he had been trying like hell.

And now it was coming back to him.

To haunt him? It was difficult to determine. Rudolph shrugged mentally. Whatever, he had made a bargain, and now he was obligated to live up to the remainder of his part. The endless supply of Vatican money had never dwindled, and his life up to this point had been every bit as comfortable and rewarding as they'd promised.

The Mercedes rolled to a solid, silent halt at a rear entrance to the *Governorate*, where he was met by Father Orlando, a youngish, extremely reticent priest. Rudolph studied the Old World decor of the building's interior as the priest led him through the halls. It had been many, many years since he'd been in this place. He was not surprised to discover almost nothing had changed. The Church was nothing if not traditional.

Up the elevators, down a long hall, and into a conference room where Paolo Cardinal Lareggia sat at the head of a polished conference table that might have served as an aircraft carrier for a small country. The other two were also present, folders and notebooks stacked in front of them. Krieger recognized the nun and the priest easily. Other than the usual insults of time, both appeared surprisingly vigorous and healthy. However, Lareggia's outrageous obesity shocked the physician. Everything about the man was almost perfectly round. He was cholesterol personified, a heart attack waiting to happen ...

"Dr. Rudolph Krieger, welcome!" said the Cardinal, standing graciously, revealing his expansive abdomen. "I trust you remember Sister Victorianna and Father Francesco ..."

"Yes, I do," said Rudolph, trying to bring a courteous smile to his face. "It's been a long time, hasn't it?"

Lareggia nodded. "For all of us. For everything."

Father Francesco smiled. "I suppose you know why you're here?"

"I have a good idea," said Rudolph. "I may be an old man, but my memory is still good."

"You will have a full staff at your disposal," said the Cardinal. "Just let me know if there is anything lacking, and you shall have it. Now, please, Doctor, have a seat."

"Very well," said Rudolph, looking across the table and selecting a chair that faced a video projector. It looked as though they were preparing for a board of directors meeting. The Cardinal resumed his seat, nodded at the nun.

"We want a complete work-up," said Abbess Victorianna. Rudolph was struck by how beautiful she still seemed to him. "Physical status and psychological."

He smiled. "Sister, I'm not trained in the latter ..."

"I'm sure you know enough to be competent," said Cardinal Lareggia. "Besides, your support staff will include some psychiatric people."

Krieger nodded. "Very well, but how is all this activity being explained?"

"We are part of a Curial Committee investigating miracles," said Father Francesco, who was smoking a dark-leafed cigarette—much to the displeasure of the nun. "What we are asking of you is standard procedure in these matters. No one will question a thing."

"Does the Curia normally bring in foreign doctors?"

"No," said the Jesuit. "But with age comes privilege. We can do as we see fit."

They seemed to have everything planned, down to the smallest detail. Not that he hadn't expected as much. From the very beginning of their association, he'd found the trio to be as coldly efficient as any organization he'd ever known. Hard to believe they were all Italian—there was an aspect to their operation that had a distinctly Teutonic cast. He smiled to himself. Other than these three, he was the only person in the world who knew what they had apparently succeeded in doing. He wondered if they would have let him live with that knowledge all this time, if they would have trusted him for so many years, if he wasn't so necessary to the eventual follow-up. He also wondered how many others might have died because they knew even disconnected pieces of the story.

"Any other questions?" asked the Cardinal.

A few I'll never ask, thought Rudolph. Then: "Where is the young man? I thought we were going to begin today?"

"He's been resting from his flight," said Lareggia. "He is being brought here as we speak."

Rudolph nodded. He had a sudden craving for nicotine, though he'd given up his pipe more than five years earlier. "Does he know the entire story yet?"

Father Francesco smiled, chuckled to himself. "He knows nothing at this point. We plan to 'educate' him gradually, after he becomes acclimated."

"I felt it might be wise for you to be present when we eventually tell him," said Sister Victorianna. "When we reveal everything to him, it would be best if you explained what you did in your own words."

Krieger nodded. "I am available as long as you might need me. Is there anything else I should know?"

Victorianna briefly recounted the story of Sister Etienne

being in a state of shock after experiencing a vision, a possible revelation, which could be connected to the issue at hand.

Although he said nothing, Rudolph was inclined to pass off such things as "visions" and other religious experiences as utter foolishness. To these people, such things were normal, but to see a cause-and-effect relationship between Etienne's breakdown and what he'd done seemed silly and presumptuous. Up until this very moment, Rudolph had tried not to think very much about why he had been airlifted from his pastoral home into the heart of the Vatican. He had not wanted to accept that he was finally facing up to the responsibilities and mechanisms he'd set in motion so many years ago.

What the hell had he done?

What did it all mean?

The questions caused him to smile to himself. He was certain many men had asked themselves the same questions over the centuries. Funny how they seemed to apply to so many situations . . .

A light tapping on the conference room door caused everyone to look in that direction. The swarthy face of Father Orlando appeared.

"Excuse me, Your Grace. Father Carenza is with me."

And then, suddenly, it sank in. He was finally going to be meeting the boy . . . the man, actually. All the time and all the work of long ago was being yanked out of the world of theory and made real.

Cardinal Lareggia stood up, backing away from the table to give his stomach its sway. "Send him in. And leave us," he said.

Orlando nodded, disappeared for an instant, then escorted a young man in a black cassock into the room. "Father Peter Carenza," said the Curial assistant, as though announcing a visitor to a royal court, then slipped silently away.

In that moment before the door clicked shut, Rudolph Krieger took Carenza's measure. He was tall and lean; his posture suggested a muscular, athletic body. He had dark eyes and hair, a classically aquiline nose, and a strong jawline.

High cheekbones gave his face an angular, extremely handsome aspect. His olive complexion seemed to radiate good health, and the spark of high intelligence capered behind his eyes. Here stood a man who could have been an athlete, a movie star, anything at all—and they'd made him a priest. What a waste, Krieger thought.

"Welcome, Father Carenza," said Cardinal Lareggia, who appeared unable to hide the awe he was feeling. The large man had trouble getting out his next sentence. "Please, have a seat."

"Thank you," said Carenza, sitting at the far end of the table. He seemed only slightly intimidated by everyone staring at him, determined to hold his own.

The Cardinal looked at Father Francesco, nodded. The Jesuit stood up and faced Carenza.

"I am Father Giovanni Francesco. Normally I serve as Papal Liaison for the Society of Jesus. Today I function as part of the Committee on the Investigation of Miracles. My colleagues . . ." Francesco introduced the others, with their titles. Even the normally brusque Jesuit appeared tempered in the presence of Carenza. Francesco gave Krieger's credentials simply, stating that he was a retired scientist and winner of the Nobel Prize.

Carenza leaned forward, apparently impressed but hesitant, perhaps confused. Krieger felt sorry for him and for what was to come his way in the next few weeks.

"For the next day or two, we will want to put you through a series of examinations. Nothing serious," said Krieger, "just a baseline physical, and some specially designed tests."

"What kind of tests?" asked Carenza. There was no suspicion in his voice.

Krieger cleared his throat. "Tests which will determine whether or not you show signs of psychokinetic ability, and also tests of a more psychological nature."

Carenza smiled. "You mean you want to know if I'm nuts."

Krieger liked the young priest's candor. "Not exactly, but yes, I suppose you could say that."

"Listen, Dr. Krieger, I didn't ask to be interviewed by any miracles committee. I'd rather just forget the whole incident—instead of having it dissected like a dead frog."

"Please, Father, there is no need to be alarmed," said Victorianna, in an obvious effort to placate. "I assure you we understand how you feel."

"Is there anything we can do to make to make you feel more at ease, Father?" asked Cardinal Lareggia.

Carenza stared directly at him. "Pardon me, Your Grace, but I *killed* another human being. I won't apologize for being a bit sensitive about it."

Well said, thought Krieger. He liked this young man already.

"Very well, then: let's start with a few questions, shall we?" Francesco smiled. "Could you please tell exactly what happened to you?"

Krieger smiled. Carenza's presence had already produced a change in the Jesuit's demeanor. How long could it have been since the man had employed the word "please"?

"Yes, I think so." Carenza sighed, just audibly.

"If you could—we would want every detail," said the nun.

Krieger leaned back and listened to Carenza's story. True to their request, the priest tried to be meticulous in recalling everything. Sometimes his listeners interrupted, but they did so with obvious trepidation. Trying to mask their respect for Carenza proved difficult, although Francesco—true to his gangsterlike persona—appeared the least in awe. Sometimes he burrowed deep, ferreting out details that seemed trivial at best. Although Krieger was free to ask questions, he chose to remain silent. He would have plenty of time to get to know the young man and his story.

The doctor admired Carenza's toughness in spite of the ordeal he'd experienced. Killing another human being must be a terrible burden to carry, but the young priest bore it well, obviously holding on to a basic belief in his own dignity.

The initial interview lasted until past sundown. Everyone grew fatigued, but the trio never lost their basic respect for Carenza, or their clear belief in the truth of his tale. Gradually they grew more comfortable in his presence, more relaxed. Rudolph watched it in silence, waiting.

Finally, Father Orlando was summoned to take the young priest to his room. Tomorrow, the real tests would begin.

THIRTEEN

Vatican City—Carenza
August 25, 1998

After they left the committee meeting room, Father Orlando took Peter on a brief tour of the place which would be his home for the next few days—the Academy of Sciences complex. He saw the labs and the offices on the second floor, where he would be examined and tested, and was then taken to his quarters on the floor above.

His room was small and functional. The furniture was virtually without style, and the cot had a military look about it. A small bathroom outfitted with toiletries completed the picture. The rooms had the look of being hastily converted to living quarters. Perhaps they had originally been some kind of utility rooms or a small lab. Not exactly the Hyatt Regency, but it wasn't a Turkish jail either. A single window revealed a starry night above the low Vatican hills and the neatly trimmed shrubbery that graced the grounds of the Academy of Sciences buildings.

Lying on the cot, which was hard and not even close to comfortable, Peter reviewed the events of the last two days, culminating with his initial interview with the Miracle Committee. He grinned as he stared at the white stucco ceiling . . . and what a weird crew they were . . . ! The fat cardinal, the gaunt priest, and the classic nun. Strange bedfellows, as they say.

And then there was Krieger. Peter found it more than a little strange that a Nobel Prize-winning scientist would be employed by the Vatican to investigate so-called miracles. Even if he *was* retired, it sure seemed like a weird way to spend his sunshine years.

Peter's eyelids grew heavy as he continued to recast the events of the day. Though his mind kept sparking and jumping from one topic to another, his body was running down, finally succumbing to the demands of jet lag. Closing his eyes, he drifted off into sea-choppy sleep . . .

. . . and awoke for absolutely no reason in the middle of the night. Stretching, his muscles screaming from the torture of the cot, he got up and looked out the window. The city was still, blued with the night, quiet. As he stood there, collecting his thoughts, he realized there was something wrong with his situation. It was like looking at a photograph of a perfectly mundane scene, and knowing all the while that aberration lurked somewhere within the picture—if you could only find it.

Aberration?

Well, maybe that was the wrong word. But he was certain things were not as they'd been portrayed. He smiled, shook his head. He was not a particularly intuitive thinker, nor prone to instinctive feelings, but an alarm he could not ignore had been triggered deep within his mind.

Screw it, he thought as he turned to the door.

He wouldn't have been surprised to find the portal locked, but it swung open silently, inviting him into a dark, utterly silent hallway. Ambient light from fire-exit signs gave off sufficient illumination to do some exploring, and that was all he needed. His Reeboks afforded him silent passage as he walked slowly up the corridor. Locating the nearest stairwell, he descended to the second floor and the labs Orlando had shown him earlier.

If questioned, he'd have to admit he was trespassing, but

he didn't believe he was doing anything wrong. Although more than curiosity motivated him, he only wished to find out about things directly concerning himself.

Opening the second-floor stairwell door carefully, he peered into the dim emptiness of a long, featureless hall. Peter held his position for perhaps a minute, listening, waiting for a sign of anyone else's presence. Satisfied that he was truly alone, he retraced his earlier path with Orlando to the clutch of offices and laboratory rooms. The doors were locked, but the latch assemblies were old, made long before the age of Visa cards. Peter pulled out his wallet and was soon inside the room.

It would have been completely dark in the lab except for the glow of several computer monitors. He paused to let his eyes adjust to the dim illumination. The usual laboratory assortment of rubber and chemical smells assaulted him as he moved past worktables, desks, cabinets and shelves full of vials and bottles arrayed like soldiers at parade rest. He had never been much of a practical scientist, although he did have good basic computer skills. None of the other stuff in the lab would mean much to him.

Pausing before the monitor of the nearest PC, Peter studied the MainMenu screen:

PROJECT TORINO

(A) PROJECT LOG

(B) WORK FILES

(C) STATISTICAL ANALYSIS

(D) MATH FUNCTIONS

Just for fun, Peter selected the Project Log, and heard a soft beep, which sounded as a Klaxon in the quiet lab. The screen display had changed: the menu had disappeared and a blinking prompt, asking for a password, stared at him.

Knowing he had little chance of stumbling on the right access word, he nonetheless made a few entries. After several rejections, the MainMenu reappeared. The PC wanted nothing to do with him. Okay, fine. I can take a hint, he thought.

At one end of the lab another ordinary door guarded a smaller room. Another flash of Peter's credit card and the simple lock surrendered. He stepped into a large, dark office. Bulky half-shapes and shadows defined bookcases, a large oak desk, specimen cases, and file cabinets. Heavy drapes covered the room's single window, and Peter decided he would chance the light from a small, cantilevered halogen lamp on the big desk. It was doubtful anyone would be in the gardens beneath the window at such an empty hour.

Clicking on the lamp, adjusting its balanced arm so that it burned close and low to the desk blotter, he allowed his eyes to acclimate to the light. Scanning the bookcases, Peter noticed whole shelves of titles on microbiology, genetics, semiology, and other arcane subjects. This was probably where Krieger would be working, probably where he'd worked in the past. Peter had gotten the impression during the day's session that Krieger had been associated with the committee for a fair amount of time. That he had his own work space and office in the Vatican Academy suggested the same conclusion.

Anything interesting or revealing would probably be contained in the file cabinets, but Peter had no idea where to search. Rather than poking about randomly, he took a pragmatic approach, and just to be contrary, he started with the end of the alphabet instead of the beginning.

An hour later, with his thumbs sore from paging through numerous folders, he finally touched on something that got his instincts kicking. All the files under the title "Torino" had been removed, replaced by a sealed plastic card that said: CLASSIFIED—SEE COMPUTERIZED FILES.

Well, he'd already tried that. "Torino," whatever that was, clearly meant something to Krieger and the Miracle Committee. Peter checked his watch—still an hour and a half before he had to get out. Nobody would be coming to work much before 5:00 AM.

The files contained acres of cross-indexed information,

journal abstracts, statistics, graphs, charts, tables, and other scientific arcana. And each time something referred to "Torino," the path leading from it had been excised. Peter grew weary and frustrated. Maybe he was wasting his time. No sense playing detective when he didn't know what he was looking for.

But something kept kicking at his subconscious like an annoying kid who simply won't go away. When he finally got around to rummaging through the big desk he discovered Rudolph Krieger's private journal. It was handwritten in German, but Peter's classical Jesuit education would allow him to translate. Slowly, he started reading the words that would change his life irrevocably.

Written in clear, Teutonic hand, Krieger's notes in a folio-sized ledger began with the date January 15, 1968.

"This contains what we believe to be blood samples," Father Francesco told me. The angular, athletic man in his late thirties was holding a glass vial containing six lengths of dark-stained thread.

Accepting the vial, I held the glass up to the light at my workbench.

"First," said Father Francesco, "I want you to verify the existence of human blood on these threads. Others are also working on this question, but I prefer to trust the results of a Nobel Prize winner."

Basking in the warm praise of my recent accomplishment, I promised him I would have incontrovertible answers within several days.

Tests I had perfected during the previous decade would now yield conclusive information from fragments even as small as the tiny linen threads. The peroxidase method could confirm the existence of a drop of human blood on a man's shoe, even if it had been supposedly wiped clean. The idea was to find a trace of hemoglobin, the substance that imparts to blood its distinctive red color. I knew I could do it.

Peroxidase, a component of hemoglobin, remains stable over long periods of time—even centuries—and would reveal itself under the microscope as pink stains when treated with test solutions of phenolphthalein.

The tests were positive, but just to make certain, I repeated the technique several times. I then sent a simple report to Father Francesco: without any doubt, the linen threads contained samples of human blood.

Today, all three of them came to see me in my new laboratory. Besides the wolflike Jesuit, there was a Cardinal named Lareggia—a big-boned man with a tendency toward obesity. Still, he looked very strong and capable of taking care of himself, as if he would be more comfortable in a dockside bar than a church. The third member of the visiting party was a nun. Her name was Victorianna and she was, quite frankly, one of the most beautiful women I had ever seen. Even though she wore the starched habit and cowl of her order, I was transfixed by her flawless complexion, her fawnlike eyes, and the delicate perfection of her features. Why would such a woman hide herself in a convent?

"We are pleased with your results, Dr. Krieger," the Jesuit said. "And we're ready for the next step."

I asked him what that might be.

"A complete analysis," said the Cardinal.

They want me to find out *everything* about this blood sample. In addition, they wanted me to obtain a genetic blueprint of the person whose blood this represents.

I can remember my pulse actually jumping. What they asked of me would place my work on the cutting edge of biochemical research! I couldn't imagine being more fortunate.

I told them it would require analysis of the nuclear DNA itself. I did not want to think about how such a project might be managed, but I informed them I would need a small staff and some very expensive equipment.

The Cardinal acknowledged me with a slight wave of the hand. "Do not worry," he said. Even the price of an electron microscope did not startle him.

I suddenly realized how serious these people were. What in the world was going on?

Of course, as any research scientist will tell you: don't question anyone when they've got their checkbook open. But part of what made me a good scientist was my natural curiosity. I could not stifle the questions already forming in my mind.

I explained my vision of a very intensive project and expressed my need to set up a schedule. I asked about a timetable and an ultimate goal.

The timetable, they said, was as soon as possible. The ultimate goal was rather complicated. I nodded, but stressed my need to know the reason for all my work. Knowing that would influence the way the work was done.

Father Francesco looked at me, but said nothing. I got the impression he was, as the Americans say, "sizing me up," deciding whether I was worth the trouble. For the first time I sensed an element of danger in the Jesuit. Priest though he was, Francesco had the eyes of something as coolly efficient as a reptile ... and he scared me.

The nun spoke at length. Her English was flawless. She had researched my work thoroughly and was conversant in cell biology. She knew of my follow-up to the experiments of Watson and Crick and others who are pioneers in the fields of gene-mapping, splicing, and engineering. She even referred to my paper on transfer RNA as a "classic."

She went on to mention my interest in the work of people like Steptoe and Edwards, and Shettles and Bevis. I was stunned—how could these people know so much about me? I was beginning to feel a bit uneasy, and I asked them point blank why they were so interested in cell physiology and recombinant DNA manipulation.

Was the Pope preparing a new encyclical on birth control and artificial insemination?

I pushed on. What specific work are we talking about, I asked. *Ex utero* fertilization, artificial insemination, cloning? What, exactly, did the Church wish to accomplish?

The Cardinal smiled at me and said: *all of those things*.

I felt more confused than ever. What on earth did these people want?

I asked them one more time to spare me the drama and the cryptic responses. Enough was enough.

The Cardinal raised a single finger several inches above the desk. It was enough to command everyone's attention. He sighed and agreed to tell me the whole story, but cautioned me on the utter seriousness of their endeavor. I was sworn to secrecy and threatened with death.

The very idea of a priest threatening murder seemed absurd, but as I stared into the cold well-dark eyes of Francesco, I knew the man had spoken sincerely. If I ever revealed what they were about to tell me—I would be a dead man. Incredible.

Lareggia nodded to the nun, and she asked me an intriguing question: did I think it possible to obtain enough genetic information from a blood cell nucleus to successfully re-create the genes through recombinant DNA techniques?

Her question so stimulated my scientific mind that for an instant I forgot my predicament. It was a challenging concept, however, initially suggested by David Silva at Stanford.

Victorianna verified my response, quoting chapter and verse from Silva's speculative monographs on recombinant research and cloning. "Bringing Back

Mozart" was published in the popular press—Scientific American—but was largely ignored by most scientists.

Then Victorianna asked me the pivotal question: did I believe Silva's idea was achievable? *Could I recreate the dead by cloning them from nuclear information left in their physical remains?*

I was stunned. The nun smiled at me; I remember her being incredibly beautiful at that moment—almost angelic. She nodded. Yes, she wanted me to recreate the dead.

I paused to consider how much preparation would be required, how many experiments would be needed to verify the complex steps in such a process. My mind leaped ahead, and I almost became lost in reverie. Then I looked at them and asked a very important question: did the blood samples I was given contain the nuclear material—that is, the white cells—that I would be recreating?

All three nodded. The nun added that the donor was deceased, but I had already assumed that.

Lareggia looked at me squarely. He told me the blood and thread samples were taken from something the Italians call the *Santa Sindone*.

My Italian is not good, but I recognized the phrase. I can still recall the sudden sensation of disequilibrium that hit me at that moment. My vision blurred and the room spun around me like a carousel. These people were brilliantly insane, their plan equally so.

Santa Sindone: The Holy Shroud.

The Shroud of Turin.

They wanted me to clone Jesus Christ.

Book Two

"And there followed him great multitudes of people from Galilee, and from Decapolis, and from Jerusalem, and from Judea, and from beyond Jordan."

—Matthew 4:25

FOURTEEN

Vatican City—Carenza
August 26, 1998

His first reaction was laughter.

Uncontrollable, semihysterical. His laughter reverberated in the small room. It had a hollow, counterfeit sound, as if it came not from within him, but from the cold outer hull of the world. The memory-echo of the sound immediately haunted him, making him feel helpless, weak, defeated.

The idea was so absurd! For a time, his mind—trained in the ways of classical theology—refused to take a firm grip on the concept. No way. Impossible. Some kind of joke.

But he knew it was no joke. And it didn't take a fool to see the pieces of the puzzle all lying there in front of him. There were just enough ego and genuine emotion in Dr. Krieger's journal to make the account completely believable. Sitting back in the desk chair, Peter drew in a deep breath, exhaled. He felt shaky, queasy.

He forced himself to think, to accept the barest possibility of what the evidence suggested. My God . . . could such a blasphemy be possible? It seemed so. The time frame: just over thirty years since the first entry in the journal. Krieger's involvement, then *and* now. Peter's "miracle," and the committee to investigate it.

Again he lapsed into a fuguelike state. His senses dwindled—sight, sound, touch all deserted him as he drifted helplessly in the void created by knowledge that did not fit within the prescribed boundaries of the world he had known only minutes ago. It was unthinkable . . .

Time fell away from him like shattered crystal. He did not hear the footsteps behind the office door, nor did he at first feel the powerful hand grip his shoulder.

"I'm sorry, Father, but you will have to come with us," said a voice.

Peter's awareness slowly resurfaced. He looked up. Father Orlando stared at him from beyond the dim light of the desk lamp. Beyond him, shrouded in shadow, stood the scarecrow-thin Francesco.

Peter's reaction was pure instinct, totally somatic. Without realizing he was moving, Peter sprang up from the chair as though it were an ejection seat in a jet. His raised forearm caught Orlando under the chin, stunning the man and sending him backward into Francesco. While both men were still falling, Peter was already running out the door, through the dark lab, and into the silent corridor. He gave no thought to where he was going. He was in trouble and he was running away from it.

The long hallway stretched away from him, ending in a square black vanishing point. It was like staring down a mineshaft, and as he ran forward, he had the sensation of rushing downward into the earth. Disoriented, he passed countless doors, and still the corridor raced ahead of him. Behind him the sounds of jagged breath and heavy footfalls grew nearer. Stopping, in almost total darkness, he yanked on a doorknob. Locked. No time to get out a credit card now, though.

The sounds of pursuit closed in. They were going to get him. Just a matter of time. Peter started running again, but his coordination seemed out of whack. His knees weren't working right, his feet slapped at the floor. His breath stuck in his throat and his tongue was so dry and swollen it felt like it might choke him. He felt as if he were trying to run for the first time in his life.

As Peter reached a T-junction in the passageway, Orlando caught him in a flying tackle around the knees. He went down like the end of a whip being snapped. His head hit the tiled floor, and with a burst of light behind his eyes, he fell into darkness.

"Is he all right?"

The voice was soft, solicitous, female.

"Yes, he will be fine," said the other in a light German accent.

Peter felt a wave of sensation slowly pass over him, his entire body coming back to life with a tingling sense of weightlessness. He lay on his back, looking up at a circle of four faces, feeling like an accident victim on a night-slick street. The confines of his spare little room took shape beyond the people looming over him. The side of his head throbbed and his cheekbone felt numb.

The memory of what he'd learned slowly returned. It was still crazy. Still impossible.

Krieger and the "committee" were staring at him.

"How much did you read?" asked Francesco.

"Enough," said Peter. "Enough to think I understand why I'm here. Enough to know you're not any committee on miracles."

"We didn't intend it to be like this," said the nun.

Peter chuckled grimly. "Really? What had you planned—maybe a little surprise party? 'Guess what, Peter Carenza? You're not who you think you are!' C'mon, people, this whole thing's ridiculous!"

"In your heart, you know that is not true," said Cardinal Lareggia. He had constructed an expression of consummate sincerity, but his face wore it like a cheap mask.

Peter shook his head, wishing he could wake up from the surreal dream his life had become. He closed his eyes to shut them all out, and Francesco touched him gently on the shoulder, speaking to him in an uncharacteristically devout tone.

"You know the truth, Peter! The good doctor cloned a baby from Christ's blood. The baby grew up into a man. And *you* are that man. *You* are the Saviour."

"No ... I can't be!"

"You have the power, Peter," said Lareggia. "Look at what you did to your assailant. Accept it!"

Peter shook his head, turned away from them. What the hell did they want from him?

"This is some kind of trick, right?" he said accusingly. "Some kind of weird psychology experiment."

Lareggia smiled. "He is persistent," he said to his Jesuit partner.

"Wouldn't you be?" asked Victorianna, placing a motherly hand on Peter's shoulder.

Of the four of them, he intuitively liked the nun the most. As to whether he trusted her more than the others, well, that was hard to say.

Probably not much, he thought. The whole bunch of them were insane. They had to be.

"Peter, we still need you to submit to a series of tests," said Cardinal Lareggia. "Doctor Krieger will supervise everything."

God, they weren't going to ease off, were they?

"What do you want with me?" he asked out of desperation.

"All will be explained in due time," said Francesco. "After we have examined you. After you are more comfortable with your true identity."

"Look, you people are nuts! I'm Peter Carenza! Don't you think I would know it if I was Christ!?"

"Jesus did not manifest his divine nature until he entered his thirtieth year," said Cardinal Lareggia.

"As you are now doing," said Victorianna as if praying.

"Oh," he said. "You mean I'm the Son of God, but I don't know it yet?"

She nodded.

"Well, that certainly explains everything."

Peter shook his head. It didn't matter what he said to these people. They were convinced of the success of their plans. He had to get away from these religious fanatics.

"We have records of everything we did," said Krieger. "Everything is documented. It took months to perfect the fertilization process *ex utero*. Then we had to create the proper growth medium. We needed to find a way to keep the embryo alive until it reached the blastula stage. Steptoe and Edwards had attempted implantation with sixteen-cell embrycysts. I'd always believed this was a mistake."

"What are you talking about?" asked Peter absently, not really wanting to know. Krieger seemed to be trying to convince him of the truth as he saw it—as if the science would impress reality on Peter.

The doctor looked steadily at Peter with steely, gray-blue eyes. Eyes as hard and cold as grapeshot. "I'm talking about the way you were *born*, son."

The words pierced him, stinging him with their venom. Could what he was saying be true?

"We even recorded it on film," said Krieger. "From the implantation to the birth."

"The *virgin* birth," said Lareggia—his tone worshipful.

"That's right," Victorianna added. "Your mother was a virgin."

These people were incredible. Never short on surprises, that was for sure. He shook his head again. He had to get out of here!

"Why don't you just stop all this bullshit and leave me alone!" His voice shook with anger.

"Calm down, Father," said Francesco, reaching for him.

Peter resisted his touch, trying to rise from the cot. But his four tormentors formed an efficient barrier of bodies all around him. He swung his arms wildly. Everyone stepped back except the Jesuit, who waded toward him like a boxer. "God forgive me!" he cried.

Francesco's left hand flashed and was crossed by his right hand. Stunned by the sudden impact, Peter went down and the lights went out again.

When he awoke this time, he was alone in the room. Sitting up on the cot, Peter rubbed his eyes, massaged his temples. He had either the vestiges of a migraine or the beginning of a new one—he didn't know which. His arm hurt; he spotted the needle mark after a moment's search. He moved to the door and tried the knob, but it was locked. He tried his credit card trick, but the sloped face of the latch bolt faced the hallway. No plastic tricks this time.

So his room had become a cell.

They had imprisoned him. And he was supposed to be their Saviour?

Right.

Peter smiled sardonically, returned to the cot and threw himself onto it. At the same time, the latch clicked and the door opened to reveal Rudolph Krieger, looking somewhat contrite and carrying a gladstone bag. Father Orlando stood behind him, facing outward, down the long, empty corridor.

"Hello, Peter. May I come in?" Krieger stuffed a key into the outside pocket of his white laboratory coat.

"It looks like you've already done that."

The scientist closed the door behind him, sat in the lone chair. He placed the battered physician's satchel on the floor, then folded his hands in his lap.

"I'd like to apologize for everything that's happened since last night. Especially your being locked in," said Krieger. "This was Father Francesco's idea. 'Until you are acclimated,' he said."

"Ah yes, Father Giovanni Francesco. A unique man," said Peter. "Not just anybody can say he's given Jesus a right cross to the jaw."

"No, I suppose not . . ."

"What time is it?" Peter's time-sense was shot, destroyed by jet lag and drugs.

"After eight PM I gave you a sedative. You've been out for more than fourteen hours. Do you feel drowsy?"

"No, not really. I feel pretty refreshed, actually."

"Good," said Krieger. "Direxin is supposed to leave you feeling that way."

"Better living through chemistry, right?"

Krieger smiled thinly. "I have to examine you. Do you object?"

"Yes, but does it make any difference?"

"Unfortunately not."

"Aren't you afraid I might zap you with one of my lightning bolts?"

Krieger stared off at the ceiling for a moment, then into Peter's eyes. "Actually, the thought never occurred to me ..."

Peter sat up, looked at the man who had won a Nobel Prize for his work and insights. Though well into his sixties, he cut a lean, energetic figure. His silver-gray hair was thick and healthy-looking.

"How do I know you're all telling me the truth? How do I know this isn't some crazy psychological experiment?"

Krieger exhaled slowly. "You read my journal. We have tons of documentation; we have films. I swear to you, it is all true. Besides, you have seen proof—you have *provided* proof."

"What happened with that mugger ..." Peter said, "that doesn't prove that I'm ... that I'm who they say I am ... just that there's something strange going on."

"Philosophically, I suppose you're correct. But I can tell you differently."

"Do *you* believe I'm the Son of God?"

Krieger coughed gently into his hand. "I don't know. It's something I've thought about a lot over the years. The only thing I know for sure is that you are a genetic duplicate of the man who bled into that shroud. Religion is one of the things I've never really reconciled in my mind."

Peter nodded. "Well, that's a safe answer, I guess. What about my mother? What can you tell me about her?"

Krieger shrugged. There was an aura of sadness about him. He had achieved greatness, but wore it like an ill-fitting suit. "There's not much to tell. She was a nun. I met her when she was a pretty little girl, only eighteen."

"And she let you impregnate her? No, she was probably *ordered* to do it. God's will or some such thing, right?"

Krieger chuckled. "Well, almost. They told her to participate in the experiments at the wishes of the Pope."

"And what happened to her after you'd finished using her?"

Again the sad shrug. "I don't know. I assume she returned to the convent. I really couldn't say."

"Which convent?"

"The Abbey of Poor Clares, as I recall."

"Is it anywhere near here?"

"I'm not sure, but I think so. Why?"

Peter looked at the man who slumped before him. "Don't you think it's natural for a boy to want to see his mother? His real mother?"

"Oh yes, I suppose you would. I'll ask the cardinal for you."

"Why can't I ask him myself? Am I going to be kept prisoner here?"

"I don't know," said Krieger, reaching for his bag of tricks, pulling out a sphygmomanometer and a stethoscope.

"What do they want with me?" asked Peter, trying to keep the desperate tone from his voice. "Assuming what you all say is true, why did you do it? Why would anyone *want* to do such a thing?"

"Please take off your shirt," said the doctor.

"There's nothing wrong with my blood pressure. Put that crap away and answer my questions."

Krieger looked at him for a moment, down at his instruments, then back again. "You're right," he said, and packed up the gladstone.

"So. What do they want with me?"

Krieger chuckled, shook his head. "You mean you really don't know?"

"I have an idea. Let's just say I want someone to tell me."

Krieger sighed heavily. "It's the Millennium, son. If we had a dollar for every person who's predicted the end of the world next year, we would be rich men."

Peter nodded. His worst fears, the craziest suspicions he had refused to acknowledge, were made real. "And I'm supposed to be the Second Coming. That's ridiculous!"

Krieger clicked the latch on his satchel.

Peter stood up, paced about the small space. "What are they planning to do? Sit around and watch me until I start turning water into wine?"

"Well, I think they want to 'prepare' you for your destiny," said Krieger. "I think that was the way the Cardinal phrased it." The old man stood up. "I'll come back later. You've got to calm down, Father."

"No, I've got to get out of here."

"You can't," said Krieger.

Peter chuckled softly. "Watch me."

"What do you mean?" Krieger looked at him with a truly puzzled expression.

Without thinking about it, Peter lunged for the man, grabbing him in a throat-hold. With his forearm pressed against the doctor's larynx, Peter forced him to his knees. Krieger felt thin and frail under his grip and he hoped he wasn't hurting the old guy.

"Stay on your knees and you'll be okay," he whispered. The doctor nodded, and relaxed. Taking the key from the outer pocket of Krieger's white coat, Peter felt immediately safer. Just knowing he wasn't locked in gave him confidence. He tied Krieger with strips of bedsheets, then placed him gently on the bed.

Searching his room, he was surprised to find that he still had everything he would need—passport, money, credit cards. Quickly he changed into a sweatsuit, then stuffed several extra sets of clothes into a small airline carry-on bag.

"I'm sorry about this, but I'm going to need all the time I can get. You understand, don't you?"

"I suppose so," said Krieger. "But I should tell you, son—you don't know who you're dealing with."

"What do you mean?"

"These people are very powerful, and they believe they are doing God's will. They believe they are bringing about the Second Coming and that the world will finally be returned to Paradise."

"That's what they want me to do? Bring about Paradise?"

"In a nutshell, yes."

"I can't stand this. I need time to think. I can't stay here. I need some time."

"Be careful. Francesco can be a ruthless bastard. He's more hood than priest. He'll do whatever he has to do to catch you. You'll never get out of the city."

"Anybody else out there besides Orlando?"

"No, just the regular security people. Lareggia didn't want to arouse any suspicions."

"Good . . . so not many people know I'm here."

"Don't count on it," said Krieger. "You never know with these people."

"You make them sound pretty rough," said Peter, almost smiling at the thought of the huge Cardinal huffing after him along a dark, rain-shined alley.

"Let's say they *know* some rough people. You'll never make it."

"Well, I'm going to try," said Peter. He tore off a strip of sheet, ready to gag Krieger. "Now, if you don't mind . . ."

Krieger obligingly opened his mouth to reveal long, yellowing teeth.

Being careful not to tie him too tightly, Peter finished the job and moved to the door, unlocking it. He opened it a crack and peered out into the darkened hallway. Orlando detected the sound, immediately turning around. Before he could react, Peter threw his full weight against the door. It sprang outward, the outer edge colliding with the priest's right temple. Stunned, he wobbled in front of Peter like a dazed boxer.

Before Orlando could recover, Peter launched himself forward, kicking the man squarely between his legs. Feeling the other man's testicles collapse beneath his foot made Peter queasy.

But it was a lot worse for Father Orlando.

Doubled over, sucking violently for air, eyes rolled back into his head, Peter wondered if the priest even felt the roundhouse to his jaw.

After dragging the unconscious man into the room and tying him up, Peter realized for the first time that he'd passed the point of no return.

Leaving Orlando beside the cot, Peter smiled good-bye to Krieger. He got the feeling the old scientist approved of what he was attempting. With a half-smile, he closed the door and locked it, then ran down the long dark corridor. His heart hitched and sputtered like a broken sewing-machine motor, and his mouth was like dry cotton, but he pushed on until he located a stairwell.

Taking the steps two at a time, he plummeted downward to the ground floor. He didn't know what he would do if he encountered a security guard, and so he tried not to think about it. The only thing he wanted to do was get out of the building, just be in the open air, free of this place. Then he would worry about what to do next.

He reached the first floor, peered out the fire door, and saw no one in either direction. The seemingly endless hallway was dimly lit by widely spaced night-lights. He moved along the shadowy corridor, feeling completely vulnerable. His Italian was not good enough to fool anyone for very long, and surely the security guards would accost someone carrying a small bag through the halls of a deserted government office building, especially at this hour. Was Lareggia still in the building? Had he alerted the guards to be extra cautious tonight?

Taking no chances, Peter slipped into an open lavatory door and moved to the back of the room, where a single window peered out upon a garden and courtyard. He slipped off one shoe as he inspected the edge of the glass for any alarm systems, ready to break the pane. Then, embarrassed, he discovered the window was unlocked. Raising it slowly, quietly, he slipped over the sash and dropped the six feet or so to the soft earth.

Free!

The feeling flooded through him like a powerful liquor. He paused for a moment to get his bearings, then set off at a steady jog, heading east. He ran past the statue of St. Peter, turned north on the Viale Del Giardino Quadrato. He kept up a constant pace as he hit the Via Germanico, a fairly large avenue which angled east, away from the Vatican. If he kept traveling east, Peter knew, he would eventually lose himself in the twisting streets of Rome.

The minutes passed but Peter did not tire. His regular jog through Brooklyn was paying huge dividends as he gradually put a good distance between himself and Vatican City. Despite the darkness, he kept to the side streets. There was nothing that odd about an evening jogger, but he didn't want to attract any attention at all.

After about half an hour of running he began to feel the strain, so he stopped at a small al fresco cafe for a Perrier. He needed to consider his options. He knew he didn't have much time—if he was going to leave the country he had to do it soon. He had no idea when the authorities would start looking for him.

Walking quietly to a main thoroughfare, he hailed a cab.

In the taxi, on the way to the airport, he thought about his next step. He knew he could not contact anyone through whom they could trace him. They would be on Daniel Ellington in a heartbeat. Sobieski too. The city whirled past the taxi's window like the lights of a carnival, and he felt totally alone. There was no one in the world, it seemed, who could help him.

FIFTEEN

Manhattan, New York—Windsor
August 26, 1998

Maybe James really *was* the asshole her friends had been telling her he was?

The question lingered in Marion's mind as she listened to him speak in rushed, slurry tones.

". . . and it's not that I don't love you or anything like that," he said. His voice battled for prominence with loud, trendy music. Why did nightclubs always locate the phones right next to the stereo speakers? Which segued right into her next question:

"James, why did you have to go to a bar to call me?"

"Huh? What?"

"It's bad enough you didn't want to talk about things face to face," said Marion. "But I can understand that, I guess. A phone always makes it easier. It's less personal that way."

"C'mon, honey . . . It's not like that at all." He paused and she could hear ice cubes clinking in a glass, hear him swallowing.

"Is this where you say it's not over, that you just want to take some time out?" Marion almost laughed, but she tried to retain some control. "Or how about: 'I think we should see other people for a while'?"

"Marion, please . . ."

"What's the matter, James, did I blow all the lines you'd rehearsed?"

"Hey, look, I'm trying to be serious and you're being sarcastic. What's the matter, Marion? Can't deal with reality?"

The bastard had a lot of balls, she had to give him that.

Reality! What did he know about reality?

Living down in Soho, living off his father's ever-dwindling trust fund while he struggled to reinvent Jackson Pollock. The only thing James Murdoch Cassidy III had succeeded at so far was keeping Pearl Paint in the black.

These thoughts flashed at light-speed through her mind, part of her wanted to spew them out like venom because he was hurting her. But another part of her was tired. Tired of going through the now-familiar mating and parting rituals of urban professionals.

So she only said: "The only reality I'm aware of, James, is that you're bored with our relationship, and therefore, it's over, right?"

There was a pause during which the receiver carried only

the electric lyrics of love from this week's hot new female singer.

"Yeah," said James, finally. "Yeah, I guess that's it. I guess that's what I've been trying to say. I'm sorry, Marion."

"Don't be sorry," she said, unable to hide the bitter aftertaste of her own words. "There're eight million stories in the Naked City, remember? This has just been one of them . . ."

"Marion, I hope you're not upset—"

Goddamn him! What did he *think* she was? Ecstatic?

"No, of course not! I'm not upset! What's a year and a half of emotional investment? We're all going to live forever, didn't you hear the news?"

"Well, listen . . ." he said lamely, "if there's anything I can do . . ."

"Yeah, right, buddy. There is one thing you can do. You can go fuck yourself!"

She slammed down the receiver and stared at the phone blankly. In spite of herself, hot salty tears broke from her eyes, cutting into her cheeks like acid. Getting up, she walked to the bathroom, grabbing a Kleenex from its flowery dispenser box.

She knew she shouldn't be acting like this. Especially since she wasn't sure she even loved him anymore. Hell, if she'd ever loved him. But if that was the case, why did she feel so bad?

It was more than the rejection or the fear of being alone, Marion knew.

It was the time.

A year and a half was a decent piece of her life, damn it. Her last birthday had been her thirtieth, and for the first time she had experienced the pangs of lost youth. The older she grew, the harder it was to get away from the idea that time was running out.

How many chances do you get? How many times can you blow it before it's all over?

Wiping away the tears, she took several deep breaths, walked to the window, and looked out on Riverside Drive and the flat, dull-green swath of the Hudson. It was late afternoon and the city was hotter than a cheap laser. Air conditioning kept her insulated from the heat; reflecting on that, she wondered if perhaps her job was doing the same thing to her personal life.

Working in television, gaining the quasicelebrity status inherent in a broadcast position, she had slowly discovered, did a tap-dance on the nonprofessional hours of her life. Men were attracted to her quite naturally, and they seemed initially to enjoy the mystique surrounding her as an on-screen personality. But as familiarity grew, as intimacy flared and finally raged, she also noticed the growth of real resentment in the men she'd dated since coming to New York.

The male ego, apparently, was not built for dating a female TV star. Well, not really a star, she corrected herself, but at least she was a recognizable person.

Strangers were constantly coming up to her and starting conversations, relating to her on a level of intimacy and familiarity that normally did not exist between people unknown to each other. But New Yorkers were used to seeing her and hearing her address them in their living rooms each night. That's pretty intimate. And it was hard for guys to handle.

After a while James began to resent, and then openly loathe, all the rude interruptions whenever he took her out. It was a pattern she had seen and felt before, with the men before him, and she wondered if the pattern would ever be broken.

Then there was the issue of her healthy salary. Despite almost two generations of women's liberation, a lot of men still didn't like the idea of being involved with a woman who made more money than they did. Welcome to 1955.

Well, the hell with all of them.

The phone rang. Its shrill, electronic insistence stung the silent air of the apartment.

Damn him!

"Listen to me, James!" Marion half-yelled as she picked up the receiver. "I don't want—"

"Excuse me . . ." said a female voice. "Is this Ms. Marion Windsor?"

Clearing her throat, Marion tried to sound professional. "Yes it is, who's this?"

"Ms. Windsor, this is Pam at the switchboard. I just got a call from a Father Peter Carenza. He says he's in Rome, at the airport, and he needs to talk to you right away. He doesn't have your number, it's unlisted, and nobody would give it to him. He talked me into calling you—I hope you don't mind."

Instantly her journalist's instincts clicked into place. She automatically reached for a pen and pad. "No, of course not! What's the matter, did he say?"

"He sounded pretty excited. He said it was extremely important that he speak to you, that it was an emergency."

Peter Carenza in Rome. What was going on? "Give me the number, Pam."

She wrote down the string of digits, hung up, and immediately punched in the transatlantic call. The phone only rang once before she heard the priest's resonant basso voice. The connection was amazingly clear.

"Ms. Windsor?" he asked. There was a hitch in his voice, and she could hear the idiot-thrum of crowds in the background.

"Yes, this is Marion Windsor, what can I do for you, Father?"

"Listen, I don't have time to explain everything. I'm sorry to call you at home, but they said today was your day off. I'm in some trouble, and—"

"Trouble?" The word, and the way he said it, spiked through her nervous system. She felt instantly alert. "What kind of trouble? Are you hurt?"

"No, I'm okay, but I have to get out of the country right away. I'm catching a ten-thirty flight on TWA. It's supposed to arrive at JFK around ten tonight, your time. Can you meet me there?"

"At the TWA terminal?"

"Yes, that's right."

"Well, yes, I guess so. Father what's going on?"

"No time to explain. Listen, I know this might sound funny, but I need a place to stay. Can you help me?"

She was so surprised, she said nothing.

"Look, there's nobody else I can ask!" he said, filling in the dead space. "Nobody I can trust. They don't know I know you . . ."

"Father—"

"And wear sunglasses and a hat!" His voice peaked, and she could feel the fear leaking out of him. "Don't let them recognize you if they're waiting at the airport!"

"Father, don't let who—?"

"No time! My plane! Can you be there?"

"Yes, of course," she said in rush.

"Good-bye, Ms. Windsor. God bless you . . ."

She wanted to ask more questions, but he was gone. The silent receiver mocked her for a moment, then emitted a pizzicato of clicks before a dial-tone finale.

What was going on? Her head still throbbed from the confrontation with James, and although Marion wasn't a big drinker, she definitely needed something right now. A glass of zinfandel or maybe some brandy.

That priest was very strange. From her first contact with him, there was strangeness, mystery, even the suggestion of the bizarre. She remembered what Huber had told her and what her videotapes of Esteban and Peter Carenza himself showed. Now Peter was talking the standard paranoid/conspiracy rap. About "they" and "them" and what "they" knew and what "they" didn't know. It all sounded so familiar, but in this case, she sensed an honesty, a sincerity about Peter Carenza.

She'd already told him she would meet him at JFK, so there was no turning back. There was some detective work to be done, figuring out which flight he'd be on, where and exactly when he'd be coming in. Plus he'd have to go through the whole customs drill . . .

If somebody really was after him, "they" would have plenty of chances to nail him. Marion gulped the rest of her wine, poured another glass. This might turn out to be exciting.

Well, she could use a little intrigue in her life right now. If nothing else, the diversion would keep her mind off James.

SIXTEEN

Rome, Italy—Targeno
August 27, 1998

He was working late in SSV Records when Father Francesco beeped him on his portable digital phone.

"Yes, Father, what can I do for you?"

"I need your help," said the Jesuit. The edge in his voice indicated either fear or barely controlled anger. Knowing the old man as he did, Targeno would have wagered on the latter.

"It is the middle of the night. Can this wait till morning?"

"If that were true, I would have called you in the morning."

"All right." Targeno sighed as he reached out and disabled the CD scanfax. There would be no more research tonight. "What do you want?"

"There is an emergency. Listen." Francesco recounted the escape of an American priest being held under observation by the Curia's committee on miracles. A psychologically disturbed priest who was now on a flight back to America.

Targeno chuckled into the mouthpiece of the portable phone. "You want me to chase down a runaway priest? Are you serious?"

"I have already made arrangements for him to be met at Kennedy International," said Francesco. "But I want to be certain there are no mistakes."

Targeno paused, letting him twist in silence for a moment. Then: "You are not telling me everything. What is going on?

First this business with the nun. And now I am supposed to chase down a psycho priest?"

"I am telling you all you need to know."

"Wrong. I need to know everything!" he hissed into the phone. "If you think I am strolling into a situation without knowing the details, you are crazy! That is how people get killed, Father."

The Jesuit chuckled softly. "Is *Il Chirurgo* afraid of a crazy priest?"

"Only dead men know no fear," he said.

"Besides," said Francesco, "why should I tell you everything I know when you do not follow your own advice?"

"What are you talking about?"

"Your report on the nun. If she told you nothing, why did you spend almost three hours with her? Sister Victorianna told me of your visit. Three hours is a long time for nothing."

Targeno smiled. "Looks like we have each other by the *cogliones*, Father. I think we will both get what we want if we both start singing."

There was a silence on the other end of the line for a moment.

"You are a sheep-fucker . . ." said Francesco. "All right, but not over the phone."

Targeno smiled. In his business, he'd long ago learned that information, not money, was the most valuable bargaining chip. If you had some, you could always get something in return.

"Very well," he said. "My office in a half-hour. I will have a pass waiting for you in the lobby."

"We are wasting time, you know." Francesco's voice registered the compromise, but he attempted one last dissuasion.

"Either we deal, or I do not chase down your boy."

"Half an hour," the Jesuit said, and terminated the connection.

Targeno gathered up the papers he had faxed from Information Retrieval and left the area. Half of what Francesco would probably tell him, he had most likely already gleaned himself from the computer records. Access to the cross-indexing of so many databases yielded many interesting tidbits. He already had pieced together a fascinating portrait of Sister Etienne, an apparently innocent nun.

Perhaps the Jesuit could tell him why a German scientist had been hired to oversee her pregnancy? Or why she claimed she could only tell her *son* or the Pope the contents of her vision?

Checking his watch, Targeno entered the elevator that would take him to his cubicle. He had the feeling he had already collected all the puzzle pieces, and needed only to fit them together.

Therein lay the best part of his job. After a while, assassinations got to be a bore.

SEVENTEEN

Queens, New York—Carenza
August 27, 1998

The HST jetliner touched down at JFK exactly on schedule, and Peter felt the first suggestions of relief since the madness had begun. He still wasn't sure what he would do beyond the next day or two, but he felt better just being back in the States, away from those Old World zealots and their revelations.

The flight had seemed endless and he'd been unable to stop replaying the events of the past few days.

Insane. Ludicrous. Impossible.

It had been all of that. But there was a part of him that kept wondering what if . . . ?

What if it were true?

The idea of a man being cloned from the genetic blueprint

of the blood of Christ was staggering in and of itself. But to even begin to think that the man in question could be Peter Carenza—

No. It was stunningly absurd.

How could he be that person? To be, as they claimed, Christ himself?

A flight steward touched his arm lightly. Peter looked up at the young man blankly.

"It's time to deplane, sir."

"Oh yes," said Peter. "Sorry . . ."

Getting up, he grabbed his little bag, and followed the rest of the passengers down the aisle to exit into TWA's own International Terminal. Peter followed the signs down a long ramp to Passport Control. The line for U.S. citizens moved quickly and he passed through toward the routine customs check.

Customs. In the confusing storm of his thoughts, he'd forgotten about the procedure.

"Excuse me," he said to an airline employee as he reached the end of the ramp. "If I'm going to meet someone, somebody who's supposed to pick me up, where would they be?"

The young woman smiled at him graciously.

"They would have to be waiting in the terminal lobby. No one's allowed in this area without a ticket or a boarding pass."

Thanking her, Peter joined the flow of passengers to the customs area. There were seven functioning checkpoints, so the lines were moving fairly quickly. If Father Francesco and his band of merry men had discovered which flight Peter had taken, somebody would be waiting for him somewhere along the line.

Customs might not be the best place to cause a scene, or, contrarily, it might be the best place. But was it possible that the Vatican had men secreted within a U.S. government agency?

Anything was credible, especially assuming that most government jobs were carried out by lazy, uninspired work-a-days who wouldn't notice a spy or a plant unless his pants were on fire.

But there were seven customs agents working. Unless all of them were Vatican operatives, it would be difficult to detain him here. Peter's chances of selecting the line controlled by one of Francesco's men were like playing Russian roulette. Though customs was a perfectly logical place to publicly detain a person, it was almost impossible to ensure that the prey moved through the correct line.

Peter queued up behind a stout woman carrying several large bags. The line moved forward, and Peter studied the faces of the customs agents. At least half of them looked pleasant and were even smiling as they went about their jobs, usually just asking a few questions. No one seemed to be paying any attention to him as he approached the bank of inspection stations. But of course that's exactly the way they would act if they wanted to lull him into a false sense of security.

Damn! Paranoia was a wondrous affliction! No matter what path of thought you chose, there was always a flip-side to make you wonder what was really going on.

The fat woman hefted her luggage onto the low tables where the agents worked. The black man who inspected her bulging vinyl and nylon bags was young and courteous. He was articulate and charming, and Peter had a hard time imagining such a person working for a wolfish type like Father Francesco.

"Aha," said the agent in a soft voice. "What's this?"

He fished out several bottles of white wine and another of red.

"Do I have to pay a duty on those?" asked the woman. "Did I do anything wrong?"

"Well, I don't know, ma'am. Do you intend to drink these yourself, or were you going to sell them?"

"Oh, no, they're for me. Honest."

The agent smiled. "No problem, then." He checked off a space on a form on his clipboard, continued looking through the remainder of her things. After he passed her through, the

agent smiled at Peter and looked down at his sports bag with
surprise.

"That's it?"

"I like to travel light." Peter smiled back at him, hoping
that he did not appear too nervous.

"I guess you do . . ." The agent unzipped the bag, passing
over Peter's wallet and assorted toiletries, then paused when
he saw the black clothes, the roman collar.

"You're a priest?"

For an instant, time stopped. Peter didn't know how to answer. Had they all been told to look for a priest? What the
hell should he do?

Without a discernible pause, Peter yanked his passport
from his sweatjacket pocket. "That's right. I'd been called to
the Vatican on short notice."

The agent nodded, handed back the document. "I see. An
emergency with God, eh?"

Peter chuckled as he shared the small joke with the young
black man. The agent quickly rezipped the bag, pushed it
back to him.

"Thank you, Father. Have a nice evening and welcome
back."

"Thank you," said Peter as he grabbed his bag and escaped
the customs bottleneck. He headed down another corridor to
the terminal lobby.

Along with a steady stream of travelers coming from various international flights, Peter entered a large open space
where crowds of people stood searching the faces of the new
arrivals. Parents awaited sons and daughters; lovers longed
for lovers; drivers held up handprinted signs for people they
wouldn't recognize; families fidgeted in wait for fathers and
mothers.

Slowing his pace, he scanned the crowd for someone who
looked something like Marion Windsor. He noticed a girl
with a scarf and billowing cotton skirt, but her puffy, thickly
featured face was that of an Eastern European peasant. Another woman in a straw bonnet with a satin ribbon looked at
him for an instant, then continued to search the pack of new

arrivals. Suddenly there was a blur of motion from his left as a young woman wearing an Aussie hat, a baggy khaki shirt, and shorts grabbed him by the arm. Her hair was pulled up underneath the hat, and she wore sunglasses.

"How do I look?" she asked, smiling as she began guiding Peter toward the exits. He looked at her, and even though he knew she was Marion Windsor, he marveled at the effectiveness of her disguise.

"Fantastic!" he said, feeling the soft yet firm touch of her hand on his arm. Several times she brushed close to him and he could feel the fullness of hip and breast unique to the female body.

"See anybody or anything funny?"

"Not yet. I was wondering about customs but that seemed to go okay. What about you?"

"Nothing. Either they're really good, or there's nobody around." She looked at him through her amber lenses and smiled. "Don't worry, I'll get you out of here."

He scanned the area ahead as they walked through the crowds, looking for anyone who seemed to be watching them. Everything seemed so ordinary, so damned normal. That's when they were going to strike, he knew it, just when he let his guard down completely.

"Did you bring your own car?"

"No, I borrowed my girlfriend's."

"Good idea. If anybody sees us, they'll have a harder time tracing us."

"I already thought of that," said Marion.

Even as they walked, even while looking around, Peter had been staring at her face. She had the most intriguing mouth he'd ever seen on a woman. Her smile was so engaging, so unique; the kind in which you swore you saw every one of her teeth for the briefest of instants. Amazing.

"Maybe we've seen too many spy movies," he said.

"This way," said Marion, pointing to an escalator leading down to street level. She still clung to his arm like a woman who's waited a long time to see her man, and Peter found himself enjoying the contact. He was certain he and Marion looked convincing as a pair of adventurous, athletic young lovers.

They passed through the pneumatic glass doors. Peter saw the yellow hulks of the taxis awaiting fares and the entrance to the parking lot beyond. He stepped forward just as a sky-cap pushing a luggage-carrier darted in front of them.

"Excuse me, sir," he said in a deep voice. Peter glanced at the tall, broad-shouldered man—who suddenly did not look very much like your average skycap.

Before they could step around the obstacle, another skycap appeared on their left and reached out as though to assist Marion and gripped her by the arm. There was no way for Peter to reach around her to free her; the other man stepped close. The one holding Marion's wrist produced a handgun. It was an angular, chrome-polished article of menace with a matching silencer, pointed at Peter's midsection. He felt the bottom drop from his stomach and his mouth go instantly dry.

These guys were good. They had moved in without being noticed and had quickly neutralized their prey. The unarmed man had a tight grip on Peter's upper arm. Peter glanced about like a cornered animal, but could see immediately how bad things looked. The large concrete support pylons covering the departure area afforded lots of shadowy protection from the notice of others.

"You have to come with us, Father. I think you know why . . ." said the one with the gun. His baritone voice was smooth, and he was smiling like a stand-up comic, but there was an unmistakable chill in his eyes.

Tensing up, Peter tested the strength of the man to his right. The big guy was strong, no doubt, and Peter wondered how badly he would do against him.

"What's going on here!?" cried Marion, trying to back away from the man with the gun. "Peter, my God!"

Her expression displayed total helplessness and terror. Seeing her like that, Peter hated himself for involving her. She thought she was helping a troubled priest, but she was actually making the descent into the maelstrom.

He had to *do* something.

Forcing himself to smile, he looked directly into the ball-peen eyes of Chrome Gun. "You aren't going to use that thing," he said. "That's the one thing you *can't* do to me. Francesco told you I don't get touched, right?"

The man didn't respond, but he didn't have to. There was moment's hesitation as the two thugs reassessed their options. Peter'd scored the points he might need. Then:

"He didn't say nothin' about this one," said Chrome Gun, suddenly flashing the silencer up into Marion's face. He reached up, as if to remove her sunglasses. "Too bad, too. She looks like a pretty one, eh?"

As his hand touched the cheap plastic frames, Marion reacted.

Spinning and lashing out at the same time, she executed a martial arts move with stunning perfection. One hand seized the man's gun arm, her other snapped down with shattering force. The angle was precisely measured and the man's ulna cracked like a dry twig. His scream masked the clatter of the gun on the pavement. It had happened so fast, both Peter and the muscular thug at his side were shocked into immobility.

"Peter! Move!" she cried, then reared back to deliver a side-kick to Chrome Gun's belly. Bent double, the guy caught Marion's power-punch to the temple and went down hard. But even before he hit the concrete, his partner had thrown himself for the gun. Peter stood by helplessly, watching the broad-shouldered thug grab the weapon and roll back toward Marion, who was only now turning away from her handiwork to deal with the other half of the problem.

"Okay, lady!" he screamed, holding the shining piece steady. "You move, and I gotta do it!"

Though Marion's eyes remained masked behind dark plastic, Peter could see the defeat in her face. She had begun to coil for another attack, but suddenly her body went limp.

"You bastards! What do you want with us?"

Big Guy sort of half-smiled and nodded toward Peter. "They want him back. Now."

"What for? For God's sake, Peter, what have you done?"

"You wouldn't believe it if I told you. Look, I'm sorry I dragged you into this."

"Shut up. We're getting out of here."

"What about your buddy?" asked Peter, looking at the still unconscious figure at his feet.

"Fuck him," said Big Guy. "They'll clean this mess up later. I gotta get you outta here. Now."

He gestured quickly with the gun toward a black Accura at the curbside. "Okay let's go. Get in the car."

Marion's shoulders slumped even lower as she began walking toward the sleek vehicle. Peter paused one last moment.

"What're you going to do with her? She didn't have anything to do with this."

The man shrugged. "I don't know. Nobody said anything about anybody else. She comes along until they tell me what to do with her."

Peter didn't like the sound of that last line. "And what happens if they tell you to kill her?"

The assailant smiled. "Hey, everybody's gotta make a livin', right?"

Marion stopped in mid-stride, obviously chilled by the thug's implication. Peter could almost feel the acidlike scent of her dread. Without thinking, he reached out, grabbed the guy's thick forearm.

"No," Peter said softly.

The thug's eyes met his, and in that instant of silent contact, Peter knew what was going to happen. It was like looking into a bottomless pool, into that place where lay his deepest fears and desires. The immediate future uncoiled before him like a long, white snake, poising to strike.

"Get in the car. *Now!*"

The chrome gun moved in Marion's direction, and Peter tightened his grip on the man's tree-trunk wrist. An instant of dizziness ripped through his head like a buzzsaw, followed by a sense of utter *clarity*. It was a clarity of purpose and sensory input. The strength of Peter's hand seemed to be increasing exponentially as each second ticked away. Big Guy was suddenly reeling backward away from the Accura, his gun hand waving randomly in the air. Peter felt the guy's radius and ulna cracking beneath the flesh like broomsticks wrapped in a wet towel. Still he continued the pressure.

"No," Peter repeated, softly. He was certain the single word had been heard, even through the other man's screams. Eyes bulging, mouth twisted into a ragged circle of torment, the thug leaned into Peter, aiming the gun at his stomach. Releasing the crushed left arm, Peter lunged for the gun and wrapped his fingers around both bright chrome and the guy's hand.

There was the softest sound, like the breath being forced from the chest of a small animal, and a 9mm shell spanged into the outer shell of the black sedan. A stinging flash of dizziness crossed Peter's forehead, and again the sensation of absolute clarity came to him.

This bastard had tried to kill him. Kill Marion.

Another *pfffftt!* The slug thonked into the side of the car, and Peter could feel the subtle aftershock under his grip. There was a pungent smell of cordite, mixing quickly with a stronger, darker odor—the smell of burning flesh.

The thug's screams reached a new octave of agony as he tried to dance away from Peter, who looked down to see a blue aura surrounding his hand, the gun, and the other guy's hand.

Only there wasn't much of a gun anymore, and less of a hand holding it. Running like liquid mercury, the molten metal of the gun poured through Peter's unscathed fingers. He watched the polished teardrops fall to the concrete like silver rain. It was beautiful and horrific at the same time.

The guy's hand had been reduced to charred, flaking bits of bone. The intense heat had vaporized his flesh and carbonized his skeleton in an instant. His frenzied dance parted him from Peter as the rest of his arm fell out of his sleeve like ashes down a coal chute. The blue aura vanished when the contact with Peter's hand was broken. All through it, the thug continued to scream.

Mute, stunned, Marion looked from the hideous scene into

Peter's eyes. *Who are you?* her gaze asked. Fear lurched behind her sea-green pupils, but so did something else.

He hoped it was respect.

Everything had happened so fast, it was hard to believe that only seconds ago, they had bumped into a couple of pseudo-skycaps. In the tradition of all New York cabbies, the waiting drivers had ignored the entire confrontation. If anyone had seen the results of Peter's counterattack or heard the agonized screams from the one-armed man, nobody was letting on.

"Come on," said Peter, reaching out to take Marion's hand. "We've got to get out of here!"

She looked at him like that was the last thing she'd want to do with him, but she nodded once, accepted his hand and let herself be led into the parking lot.

"Where's the car?" he asked.

Marion tugged at Peter and they ran in a half-panic. She fumbled with the door-lock before they could scramble in. She drove in silence glancing over repeatedly at him. His face burned with a flush of embarrassment, like a boy who's been caught stealing cookies. Her gaze was both fearful and intimidating.

"Where're we going?" he asked. "Your place?"

The lights of Ozone Park blinked past the window behind her head, creating a halo in her auburn hair. She looked very beautiful.

"No," she said finally. She checked the rearview mirror for a moment. "It doesn't look like anybody's following us . . ."

"That was a hell of a show back there," Peter said, trying to smile. "When did you learn all that ninja stuff?"

"It's *tae kwon do*. I've been studying it for years . . ." She paused, rubbed her eyes. "But I don't think that's the burning issue of the day—if you'll pardon my pun."

Peter looked down at his hands, knowing what she meant, trying to fathom how she must be feeling right now.

"You saw what happened?" he asked lamely.

"Father, how could I miss it?"

Peter exhaled, shook his head. How could he ever explain? Would she believe him? Did it matter?

"Listen," Marion said, touching his arm softly. "I don't know what's going on, but I've got to tell you, you've got me freaked out. First somebody who tries to mug you gets hit by lightning—only the M.E. says it was more like a microwave—and now . . . I saw what you did to that guy and his gun. Pardon me for asking, Father, but what the hell's going on with you?"

"Could you please call me 'Peter'?" he asked, not really knowing why.

She nodded, waited.

The car barreled its way along the Belt Parkway as he glanced out the window. A freighter loomed beyond Gravesend Bay, and the towering lights of the Verrazano-Narrows Bridge grew even larger as Brooklyn unfolded to their right. He felt like he was hurtling forward into a terrible darkness, upon a journey he couldn't make alone. The car exited at Ocean Parkway and headed north.

"All right," he said in a half-whisper, "I'll tell you everything I know."

Marion glanced over at him then went back to concentrating on the traffic, which had become suddenly heavy. "Not now," she said. "We're almost there."

Sinking back into his seat, Peter nodded.

She turned on Avenue H and headed east till she reached Ocean Avenue. Waiting motionless, in silence, for a moment, she decided they hadn't been followed. She exited the car, and Peter followed her lead.

"Where are we?" he asked.

"My friend, Suzette, lives here." She pointed to a bungalow surrounded by trees, then held up a house key. "She's in Nags Head for two weeks and I told her I'd water her plants while she was gone."

"Okay."

"Let's go," said Marion, leading the way up the walk to the porch, and through the front door.

The living room was wellfurnished in a contemporary

style. The bookcases and framed artwork bespoke a person of intelligence and culture. Exactly the kind of friend he would have expected Marion Windsor to have.

"I don't know about you, but I need something to drink," she said, going to the kitchen. "Suzette always has a couple of bottles of wine around. Red or white, Father? I mean—Peter."

He sat on the couch, smiled. "Red will be fine—if it's okay with you."

"Listen," she called from the other room, "after what I've been through tonight, the color of my wine isn't going to score too many points, if you know what I mean."

She entered the room with two half-full goblets, handed him one, and joined him on the couch. She'd discarded the Aussie hat, and her hair fell down past her shoulders in a red-brown cascade. Even in the dim light of the room, highlights gamboled brightly.

Peter sipped the wine, then gulped down most of it. He was breathing raggedly and his pulse had begun to jump in reaction to all that had happened since he'd gotten off the plane.

"All right, Peter," she said over the crystal rim of her glass. "I think you owe me an explanation."

"I just hope you'll believe me," he said.

"After what I've seen, I think I could believe anything."

Peter nodded, looking into her eyes. "Then listen . . ."

EIGHTEEN

Rome, Italy—Targeno
August 27, 1998

He watched the Jesuit pacing about the room. He'd never seen the man so agitated or anxious. Having just received the news that Peter Carenza had escaped detention at JFK, Father Francesco seemed disoriented, unable to think or function in his usual Machiavellian manner.

Targeno lit a Turkish cigarette, sucked the thick smoke deep into his lungs. The hot gases seared his delicate nasal passages as he exhaled.

"We have been playing games for hours, Giovanni," he said. "Is it not time we were honest with one another?"

The priest glared at him.

Targeno smiled. "Things do not add up. So far we have traded information the way children on a street corner swap candy, exchanging flavors neither one of them like."

"I have told you everything I can." Francesco turned to the window.

"I do not think so." Targeno's voice rose sharply. "Listen to me! Masseria's goons blew the assignment at JFK. I do not know how two trained agents could be stopped by a single priest, but believe me, I *will* find out."

Wheeling from the window, the Jesuit glared at him. "I *cannot* tell you anything else!"

"You have not told me goat-turds!" Knowing the impact of his next words, Targeno spoke quietly. "You and your friends hired a German scientist to artificially inseminate a naïve little girl just dumped into a convent."

Francesco nearly jumped out of his skin. "What? How did you—"

"I discovered it on my own." Targeno knew it was only a matter of time before he got all the information he wanted. "We keep going over the same barren landscape, Father."

Francesco slumped into a chair, exhaled dramatically. A sign of surrender? "There were two others involved . . ."

"I already know that too. Cardinal Lareggia and the Abbess Victorianna. The only other person who knew anything was the late Pope."

Francesco seemed surprised. "How could you possibly—?"

"Some crumbs gleaned from the nun, some from my research into the files. I also know you received a scrambled message from Carenza's pastor in America, who used the code name Bronzini."

Francesco's mouth hung open.

"I assume the pastor told you something which warranted your summoning Carenza himself. I am still running some checks on Carenza in America. If anything out of the ordinary has happened to him lately, I will soon know about it."

"You are incredible," said Francesco. His voice conveyed a mixture of disgust and admiration.

"If you think you can keep the whole story from me after dropping me into its center, then you have never learned who I am." Targeno drew dramatically on his cigarette. "A little intuition and a little guessing." He smiled. "That is how I have stayed alive all these years."

"Yes, I suppose you are right. I always knew you were good. I should not be surprised at what you learn when your skills are pointed at me."

"So who else knew about your little experiment?"

"The Pope, as you surmised. He knew what we had planned. He approved of everything."

"What about the current Holy Father?" He purposely employed the euphemism for satiric effect.

Francesco shook his head. "He knows nothing. None of the Popes after Paul VI knew anything about the project."

Targeno nodded. "So you stole the baby, locked him into the Church, then sent him to America. Why? And now you want him back and he doesn't want to stay. I want to know *why*."

Francesco shook his head, buried his face in his spindly, long-fingered hands. "I did not expect Carenza to do anything like this. Either he does not believe what he learned about himself, or he is terrified by it. Regardless, he does not want to accept the path we have set him upon."

Targeno moved to the Jesuit's desk, leaned down over the older man. "That is *precisely* what I need to know . . ."

"Yes?"

"Just exactly *what* did you and your little band of conspirators do to Peter Carenza to make him run like that?"

"That is possibly the one thing your research, your files, and your intuition might never tell you." Francesco leaned back in his chair, reached for a cigarette from his jeweled tobacco box.

"Maybe so," said Targeno, looking at his wristwatch, "but as we speak your runaway boy is losing himself in the great melting pot, eh?"

Francesco said nothing, but the expression of defeat on his face eliminated the need for words.

"It is late, Father. If you have nothing else to say, I have got work to do. *Other* work."

"I will get Masseria to order you to help me."

Francesco's last-ditch threat was pathetic. Targeno looked at him and smiled. "Do you actually think Masseria can make me do anything I do not want to?"

"What does that mean?"

"I have always wanted a long vacation—and I have never seen all there is to the USA. I could spend lots of time and money traveling around the country. I might never look for your priest, and no one would be the wiser."

"You would not do that."

"Listen, Father. You may think I am just a pawn in all the

games you play, but I tell you Targeno is one piece who thinks for himself!"

"Damn it! I cannot tell you anything else!" The Jesuit was close to tears. Frustration drove him to the limits of self-discipline.

"You must, or I cannot help you." *Let the bastard cook in his own juices just a little longer.*

Francesco shook his head, again burying it in his hands. "No one else must know the secret . . ."

"Try this on for size," said Targeno. "In 1969, when Father Masseria was young and only beginning to learn how to be a Jesuit thug—working for you—he was questioned about the disappearance of another of your employees."

"Who?" Francesco's olive complexion had become suddenly ashen.

"A seminarian named Amerigo Ponti. He vanished the night after being assigned to a Vatican Commission to study the *Santa Sindone*."

Francesco slapped his fist on his desktop. "Goddamn you . . ."

Targeno smiled. "Eventually I will know it all, but it will take much time, and by then, your boy may have permanently disappeared."

"Even the sheep would not have you!"

"True." Targeno chuckled. He knew he had Francesco now. "Are you ready to give me some answers?"

"Yes, goddamn you! Yes . . ."

Targeno sat in the chair facing the large desk. Deep in the core of his being, a feeling of satisfaction blossomed like a new sun being born. Money was not the most valuable or desired commodity in the world. There was something better.

Information.

Anybody could steal money. But only a master could extract information.

"I must warn you," Francesco said dramatically. "What I am about to tell you is—"

Targeno waved him to silence. "I know, I know. Top secret

and all that, right?" He wanted to chuckle. "Please, 'Vanni, I have heard this sort of thing all my life."

"That is not what I meant," said the Jesuit, letting his anger seep from behind the edges of his mask of resignation. "You think you are so smug, Targeno. What I'm about to tell you is the craziest story you'll ever hear. But, believe me, it is completely true."

NINETEEN

Brooklyn, New York—Windsor
August 27, 1998

"Do you really expect me to believe you're Jesus Christ?" asked Marion. She tried not to think how silly she sounded. After what she'd seen and heard, she didn't know what to think, but Peter's explanation stretched her credulity beyond its limits. She felt disconnected from solid reality. She felt like she had in childhood when walking out of a Disney movie—knowing that it had all been a fantasy but wishing it were true somewhere in the universe.

"How can I ask you to believe something I don't even believe myself!" said Peter. "I'm just telling you what they told me."

She looked at him draped across the couch, his dark hair flying in every direction, his dark eyes half-lidded. He looked damned sexy. Sorry, Father, but you do. Full of wine, he was slowly getting stoned. Well, he probably needed it. If what he said was true, what Peter Carenza had gone through in the past twenty-four hours was enough to put anybody into the bottom of a bottle.

"I know," she said. "But it just sounds so absurd, so unbelievable."

"Yeah, yeah . . . I've been over all that in my mind. Lots of times."

The after-image of the blue aura burned abruptly in her mind's eye. The twisted face of the goon leered at her as he pirouetted once again through his *pas de doleur* while the bones and flesh of his arm turned to powdery ash. She'd seen it happen. No denying it or trying to explain it away. Peter Carenza had somehow zapped the guy—just like he'd zapped that mugger in the alley.

"What are we going to do now?" She sat on the edge of the couch, fighting the urge to smooth his hair, to run her hand along the edge of his shoulder and down his triceps.

He looked at her for a moment before answering. "You said 'we' . . ."

"I did, didn't I?" She smiled at him, wanting to tell him she was wildly attracted to him, that she had a bad case of the lusts. But she didn't want to scare him away or offend him. Besides, there was more to it than that.

"Because I care about you, Peter," she said softly. "Because you're a good person, and you're in some kind of crazy trouble, and—because you seem very much alone."

He placed his empty wineglass on the carpet, rubbed his eyes. "That's very perceptive. I do have one close friend, but I'm afraid to call him."

"They would know about him," she said slowly, thinking aloud. "They'd wait for you to get in touch with him."

Peter shrugged. "I guess so. I don't really know, but I don't want to take any chances. That's why I called you. They don't know you. They don't know I know you."

"You're safe here," she said, placing her hand on his shoulder. "Do you want to get some sleep now?"

"Does the Pope wear a funny hat?"

She burst into nervous laughter and he joined her. It felt good to relax after what they'd been through. It was the first time she'd seen him really smile. The sound of his laughter was a broad, healthy sound. She wished the circumstances were different, so that she might hear more of it.

"All right, come on, you can use the second bedroom upstairs. I've got to get home and get some sleep myself. I'm a working woman, remember."

He nodded, rubbed his eyes. "Thank you, Marion, for everything. The *tae kwan do* was a bonus I hadn't counted on, but it was a good one."

She smiled. "It was the first time I've ever had to use it. Good to know it works."

He got up, wobbly, and let her guide him to the stairs. "I feel like I haven't slept for a week. That wine's hitting me like a piano."

"A piano?"

"Being dropped out a window." He smiled again . . . He looked so damned good to her.

She laughed, pushed him gently upward. "You can use the towels in the bathroom. They're clean. Don't answer the phone. I'll call you tomorrow—I'll let it ring twice, hang up, then call again. So you'll know it's me."

"Ring twice, then hang up. Right." He turned and began the trip upstairs.

She watched him till he reached the top. "Peter?"

"Yeah?" He turned and looked down at her.

She wanted to ask him if he wanted her to stay, but forced herself to simply say: "Take care. Things will be better in the morning."

God, she sounded so stupid!

He smiled. "I know. Thanks, Marion. I mean it."

"I know you do. Good night."

He disappeared down the upstairs hall and she went into the kitchen to call a cab.

She didn't want to know what time it was as she watched the yellow taxi speed off, heading south on West End. The exhilaration and sheer adventure of the evening had slowly seeped away. Left behind were extreme fatigue and an odd kind of longing, as though something vital, something terribly important was suddenly missing from her life.

Entering her building, Marion nodded to the security concierge, walked to the elevators. The contemporary decor of the lobby seemed sterile. It was as though she were entering a mausoleum. The "something missing" feeling wouldn't go away, and Marion knew herself well enough to realize Peter Carenza and his special problem lay at the core.

Her heart often spoke to her like that. Sometimes she listened, sometimes not. Her professional persona sought equal time under the Fairness Doctrine, and that particular inner voice was screaming a different message: *you might be sitting on the biggest story of the century.*

She exited the elevator and keyed the lock to her co-op apartment. Urban paranoia insisted that she inspect all the rooms and closets before she could feel comfortable and resume her train of thought. The ritual was one she'd learned from her friend Suzette, and if it was a bit on the pathological side, so what? It made her feel better to know immediately that she hadn't been robbed and that no creep with a knife lay in wait for her, curled and twisted like a demented pretzel.

Once the paranoia tour had been completed, she collapsed on her bed without even getting undressed. Her body ached from exertion, but her mind was revved like a dragster's engine, ready to jump off at the lights. Her life had changed irrevocably since she'd visited the Saint Sebastian rectory, where she'd met a priest so handsome he could have been a film star, who could shoot lightning bolts from his hands and who, by the way, said he'd been cloned from the blood of Jesus Christ.

Yeah, right.

Business as usual in the world of a hustling journalist. The news of the day, or the news of the century? He might not be Jesus Christ, but he certainly displayed something beyond normal human abilities. A mutant? A freak? A monster? Whatever else he might be, Father Peter Carenza was definitely News, and she didn't know what in hell to do about it.

TWENTY

Brooklyn, New York—Ellington
August 27, 1998

When his friend didn't meet him Monday morning, Dan Ellington had become immediately concerned. When Peter didn't call to explain, either that night or in the next two days, Dan's concern had escalated into mild panic.

It simply was not like Peter to do something like that. As long as Dan had known him, Peter had been a considerate, thoughtful guy. He just wouldn't skip out on an appointment unless something unforeseen had happened.

Knowing Peter's delicate relationship with Pastor Sobieski, Dan had been reluctant to call the rectory. But three days had passed with no word from Peter. The hell with it . . .

Dan picked up the phone, punched in a number.

An unfamiliar male voice answered, identified himself as Father Ryan.

"Good evening," Dan said. "I'm trying to reach Father Carenza, please."

"He's not here right now," said Ryan.

"Well, do you have any idea when he'll be back? I had an appointment with him, but he missed it."

"I'm sorry, but I don't." Father Ryan's voice carried no suggestion of tension or dissembling.

"Well, could you please tell me where he is? Where I might contact him?" For some reason, Dan's instincts were telling him something was wrong. Remembering how upset Peter had been, and especially considering the weirdness of what had happened, he had a feeling Peter was in deep trouble.

"I don't think so," said Ryan. "Father Carenza's out of the country. He's gone to Rome."

"What?!" Dan couldn't hide his surprise. "When did he leave? What for?"

"I'm sorry, sir, but I really don't know. It was arranged by the pastor, but Father Sobieski's not here right now. And I don't know any of the details."

The man sounded extremely sincere. If he was lying, he should've been an actor instead of a priest.

"When do you expect your pastor?"

"Not until later tonight," said Ryan.

"All right, I'll give him a call tomorrow."

"That will be fine. He should be here all day."

"Okay," said Dan. "Thank you very much."

"Is there any message I can leave for him? Who should I say is calling?"

Dan left his name, then hung up.

Rome? What was Peter doing in Rome? But even as the question formed in his mind, Dan imagined the old pastor getting cranked up about the "miraculous" overtones to Peter's mugging. As a Jesuit, Dan was painfully aware of the old committees in the Vatican Curia devoted to the study of miracles. Although most modern Jesuits considered the committees silly, and a general embarrassment to the Church, he was certain the "old boy" network in Rome would be anxious to learn what had happened to Peter.

Rome. The more he thought about poor Peter being dragged before a bunch of old Cardinals, the more it made sense.

And the less anxious he felt. It still bothered him that Peter hadn't called before running off to the Vatican—or after arriving. Still, knowing Peter, he was probably afraid to incur the expense of a transatlantic call—even if that call would be paid for by the wealthiest church in the world.

Well, tomorrow was Dan's day off. He didn't have anything to do, so he'd have plenty of time to catch Sobieski and find out exactly where Peter was and when he was due back. He picked up the Cable Guide and checked out the late movie on Cinemax.

A light tapping on his door awakened him. The television driveled on into the dark room—a badly dubbed foreign film. Dan rubbed his eyes as he realized he'd fallen asleep during the spy thriller and lost track of time.

Tap-tap . . . Tap-tap . . .

The soft sounds drew him into full wakefulness. Looking at his watch, he was surprised to see it was after 2:00 AM.

Who the hell could be knocking at this hour?

Dan moved to the door and looked out the peephole. In the dim light of the faculty apartment building hallway, he saw the figure of a man in a dark suit, wearing a fedora. His features were indistinct.

"Who's there?" asked Dan.

"Father Ellington?" said a muffled voice.

"Yes?"

"I'm Detective Benjamino Ortiz from NYPD. I'd like to ask you a few questions."

Was this guy nuts? "Detective, it's two in the morning. How about tomorrow?"

There was a short pause, then: "Father, it's about your friend, Peter Carenza . . ."

Peter! Without thinking, Dan unlatched the steel door. It opened to reveal a tall, broad-shouldered man wearing a dark gray, stylishly tailored suit, an expensive-looking shirt, and a designer tie. His face was lean and deeply tanned; high, angular cheekbones accented deeply set, large brown eyes. The man's unlined face gave no clue to his age; Daniel thought he could be anywhere from thirty to forty.

"Good evening, Father," the man said, stepping forcefully into the room.

Automatically, Daniel backed out of his way. The man moved with such grace and power, he commanded immediate respect.

"You said something about my friend, Father Carenza—is there anything wrong?"

"I don't know," said the detective. "That's what I'm here to find out . . ."

He stood very close to Daniel, radiating an aura of strength and menace. Now that he'd spoken more than a few words, Dan realized his accent wasn't quite Spanish. Dan frowned. He had no reason to fear a policeman—unless this guy wasn't a policeman . . . Damn! He'd been stupid to throw open the door like that!

The man must have read the apprehension in Dan's face. He stepped even nearer.

"Something wrong, Father?" Was that a smile beginning to form?

"You said you were a detective . . ." said Daniel. "But you didn't show me your badge."

"That's because I lied." He chuckled darkly. "Bless me, Father, for I have sinned."

"Who are you? What do you want with me?"

"I'm looking for Peter Carenza." The man seized Dan's shoulder in a powerful grip and forced him toward a chair in the breakfast nook. "Sit down, please. We must talk."

"Look, I want to know what's going on here! You just can't come busting into my place and—"

The blow came from nowhere. So quick, so fast, and delivered with such power, Daniel felt like he'd been decked by an anvil. The entire side of his head throbbed with violent bursts of pain. White, numbing pain.

"Shut up, please," the false detective said in his whispery baritone voice. He was terribly calm and businesslike.

Daniel couldn't speak. His words were slurred moans.

"Peter Carenza is your friend, I know that. I want to know where he is."

Daniel forced himself to speak clearly. "He's in Rome."

"He's *not* in Rome. I've just come from there. Don't fuck with me, Father!"

Not in Rome? What was going on here? This guy, whoever

he was, assumed Dan knew more than he really did. "Then I don't where he is, honestly."

The invader smiled. "Father, believe me. If you know anything about Carenza, I will discover it. You can either tell me easily, without pain, or you can tell me with a great deal of pain."

Daniel slumped in his kitchen chair. The pain in his jaw had dulled to a low, pulsating ache. His ear had stopped ringing. He looked at his questioner. There was something reptilian about the man.

"Look, I don't know anything, really! He was supposed to meet me Monday, and he never showed up. Just tonight I found out he'd been sent to Rome."

"He's not there now," said the man, leaning down to peer into Dan's eyes. "Your friend escaped and took a plane back to New York. He's been back for more than twenty-four hours."

"Escaped? Was he a prisoner?"

The man chuckled. "Yes, I guess you could say that."

Dan's mind was racing. He strove to keep calm. "Listen, I'm telling you the truth. I don't know where he is."

"We'll see about that," said the man, smiling again. He withdrew a small leather case from an interior coat pocket, opened it slowly to reveal a long, wicked-looking hypodermic syringe. From another pocket the man produced a small drug vial.

In an instant of pure, terror-driven reaction, Dan swung his arm and struck the hand holding the syringe case. Its contents fell to the floor and shattered.

The man who called himself Ortiz just smiled. "Oh that is unfortunate. You don't like needles, Father? Your life would have been so much easier with just a small amount of xylothol. Now, I am afraid I will have to use more old-fashioned means . . ."

A blur of movement in the corner of Dan's eye terminated in a starburst of pain at the base of his skull. Then everything just went black.

A splash of ice water in his face brought him around. After a moment of total disorientation, Daniel assessed his situation. He had been stripped naked and bound tightly to the chair with telephone cord. There was enough slack in the wire to allow circulation, but any thought of breaking free was absurd. This guy was a pro, no doubt about that.

The torturer stood before him, carefully arranging a variety of tools and kitchen implements in a row on the dinette table: knives, a corkscrew, a cheese grater, an electric hot-plate, an ice pack, a Black and Decker wireless variable speed drill, a pair of needle-nosed pliers, and a pair of channel-lock pliers. The countertop next to the sink displayed an array of open jars, cans, and other containers.

"You certainly keep a well-stocked home, Father," said the man, gesturing at the table and smiling. "You must have known I was coming."

"Look, I've told you all I know. What the hell do you want with me?"

It sickened Dan to hear the pleading in his voice, but he felt so incredibly vulnerable. With his legs spread apart and his ankles tied expertly to the back legs of the chair, Daniel felt embarrassment and fear. His penis had shriveled to a nub and his testicles had pulled up close to his body.

The man picked up a small paring knife, moved to Daniel's left and casually inserted about a quarter inch of the blade into the skin of his forearm. Daniel watched with horror as his flesh was violated. His mind sparked, more from the audacity of the act and the shock than the pain.

Calmly the man held the blade in place. Surprisingly little blood escaped the wound.

"I'm going to ask you a question," he said. "If I don't like the answer, I'm going to filet your arm as if it were a fish."

"Please . . . what do you want from me?"

"Answers. Only answers. Now, tell me: do you know *why* your friend went to Rome?"

"No."

The blade moved half an inch up his arm. Blood spurted, and the torturer reached for an open box of baking soda. He shook some into the wound. "Next time I'll try some salt, eh?"

"I *don't* know why!" screamed Daniel. His arm felt wrapped in a cocoon of tingling fire.

"You mean Peter Carenza told you nothing of his recent . . . experiences? His troubles?"

"I don't know what you mean."

The man smiled. "Do you know what my colleagues call me?"

"Huh?" The question made no sense.

"*Il Chirurgo*. It means 'the surgeon.' "

He guided the blade another inch closer to Daniel's elbow, running the tip along the edge of the ulna, careful to avoid any major blood vessels. Unable to look away, Daniel watched his skin being parted as casually as if the man were slicing into a juicy steak. The "surgeon" shook a box of salt over Dan's arm. This time the pain threatened to white out his senses. Fireworks seemed to sputter before his eyes.

"That's shit, my friend," said the man in his terribly soft voice, like a hammer wrapped in velvet. "You're lying."

"No!" Daniel screamed, wondering if anyone else in the building could hear him. "He told me about the mugger! The lightning! That's all I know!"

The phony policeman nodded. "Perhaps. Perhaps not."

"Oh God, it's true! Please believe me!"

"Do you know why Peter Carenza was taken to Rome?"

"No, but . . ."

The knife's tip touched bone and a new shellburst of agony shocked through Dan. Sweat ran from his pores like blood.

"But you have suspicions, don't you? Tell me about them."

Through clenched teeth, fighting back bitter tears, Daniel briefly outlined his supposition that Peter had been summoned by a miracle investigation committee.

"Now isn't that a nice, convenient answer?" The man scraped the blade along the bone, flensing back the flesh. Dan was bleeding slowly, probably due to his body's gradual lapse into shock. The pain was so all-consuming, so beyond all thresholds, that Dan had begun to look at his ruined arm as though it belonged to someone else.

He could hear himself screaming weakly, almost whimpering. "I'm telling you the truth. What's the matter with you?"

"No, I don't think so. What you're telling is the party line, my friend."

"No . . ." Dan moaned. "No, I'm not."

The man bent to stare directly into Daniel's eyes. "Now you listen to me. What you're telling me is exactly what those goons in the Vatican want everybody to think! How could you know what to tell me unless you've talked to Carenza?"

"I haven't talked to him! I swear to God!"

"Do you?" The questioner picked up the Black and Decker, squeezed the trigger lightly. The tool whined into life, drill bit turning slowly. The slow keen of its electric motor sounded horribly obscene.

"Oh God, I'm telling you the truth . . ."

"We'll see." "Ortiz" held open Daniel's palm and pressed the sluggishly-turning drill bit into his flesh. With inexorable slowness the steel churned through the center of his hand. Bursts of pure torment blanketed his brain like the static between radio stations. Dan screamed hoarsely, pain searing his vocal cords.

Once the drill had passed all the way through, the man reamed it up and down several times before beginning again in the center of Dan's other hand. Just as the bit curled off the first layers of skin, he paused, looked at his captive's face.

"Anything you want to tell me?"

"I *swear* to you! I haven't talked to him. I *haven't* seen him!"

"Then how did you know that 'miracles' crap!?"

"I'm not stupid! That was the most logical reason to have him there!" Daniel had trouble keeping his thoughts straight. Waves of pain crashed over him, scrambling his thinking. "I've told you everything I know. Please, believe me."

Ortiz plugged in the one-element hot-plate Dan used to

perk coffee. Within a minute, he held a neonlike orange sworl in his hand. "Now, that looks nice and toasty, doesn't it?"

"Please . . ." said Daniel, unable to take his eyes off the glowing heating element.

"It is said that the tips of our fingers have more nerve endings than anywhere else in the body. Do you believe that?"

"Yes," he heard himself saying insanely.

"Now, I'm going to ask you—where is your friend, Peter Carenza?"

"Oh, God, I don't know . . ."

"Yes, you do. You must."

The man held Dan's left hand in a viselike grip, forcing his fingers back and up. With deliberate slowness he pressed the hot-plate against the tip of Dan's middle finger. With a loud, steaming hiss white-hot pain flashed and popped through Dan like a broken high voltage wire. Pain shorted out all sensation. Dimly, Dan felt pressure as the element was pushed harder against his finger. There was a crackling sound, followed by a *pop*, and the smell of charred meat.

Daniel screamed weakly, exhausted from pain, driven beyond sound. Sweat dripped into his eyes, mixing with tears to form a burning acid under his clenched lids. His stomach heaved and lurched. A hot column of vomit and bile surged up and down his throat, threatening to choke him. Suddenly a warm stream of urine burst from him, staining the chair and running down his leg.

"So messy," said his tormentor.

"Please . . . No more, please."

"Where is Peter Carenza?"

"I don't *know*!"

"Does he have any other close friends?"

"I don't know . . ."

Ortiz pressed the hot-plate against Dan's index finger. Skin burned and steaming capillaries burst. The pain novaed-out his thoughts. He was going to pass out . . .

Cold water stung his face, shocking him into wakefulness.

"Is there anyone else he might go to?"

"No, no. I don't know." He was weeping.

"I think you do," said the man. He put down the hot-plate, reached for the ice pick.

TWENTY-ONE

Brooklyn, New York—Carenza
August 28, 1998

When he woke, he felt as though he'd risen from the dead.

Peter smiled. Maybe that wasn't the best colloquialism to employ just now. Shaking his head, he sat up and rubbed his eyes. He wasn't even sure what day it was, much less the time. The evening on the couch, the wine, the conversation with Marion Windsor seemed a very long time ago.

He staggered into the bathroom, only half-noticing the incredible panoply of female cosmetics covering the vanity countertop. He peed like he'd never had the chance in all his life, then moved to the sink to splash some water on his face. More awake, he looked in the mirror. He felt as if his face were changing somehow. His familiar boyish features were hardening, fading away, and it bothered him. The suggestion of lines and creases around his eyes and mouth. He wanted to chalk it up to fatigue, or even the good old aging process, but he knew the events of the last week had catalyzed any differences he now noticed in his appearance.

When he reentered the bedroom he noticed the Westclox on the dresser ticking past 4:17. The hazy light coming through the chenille-curtained windows meant afternoon sun. Could that be right? Had he really slept through the night and half the next day?

He shook his head, sat on the edge of the bed, and slipped

into jeans and a cotton shirt. Guess that's what jet lag and a good fight with a couple of killers can do for you . . .

When he descended to the kitchen, he found a note from Marion. Since it was Friday, she wrote, she would be working the evening news slot and would be finished around 8:30 PM. She would call him then. Peter smiled as he crumpled up the note and dropped it in the trash. He hardly knew the woman, yet he felt like she'd been his friend all his life.

The bizarre events of the last week had thrown them together, and after the scene at the airport, they seemed almost fated to be close to each other. You don't save each other's lives and maintain a casual attitude, he thought with a smile.

Of course, you don't tell someone you're the Son of God every day, either.

The Son of God.

Peter remembered the previous evening, when he vaporized the guy's arm. Although he'd been trying to avoid thinking about it, his subconscious wouldn't let it go. Thinking back to the precise instant, Peter reflected that he'd felt almost able to make the blue fire appear. He couldn't actually control it, but he thought he might be able to bring it on when he needed it. Extreme stress or danger apparently was the trigger.

If that was true, then maybe he could *learn* to *really* control it. He'd read, in Charles Fort's *Wild Talents*, about bizarre cases of spontaneous human combustion—people who suddenly burst into flames so intense that their bodies were carbonized within seconds—and wondered if his own "ability" was part of the phenomenon.

He shook his head, sighing with exasperation. Why was he still grasping for rational or even quasirational explanations for who and what he was? The Vatican had offered him the cleanest possible exegesis; he just didn't want to accept it. He was getting sick of all the mental gymnastics.

Peter walked into the kitchen, rummaged through the refrigerator and found some juice and seven-grain bread. A two-slice toaster stood on a nearby counter.

There had to be some basic flaw in the Vatican gang's argument. Perhaps their procedures had produced only another test-tube baby. He certainly didn't *feel* like God. Not even His Son.

He smiled as the toast popped up. His thoughts were so absurd. And yet—the physical evidence, and the testimony of very serious men and women, couldn't be easily dismissed.

As he buttered the toast, poured a glass of orange juice, he wondered how long he would be plagued with thoughts like this. Maybe for the rest of his life . . .

He hoped it wouldn't drive him crazy.

Marion's support had been the only *real* thing in the last week of his life. Daniel Ellington was the only other person he could trust. His closest friend deserved to know what had happened—and Peter would certainly welcome his input. Peter reached for the phone, punched in the number for the Fordham English department, and hoped he'd remembered it accurately.

When Dan's receptionist answered, Peter smiled. Good. This is what I need. We'll meet for lunch or something.

"Daniel Ellington, please . . ." he said.

"Oh, I'm sorry, but Father Ellington's off today. Would you like to leave a message?"

"He's not coming in at all today?"

"Well, we're not expecting him."

"So he wouldn't get my message till tomorrow?"

"I don't think so," said the young woman.

"All right," said Peter. "Thank you very much."

Holding the receiver, he dialed Dan's apartment number.

He let it ring twenty times before hanging up. Figuring his friend might be in the shower, he finished his meager breakfast, cleaned up the mess, and called again. Still no answer.

He decided to wait until Marion contacted him. Maybe they would ride up to the Fordham campus together.

"Did you watch me on the news?" she asked with a reproving, somewhat flirtatious smile.

"I forgot, honest," he said. "I've never been a real news-addict. I watch once in a while, but everything is too politically oriented for me. Politics is boring."

"That's okay, I was just kidding," she said, as she turned her Mazda east on Atlantic Avenue. "It was a terrible show anyway. Nothing really going on tonight."

"No splashy murders or government scandals, huh?"

"Peter, are you trying to be snide?"

He smiled. "Had to resort to a second-rate warehouse fire for good video, I'll bet."

Marion sighed as she dodged the slower traffic in the right lane. "Are you that cynical? Are we that predictable?"

He shrugged. "There does seem to be a pattern to TV news. The producers have stumbled onto a formula that works, something the average viewer's comfortable with. I can understand that. If it's not broke, don't fix it, right?"

"I guess so," she said, almost sadly.

"Hey, I didn't mean to bring you down," he said. "I'm sorry."

"It's okay," said Marion, pushing a lock of her auburn hair away from her face. "It's just that I really like my work, and I want to think I'm doing something meaningful. I guess I get caught up in the glitz that comes with the territory, and I forget what it's like on the other side of the screen."

"Marion," he said, touching her arm for the briefest of moments. "I'm sorry I made that remark. It was uncalled for, and you don't have to defend yourself to me."

"Peter . . ."

"I mean it. Look, you've helped me through some unbelievable stuff already. I want you to know I appreciate everything you've done. I don't know why I was talking like that."

She looked at him for an instant before returning her attention to the traffic. Her green eyes were as deep as the sea; Peter was fascinated by the effect on him of a single glance from her. The last time he'd let himself admit to such feelings about a female, he was still in prep school. Of course, an adolescent boy's glands generate a lot more than just feelings . . .

"Thank you, Peter," she said. "But you shouldn't apologize for making me think."

They rode in silence for a few minutes, headed north on the Van Wyck Expressway. There was no easy way to get from the heart of Brooklyn to the heart of the Bronx. This late in the evening traffic was fairly thin as they approached the lights of the Whitestone Bridge. Peter wondered aloud why he couldn't reach Dan. "I hope everything's okay," he said.

"You said it's his day off. Maybe he left town, visited his relatives, something like that."

"Nah, they're all in the Midwest," said Peter. "I don't know—I just have a weird feeling."

She reached out and touched his hand, letting her long-nailed fingers entwine with his. "Hey, your friend's fine. You'll see."

"Thanks," he said, squeezing her fingers, then purposely breaking the contact. Her closeness made him uncomfortable; her touch made his pulse pound.

They drove on in silence, over the Whitestone, along the Cross Bronx Expressway and Bronx River Parkway, then through the park to Fordham Road. As the campus appeared on the right, Peter felt inexplicably apprehensive.

"Where am I going?" asked Marion as she pulled into the campus.

"Follow this road around to the right. The apartments are down behind that row of big buildings. Off on the left—see them?"

Marion nodded, turning the steering wheel, accelerated toward several rows of faculty housing. Peter directed her to the parking lot in front of Dan's building.

"That's his car," he said, pointing to a low-slung Pontiac.

"Are you sure?"

"Almost positive. I remember him calling the color 'midnight blue'—'the color of the notes from a jazz trumpet, if they could have any color at all,' is the way he'd described it."

"Sounds like your friend Dan has a bit of the poet in his soul." Marion smiled as she killed the ignition.

Peter shrugged. "He's a Jesuit. He thinks he's got a bit of *everything* in him!"

She laughed nervously as she opened her car door and got out. Peter exited on his side and walked over to look into Dan Ellington's car. Empty. The hood was cool.

While Peter checked the car, Marion had been studying the small two-story building, which had two apartments on each floor. Together, she and Peter approached the blank, steel door of Dan's flat. Peter felt a slight tingling sensation throughout his body. He was sensing something, but he didn't recognize what his awareness was trying to tell him. The upper landing was hot and humid, and quiet as a grave.

He knocked several times, waited, knocked again.

Marion stood beside him, but said nothing.

He knocked again. "Dan!" he said loudly. "It's Peter! Are you in there?!"

"He's not there," said Marion. "Let's—"

"No, wait!" The tingling increased. The sensation was mesmerizing. "No, he's in there! I can feel it!"

He began pounding on the door, screaming Dan's name.

Then they heard the single, choked sound from behind the door. A muffled, strangled utterance. Not really a word, just a solitary syllable.

"Did you hear that?" shouted Peter. He threw himself at the door, but it remained firm. "He's in there! I knew it!"

"Oh my God . . ." Marion's voice was a hoarse whisper.

"Dan, it's Peter! I'm coming in!"

"Peter, be careful. Maybe we should get some help . . . ?"

"No! He needs us! We've got to get in *now*."

Peter placed his hands on the doorknob and the tumbler for the deadbolt. He tried to relax, to push all extraneous thoughts from his mind and just think about the locks on the door and how they were in his way, how they need to be removed. He tried to recall the fleeting sensation he'd had that morning, when he'd been thinking about his "talent." The power lay within him; he just needed to learn to harness it, to use it.

But how!

He pressed himself against the door, futilely. Trying to will the energy out wasn't working. He had to let go somehow, to be subsumed into the energy-flow. Somehow, before, his mind had cut loose from time—and at those moments his talent surfaced.

"Come on!" cried Marion. "We've got to get some help. We'll never get in!"

"No!" he screamed. "No!"

Another single cry for help seeped through the frigid metal barrier.

Suddenly he was angry with Marion for not believing, for wanting to abandon Dan at the moment of his need. Angry because the damned door was keeping him out of there. The urge to grab her by the throat and shake sense into her shot through him but instead he leaned into the door.

A flash of blue-light radiated off the metal as the knob and tumblers and one whole side of the steel slab blew inward in a superheated explosion. The rest of the door swung violently on its hinges, sending Peter sprawling into the room. Heavy smoke hung about like laundry on a line; as he struggled to his feet he could see nothing.

Dan's muffled voice cut through the mist like a warning beacon. Peter moved into the smoke, dissipating it with waves of his hands.

Like some grotesque monster materializing out of the fog, the grossly altered figure of Daniel Ellington appeared to him. Peter's gaze locked into his friend's, and for an instant the eye contact held them as one. Behind him, Marion stumbled into the room, fighting off the smoke.

Peter heard her scream as he surveyed what had been done to his friend, who sat slumped and bound, naked, to a kitchen chair. The slow rise and fall of Dan's chest, his occasional moans were the only way to know he yet lived. One arm had been sliced open like a deboned slab of meat; his hands and fingers were cauterized, burned down to nubs; his lips were stapled together, his eyelids razored off and the corneas crusted over; an ice pick had been pushed up his urethra.

The bastards!

Tears streamed from his eyes; he felt Marion's hands on his shoulders. She was shaking and sobbing with a combination of fear and pain and disgust.

"Help me," he said softly. "We've got to get him out of that chair. Come on, now!"

Marion clung to him, shivering, wracked with sobs. "Oh my God . . . Oh my God . . ." she kept repeating. "What happened to him?"

"They're looking for *me*, Marion. This is how they think they'll find me." Peter pulled the phone cord from Dan's legs, carefully unbound his wrists. He looked at his friend's face, the muscles and skin slack and bruised, his eyes rolled back into his skull.

"Is he . . ."

"Yes, he's still alive. Help me lay him on the rug." Peter's tears ran hotly down his cheeks as he spoke. "Dear God, Dan, who did this to you?"

His friend forced a moan through his stapled lips, flicked his eyes from side to side. Marion helped ease him to the floor, obviously fighting an urge to give in to hysteria. Just looking at the poor man in front of her must have taken all her strength.

"I'll call for an ambulance," she said hesitantly.

Peter nodded. She moved away quickly, looking for the phone.

"We're going to help you, Dan," he whispered to his friend, as he cradled him in his arms. Though he managed to keep from openly sobbing, tears still flooded down his face. "It's going to be okay, everything's going to be okay."

"The phone's been yanked out!" said Marion, getting panicky. Peter was about to tell her to try another apartment when several teardrops fell from his cheeks and splashed upon the ruined flesh of Dan Ellington's arm. Peter was stunned by what happened next.

"I said the phone's dead!" cried Marion, hurrying back into the room.

"Marion, look!" he cried.

She knelt down next to him to see the flayed muscle and bone of Dan's arm bathed in a soft blue aura.

"What's happening?"

Peter touched his cheek, then pressed his wet fingers to her own cheek. "My tears . . . they touched him there."

"Oh Peter—My God, what's happening!?"

Peter slowly stroked his damp fingers along Dan Ellington's arm. The intensity of the aura increased with his touch and as he slowly traversed the length of the ravaged flesh it began to heal.

"Oh . . ." he heard himself whisper. "I don't believe this . . ."

Marion began whimpering. Within seconds, Dan Ellington's arm had become whole again, the flesh pink and new like a baby's ass. Peter rubbed his fingers across his own face, trying to pick up the remaining moisture from his tears. He grabbed the stubby, charred remains of Dan's fingers, caressing them gently as the blue aura again burst into life and the healing began anew.

Fresh tears seeped from Marion's eyes. The strength of her sobs doubled her over.

"I don't believe this! I don't believe this . . . !"

Dan's muffled moans seemed softer now, as though he experienced some sort of pleasure. When Peter touched a fingertip to his friend's stapled lips, the metal fasteners dissolved through the savaged flesh and fell away harmlessly. Peter's hand, laid gently upon Dan's eye sockets, restored his vision and fluttering, long-lashed lids. As Dan began to cry, Peter removed the ice pick, as carefully as possible.

By this time the aura had expanded to envelop all of Dan's body. Like St. Elmo's fire, only centimeters away from his skin, it shimmered with a neon intensity.

Marion whispered in Peter's ear as she looked down at Dan. "Peter, he looks beautiful. Oh, God, look at him! He's beautiful!"

"Peter . . . ?" Dan looked at him, totally perplexed. His voice was ragged.

"Yes, it's me."

"What's happening to me?" Dan's voice contained fear and wonder in equal parts.

"You're going to be all right now. Just take it easy."

Marion got up, looked hurriedly about the cluttered apartment until she found a closet. She pulled a coat from its hangar and returned to wrap it around Dan Ellington. Peter smiled. Modesty was the least of his friend's concerns at this point.

"Was I dreaming?" asked Dan. "What happened to me?"

"Who *did* this to you?!" Marion's voice quavered, but she fought to get it under control.

Dan looked at her uncomprehendingly.

"Uh, this is my friend, Marion Windsor," said Peter. "She helped me."

Dan nodded, still recovering from the gross shocks to his mind and body. He touched his face tentatively, looked at the tips of his fingers as if not believing the reality of the soft, pink flesh.

"I don't know who the son-of-a-bitch was . . ." Dan shook his head. "Said he was a cop and had news about you. Peter, what happened?" He paused, took a shaky breath. "How did you do this? That guy cut me up like a birthday cake! Oh, Jesus . . . I don't believe this!"

Peter started crying again. "I'm sorry, Dan. Oh, God, it's my fault that this even happened to you . . ."

Daniel reached out and hugged his friend, pulling him close.

"When did this happen, Dan?" asked Marion.

"Late last night." He relaxed his embrace.

"Didn't anybody hear what was going on?"

Dan shrugged. "It's a small building and it's summertime. The other three guys are all on vacation. I was the only one dumb enough to teach a summer session . . ."

"Can you describe the guy?" asked Marion.

"I don't think I'll ever forget him." He looked at his hands.

"Peter, the guy *mutilated* me! Now look! What's going on here?"

Peter nodded.

"We've got to get the police," said Marion, standing up, but not knowing where to go next.

"No," said Peter.

"Why not?!" Marion looked at him in total surprise.

"What could we tell them?" Peter asked. "That Dan was tortured, but that he's better now? What evidence could we offer them? And if by some chance they believe us, what then? The man who did this was a pro, dispatched by the Vatican. The cops could never find him—and we'd look like fools—or madmen."

"You're right," said Marion.

Dan slowly stood up, drew the long coat about his body. He inspected the partially incinerated door.

"Couldn't find a locksmith, huh?" He grinned, shook his head, then moved slowly to the couch where he collapsed into its familiar cushions. He looked at Peter warily. His eyes revealed a conflux of feelings—fear, disbelief, shock, even a touch of adoration. "You've got to tell me what the hell's going on."

"I know," said Peter.

"It's a long story," said Marion.

Daniel essayed a shaky smile. "I think I owe you at least the time it'll take to tell me," he said. "Believe me, I'm listening."

TWENTY-TWO

Brooklyn, New York—Windsor
August 28, 1998

Being followed seemed like the only thing Marion could think about as they drove back to Suzette's apartment. The man who'd tortured Dan was following them, was going to kill them.

"There's nothing back there," said Peter, checking the darkness that trailed the Mazda down the Van Wyck. "You can relax."

"Unless he put a bug on the car. Then he could track us electronically," said Dan, hunched up in the minimalist back seat of the sleek vehicle.

"That's a cheerful thought," said Marion.

"Well, we could leave the car at a garage for the night. Take the subway the rest of the way," said Dan. "Maybe you could get somebody from the TV station to check the car tomorrow."

"Not a bad idea," she said. Dan's voice sounded so normal it was startling. Like the clash of cymbals, the memories of Peter *healing* Dan brightened in her mind. Maybe Peter still couldn't accept who he might be, but he sure was doing a lot to make a True Believer out of me!

Watching that glow around Dan's body, seeing all the blood and ravaged flesh just . . . *disappear*, had been the most beautiful experience of her life. To be a witness to such a thing! Just thinking about it brought a lump to her throat, fresh tears to the corners of her eyes. Even while Peter had recounted his unique tale to Dan, Marion had been weeping from the power she had seen. She'd watched the Jesuit calmly listen to every detail, never interrupting, never commenting. She could almost see the man's mind weighing and analyzing every word, every aspect of the story.

"You know," Daniel Ellington had said quietly, "it doesn't sound that crazy to me. When you think about it, it all makes rather good sense, really."

The young Jesuit had described the plausibility of the science involved, then cited the "talents" Peter had exhibited for healing and destroying. As Marion listened to Dan drone on in a perfectly calm, logical voice, she began to think she might be able to believe the unthinkable.

Dan had summed it up best of all. "Let's face it, Peter," he'd said. "After what you did to me tonight, I would have no trouble believing you might be the Son of God."

And Peter had reacted pretty strongly against that. He kept insisting that he was just an instrument, that for some reason God was acting *through* him, that God was merely using him.

But using him for what?

They had no answers.

The more Marion thought about ditching the car and getting it debugged by one of the station's techies, the more the idea appealed to her. She explained her thinking as she left the highway, heading for the big parking garage near the Queens Center Mall. The car would be safe enough there overnight.

"Sounds good to me," said Peter. He looked at her and smiled halfheartedly. He looked scared and lost, like he had not the slightest idea what he might do next. They were going to have to spend some time planning their next moves.

Several minutes later, the three companions were riding the G train west. The line looped around to the south, past Greenpoint into the heart of Brooklyn. Marion had never liked riding the trains at night, and as a rule, never did. But as she stood by the gritty, paint-speckled door of the car, with Peter Carenza standing by her side, she knew she was safe.

"I don't think you have much choice, Peter," Daniel said, holding a bottle of Heineken in his freshly healed right hand. "You've got to get outta Dodge, buddy."

Peter looked decidedly distressed. "But where do I go? I can't run forever."

"No, but there's a guy looking for you right now who's probably the baddest news this side of King Kong."

Peter forced a smile. "Where do I go?" he repeated.

"I wasn't kidding—I don't think you have much choice but to head for western skies." Daniel took a long pull from the green bottle. "New Jersey's a good place to start."

"I don't have much money. I don't even have a car."

Daniel waved off the objections. "I've got money."

"And I've got a car," said Marion, surprised by her own impetuous words. Apparently her subconscious had already made a decision. The offer had come out without hesitation.

"Your *car*? You'd give me your car?" Peter looked absolutely stunned.

"Not exactly," said Marion, smiling. "I'd be driving it."

"I can't believe this! You mean you would come with me? How? Why?"

"I haven't had a vacation in three years. My boss owes me," she said, wondering if that was completely true. She'd probably have to beg for a leave of absence in promise for an utterly unmatchable story when she returned. That last thought burrowed deep into her conscience—she wasn't doing all this just to get the story of the century, was she?

No. It was more than that.

But that was sufficient explanation for anybody who asked.

"Count me in," Daniel was saying. "I can't let you run from this guy by yourself. I owe you."

"You don't owe me anything."

Daniel smiled. "Says you. I'm coming, okay?"

"But we don't have a plan—"

"We'll make one," said Daniel.

"And we'll make it work," added Marion.

She was suddenly suffused with a sense of adventure and excitement she had never known before. The feelings were oddly intoxicating. She felt no danger, nothing but security in the knowledge that she was doing the right thing.

She looked across the room at Peter Carenza, and for the first time Marion Windsor grappled with the thought she might truly be falling in love with him ...

TWENTY-THREE

Du Bois, Pennsylvania—Carenza
August 29, 1998

Things were happening so fast, Peter was having a hard time adjusting to all the changes in his life. The rectory at Saint Sebastian's already seemed distant, alien. It was as if his identity as a parish priest belonged to another person. Slowly he had begun to think of himself differently. Maybe he *was* a special person. If God had chosen him to do a special task, then maybe he'd better start getting used to the idea. He had to admit he was getting more comfortable with his ... special abilities. Ever since he saw the healing, he'd definitely felt better, knowing he wasn't built purely for destruction. He could learn to live with his new abilities, and learn to control them. He was more confident that he would eventually hold the power, so to speak, over his power.

He watched the green semimountainous terrain of northern Pennsylvania spool past. It was his turn in the cramped back seat of the Mazda as he, Dan, and Marion motored west on Interstate 80.

Having made up their minds to protect him, his two friends had acted quickly and in concert. After a station security tech, grumbling at being rousted out of bed, had declared her car clean, Marion had purchased the necessary supplies and equipment for a cross-country camping trip. Though Dan had plenty of camping gear, they'd decided not to risk the trip back to his apartment, in case the Vatican's agent had bugged the place. They borrowed a small trailer from WPIX and headed north and west to the George Washington Bridge with the radio playing loud rock and roll. Once into New Jersey, they stopped at a K-Mart to buy the few things they hadn't found at the Herman's in Queens.

Dan and Marion seemed to be caught up in the spontaneity of the moment. They were like a couple of little kids running away from home, like Huck and Tom seeking adventure on the Mississippi. Peter wished he could feel so cavalier about what they were doing.

For Peter, it was an exhilarating but threatening experience. Most of his life had been planned and scheduled and ordered. He'd always known what he was going to do. He wasn't used to this kind of freedom—in fact he almost felt guilty at being suddenly free of obligation, duty and expectation. He was afraid he wouldn't know what to do without an outwardly imposed structure.

Towns slipped past them, and as Peter read their names on the signs, he wondered what small dramas were being played out in their thousands of homes. Stroudsburg, Fenridge, White Haven, Mooresburg, New Columbia, Clintondale. So many places he'd never see, full of people he would never meet. Already this journey was opening up his mind to a whole new range of experience. Perhaps he would not regret running away from the only life he'd ever known.

"I'd forgotten how pretty everything is when you get out of that ridiculous city," Marion shouted over the back beat of an old Rolling Stones song.

Daniel turned down the volume and spoke. "We're just about clear of the Appalachians now. Beautiful, isn't it?"

"We're going to need some gas," said Marion. "There's an exit coming up, okay?"

"Fine with me," said Peter. "It's getting late. Maybe we should start looking for a place to put up for the night, too."

Marion exited south on Route 219 and headed for an old red brick grocery story with a pair of Chevron pumps out front. A big maroon Harley touring bike was canted over by the door and a young blond girl in leathers was leaning against it. She looked oddly at Peter and the others as they exited their car. Taking a step toward the door of the grocery, she hesitated, then returned to the bike. The travelers passed her and entered the store.

None of them saw the kid with the gun right away.

"Can we get some gas?" Marion asked a middle-aged woman in a white apron at the counter. The woman was emptying the cash drawer into a small brown paper bag. She looked up, startled, as Marion approached.

"I—"

"Hey, what the fuck's this!?" The slightly high-pitched voice belonged to a boy in his early twenties. Dressed in bike leathers, he held an automatic pistol in one hand and a large Hefty bag full of grocery items in the other. His naturally handsome features were obscured by three days of beard, road grime, and sweat. He was wide-eyed and taut-jawed; his gunhand waved the weapon erratically.

"Oh shit," said Daniel. "I don't believe this . . ."

"Believe it, man," said the kid, looking frantically from one person to the other. "Okay, everybody! Everything outta your pockets and on the counter. Now!"

"Just do like he says," said Daniel, slowly reaching into his jeans for his wallet and folding money.

"Okay, take it easy," said Marion, opening her shoulder bag. Peter hadn't moved. He kept looking at the kid, trying to get a read on him. Despite his appearance and his jacked-up motions, Peter didn't think the kid was on any drugs. Fear and confusion, desperation and need, capered behind the boy's eyes.

"Look," Peter said. "If you've got trouble, maybe we can help. You don't have to do this."

The kid looked at him, forced a laugh. "Man, don't preach

to me! You *are* gonna help—you're gonna give me all your money right now!"

"I don't think so," said Peter.

He said it in such a flat, emotionless tone that the young thief did a double-take.

"What? What'd you say?"

"I said we're not going to give you our money."

"And why not?"

The kid shifted his feet, tried to sneer but failed miserably. He pointed the gun at Peter's face, but his motion was hesitant, as if he knew it wasn't going to faze the tall, sinewy man.

"Because . . . because I can destroy you—if I want to."

Peter could feel everyone's gaze upon him, like headlights pinning a deer against the dark matte of a night road. He could hear the heavy echo of his own voice. "You know I'm telling the truth, don't you?"

The kid started to answer, then held back. His eyes locked with Peter's.

Peter stared into him, never flinching. He could feel his body beginning to tingle. The summer-air-before-lightning feel told him the power was gathering. If the kid tried anything, he could fry him like a moth in a purple bug-zapper. No, that wasn't quite right. The way he felt right now, the way the forces were boiling and twisting inside him, he didn't need the kid to start the action. He no longer required a catalyst to bring forth the awesome energy.

Peter realized, with a suddenness that was deafening, that he now had control of his power, whatever it was. He accepted the knowledge without question or fear.

"Who *are* you, man?" The kid seemed to feel the shift in Peter's soul.

"I'm whoever you need me to be," said Peter. "Put down the gun and let us help you."

The kid forced himself to break eye contact. He wheeled and pointed the automatic at Marion, then Dan, then the clerk.

"I'll kill 'em, man! If you keep fuckin' with me, I swear I'm gonna kill 'em!"

The front door opened and the long-haired blonde sauntered in.

"C'mon, Billy! What're you waitin' for?—the whole town's gonna be in here before you're done."

"Shut up, you little bitch! Just you shut up, Laureen!"

"Put down the gun, Billy," said Peter.

"Fuck you, man."

Resisting, against his will, Billy stared into Peter's eyes.

"I can't let you do this, Billy."

The gun began to glow a deep, cherry red. Its metal surface seared the flesh of Billy's hand with a loud, serpentine hiss and a puff of white smoke. The boy dropped the weapon; before it hit the floor it had lost its shape, melting into a dull lump of bubbling lava.

Screaming like a baby, Billy staggered toward Peter, his still smoking palm as black as a burned steak. "My hand! My fuckin' hand!"

He kept repeating the words as if they were a litany. The blonde had turned, racing for the door, but Marion grabbed her. She yapped like a small dog until Marion slapped her across the face. Good for her. The red-haired store clerk had started crying as she backed into the corner.

Billy tried to take a swing at Peter with his good hand, but he blocked it easily, and grabbed the wrist of the boy's burned hand. Slowly, Peter stretched out with his index finger toward the charred flesh. Terrified, Billy tried to pull away, but Peter's movement was inexorable, determined.

When he touched the boy's ruined palm, the now familiar aura shimmered like blue neon. Tears burst from the boy's eyes as he watched and felt his burns healing. After a moment, Peter withdrew his finger; the flesh was whole and pink. He glanced over at Daniel and Marion. The Jesuit's face was a mask of stolid acceptance. Marion looked like she might start crying.

"My hand!" Billy sobbed out the words through his tears. He dropped to his knees, unable to stop looking at his reju-

venated skin. "My hand ... ! Jeez, mister, who *are* you?"
There was no anger in his voice now, only awe.

"Praise Jesus!" cried the store clerk as she bustled out from
behind the counter to grab the boy's hand. "Praise the Lord
Jesus! We've seen a miracle!"

Billy's girlfriend pulled away from Marion, and slid down
beside him. Grabbing his hand, seeing its healthy glow, she
too began whimpering.

"How'd you do that, man?"

"It's a miracle!" crowed the red-haired woman as she
wiped her hands nervously on her apron. "It's a sign from
the Lord!"

Billy and Laureen stood up slowly. The boy cleared his
throat and wiped his nose on the sleeve of his leather jacket.
He looked down at the still cooling lump of steel, then up at
Peter and half-smiled. "I'm sorry, man. For what I did before.
I didn't mean it. I'm sorry."

Peter nodded. "I know you are. But why did you do it?"

"Just got married," Billy said, looking down at his shoes.

"Billy, shut up!" hissed his wife.

"I lost my job. We needed money. Bad."

"Bad enough to shoot somebody?"

Billy grinned self-consciously; there was a rough-edged
handsomeness about him. "Hell, it wasn't even loaded ... I
just didn't have any place left to turn, you know?"

Peter nodded. "I understand."

Billy looked at him squarely once again. "I got a real
funny feelin' when I first saw you. What're you, like Super-
man or somethin'?"

Peter smiled, put his hand on the boy's shoulder. He was
basically a good kid, driven by desperation. Peter had seen
many people with the same look in their eyes.

"Billy," he said softly, "I don't know who or what I am
just yet. But I plan to find out."

"You're a miracle-worker, that's what you are, mister," said
the counter clerk. "I never seen nothin' like that. Our pastor
says the Millennium's comin' and that there'll be signs and
portents—just like what you done. You're a *sign*, mister!"

Peter looked at Billy, smiled. "Why don't you clean up the mess you made."

Billy nodded, turned to pick up the bag full of pilfered goods, then looked back at him. "What am I gonna do? We don't have any money. No place to live."

Without thinking, Peter heard himself say, "You can come with us."

"Where're you going?"

Peter shrugged. "I don't know."

Daniel moved close to him, whispered softly, "You sure you want to do this?"

Peter looked at him and shrugged. Turning to the store clerk, he asked: "Any place nearby to camp?"

"Take 219 north to Treasure Lake. Lots of campgrounds around there," said the woman. He found the bright light burning behind her eyes a bit zealous.

Peter looked at Billy and Laureen. "Know where she's talking about?"

Billy nodded hesitantly.

"Want to lead us up there?"

"Yeah, I guess," said the boy, shrugging.

"Okay, then," said Peter. "Clean this place up for the lady and meet us outside."

"Yes sir," said Billy.

Marion and Daniel followed Peter out to the gas pumps.

"I don't know if this is a good idea," said Marion as she unlatched the nozzle and inserted it into the side of the Mazda. She pushed her long hair back from her face. Peter thought she looked harried and confused. "Are you sure we can trust them?"

"No, but they seem like okay kids. Just scared and crazy. Kind of like us, really."

"Yeah, but we didn't try to rob anybody with a gun," said Daniel.

Peter smiled. "Hey, who knows what we might have to do before we're through."

"Don't talk like that," said Marion. "It frightens me."

"Sorry . . ." Peter touched her shoulder for a moment. He

felt comfortable being close to her. It was a new experience for him.

"It looks like you've gotten some control over . . . over what you can do," said Daniel.

"Yeah," said Peter. "I think so. It's not something I can really think about, though. I have to kind of just let it happen."

Daniel nodded. "I'll take your word for it."

Marion topped off the tank and returned to the store to pay the clerk just as Billy and Laureen came outside. They climbed aboard the big Harley and Billy kicked in the engine.

"You gonna follow me?!" he yelled above the barely muffled purr of the twin cams.

Peter nodded and waved. Marion returned with the red-haired clerk. The big woman in the apron approached him, held out her hand. "Mister, I just wanna thank you for what you did. It was a sign from God, I know it was. I always knew I would witness a miracle before I died, and I wanna thank you for it—whoever you are."

"My name is Peter," he said, smiling and gently shaking her hand.

"I'm Gretta Stowe. Thank you so much, Peter." She was staring at him with what could only be called adoration. It made him damned uncomfortable.

Marion keyed the Mazda's ignition, and he used the sound as a cue to break contact. "Good-bye, Ms. Stowe."

Billy cranked on the Harley and the maroon bike lurched crazily from the gravel lot onto Route 219.

Gretta Stowe watched Peter as he settled into the car's passenger seat and Marion let out the clutch. The red-haired woman cupped her hands to her mouth and yelled: "Praise the Lord!"

TWENTY-FOUR

Du Bois, Pennsylvania—Ellington
August 29, 1998

Dan had the feeling he was witnessing a historic event. He'd been standing in the back of the Grace Pentecostal Church of God—originally a feed and grain store—for more than an hour, watching and listening to his closest friend talk to about thirty rural souls.

It didn't look like anything special. Peter stood before the group, dressed in a pair of jeans and a polo shirt, charming the hell out of them with his big, dark eyes and his natural orator's voice. He spoke with the right cadence and perfect timbre. It was like hitting a 95-mile-per-hour fastball or taking an S-turn at five gees—some people had the right stuff, some didn't. Peter definitely did. When he spoke, you couldn't help but listen.

Daniel shifted in his metal folding chair and glanced at Marion, who was taking notes in her journalist's pad. Her little Sony audio recorder was cranking away. She looked at Dan and managed a half-smile—as if to say, What have we gotten ourselves into now?

Daniel smiled back, then looked toward Peter, who leaned against the side of the pulpit, his left arm casually draped over it. He could have been standing on a street corner, rapping about the latest song. But his small audience, including Billy Clemmons and the sultry, long-haired Laureen, hung on his every word. Daniel shook his head slowly. He wondered if Catholics were still called "Papists" in backwoods places like Du Bois ...

Peter's discourse was general enough to allay any suspicions of Catholicity. He'd begun the "meeting" by allowing Billy Clemmons and the red-haired woman from the grocery to give witness to the miraculous events of the afternoon. Although Peter disclaimed any responsibility for what had happened, always stressing that he was only an instrument in God's steady hand, Dan could tell the people wanted to hear something different. They loved him, there was no doubt about that. His delivery, the casual, sincere way he involved every member of his audience, made people trust him. He was telling them what they wanted to hear about love and faith and the fear of God as the end of the Second Millennium rolled on.

For the last year or two, the religious tenor of the country had been changing. People were lapsing into what Dan had termed an *apocalyptic mood*. A majority of the American population believed that when the century ended, the world would be irrevocably altered. As the years toward the end of the century fell away, the media had mapped a steady increase in church or temple attendance for all the organized religions. Part of the increase could be attributed to the demographic "bulge" of postwar baby-boomers who were now slipping into middle and retirement age and returning to their various faiths. But part of it was due to superstition. Though the world trembled on the threshold of the twenty-first century, most people were as superstitious and insecure as they had been a thousand years before.

On top of the usual mess was an explosion of fringe organizations, "new" churches, and apocalyptic movements that were springing up like after-the-rain mushrooms. Many were transparent ruses, set up only to capitalize upon people's natural fears, but some were sincere—and some were dangerously unstable.

Dan thought the approaching turn of the century might be the most bizarre, the most embarrassing carnival yet foisted upon the people of the world.

Watching his friend speak, Dan hoped Peter was not doomed to become part of the sideshow.

He hadn't wanted Peter to get involved with this little country church. But it would have been hard to turn down the delegation who'd showed up at the Treasure Lake campgrounds several hours back. The grocery clerk had raved to the Grace Church's pastor and the town's sheriff, convincing them to pay a visit to the strangers by the lake. Peter had no choice but to accommodate the locals.

Dan checked his watch and slipped out the door to have a cigarette. He'd been trying to quit for the last year or so—without success, even though he'd started smoking the nicotine-free brands. Obviously his was a psychological rather than a physical or chemical addiction. He smiled to himself . . . maybe he could just get Peter to zap him with a cure.

"Well, what do you think of all this?" Marion's voice drifted to him like a scented breeze. She'd come up beside him so quietly he hadn't noticed.

Looking up at the night sky, he was amazed, as he always had been, at the sheer number of stars in this corner of the galaxy. It helped to be up in the Appalachian foothills instead of on a street corner in the Bronx. Back there, Dan mused, if he looked up at night he'd be lucky to see a street light.

"Well," he said, "it'll give me some good material for my what-I-did-on-my-summer-vacation essay."

"Yeah, me too. Seriously, though . . ."

"Okay. What do I think of all this? Personally, I don't think we should be doing anything to draw attention to ourselves." He took a long pull off his cigarette. They didn't taste much different than the ones laced with good ole Saint Nick.

"My sentiments exactly," said Marion. She looked up at the sky, crossed her arms under her breasts. A small silence passed between them, then: "Have you been listening to him?"

Dan smiled. "Yeah, he's pretty convincing. That boy surely do have a silver tongue, don't he?"

She laughed. "What made you become a priest, Dan?"

"Changing the subject?"

She shrugged. "I do it all the time. I'm a news-hound, remember?"

"Why do you ask? Because I don't 'seem' like a priest? Don't act like one?"

She grinned. "Yeah, I guess that's part of it."

He exhaled slowly, studying the thin stream of smoke as it mingled with the crisp evening air. "Okay, why a priest? I really don't know, anymore. I come from a strict Catholic family in Syracuse. My mother's brother was a priest, a Jesuit, and I always thought he was a great guy. Real intelligent, full of curiosity and personality."

"And you wanted to grow up like him?"

"Kind of. My father died working for the railroad when I was only five—got in the way of the wrong boxcar is the way the story gets told. After that, my uncle was pretty much my only male role model. I guess it was expected all along that I was going to be a priest. It's an honor in strict Catholic homes to have a son with a calling."

"Calling?"

"Catholic buzz-word, sorry. It means, supposedly, a divine request from God to become a priest."

" 'Supposedly'? Why, Father Ellington, do I detect a trace of cynicism in your heart?"

Dan smiled, flipped his cigarette into the parking lot. "Well, if not my heart, at least my voice."

"Want to explain?"

He took a deep breath, exhaled. The air was crisp, terrifying clean. "Well, in addition to the seminary and the theological stuff, the Jesuits put you through a tough academic program. I've got a Ph.D. in English and Comparative Literature. You know how it is—you get all that education and somewhere along the line you learn how to think. I mean really think—for yourself."

"Sure," she said, smiling. "And then, for a while, nobody can tell you a damn thing."

"Right," said Dan. "But the important thing is that you

learn to always ask the next question. You know what I mean?"

"I think so. Never be satisfied with prepared answers, with programmed responses . . . My business is a lot like that too."

"Exactly. The Jesuits consider themselves very progressive and scientific. So they gave me all these intellectual tools and told me to shoehorn them into a medieval, dogmatic way of seeing the world. Marion, I'll tell you—it's tough."

"I'm sure it is."

"And I'll be honest with you. Before this business with Peter fell into my lap, I had started to lose my whole sense of perspective."

"What do you mean?"

Dan shook another cigarette from his pack, lighted it. "I mean I was having a real psychological crisis. In the seminary, they call it 'loss of faith syndrome,' and they try to teach you ways to safeguard against it or cope with it."

"And it happened to you?"

"Yeah. Big time. I don't want to get into a long theological discussion, but I've been having serious doubts about everything. Sometimes the idea of a supreme being is baffling to me; other times, it seems downright silly. The idea of our consciousness surviving death—well, it sounds like a great idea, but . . ."

"I know," she said. "I have the same thoughts. Most of the time I try to put them out of mind."

"Yeah, it's better to worry about the next one-day sale at Macy's." His voice was cutting.

"Hey, did I really deserve that?" Her big green eyes were smiling at him.

"No, you didn't. Sorry." He almost sighed.

"You're forgiven." Marion Windsor smiled a natural smile, full of grace and beauty. She was an intriguing woman. "You were saying something about Peter . . . ?" she asked.

"Yeah, right. Peter. I mean look what's happening to him— zapping a mugger? Burning a guy's arm off!? I hear all that and, the way my mind works, I'm right away trying to come up with rational explanations, scientific reasons to make it all plausible.

"I mean, miracles and direct intervention don't happen every day. We're not prepared to accept such things."

"The more we learn, the more we realize we don't know."

"Yeah, that's definitely part of it. But Peter touched me and made all those faith-healers look like trained-animal acts! C'mon, Marion—I don't know about you, but I'm never going to be the same after going through that. After seeing it, *feeling* it!"

"It *is* miraculous, isn't it?"

"What else can you call it?" Dan inhaled, blew out a thin line of smoke.

"Do you think he's Christ?"

Dan chuckled nervously. "Just the idea bothers me. I don't know who or what he is. But if they really did clone him from the blood on the shroud, then, yeah—genetically, he *is* the guy who was crucified and wrapped in that sheet. If the guy in the shroud was Christ, then so is Peter."

"Whenever I let myself think about it, I just feel stunned."

"I know—like this can't really be happening."

"But it *is*," said Marion.

"And yet, Peter keeps telling us he doesn't feel like God . . ."

Marion nodded. "Maybe, but I feel he's . . . changing somehow. I haven't known him long, so maybe it's not my place to say that, but it's what I feel."

"I've had the same feelings," said Dan, "and I've known him a long time—if anybody should notice him acting differently, it should be me."

"Like today, with Billy, he seemed so *sure* of himself."

"Yeah," said Dan. "He's learning to use his powers."

"Did you ever wonder what else he might be able to do?"

Dan smiled weakly, took the final drag off his cigarette and flipped it onto the gravel. "You mean things he hasn't discovered yet?"

Marion swallowed, nodded.

"Oh, yeah," said Dan. "And I don't mind telling you—it's kind of scary."

Peter sat in the back seat of the Mazda as they returned to the campsite. As he spoke, Dan could detect in his voice an enthusiasm and excitement he'd never heard before. Dan wasn't sure if that was bad or good.

"So much has happened lately, I'd almost forgotten how good it is to give a sermon," Peter said as they drove north on 219. Only a suggestion of the thick, leafy forest on both sides of the two-lane asphalt was visible in the beams of the car's headlights.

"Really?" asked Marion. She could see the single head-lamp of Billy's Harley close on their tail.

"I felt so in synch with them, couldn't you tell? They really needed me tonight. They want me to come back when the rest of the congregation can be there."

"Aren't we suppposed to be moving on?" asked Dan. "Keeping a low profile?"

"I know," said Peter. "It's hard to explain, Dan, but I feel like I've *got* to talk to these people. They're so hungry for guidance. They're scared, uncertain. Confused."

"Kind of like us, eh?" said Marion.

Ignoring her remark, Peter continued ebulliently. "Maybe *this* is what I was chosen for—to get out in the world with the people, to get my hands dirty and help everybody, any way I can!"

"You've got a point there. Maybe."

"Out here, on the road, the thought of being cooped up in that rectory for the rest of my life seems silly. *This* is where I belong."

"What about the Vatican?" asked Marion. "What about the guy in the black suit who almost killed Daniel?"

"I know, I know," Peter said, "but . . ."

Dan looked at his friend. Peter's eyes were like beacons, so suffused with energy did he seem. His soul seemed to be shining. Marion was right. Peter *was* changing.

Dan said, "But *what*? Do you want to get caught?"

"Yes," said Marion, "I thought that was the whole reason we ran off with you—to help you stay hidden, to protect you."

"I know," said Peter. "I realize all that. I haven't forgotten. It's just that I've been thinking, and maybe low-profile isn't the best way to play it."

"What do you mean?" asked Dan.

"I mean if I get out among the people, and let everybody see me, then maybe the Vatican will be afraid to make a move on me."

"Hmmm," said Marion. "He has a point. Maybe."

"Sure! Listen, if we keep low, don't let anybody know us or see us, and the 'Man In Black' finds us—what do you think's going to happen?"

"He could sic the Vatican on you, and kill Marion and me," said Dan. "And nobody would ever know it."

"Right. Our anonymity can work against us as much as for us. Think about it."

"I don't know," said Dan. "I think we're taking a terrible chance. You didn't see this guy. You don't know him like I do."

"Well," Peter said, "I have a few 'talents' of my own, don't forget. I don't think we have anything to fear from anybody."

"Except maybe ourselves," said Marion. She didn't turn her head away from the dark road ahead. Dan could see the tension in her features.

"Huh?" Peter looked at her. "Why do you say that?"

Marion looked at him, then Dan. "I don't know about you guys, but I'm still scared."

TWENTY-FIVE

Clearfield, Pennsylvania—Targeno
August 30, 1998

"That is correct—Clearfield," he said. "It is a very small village in Pennsylvania."

This call to the Vatican was his first report since coming to America. Targeno was shaken by what he had learned, but his training and his years of experience kept him from letting it affect his performance. But he did not like the implications of that knowledge . . .

"Have you had trouble tailing them?"

"Of course not. The bug in their car transmits everything I need to know."

"Excellent. When will you bring him in?"

"Not so fast," said Targeno. "There is much to do. And some interesting things you should know first."

"I am waiting," said Francesco.

And wait you shall, thought Targeno. Until I am ready to give it to you.

"They have stopped for the night. Tomorrow, I shall interrogate some of the villagers."

"For what?" The Jesuit sounded impatient.

"Because I need to know what he has been doing. I have not dared any close-up surveillance since he left New York. He's traveling with two other people. I need to know more about their arrangement."

"I don't give a damn about the 'arrangement'! I just want him back," said Father Francesco. His voice was so clear, he could have been in the next room instead of thousands of miles distant. Despite Americans' complaints about their phone companies, the technology was superior to any in the world.

"I know, I know," said Targeno.

"Very well. Tell me . . . who are these people he's traveling with?" The Jesuit's voice was colored by anxiety, but he was doing his best to disguise it.

Targeno exhaled slowly. "His friend from the seminary, Ellington. You should have a file on him already."

"Affirmative. Who's the other one?"

"Marion Windsor. Local TV journalist in New York. There was no record of Carenza knowing her. Either he has been very careful about it for some reason, or their friendship is something new."

"Your feelings on this?"

Targeno lit a Turkish cigarette. The smoke drifted up into the cool air. On the road, an eighteen-wheeler punched a hole in the night. Noisy as hell. "I believe," he said, pausing to take a drag, "they met recently. The most obvious conclusion is that she was investigating the incident with the mugger."

Francesco's veil of control and detachment began to slip. "You don't think he is fucking her, do you?"

Targeno chuckled. He knew it was irritating his superior. "Such language from a prelate!"

"Don't shit around with me," said Francesco. "Just answer my questions."

"I have no idea at this point. But I tell you—having seen her, if he is not, he is truly a fool . . ."

"You dare to blaspheme so casually?" Francesco's voice dripped with sarcasm.

"Is it blasphemy if I do not believe he is who you claim he is?"

"You do not believe?"

Targeno inhaled, exhaled heavy, acrid smoke. "I do not know what I believe. I have heard your story and I confirmed the incident at the airport, but I do not know what to believe."

"You pragmatic ass!" said Francesco. "How can you doubt the facts?"

Targeno chuckled again. "And I have not even told you the latest."

"What do you mean?"

"I interrogated his friend, Ellington. He broke my hypo, so no drug-therapy."

"Meaning?" Francesco's tone became one of concern.

"Meaning I had to get out the toolbox." Targeno smiled.

"You disgust me."

"And yet you keep coming back to me. I must be doing something right."

"Enough!" said the Jesuit. "Tell me!"

Briefly, Targeno listed the degradations he'd inflicted on Ellington. He told Francesco that after the torture session he'd kept the priest's apartment under surveillance until Carenza and the woman arrived.

"After I planted the bugs on the woman's car, I waited. When they departed, Ellington went with them."

"What are you saying?"

Targeno said smiling. "He was completely healed."

"Healed?"

"There wasn't a mark on him. It was like I had never touched him."

"So Carenza restored him!?"

"What else could have happened? I'm telling you, 'Vanni, I carved him up like a goose!"

"The Lamb of God," said Francesco. "We've really done it!"

"So you say . . ."

"You're a fool," said the Jesuit. "He burns off your mob-buddy's arm, he heals one of your victims, and still you do not believe!"

"I only believe in myself," said Targeno. "This man is just a freak to me."

"A freak with a power you do not understand. A power you cannot match." Now it was Francesco's turn to chuckle. "I think you fear this man."

"Perhaps. A man who knows no fear usually does not grow old."

"All right," said Francesco. "What next?"

"I will continue to track him electronically. I can follow up on his activities by asking the right questions. I need to learn more about my prey before I bag him. Habits. Needs. Plans. All this will determine my strategy. I cannot just walk up to him and order him back to Rome. And we already know force will not work."

"Whatever you do, Targeno, no harm must come to him."

"I understand that. Do not insult me."

Francesco laughed softly, briefly. "I didn't think that was possible. Nevertheless, I must tell you—if you damage the goods, you will be punished with what you would call 'extreme prejudice.' "

"Is that a promise?"

"Unfortunately, yes."

"Good-bye, Father," said Targeno. "You will not hear from me until I can tell you something new."

Terminating the connection, he returned to his rental car, a low-slung, black wedge with opaqued windows and a high-performance engine. On the front seat, his briefcase lay open, revealing his KU-band scanning device. The blinking cursor on the map-display grid indicated the position of Windsor's vehicle. He had planted two bugs on it when she parked on the Fordham campus—one a clumsy counterfeit. He knew if it were found, the odds were whoever did the checking would assume he'd successfully cleaned the vehicle. Only a high-level pro would even think to look for a wafer-thin ceramic beacon that looked like nothing more than a speck of dirt on the license plate.

Targeno leaned back in the reclining seat behind the steering wheel, to light another cigarette. As he savored the harsh, heavy taste of the latakia blend, the scanner beeped. The cursor pulsed as the grid map coordinates began to move and change.

They were moving out, but they would not be lost in the wilderness.

Targeno's thoughts were calm, but there was an unwelcome edge to his emotions. Something the Jesuit had said was repeating in his mind. There was no doubt—Targeno feared his prey. This was a healthy posture when dealing with the unknown. But did he really not care about Carenza's true nature?"

Could this man really be Christ?

If so, then the whole game of cat-and-mouse was reduced to plain silliness. There was an old American saying: You don't fuck with King Kong. Surely a corollary would be that you don't fuck with the Son of God . . .

TWENTY-SIX

Warrenton, Indiana—Windsor
October 14, 1998

After the "Miracle at Evansville," there was no keeping a lid on the story. Events moved at a geometric rate, and Marion had to fight the feeling she was going to be overwhelmed by what was happening.

Unbelievably, the small group of travelers had spent more than six weeks in Pennsylvania, stopping in one small town after another. Daniel had wanted to get away from New York, but Peter had warmed to his audiences. Finally they'd headed west again. Marion drove her Mazda into Ohio via Interstate 80 at Youngstown. Billy and Laureen, on their Harley, followed them west through Akron and onto I-71, angling southwest into Columbus. Autumn was in full swing and the college town looked good in orange and brown.

Marion and her merry band stopped for lunch and gas at a diner just south of the town center, then resumed their journey on I-71. The day's plan was to put as much distance between themselves and New York as possible. They bisected Cincinnati and rolled on into Kentucky, hugging its western border, along the Ohio River basin, until they reached Louisville. Marion had never been through that part of the state. The grass really did look blue.

At that point, a decision was needed—west to St. Louis or south to Nashville. Billy and Laureen wanted to see the country music capital of the world; Daniel had no preference. Peter had been oddly quiet through most of the day, staring out the window for hours at a time. He voted for St. Louis but without much enthusiasm.

As the tie-breaker, Marion let her prejudices rule. For no other reason than her absolute loathing of country music, she opted for the Gateway to the West, and guided her car onto Interstate 64, heading into Indiana.

Southern Indiana is as flat as a pool table and, other than the Hoosier National Forest, almost as barren. When the sun hits the horizon, Marion discovered, it gets dark in a hurry. As evening covered them like the dome on a fancy dinner plate, the talk drifted onto subjects like food and sleep. Great ideas. Marion loved her car, but after a long day at high speeds, tension and fatigue had pushed her to her limits. Time to call it quits.

She planned to keep a journal of their trip, and had been mentally composing some entries as she drove the endless highway. Though she'd made a few notes on their sojourn in Pennsylvania, she needed to do some serious work, to get some of her impressions, memories, and maybe even some of her apprehensions, down on paper.

When she exited the interstate at a forgettable place called Warrenton, the local radio station's evening news segment reported the latest developments in a labor riot taking place in nearby Evansville. A large Korean automobile manufacturing plant had been plagued by factory workers' unrest for the last three days, following the announcement by the Yusang Motor

Corporation that all plant employees would be required to participate in mental and physical fitness regimens. Local news spots relayed tales of bloody violence between state police, Yusang security personnel, and the several thousand employees demonstrating just outside the auto assembly facilities. One worker had been killed by security employees, and the factory had essentially been under siege ever since. Marion had been assigned to powderkeg scenes like that, and she felt immediate empathy for her colleagues down in Evansville.

"Sounds pretty bad," she said as they pulled up to a Po Folks restaurant just off the exit. The deep rumble of Billy's cycle resonated through the car's interior as it nestled in beside them in the parking lot. Marion got out of the car as Billy and Laureen climbed off the bike.

"Yeah," said Daniel as he pushed her seat forward, and climbed out. "I'm starving. And if you don't mind my quoting Billy, 'I gotta pee like a racehorse.' "

Billy laughed, slapped Dan's shoulder.

Marion smiled, slammed the car door. She wondered if all Jesuits were like Dan. Everyone turned toward the restaurant entrance—except Peter, who remained seated in the Mazda's passenger seat, staring straight ahead.

"Peter, is something wrong?" Marion asked, leaning down, looking at him. He looked relaxed, well-rested, and as usual, handsome in an unobtrusive, Gregory Peck kind of way.

"No, not really. I was just thinking about that riot. It's so close. Maybe we should go down there and help."

"Help? What could *we* do?" Marion's pulse jumped up about twenty beats per minute.

"Use your martial arts?" He looked at her and smiled.

"Oh, Peter . . . really." She laughed, shortly and without humor. "Everybody's hungry," she said, trying to remain casual. "Are you coming?" No one else had heard his remarks, and she wanted to keep it that way. Peter had been so quiet all day . . . It was unnerving, and for some reason his interest in the labor riot deeply disturbed her—though she didn't know why.

"Sure, I'll be right there. Go on in."

He made no effort to move from his seat, still gazing at a distant horizon, as though he could see something she couldn't. Well, maybe he could. She considered waiting for him, but didn't want to seem pushy. Against her better judgment, she left him and walked into the restaurant.

Daniel, Billy, and Laureen were sitting at a table near the door, perusing menus.

"Where's Peter?" Daniel asked, pushing a length of blond hair from his forehead. He looked like an eternal surfer-boy.

"Still out in the car. He'll be right in." She picked up her menu, scanning it, but not reading a damned word. "Dan, did he seem funny to you today?"

"I don't know. Kind of quiet. Moody, maybe."

"As far as I'm concerned, Peter can act any way he wants," said Laureen. She spoke with such reverence, it was almost comical, especially with her words so opposed to her look: archetypal biker-chick.

"Yeah," said Billy, holding up his hand as if offering proof of his newfound devotion.

Marion looked at Daniel. "You know him better than the rest of us. Would you say he's moody, unpredictable?"

"Heh!" Daniel shook his head. "I'd say he's usually exactly the opposite."

The waitress appeared wearing a blue calico dress and a white apron. She smiled through her myriad freckles. After ordering the perfectly outrageous chicken-fried steak, Marion looked toward the entrance for Peter.

What was he doing out there?

"I'm going to go get him," she told the others as she headed for the door.

When she found the car locked and empty, she was not surprised. She'd expected it since she'd stepped into the restaurant.

Route 41 was a four-lane highway through nothing but dark, desolate farmland. They found a campground and dumped the trailer before heading south in search of Peter. Between Warrenton and Evansville towns were infrequent and practically invisible. Billy and Laureen pushed their bike up into the nineties, taillighting off into the night. More wary of Hoosier state troopers, especially as they got closer to the riots, Marion kept the aerodynamic RX-7 just under the speed limit.

Daniel sat beside her, watching the road and gnawing on a burger from McDonald's. The waitress at Po Folks had been stunned to see them bolt the place so fast.

They drove in silence for almost ten minutes, both lost in thought. Marion wondering what they would find at the factory, and what they would do about it. She wondered if Daniel's thoughts were similar. A luminescent green highway sign announced Evansville's city limits. They passed the municipal airport and lots of small cross-streets. Billy and Laureen were waiting for them at a Union 76 station at the intersection of St. George Road. Marion pulled in and asked the attendant for directions to the Yusang plant.

"You don't wanna be goin' there, lady. 'Less'n you're a reporter."

"I am a reporter."

"Figures . . ." The guy smirked at her, looked at Billy and Laureen on the touring bike. "Okay, stay on Route 41 'bout a mile to Division Street, then hang a left. Take Division all the way out past the hospital, just keep going till you see the plant. And believe me, you won't be able to miss it."

Marion thanked the guy, signaled Billy to follow, and pulled out of the station.

She drove in silence, glancing over at Daniel several times. He was looking straight ahead, tight-lipped, as if searching for something along the dim streets. A panorama of flashing lights from fire trucks, police vans, and media vehicles announced the beginning of trouble. Cops and other uniformed types swarmed all over the area. Smoke bombs and the afterstench of tear gas smudged the sky; the thrum of a huge crowd resonated in the air, rising and falling like an endless chorus of summer cicadas. The distant echo of a bullhorn carried a distinctly hostile voice, perhaps a labor leader.

At the front gates, a forklift held a big pallet high. Behind the lift soared a set of high steel-reinforced gates; looming above everything, like a Martian machine from *The War of the Worlds*, stood the superstructure of a water tower with the word YUSANG branded across its oblate swell. Two men stood atop the lift's pallet, high above the crowd, getting them worked up. Police in riot gear and firemen with crowd-control hoses scuffled with the edges of the large, seething mass of bodies that surrounded the entrance to the auto plant. People were screaming and shouting at the cops. Fistfights broke out sporadically. Paramedics wheeled a gurney along the edge of the crowd, its bloody passenger half-hanging off the cart.

"Oh man, this looks like shit," said Daniel.

"I've seen worse," she said. "Remember the food riots in the Bronx?"

Daniel rolled his eyes. "Who doesn't?"

"C'mon. If Peter's out there, we've got to find him." Marion popped the trunk latch, opened her door.

"Are you sure you know what you're doing?"

"No." Walking around to the trunk, Marion retrieved her mini-camcorder from its shockproof case. She clipped her press credentials to the lapel of her jacket, then handed Dan a portable quartz lighting rig. "You've just become a news-rat," she said.

He smiled, glanced briefly at the handles and controls for the lights. "Pretty ballsy, Marion."

"Thank you," she said, grinning. "Now, let's go."

Billy pulled alongside the Mazda, raised his goggles. "Wooooeee!" he yelled. "Looks like my kind of par-*tay*!"

"Knock it off, Billy," said Marion. "We're here to find Peter and get out. You hear me?" She spoke sternly.

"Hey, just kidding, Marion," he said. "I'm reformed, re-member?"

"So you tell me. Listen, Billy, just find Peter, okay?"

"I'll do my best," he said, wheeling his bike to lean against the nearest light pole.

"Laureen, you better stay here at the car where it's safe."

"Fuck you, Billy! I ain't gonna miss nothin' cuz o' you sayin' so."

Billy shrugged and led her toward the crowd. So much for chivalry, Marion thought.

"Okay, let's move in, toward the action," she told Dan. "Keep your lights at low power and we'll make like we're shooting."

"We're not?"

"Not necessary. We just have to look good."

As they moved closer to the gates, Marion saw more and more devastation. The tactical police squads had been busy knocking heads and shooting off their weapons. Though the violence had for the moment subsided, it seemed ready at any moment to sweep through the crowd in ocean-like swells. The TV equipment made Dan and Marion practically invisible to cops and demonstrators alike. It was a common phenomenon. The camera gave her carte blanche. Everybody wanted to be on TV—for whatever the reason—and if they screwed around with you, they might blow their only chance.

The guy on the bullhorn incited the protestors to storm the front gates. Catch-phrases about power and control sprayed over the crowd like lighter fluid over hot coals. The air almost crackled with tension. Things were on an ugly upswing, and Marion hoped her camera-armor would protect her and Dan as they moved into the edge of the mass of factory workers. As she looked around at some of their faces, trying to personalize them, to draw individuals from the bloblike mass, she was surprised to see so many women in the ranks.

Suddenly, they came upon Billy and Laureen. An anonymous arm reached out and grabbed Laureen's shoulder, holding her while another man fondled her nearest breast. She wheeled and spit at the molester, kicking him between the legs. His scream was lost in the general din of the crowd, as he was pulled back into the shifting pack. Laureen stood her ground and glared defiantly around her.

"We found 'im!" yelled Billy.

"Where?" Marion's voice sounded weak and thin, in the midst of all the noise.

"Right up front. He's arguing with some of the guys with the horn."

How had Peter reached the scene so fast? Later she would learn he'd coaxed a ride from a county police officer, but at that moment, she couldn't imagine how he'd worked his way into the very center of the action so quickly.

"Great. Just great," said Dan. "How're we going to get him outta here?"

"We've got to try," said Marion. "Key those lights up to the max, and the zoom mike too, and follow me."

As they shoved through the workers, the mike began to pick up the words of Peter and the labor leaders

". . . and who the fuck are *you* anyhow?" said one man, who wore a white hard hat.

"I'm your friend," Peter said, smiling.

"Yeah, I'll bet," said the second protest leader. He tilted back his Beech-Nut baseball cap, and jumped down from the forklift pallet to confront Peter. "Ten bucks sez yer one o' them Fed infiltrators. So get lost, buddy, afore you lose some of them pretty teeth."

The crowd thrummed about her but Marion concentrated on the conversation echoing in her headphones.

Peter placed his hand on Beech-Nut's shoulder. "But I am your friend. You do believe me, don't you?"

It was the touch that did it. Or maybe it was just Peter's tone of voice. Whatever, Marion noticed a sudden change in his adversary's demeanor.

"Yeah, okay. What, uh, what can I do for you?"

"Help me up there with your buddy." A moment later he climbed up to join the guy in the white hard hat.

Marion and Dan had eased through the pack of workers, who, for the most part, backed off to let the camera get as close as possible. Most of them made a point of looking directly into the lens and the lights. Some things never change, she thought. A new voice boomed over the bullhorn—Peter's.

It was funny. She'd never been much for churches or sermons or preaching, but there was something about Peter's voice, or his delivery, or the cadence of his words—she wasn't sure—something that made people pay attention. What he was saying didn't seem to be as important as how he was saying it. Even though Marion was focusing her attention on maneuvering through the crowd, a part of her still listened to him, as though she tuned to his words automatically, naturally.

He was telling the workers things they didn't want to hear, but they couldn't stop listening. Marion decided to switch on the camera. She had a feeling something interesting was happening. Clearly, Peter was influencing the mob. Almost as soon as he'd opened his mouth, the general restiveness of the crowd began to lessen. Within sixty seconds, everyone was paying attention.

How did he do it?

"Each one of you knows as well as I: violence is not going to solve any of your problems," he said, with just enough authority in his voice to make the words count.

Initially, when the crowd realized he wasn't up there to incite them to gut the Yusang plant and its managers, they had yelled for him to be silent, to go away. But their roar stopped almost immediately . . . because it was Peter speaking to them. There was something scary about his effect on people. Marion considered the implications of this as she let her camcorder roll. His power was hypnotic, pervasive, and utterly compelling.

"You must ask yourselves what you are really doing here. Risking your family's security and your own health and safety? For what? Because you don't want to be part of a corporate fitness program? What are you afraid of? Feeling better? Living longer? Being more productive?"

Marion listened, and watched the crowd's reaction. She was puzzled. Peter wasn't saying anything earth-shaking; his logic, while solid, was neither unassailable nor overwhelming. Yet they were rapt. As he spoke, Marion sensed an element of *control* lurking just beneath the surface of his words.

It was as scary as it was impressive. People were calming down, lowering fists and protest signs.

Everything was going fine until the carbomb went off.

Later, Marion learned from Billy that the bomb-makers, after hearing Peter's words, had decided to defuse the device and remove it from the Yusang Security cruiser. But somebody had pulled the wrong wire . . .

Like a desert flower blooming in the night, the patrol car erupted in an orange, concussive blossom. The explosion stunned everyone; the crowd was showered with hot shrapnel and body parts.

The cops and the plant security people tried to maintain control. While the mob stood transfixed by the horror of the moment, a squad of tactical police fanned out behind the trailing edge of the crowd. Plant security trained their own riot gear on the leading edge, and the firemen opened up with their hoses. It was a synchronized operation, like a blitzkrieg.

A volley of rubber riot-slugs peppered the crowd. Water cannons body-slammed the workers to the ground. It was like being caught in a hurricane at Times Square on New Year's Eve.

"Oh no!" cried Dan. "The bastards!" He shouted Peter's name, but his voice was lost in the white noise and confusion of the sneak attack.

"We've got to get him!" yelled Marion, trying to push forward. The pack of bodies around her allowed no movement.

Plant security forces opened up with a second, heavy fusillade of rubber bullets, pummeling the front wave of the workers senseless. Up front, Peter and White Hard Hat looked down at the mayhem in apparent helplessness.

Locked into the center of the mob, Marion and Dan were somewhat insulated from the heaviest assaults of water and bullets, but there was no chance for escape. The vast sea of bodies surged and eddied in all directions; she and Dan had no choice but to be carried along on the ever-changing currents. She'd lost track of Billy and Laureen, and now even Dan was being pulled away from her.

Anger whipped through the mob like a forest fire. They

stormed the gates. Weapons appeared in the workers' hands. Like a huge amoeba, the mob surged toward the gates—and Peter. It was as though they blamed him for the turn of events; he'd become the first object of their attack. Marion knew they were going to kill him.

Looking through the lens of her camcorder, she saw Peter standing on the raised pallet with his hands outstretched. He shouted—and though he had no bullhorn, she could somehow hear his words.

Everybody could.

"No! You must stop this!"

Like a sonic boom rolling across an Indiana cornfield, his voice echoed over the mob. Cops, guardsmen, workers—all turned toward this single man as he commanded them to be still.

And they *were* still.

For an instant, it was so quiet, so utterly and deathly quiet, Marion felt her flesh go cold.

Then Peter raised his arms and lightning flashed. Out of nowhere a rainstorm swept down like an attack of the Valkyries. Everything was drenched instantly. The fire hoses were still blasting away, but nobody cared. People went crazy. Close to Peter, someone fired a shot into the air. Others followed. Brickbats flew toward the platform where Peter stood defiantly above the crowd.

Flashes of lightning kept freeze-framing the scene in hard black-and-white tabloid shots. Marion was almost lifted off her feet as the crush of bodies moved in concert toward the plant's gates. Somehow she kept the camcorder rolling. A bolt of lightning grounded at the water tower, creating a spectacular display of yellow-white sparks.

Thunder cascaded; the crowd paused for an instant, reeling from the combined forces of rain and wind.

"You're going to stop this!" Somehow, Peter's booming voice rolled across the riot like a prairie fire. *"NOW!"*

Dan had struggled back to Marion's side. He wrestled with his light-rig, trying to protect it from the mob. Lightning crashed again. A hand grabbed for the camera and Marion wheeled to smack it away. Someone yelled, pointing at the gate. All around her, people began looking up—their faces expressing something between fear and awe.

"Oh my God . . ." she heard Dan mutter behind her.

Saint Elmo's fire danced about the water tower as if it were the mast of a storm-lashed clipper. Turning, she saw Peter, still astride the forklift pallet. Lightning framed him in stark contrast to the rain-slashed night.

Though the lightning flash faded, Peter, shockingly, remained lined in light. He glowed with a fire that coruscated madly about his body. He stood rigid, arms outstretched in a cruciform posture, above the crowd. The glow grew stronger, and for an instant Marion thought he rose above the platform. The crowd gasped collectively. It was the sound of awe on the edge of panic.

"Leave this place," Peter said, softly now, yet clearly audible despite the clamor of the storm and the crowd. He raised one hand, pointing toward the water tower, which exploded as if from a missile strike. But instead of super-heated water and sizzling chunks of shrapnel, the air was filled with petals of pink roses. Marion watched one delicate pink speck flutter down from an impossible height, tracking its descent, until it lightly brushed her cheek. There was a hint of fragrance and then nothing as it fell to wet, shining asphalt and disappeared.

The storm had vanished. The sky was clear. Stunned, Marion blinked, looked again at Peter—and everything had changed. The light, the aura, the rose petals—gone.

No one spoke. No one seemed capable of anything but wandering off, like zombies in a B movie, lost in the myster ies of their own thoughts. The huge mass of protestors turned away from the factory gates, colliding with each other, stumbling on.

Marion felt drained, sucked clean. What had just happened? Her heart was thumping crazily in her chest. If she hadn't been white-knuckling the camcorder, her hands would be trembling. The night suddenly seemed heavy and oppressive as a mildewed blanket. Peter had disappeared into the darkness.

"Did you see that?" Dan asked quietly, breaking the silence.

"I think so," she said, equally softly.

"Rose petals. I saw rose petals." She could hear the shock in his voice.

Shaking her head, Marion turned back toward the car. Where, moments before, a mob had rampaged, bare concrete gleamed wetly.

Billy and Laureen ran up to them.

"He is Lord!" shouted Billy. "He is Lord!"

"Be quiet, Billy," she said harshly. "Please be quiet."

"But it's true! And you know it." Suddenly he fell silent.

All around them cars and vans slunk off into the night. Fire trucks rumbled away from the perimeter of the parking area. Reaching the car, Marion keyed open the trunk and stashed the TV gear. Dan helped, then put an arm around her shoulders.

"What are we getting into?" he asked.

"I don't know," she said, "I just don't know."

Turning around, she saw Peter standing by the hood of the car. He had seemed to have just materialized there, and Marion felt a chill touch her between her shoulder blades.

Peter regarded his friends with a small grin that could only be called sheepish.

"You see," he said, "I knew I could help."

"Yeah, buddy!" said Billy.

"Should we leave?" Marion asked, gesturing at the rapidly emptying lot. A police patrol was rousting stragglers.

Peter shrugged. "Why not?"

Without another word, they climbed into the car. Billy and Laureen mounted their Harley and led the way north. Peter instantly fell asleep in the jump-seat of the Mazda, leaving Dan and Marion to their thoughts. She was too stunned, confused, and just plain upset to do much talking. Dan seemed to want to unload, but he looked at her and remained silent.

Later that evening, after they'd returned to their campsite

and bedded in for what was left of the night, Marion woke. She got up and sat on her front bumper and contemplated the endless spawn of stars in a now-clear sky.

She had begun to see where their adventure was heading. She knew it would only get harder and harder to ignore the signs and parallels. Comparisons would be obvious and well-deserved. She also knew she had the inside track on the most explosive story of the decade, maybe of all time.

She wondered if she had the strength and the courage to stick it out.

BOOK THREE

"Again, the devil taketh him up into an exceeding high mountain, and showeth him all the kingdoms of the world, and the glory of them; and saith unto him, All these things will I give thee, if thou wilt fall down and worship me."

—Matthew 4:8-9

TWENTY-SEVEN

Bessemer, Alabama—Cooper
October 15, 1998

"Okay, boys and girls!" cried the Most Reverend Freemason Cooper. He adjusted his Sennheiser headset, careful not to disturb his carefully set and sprayed helmet of silver hair. "Let's see what's evil in the world tonight!"

Seven o'clock at the southern mansion of the Reverend was always a special occasion. Every weeknight Cooper and his aides gathered in his leather- and oak-appointed study to watch the evening news. In an adjoining room, separated by a glass wall, but in full view of the assemblage, were four wall-mounted big-screen Sony TVs. Each set was tuned to a different network, and monitored by a "media-hawk," as he called his four headphone-equipped assistants. The setup looked like a miniature NASA mission-control.

Cooper swiveled his chair away from a desk so big it could have had its own heli-pad and toward an electronic console that rose up out of the floor at the touch of a button. It had more switches, slides, and touch-pads than a mixing board, plus an ultra-rez NEC monitor; it gave him total control of all the gear in both rooms. A special comm-link connected Cooper to his hawks. Behind him, flanking him like members of a wedding party, awaited a flock of aides. Some of them sat, prepared to make notes on radio-enabled laptops that transmitted to a nearby mainframe; others stood around, trying to look ready to serve in any capacity.

Yessireebob. It surely was fun havin' a lot of money.

He picked up a thin, wrapper-cured El Cajón cigar, specially "imported" from Cuba, paused to savor its aroma. Three fingers of Maker's Mark bourbon slowly melted a single ice cube in a snifter at his right hand. The Reverend's father had schooled him on the medicinal properties of Maker's Mark many years ago. Daddy was still pickin' and pokin' at ninety-one, so maybe he knew somethin' the doctors don't, Freemason thought.

One of his aides, a young buck named Addison who looked liked an FBI agent, had a butane lighter flaring before Freemason could get the cigar to his lips. On the screens, the network logos were fading to black and the talking heads of the Grand Old Anchormen were staring out at the world. Their lips were moving but no sound penetrated the glass wall—Freemason had the gain damped down. He didn't really give a fart in a windstorm for what they were saying—that's why he paid his staff. They scanned the day's events, gleaning the wheat from the chaff, and providing the Reverend with material for his nightly satellite broadcasts. There was always plenty of controversial stuff, always something that could be twisted and turned and polished up for his use. Anything truly unusual would be brought directly to his attention.

He took his first pull of the El Cajón. It was as sweet as a young girl's quim. A sip of his iced Mark produced in his mouth a light, woodsy bouquet. Lord, life was good. Cooper looked idly at the screens as the anchors oozed into their lead stories of the night—skirmishes in South Africa as the civil war raged on. The story didn't seem on the face of it to be a message from the Lord, but what did the Reverend know of such things?

Freemason didn't concern himself with interpreting the news. That's why he paid writers. Ten of the sharpest Bible scholars in the South worked their buns down to their assbones hooking up references from Scripture with whatever was going on in the world. And my, those bright little boys and girls were good! They gave the Reverend the meanest, cleanest sermons in the Industry. There wasn't a telepreacher on the sats with half as many viewers. His Church of the Holy Satellite Tabernacle chewed up all the other teleministries for breakfast.

Freemason was mighty proud of that. His audience spanned the globe, and the money they sent him had created a monolith of power and influence and just plain opulence for Freemason and his coterie. He was riding the crest of a new wave of televangelism because his programming related directly to current events—and because he'd helped launch what he called "apocalyptic thinking." All his shows were linked, however subtly or overtly, to the coming millennium and the possible End Of The World.

For some reason, a lot of people found that a subject of great interest.

The lead story faded from the screens as the networks segued into their next segments. Unity of coverage disintegrated as the news divisions began to cater to their different priorities, different political/social leanings. It was no secret, Freemason thought, that the media'd been controlled by a buncha Hebes and homosexuals since World War II.

As he brought his snifter to his lips, he heard a change in the silence in his headset. Someone had opened the channel.

"Reverend," said Number Three, seated below the CBS screen, "I think we have something here. I'll punch it up on replay/delay for you."

"What is it?"

"You're going to want to see the whole thing yourself. It's a network exclusive."

"Well, let's get on with it, boy!"

"We're cued up now—here it comes . . ."

Freemason stared at his personal monitor, where the image of a New Yorky-looking woman appeared. She radiated health and sexiness. Her eyes were full and wide and green as the sea; her face was framed by a mane of auburn hair. She looked at the camera like she was making love to it, and Freemason Cooper was immediately in lust with her. Like every other on-site reporter, she wore a jump-suit and photographer's vest, but he quasi-uniform couldn't conceal the sensuous lines of her body. Whoever she was, she was all woman. Just the way the Reverend liked 'em.

As if in answer to his prayers, an ID print-over appeared across the bottom of the screen:

Marion Windsor—Courtesy WEVN-TV and WPIX-TV

"The violence and bloodshed which has plagued the Yusang Motor Corporation plant in Evansville, Indiana, for the past two days has come to an abrupt end. Last night, just after midnight, Central Time, an assemblage of enraged workers planned a final assault on Yusang's front gates. Harassed by police and riot-control units from the fire department, what began as a peaceful demonstration against new company policies escalated into an ugly siege . . ."

While Marion Windsor spoke, the screen displayed close-up video of tactical police mixing it up with a huge crowd of blue-collars. Water-cannon crisscrossed the crowd, battering the strikers like bowling pins. It was a familiar tableau—what made it special? Freemason was about to buzz Number Three and give his hole a good reaming when Marion Windsor came to the meat of her story:

". . . and more deaths were certain to follow, until the sudden appearance of a young man named Peter Carenza, a parish priest from Brooklyn, New York, changed everything . . ."

The video displayed a tall, sinewy man with dark hair and dark eyes standing atop a platform on a forklift. This was a priest!? He looked like a telephone lineman. The crowd surged beneath him like a cruel sea. He was speaking, but his words were blanketed by the narration. The look of cool determination in the young man's eyes disturbed Freemason deeply.

Windsor described the violence that ensued due to a mistakenly ignited car bomb. The video, amazingly clear given the circumstances, showed flares, bullets, and a hellacious rainstorm. Lightning flashed and danced against the industrial background.

Freemason watched as the young priest was enveloped by what could only be called a halo of light. Green fire danced along the metal fence and water tower behind him. A stunned silence gripped the crowd and a sense of awe and fear penetrated the flat screen of the video monitor. Iciness touched Freemason's gut.

". . . Something wondrous has happened in Evansville . . ."

A brief childhood memory flared. Cooper, aged five or six, bouncing along in the shotgun seat of his daddy's Chevrolet DeLuxe. Rain dappled the windshield as they jounced along a rutted country road; the little plastic statue of Jesus on the dashboard gave off a sick green shine. Lightning flashed, and Freemason remembered being scared by that little statue. He told his daddy, and the old man had just cackled as he wrestled with the steering wheel. Then the memory short-circuited and was gone. But for an instant, it had been painfully clear.

Freemason rubbed his lips with the back of his hand; the urge for a sluice of bourbon was overpowering, but he couldn't break his attention from the screen. Carenza raised an arm toward the water tower behind him and lightning blasted it!

Un-goddamned-believable.

Freemason's trembling fingers found the snifter, grabbed it. Bringing it to his lips, which had become suddenly cracked and desert-dry, he sucked down the liquor's woodsy bite.

". . . and the violence which has wracked this small, industrial city is over. This is Marion Windsor, reporting on the scene, in Evansville, Indiana."

Tilting his head, Cooper knocked back the rest of the bourbon and whipped his chair around, reaching for the decanter at the corner of his flight-deck desk. God-damn-it-to-hellfire, what was that all about? Why were his hands shaking? His heart thudding?

Take it easy, he thought.

Turning slowly, he glanced back at his aides. They all sported the same dazed, what-did-I-just-see look. No one spoke. "You want a file copy of that, Reverend?" Number Three's voice filled his headset.

"Yes," said Freemason, "that'll be fine."

"I've got a follow-up on that Evansville piece!" Number One piped in. "Want the feed?"

"Roll tape, Number One," said Freemason.

Normally he got a charge out of the whole media-blitz session. He loved using all the industry buzzwords and playing like he was a director or something. But suddenly, he was just going through the motions. He couldn't shake the image of that young guy, glowing in the dark.

Hastily-shot video of a striker filled the small monitor screen. The worker spoke into a mike held by an off-camera interviewer.

". . . nothin' like it, man, you know . . . I mean, here's this kinda wimpy guy, you know, and he's standin' up there, and, like, I saw him zap that water tower, man!"

"What do you mean—'zap'?" asked the unseen reporter.

"I mean, like, you know, he *blasted* it! You know, like a wizard, man. Like those guys inna cartoons."

The image was replaced by that of a young woman in fire-fighter's gear.

"It was an amazing experience. Like being in church. I've never seen anything like it. He was an amazing guy."

"Did you see where he went? Find out who he was?"

"No, I didn't . . . but I'd like to see him again."

"If you knew where he was, would you go after him? Seek him out?"

"Yes . . . I think I would."

Another sloppy video edit, and another broad, midwestern face filled the screen. Same hand-mike and anonymous interviewer.

". . . like a religious experience. Like when I was saved. It was kinda like that. First time I had the same feelin'."

Another quick-edit and the video portrayed the young-old faces of a biker couple. The boy was weathered, long-haired, and wrapped in leather. His companion was a wispy blonde whose features were on the hard side of beauty.

". . . I know 'im," said the boy. "He saved me and Laureen here."

"Saved you?"

"You bet. I hurt my hand tryin' to rob a place and Peter healed me—look!"

The boy exhibited a perfectly normal hand to the camera.

"You can say whatever you want, but I'm tellin' y'all—this guy's *real*."

"Meaning . . . ?"

The boy stared into the camera, his almost constant leer fading. "Meanin' he's what we've all been waitin' for. You saw what he did here tonight. Only one guy can do somethin' like that—and that's *Jesus!*"

Freemason punched a key on his master-board, and the NEC darkened. He'd seen enough of that shit. Damned media, tryin' to make that priest look like some kind of savior. He'd have to review the tapes, but it sure as hellfire sounded like some kind of publicity stunt. 'Course it wasn't like the Catholics to get involved in that sort of thing. The Papists had been soft-pedaling the turn of the century and the whole Millennial Movement for a damned good reason—they didn't want to be identified with the mainly fundamentalist churches backing the whole thing.

He couldn't blame them. The Church of Rome, despite being as corrupt as anybody else, had parlayed its investments, its political and technological connections well. The Papists were a strong force in the religious world. As much as Freemason hated them, he had to respect their staying power.

But if this circus stunt in Evansville was some new Vatican strategy—something to stir up the sheep and get their attention away from the satellite ministry—well, hellfire, he couldn't let them fuck around like that.

Raising a single finger brought a pair of aides to his side.

"I want more research on that Evansville story," he said. "Find out everything you can."

"You got it, Reverend," said a woman dressed in a prim business suit. Her name was Melody, and although she looked a little wholesome for Freemason's taste, he was thinking of playing a tune or two with her.

He smiled and winked at her. She returned the smile and

moved back to her laptop. The other staffer, a cracker-jack fellow named Billingsly, still awaited his orders.

"I'm going to need a strong piece on this Evansville thing," Cooper said. "Get all the poop you can from Melody, and write me a real ripper. You hear? I want to punch a few holes in this guy's sails before he even gets started."

"You can count on it, Reverend." The aide nodded, slipped away.

Freemason returned his attention to the overview of the media blitz. His hawks had all four screens running separate stories now, circling over new, juicy pieces of what the sheep called "news." The only thing interesting was the earthquake that had rocked Beijing, killing ten thousand Chinks. Served the heathens right, he thought.

As the nation geared up for another evening of prime-time narcolepsy, Freemason dismissed his cadre of aides. In a flurry of activity, sliding panels of burnished oak moved to conceal the electronic gear, bookcases maneuvered on floor-and-ceiling tracks to cover the glass wall, the control panel sank into the floor. His staff slowly filed out of the room, leaving him alone. He poured another three fingers of Maker's Mark from his desk decanter, added a single cube of ice, and lifted the snifter to his aquiline nose for a long, savory inhalation. He allowed himself only three cigars per day and he'd expended his last one during the blitz. But damn, he wanted to fire up one more tonight!

He couldn't get the image of the priest, with the light shining all around him, out of his mind. It was probably a bunch of hokum, but for some reason, Freemason was letting it rub his fur the wrong way.

A short, pudgy man entered the room through a side door. He wore a tan western shirt and tailored jeans, accented by rattlesnake Dingos. The style did not flatter his bowling-pin body, but he walked with the confidence of a man who did not care about his appearance. Though his face was doughy, his features were a bit pinched. He would have been bald except for about forty strands he insisted on plastering across the top of his head. Preston J. Pierce sat at Freemason's right hand. His official title was Chairman of the Board of CHST, Inc., but he was actually a little bit of everything from Freemason's chief procurer to financial advisor.

"Evenin', Mason . . . how'd the blitz go?"

"Okay, I suppose."

Preston looked at him askew, poured himself a dollop of bourbon over lots of ice, squirted in some Coke from the dispenser at the wet bar.

"That doesn't sound promisin'. What's the matter, Reverend?"

Freemason quickly recounted the Evansville incident and the reactions from the sheep.

Preston sipped his weak drink, nodded. "I'd say that's a development which bears some watchin'."

"Yeah, I know. Put some of our boys on this guy. See if they can find him, keep an eye on him for a while."

Preston winked, gestured OK with his right hand.

"Your steam bath's ready."

Freemason sighed heavily. "Oh yes, who is it tonight?"

"Stephanie June."

"The redhead with all the freckles?"

"You remember well," said Preston with a wonderfully perverse smile.

Freemason knocked back the rest of his drink, stood up behind his desk and stretched his six-four frame. He felt oddly tense, wary. Even the promise of Stephanie June couldn't get his mind off the video of the rose-petal snowstorm and that priest standin' up there like that goddamned glow-in-the-dark Jesus. He could almost smell the rank stink of nicotine in the cab of Daddy's old pickup.

TWENTY-EIGHT

Rome, Italy—Etienne
October 15, 1998

Why would the Abbess do such a thing to her?!

The images from the video she had been shown had stained her vision. No matter where in the white infirmary room she looked, the specter of the man called Peter Carenza took shape and filmy substance. A man, and yet more—and less—than a man. Like looking at a ghost. She saw him everywhere, yet she knew she was not crazy.

Falling back into the safety and softness of her pillows, Etienne squeezed shut her eyes ... and still she could see him. A man, dressed in black—but where his head should have been was a dark swirl like the black rose she'd seen in the garden.

Holy Mary! What was happening to her?!

She'd asked her Abbess to grant her an audience with the Holy Father. Only God's authority on Earth could understand what she'd seen. In the depths of her soul, Etienne *knew* that God was talking to her, giving her a message that must be delivered.

Why would Victorianna not listen to her?

Blinking her eyes, Etienne saw something new taking shape against the stark white wall opposite her bed, like a film being projected through a gauzy lens. A fuzzy image of the Great Wall of China, snaking across hilly terrain, punctuated by battlements and towers. Suddenly the hills beneath the Wall shook, became almost fluid. Waves of force pulsed through the earth and the Great Wall cracked and fractured like the frail shell of a dove's egg. So fierce were the shock waves that the wall seemed to explode. A hailstorm of fragments rained down on the countryside while the earth continued to sway and tremble. The sky darkened from the dust and debris thrown into the air.

Etienne could hear the cries of animals and people rising up in a chorus of agony and terror.

TWENTY-NINE

Vatican City—Lareggia
November 1, 1998

Paolo Cardinal Lareggia stood at his office window overlooking the Via della Fondamenta. It had been raining all morning, and the stone buildings looked stained and dreary. But the bad weather did not deter small knots of tourists from making their appointed rounds. Their umbrellas and rain-gear speckled the gray pavements with dashes of bright color. The contrasts mirrored Lareggia's own emotions.

Damnation . . .

The desk intercom's low-register buzz interrupted his thoughts. He turned from the window, waddled to the desk and touched a button.

"Yes?"

"Father Francesco to see you, Your Grace . . ."

Before he could say "send him in," the double doors to Paolo's sanctum sanctorum swung inward. For an instant Giovanni Francesco stood at the threshold, dramatically posed, his outstretched arms bracing the doors. The Jesuit looked thinner than usual, and Paolo wondered if the stress of recent developments was getting the best of him.

"Can you believe this!?" Francesco cried out, then turned to close the doors behind him.

"Sit down, 'Vanni . . ."

"I *cannot* sit! Have you seen the sat-casts?!"

Paolo settled his bulk into his large desk chair, steepled his pudgy hands over the blotter. "Yes, of course. You know I have."

"What is He trying to prove?!"

"Maybe He is trying to prove He's who we said He is?"

"In public!?"

Paolo smiled. "Can you think of a better place?"

"How do we know Krieger didn't *let* Peter escape?"

"We don't. But I think the old man truly wanted to examine Him. Test Him." Paolo shrugged. "Krieger is a scientist, don't forget. An opportunity to do a follow-up study on a thirty-year-old experiment is rare indeed."

Giovanni Francesco nodded. "That is true. Is he coming to the meeting?"

"I saw no need of it. But I am keeping him in Rome for the time being."

Francesco frowned as if a singularly depressing thought had just struck him. "I cannot believe we cannot get Him back. This is where He belongs."

"I thought your 'super-agent' was supposed to bring him back to us."

"He's gotten bigger than Targeno can handle," said Francesco.

"Is that what Targeno thinks?"

"Hah! Even if it was, he would never admit it." Francesco began to slowly pace. "Where's Victorianna? Is she late?"

"No," said Paolo. "It is you who are early. I expect her at any moment."

The Jesuit continued to pace slowly from one end of the large room to the other. He looked like a scraggly wolf. "I have been thinking about what we should do ever since I saw that ridiculous sat-cast."

"Not so ridiculous," said Paolo, "rather impressive, actually."

"What next, the loaves and fishes?" Francesco almost shouted as he continued to pace.

Paolo Lareggia chuckled. "They say history has a habit of repeating itself . . ." The intercom buzzed. Paolo said, "Yes?"

"Abbess Victorianna is here, Your Grace."

"Very good," he said. "Send her in."

Only one of the double doors opened as Paolo's receptionist ushered the stately nun into the room. Her long, dark blue habit almost touched the Spanish-tiled floor, obscuring her feet and making her appear to glide across the room.

Paolo had always admired Victorianna—no lust, just an appreciation of her beauty and her natural elegance. His sexual urges had been in steady decline for a long time, suppressed by age and obesity.

Old Giovanni, however, was most likely a different story. Lareggia watched the Jesuit's gaze track the Abbess. Naked lust capered behind his eyes. Lean and gaunt, Francesco probably fancied himself quite the sexual engine.

"You're looking well, 'Anna," said Paolo, guiding her to a small library table and chair to the left of his desk. "Have a seat. Will you join us, 'Vanni?"

Francesco pulled up a chair, sat down roughly. For a moment, the trio looked at one another, hoping to find a solution to their problem in the eyes of their partners. Lareggia's receptionist entered the office, pushing an ornately carved cherrywood tea wagon that carried steaming carafes of both coffee and tea. Without a word, the young priest served everyone their long-familiar preferences. He even provided Giovanni Francesco with a small vial of Montecusano brandy for his Earl Grey.

After the receptionist departed, the silence grew awkward. Paolo cleared his throat; Victorianna sipped her tea. Francesco added the brandy to his cup.

"All right," said the Jesuit at last. "Our plans have gone completely awry. What do we do now?"

"I have been thinking that we do nothing at all," said

Paolo. He gulped at his coffee, craving a sweet bun of some sort.

"What?" Giovanni stared at him wide-eyed. "He's making a public spectacle of Himself—in America of all places! He will become a buffoon! A television star!"

"Perhaps America is where he *should* be," offered Victorianna. "The prophecy of Nostradamus says the Messiah will come from the New World."

"Interesting," Lareggia said thoughtfully.

"Who cares about Nostradamus!" Francesco shouted.

The Abbess looked at him slyly. "You know, Father, I think what upsets you the most is that you lost control of this grand plan . . ."

"What?" Francesco looked at her warily.

"Did you ever *really* believe you would be able to control the Lord Jesus?"

" 'Control' is hardly the right word," said Francesco.

Lareggia chuckled. "Oh? Then what would you call sending a couple of Sicilian thugs to kidnap him?"

"I am still shocked that you did such a thing!" said Victorianna. "How could you, 'Vanni? Sometimes I think you've never had faith in what we were doing."

Francesco shrugged indifferently.

Lareggia looked at his cohort and frowned, then sighed. "There is no bringing Him back. The prophecies say he will eventually return. Perhaps we should just wait for that day?"

"Do we have a choice?" Francesco glowered at him.

Paolo reached out, touched Victorianna's hand. "Any thoughts?"

She smiled graciously, albeit a bit primly. "Now I know how Victor Frankenstein must have felt."

Paolo shook his head. "No. I think He is just learning to accept His identity."

"He should be *here* for that! We all agreed He would need special counseling, training," said the Jesuit.

"Yes," said Victorianna. "But perhaps we were guilty of *hubris*? How presumptuous, to think we could teach Him how to become the Messiah." Lareggia nodded.

Giovanni lighted a strongly-scented cigarette, inhaled deeply. "I don't like it. He should be in Rome."

"That may be true," said Paolo. "But you must admit we are quite powerless."

Francesco exhaled, shook his head in a gesture of disgust. "How could we have misjudged things so?"

Lareggia sighed. "Then are we in agreement? We will not interfere with His desire to stay in America?"

Francesco and the Abbess nodded.

"I think we should try to keep someone close to him," said Paolo. "I do not like the idea of the American media being our primary information source. Perhaps your man Targeno can still be of some use."

Francesco agreed, saying, "The media slant everything according to their own politics. Did you see the way they besieged old Sobieski at Saint Sebastian's?"

"Yes, but he handled them well. He said practically nothing," Victorianna said.

Francesco snorted. "Only because he knows nothing."

Lareggia raised his hand for both of their attention. "Where is Targeno?"

"Still following Peter's little caravan. They picked up a few followers in Indiana and are again traveling the Interstate highway system."

"Can Targeno maintain surveillance discreetly?"

"Certainly!" Francesco stubbed out his cigarette, immediately lit another.

"Very well. Let's keep him on the job." Paolo sat back in his chair. Across the table Sister Victorianna had fallen silent and was looking down at her hands. "What is it, 'Anna?"

The nun's soft gaze rose to meet Lareggia's concern. "It is Etienne . . ."

Paolo tapped the table with his pudgy fingers. He'd almost forgotten Peter's mother. "Ah yes," he said. "You said she was improving."

Despite his show of concern, Paolo didn't give a damn about Sister Etienne. She'd done her job thirty years ago; now she was of no use to the triumvirate. Her "vision" was worthless because she had refused to share it with them. Francesco's doctors had begun a drug-therapy regimen which seemed to be working, the nun was sitting up, eating, talking a little. But she continued to insist that she would speak of her religious experience only to the Pope.

"After dinner last night, I decided to try an experiment," said Victorianna.

"What did you do?" Paolo poured another cup of coffee, looked at the Abbess patiently. She had a very deliberate way of speaking, prodding her would not help.

"I thought it might be interesting to let her see her son. I showed her a disk of the Evansville sat-cast."

Francesco leaned all the way back in his chair, his thick eyebrows arched. "And . . . ?"

Victorianna's embarrassment was clear. "She reacted very badly, I'm afraid."

The men both leaned forward as the Abbess continued. "As soon as she saw Peter's face in a close-up, she started screaming uncontrollably. She started raving about seeing an earthquake, and demanding to see the Pope. We had to sedate her."

Francesco grimaced. "The Chinese quake."

Victorianna nodded, "She obviously saw it happening. She has the Sight."

Francesco threw up his hands in disgust. "It doesn't mean a damned thing! She just can't face the truth that her baby is now thirty years old—that she's thirty years older."

"That is the most ridiculous thing you have said yet!" said Victorianna. "I think Etienne dealt with giving birth a long time ago. I think this is something else."

"Is she afraid of her son?" asked the Cardinal.

"I don't know if that's the question we should be asking," said Victorianna. "Maybe it is *we* who should be afraid."

THIRTY

Bessemet, Alabama—Cooper
November 21, 1998

A digital signal sounded on the control console behind his water bed. It had been programmed to sound like a cageful of canaries singing sweetly. Like Saint Francis of Assisi, Freemason had a thing for birds.

"Gee, that sounds pretty, honey," said Stephanie June as she looked up from her work under the sheets. "What is it?"

"The intercom," he said, twisting around, reaching for the correct keypad, finding it, punching it in. "Yeah?"

"Mason . . . ?" Preston J. Pierce's voice was thin, reedy.

"Who'd you expect—Oral Roberts? Press, I told you never call me in here unless it's a barn-burner . . ."

"Did you catch the eleven o'clock news?"

"Now what do you think?" Freemason said with as much sarcasm as he could muster. Which was hard to do with Stephanie June working so hard. She was a splash of red-gold hair across his stomach, half covered by the silk sheets.

"I'm serious, Reverend. There's something I think you oughta see."

"This better be worth it, Press," he said.

Pierce cleared his throat. "Trust me on this one, Mason. Just get down to the studio as soon as you can."

"I'm coming," said Freemason.

"Gee, Reverend," said Stephanie June. "That's mighty nice of you to tell me like that. You wouldn't believe how inconsiderate most men are . . ."

"We pulled this off the eleven o'clock news," said a bespectacled, white-shirted engineer named Ames.

"Local?" asked Freemason.

"Montgomery," Pierce said, nodding. "But they were picking up a national feed."

Freemason Cooper sank into a padded leather chair and focused on a big flat-screen monitor. He and the boys were in the mansion's east wing, which had been renovated into a state-of-the-art recording and broadcasting facility. The screen flickered, then revealed the auburn-haired woman he'd seen before—and a sweet-looking piece of cake she was, too. She was standing alongside a highway, beneath a dark sky tinged with the soft glow of a distant fire. The name "Marion Windsor" and her station ID flashed for an instant across the bottom of the frame.

The words "New York" caught Freemason's attention. What the Christ-on-an-aluminum-crutch was a New York reporter doing out in Illinois? Something didn't add up, he thought as the woman began speaking.

"Interstate 64 just east of Saint Louis, near the Richview, Illinois exit, marks the scene of one of the most horrible highway catastrophes in Illinois history . . ."

Marion Windsor remained in the left foreground, but the image behind her changed, zooming in to reveal, under the harsh reality of emergency lighting, a panorama of carnage and demolition. Twisted, burned-out husks of all kinds of vehicles littered the six-lane swath of road like toys fallen off a playroom shelf. Fire equipment and rescue vans skittered across the scene in erratic paths. Body-bag crews slicked into the darkness carrying their grim cargoes. State police officers shambled by with slack faces.

"Thirty-eight vehicles became entangled in a chain-reaction collision which has thus far claimed sixty-four lives. Eyewitnesses claim the huge, multi-car mishap ensued when a tractor-trailer carrying jet fuel careened into a log-jam of commuter traffic."

The image changed again. Against the backdrop of a flaming knot of wreckage, the silhouette of a solitary figure stood out in dark relief. A man ran toward the flames, seemingly to certain death.

"What the hell's going on?" muttered Freemason. He'd gotten a bad feeling as he'd seen that damn Windsor woman opening the segment. His stomach felt like it was being chewed by squirrels on speed.

"Just watch," said Ames.

Preston J. Pierce cleared his throat, coughed nervously. He obviously knew what was coming; Cooper could hear something oddly like awe in his voice. "Aw, Jesus . . ." he whispered.

The camera followed the running man, who dodged flames and debris like a Crimson Tide tailback. He approached a vacation camper wrapped in flames, ripped open the back door as tentacles of fire reached out for him. He seemed completely unaffected by the inferno as he climbed into the vehicle.

"You are witnessing one of the most courageous and unbelievable rescue attempts ever recorded. Despite the jet fuel inferno, one man risked his own safety to seek out survivors."

The man reappeared in the doorway, cradling a small body in his arms. In an instant hungry flames rose up to obscure him. The vehicle buckled and sagged under the ovenlike heat. Fire enveloped everything, igniting the tires, incinerating paint, a raging hell in which nothing could survive. Freemason's stomach churned as he imagined dying like that—feeling your nerve endings short-circuit, your hair singe down to the bones of your skull, the liquid of your eyeballs boiling like eggs. How many seconds before you couldn't feel it anymore?

"Look at this!" cried Ames. "Can you believe this shit?"

Watching the screen intently, Freemason could see movement in the choreography of flames. The man emerged, bent over his burden, and walked slowly away from the wreckage.

"No . . ." Freemason heard himself whispering.

Still carrying the small, slack form in his arms, the man

loomed ever larger as he passed *through* the flames. For an instant Freemason thought he saw the fire bending away from the man, but that was impossible. He'd have to check it out on replay. As the man drew close to the camera, Freemason could see that the body in his arms looked like something from a Cajun restaurant.

"This man, identified as Father Peter Carenza of New York City, personally saved the lives of seven people. The little girl in this footage, nine-year-old Amanda Becker, was pronounced dead at the scene by paramedics. But Peter Carenza's miracle was not finished."

"This is it," said Preston. His hoarse voice dripped with reverence.

Carenza bent over the still, blackened form of the little girl. He was a lean, handsome man of no more than thirty. The light of a man on a mission burned in his eyes. Freemason had seen that look before, in the eyes of other determined young men, and it had always scared him.

This time was no different. Orange light flickered and wavered, giving the whole scene an eerie, otherworldly aspect. Carenza placed his hands on the charred flesh of the girl. He closed his eyes as the camera briefly zoomed in on his face. For a moment nothing happened.

"Well?" asked Cooper, smelling a stunt of some kind. Lord knew he'd seen enough in his day.

"Wait!" cried Ames. "You ain't gonna believe this!"

The girl's blackened flesh had hardened like a carapace, but as the man touched the shell it began fracturing, sending out spiderweb cracks. Slowly, the fissures widened; strong blue light burst forth from them like headlights slicing through half-drawn blinds.

Cooper sucked in a deep breath.

Carenza passed his slender fingers over the fragmented pieces of the shell. It ruptured completely, falling away from the body to reveal perfectly formed, unscathed flesh. The image shook for a moment as the camera zoomed in to examine the girl's face, cherubic and totally at rest, eyes closed, the suggestion of a smile at the corners of her mouth. Carenza touched three fingers to the center of her forehead. The blue light that had seemed to emanate from her body faded away and she blinked open her eyes. A gasp rose up from the surrounding crowd, quickly escalating into a full-fledged cheer. Carenza, looking haggard and drawn, managed a quick, engaging smile before he was surrounded by people and carried off by the exultant masses.

"This is Marion Windsor, on the scene in Richview, Illinois."

The screen faded to black.

Freemason tried to swallow but his throat was too damned dry. Turning, he found Preston already pouring some bourbon into a tumbler.

"Here, Reverend . . ." Pierce said, passing it to him.

"All right, how'd he do it?" Freemason asked after slugging down half the glass.

Ames and Pierce both looked at him like he'd just spit a lizard out of his mouth.

"Reverend Cooper," said Ames, taking off his glasses in a practiced gesture of deference and humility, then making a big deal of refitting them to his head, "Reverend, that was no trick." Though his voice shook, he spoke with conviction.

"Bullshit, boy! That was movie stuff!"

"I've put the tape through the digital analyzer, Reverend," said Ames.

"You're tryin' to tell me that's for *real*?" Freemason knocked back the rest of the Maker's Mark.

"That's what he's tellin' you, Mason," said Pierce. "And I sat here and watched him check that tape out. Believe me, it's as clean as the band on a nigger's new hat."

Freemason laughed. "That's ridiculous! Ain't no man walks through the fire like that! It's a yankee, bullstuffin' trick, I'm tellin' you!"

"You saw how he healed that girl," said Pierce, taking a sip from his own glass of bourbon. He barked out a short laugh. "Heal, hell! He brought her back to life, he did!"

"Don't talk that kind of crap around me!" screamed

Cooper. "Ain't nobody comes back from the dead! And no-body *brings* 'em back neither!"

"Uh, Reverend," said Pierce, "I think there was *one* fella who did a pretty good job on both counts . . ."

"Don't get wise with me," said Freemason. "This is some kind of publicity stunt, some kind of gag . . ."

"Looked pretty good to me," said Ames. "Actually, it looked *damned* good."

"It looks to me," said Cooper, "like somebody is tryin' aw-fully hard to get hisself in the news."

"What for?" asked Pierce.

"To get known! Why the hell does anybody do it?!" Free-mason reached for the bottle, poured another few fingers, knocked back half in one draught. "Fame! Goddamned fame is what this New York boy's lookin' for!"

"How do you know that?" asked Ames.

"Because," said Preston J. Pierce, nervously rubbing his hands together, "fame is power. And power begets wealth. Which in turn begets more power."

Cooper smiled. "Amen to that, brother." He spoke his thoughts aloud. "I was wonderin' why every time there's a story on this Carenza character, it just happens to be reported by Miss Marion Windsor. And if she's a local reporter from New York City, then what in all the Bible's books is she doin' in Illinois in the middle of the night?"

Pierce ran his palm over his nearly bald head. It was an old, twitchy habit. "That does make it all smell kind of fishy . . ."

"Damn straight." Freemason sipped from his tumbler this time. Wouldn't do to be gettin' sloshed when he had some se-rious ponderin' to do. "We got to find out who that boy is."

Cooper's long associations with charlatans and snake-oil salesmen made him extra-sensitive to a scam. Though every-thing he'd seen so far confirmed that something odd was hap-pening, he wasn't sure it was as much of a flim-flam as he wanted his boys to believe.

In fact, when Freemason reflected on Carenza's actions, he got a good case of the creeps, like when he was a kid and he'd look down the well at his Aunt Daisy's farm, down past the winch and the bucket into that dank, circular darkness, wondering what kind of holy terror lived beneath the black water. He knew there was something terrible waitin' to get him, hopin' he'd fall into the well. The whole time he was growin' up, he figured the worst thing that could ever happen to him would be to take the drop into that well.

The memory made him shudder slightly. He could almost see that terrible blackness.

"What you got in mind?" asked Pierce.

Freemason leaned back in his chair, looked up, scrutinizing the ceiling. "Call Freddie Bevins. Tell him I got a job for him."

Pierce nodded. "Do you want him to come in and talk about it in person?"

"Absolutely. This ain't no divorce work. This is serious business."

"When do you want him here?"

"First thing in the morning—and tell him to clear his schedule. Until further notice, he belongs to me." Freemason stood up. The sudden motion gave him a slight rush. He waited till the brief dizziness passed, then headed for the door.

"Nice work, boys," he said casually. "Especially you, Ames."

The video engineer smiled, adjusted his glasses. "You bet, Reverend. Thanks."

As Freemason left the room, the unsteadiness returned. He couldn't tell whether it was physical or mental, but he felt cut loose from everything familiar and potent in his life. Funny how things could change so fast. Less than an hour ago he'd been doing his personal brand of aerobics with the young redhead, but right now, he couldn't get it up if you blew compressed air up his ass.

He walked down the corridor that connected the east wing with the residential sections of the mansion. Gilt-edged paintings graced the walls. Crystal chandeliers hung from the high ceilings. The mansion was a palace built for his pleasure, and he usually derived great satisfaction from thinking about how far he'd come in life.

But that New York boy had him spooked—no gettin' around it

Maybe he'd go down and see his Daddy. The old man was gettin' kinda shaky, but he still had his wits, and he'd never given Freemason a bit of bad advice.

Zachary Stewart Cooper had a suite of rooms on the mansion's first floor. Freemason had provided him with his own staff of servants, a twenty-four-hour complement of nurses, and every creature comfort a man could ever wish for. Freemason considered it an honor to be able to take care of his father so well. All children, he believed, were in debt to their parents, and were obligated to take care of the old folks. And that wasn't no Satellite Tabernacle bull—Freemason truly believed it, in his heart of hearts. Shouldn't be no need of that Social Security nonsense. Nothin' but a fancy Ponzi scheme anyway.

He knocked on the door to Daddy's suite. A video camera checked him out and his father's voice crackled through a hidden speaker.

"That you, son?"

"Sure is, Daddy. I need to see you."

A soft digital chime played the first few bars of "Dixie," and the door unlocked electronically. Freemason entered the foyer, passed through the living room, where a black nurse sat reading a magazine, and walked down a short hallway to the large bedroom where Zachary Cooper did most of his living.

The old man had taken a fierce interest in video technology. His bedroom was outfitted with every conceivable type of equipment in the free world. From the comfort and warmth of his waterbed, Daddy Cooper could analyze, digitize, or colorize. He could perform audio mixes, video FX, dubs, assemblies, or anything else he could think of. He amused himself endlessly by creating his own video concoctions. Predictably, his earliest efforts were preoccupied with sex, but he now aspired to create True Art, and his work grew progressively more abstract, personal, and impenetrable.

All this from a man who had spent forty years on the road, the ultimate traveling salesman. Zachary Stewart Cooper could sell anything to anybody. Freemason's earliest memories of his father were of a round-shouldered man in ill-fitting suits and wide, colorful ties. The dominant image was Daddy humping a sample case only slightly smaller than a steamer trunk in and out a '54 Chevrolet DeLuxe Coupe. The old man had started out working for the Fuller Brush Company, spending weeks at a time traveling through Tennessee, Kentucky, Mississippi, Alabama, and Louisiana. Once in a while, on certain Sundays, that Chevy would roll up the driveway, and a guy in a baggy suit would jump out, carrying gifts for his wife and his little boy.

He always brought those big rainbow-swirl lollipops and balsa wood Testors airplanes, and once he'd handed over a pair of simulated pearl-handled chrome toy six-guns with real leather holsters. For Mamma, there were silk stockings and slips, department store perfumes, and boxes of peanut brittle from Stuckey's.

Freemason used to love those Sundays, especially during the Alabama summers when the trees were green and the lemonade was cool and yellow on the front porch. Seeing the door to that old Chevy swing open used to get his heart jumpin' like a jukebox. It had been a different story for Mamma, though. Half-drunk all the time, she never seemed to get too excited when Daddy'd get home.

It seemed like all they'd ever do was fight, and as Freemason got older, he started to understand why Daddy stayed on the road most of the time. That and the money, of course. Daddy worked hard and he worked long; he made a decent buck. But it wasn't until he went into business for himself, and started selling his own company's Bible door-to-door, that he made *real* money. He lugged that Bible from one little town to another all over the South.

A million towns and a million dollars.

Daddy got rich, Mamma died of cirrhosis, and Freemason

realized there was a passel of money to be made in the religion business.

So by the time young Cooper started wearing a man's clothes, the Bible company had given birth to a Church. Freemason knew the best way to spread the word and pick up new Church members was to advertise. He cut a deal with a local radio station in Bessemet and the Church of the Holy Radio Tabernacle burst upon the airways.

That, plus his inherited talent for talkin' (his father had always boasted that Freemason could "talk the balls off a bull"), made the self-ordained Reverend Freemason Cooper a regional star in the religious firmament. The natural progression to television, first locally and then nationally on the indie/syndie circuit, had made Zachary's first million look like pocket change. Then came the satellite and the superstations. After weathering the scandals of the late eighties, the surviving telesat churches had become stronger than ever as the world careened toward the end of the century. And lounging at the top of the heap was none other than the Church of the Holy Satellite Tabernacle, hallelujah, praise the Lord, and amen, brother.

Freemason blinked his eyes and looked at the old man seated in the middle of a circular bed. Like a Gandhi in pajamas, Daddy was surrounded by remote controls, consoles, and keyboards. The opposite wall looked like the interior of an edit suite. Monitors displayed a variety of moving and frozen images. It was a vast electronic palette from which Daddy could choose and create.

"Hello, son," said the old man, barely looking up from his toys. "What's up . . . ? Besides your dick, that is."

Daddy laughed at his own joke, stopped when he noticed the serious expression on Freemason's face.

"I need your advice, Daddy. Couple things on my mind."

The old man pushed his toys to the side of the bed, leaned back against his pillows. He took a hit of oxygen, looked at his son. "Take a shot, son. I'm ready."

"Have you been watchin' the news lately?"

Zachary Cooper smiled. "Peter Carenza."

Freemason couldn't hide his surprise. Ninety-one and still no moss growing under his ass. "How did you know?"

"Just a feelin'." The smile widened into a grin.

"Well, Daddy, what're you makin' out of all this?"

The old man shrugged. It was a long-practiced, beautifully enacted gesture. "It's still too early to tell."

"My question is: *who* is this guy?"

Daddy laughed. "Don't you know?"

"Come on, Daddy!"

"Well, either he *is*, or he *ain't*, right?"

Freemason didn't answer right away. Hearing his father verbalize the solitary fear that had been rattlin' around inside his head like a pea in a gourd had stunned him for a moment.

"Yeah," said Freemason, finally. "And either way, Daddy, I'd say we have a few plans to make."

Daddy laughed. "You bet yer ass, sonny. You bet yer ass we do."

THIRTY-ONE

Richview, Illinois—Carenza
November 25, 1998

"Peter, you've really done it this time," said Daniel Ellington. He was sitting at the kitchen table of a Winnebago. The spacious RV had been given to Peter by Herman Becker, father of the resurrected Amanda and owner of several car dealerships in St. Louis. The Winnebago rested on the acreage of George Affholter, a farmer whose fatal injuries had been healed as Peter bent over him on the hard asphalt of Interstate 64.

Peter sat across the table, sipping a cup of coffee.

"Yes, I guess I have," he said with a boyish grin on his face.

"How long are you going to keep this up?" asked Daniel. "This mobile, guerrilla ministry?"

"I never thought of it like that," Peter said with a chuckle, "but you know, it has a nice ring to it. Guerrilla ministry—I like that."

He peeked through the slatted blinds of the window, amazed at what he saw.

Thousands of people surrounded the Winnebego, in every direction. Some had set up tents; others sat in the open, on blankets; more just stood by. Their cars and other vehicles were scattered about Affholter's property like carelessly tossed toys. It looked like the first stages of a monster rock concert, or a demonstration on the Mall in Washington, D.C.

The thrum of the excited crowd had become a constant background noise. They'd been out there for hours. Most of them were from the small towns outside of St. Louis, some from the city itself. Mixed in were media crews from various radio and TV stations. Marion was out there somewhere, trying to deal with them and with the newspaper and magazine journalists who were also beginning to swarm about. Despite the early autumn coolness in the air, there were the beginnings of a carnival atmosphere.

"Look at this, Daniel," Peter said. "More hucksters. Inevitable I guess."

His friend carefully peered through the blinds to see a construction site lunch-wagon swinging down its panels. It was in competition with a two-wheeled hot dog stand, a soft ice cream truck, and the peanut and popcorn peddlers hawking their way through the crowd like vendors at a ballgame.

"Well," said Daniel. "It was either that or we're going to have to drag out the loaves and fishes, right?"

Peter smiled. "Don't tempt me, Daniel."

He meant it as a joke, but his friend was not laughing. In fact Daniel looked at him more seriously than Peter could ever remember.

"You, know," said Daniel, "that's not really funny. None of this is."

Peter knew what his friend was getting at. "Funny?" he said, looking for an instant into Daniel's eyes, and then into the black depths of his coffee mug. "I guess not. Sometimes I feel like I'm following some kind of script, some kind of preordained plan."

"That's crazy, Peter."

He shrugged. "Maybe. I don't know what to think."

Daniel left the table to get a fresh pour of coffee, and Peter used the moment to reflect on their time on the road. Though he and Daniel and Marion had held strategy sessions (which sometimes included the slightly whacked-out input of Billy and Laureen), Peter wasn't totally comfortable with his new public image.

Weeks ago, when Father Francesco and his cronies had told Peter the whole story, he felt outraged. His whole life had been a sham, based on a past that was a lie.

But after they'd tried to strong-arm him back to Rome, after they'd tortured Dan, Peter had decided that the only way to defend himself was to attack, face them down in the middle of the street. High noon and all that. And that meant publicity.

After the auto factory riot, he'd consulted with Dan and Marion. They agreed that he should go public—and events accelerated faster than any of them imagined.

"You know, there's one thing we never seem to talk about," said Dan as he returned to the table.

"What's that?"

"Who are you, Peter? Are you Christ? Are you the Son of God?" Dan's tangled emotions poured out. "I mean, should I be down on my knees before you? Are you the One I've been praying to all my life?"

"Daniel . . ." He didn't know what to say.

Daniel put his hands to the sides of his head as though trying to suppress the pain of a terrible headache. He looked away from Peter, staring at the laminated, fake wood of the kitchen cabinets.

"I think that's what I'm trying to find out for myself, Dan."
Peter stood, moved away from his friend. "I mean, I don't
feel like God, you know? I don't feel any different than I ever
have. I feel like plain old Peter Carenza."

"But . . . ?" prompted Daniel.

"But my life is completely different. Do you know that I
haven't said Mass *once* since we left New York? Not once!
It still feels unnatural to be without that daily ritual."

Daniel grinned sadly. "I know. I have the same problem."

"Really?" Peter felt better, knowing his lack of attention to
his vows was not so solitary. "We've been so busy . . . It's
like there's a little room, deep down in the center of my soul,
that's been locked up all my life. What I learned in Rome
threw back the bolt—and now that the door's swung open, I
know I can never close it again. The light shining out of that
room is going to light my way for the rest of my life."

"Do you feel that you're moving closer to that little
room?" asked Daniel. "Are you going to be able to look
through the door and see where that light's coming from?"

"I hope so. I feel like I'm moving toward it inexorably. All
the time."

Daniel drew in a breath, held it for a moment. "All right,
how's this? What if you decide, or discover, or accept—or
whatever—that you *are* the Son of God? What then? Have
you thought about that?"

"Not as much as I should, I guess." Peter paused to sip his
now-cooled coffee. "It makes me uncomfortable."

Daniel nodded. "I can believe that. But where do we go
from here?"

"Well, we've agreed that we've started something important out here. I've always been very popular with people.
Congregations have always liked me. So we continue, and I
keep doing the work I've always done."

"Okay, but what about everything you and I were taught?
What we believe?" Daniel began to pace within the confines
of the vehicle, his face a portrait of concern, anxiety.

"You mean about Christ?"

"That, and the Second Coming. If you're the Messiah, what's supposed to happen next? The end of the world?"

"Daniel, I don't know. I swear I don't!"

His friend smiled ironically. "Some messiah you are."

"I thought you said this wasn't funny."

"It's not, but I *am* starting to feel a little silly."

Peter looked through the blinds at the expanse of people gathered around the Winnebago. He felt responsible for all of them; he wanted to lead them as they wished to be led.

"What're you thinking?" asked Daniel.

"That even though I'm not sure about much, I know those people out there need something. And for now, at least, that something is me."

"Are you sure, Peter? It's a lot of responsibility—more than you had in Brooklyn."

Peter shrugged. "I don't have a choice. I feel their need, Daniel, don't you see that?"

"I guess I do . . ."

Looking through the blinds, Peter saw Marion Windsor, talking to a small band of casually but stylishly dressed people—obviously media. With his consent, Marion had orchestrated his explosion upon the national scene. She was an amazing woman, who reached him in a way totally new. After spending his entire adult life denying himself one of the most basic, natural drives, it was hard to acknowledge, much less justify, his feelings and desires.

But he wanted to try.

"Listen," said Daniel, interrupting his thoughts, "I'm sorry if this sounds like I'm attacking you, Peter, but this whole adventure's getting to be too much for me. I mean, sometimes I feel like I've hooked up to a runaway train."

"So do I, Daniel. Believe me."

There was a knock at the door.

"Who is it?" asked Daniel.

"Billy! Lemme in!"

Unlocking the door, Daniel opened it just wide enough to let Billy filter in. A press of bodies surged behind him, people calling Peter's name, waving their hands. The urgency in their collective voices was palpable. Peter knew he had to go speak to them soon.

Billy slipped in, then threw his weight against the door to help Dan close the portal.

"Man," Billy said, "this is amazing! Look at this!" He waved a thick stack of envelopes. "More money! We're going to be rich, man!"

"Give that to me, Billy," said Peter. "I told you before: we keep only what we need to continue. Everything else we give to the poor. Everything."

"Man, they *love* you out there, Peter." Billy was extremely animated as he piled his cargo on the table. "I never seen nothin' like it."

Peter looked at Daniel and sighed. "I'm going to have to talk to them."

"Again?"

"It's what they want. It's what they need."

Peter opened the door. An early autumn breeze touched his cheek; the crowd erupted, cheering and applauding. They reached out, trying to touch him, and he responded by smiling and shaking as many hands as he could reach. This was not the mindless adulation of fans—these people radiated warmth and love. It gushed from them in curling, crashing waves. And still their eyes burned with the fire of pure need.

The pressure of the crowd almost lifted Peter off the ground as he made his way to a pickup and climbed into the truck bed. As he began to speak, he noticed Marion and the media types on the edge of the crowd. She watched him as intently as everyone else, though she'd heard his message before. The emotions Peter felt from her were unlike those of first-time listeners.

His message was simple, basic. He spoke of humankind's common brotherhood, their need to love one another, to bond together and work toward their communal destiny of meeting the one true God. Peter claimed he was only a messenger, an instrument through which God had chosen to work. He didn't want their attention or their gifts or their money. He would use only what he needed to continue traveling through the country and help the world witness the glory and power that was God's. Despite his Roman Catholic training, he attempted to keep his sermon as nondenominational as possible, guided by the reactions of his listeners.

In fact, during this address, Peter found himself making reference to the possible dissolution of all organized religions. This was a minor chord sounded in a great symphonic movement, and Peter was almost surprised to hear himself speak so, but he did not call back the words. And if many in the crowd missed the veiled references to the need for a single unified church, others would seize upon the notion with vigor.

Peter had begun to think that it didn't really matter what he told his audiences. They were always so receptive, so prepared to accept whatever he wanted to tell them. In his early speeches he had tried to be careful not to say anything offensive. But as he grew more facile, more confident, he realized he could tell them whatever he wished. The crowds were willing to, if not immediately believe, at least consider his ideas seriously.

As he continued to talk to the midwestern masses who surrounded his truck, wrapped in their sweaters and plaid jackets and Cardinals baseball caps, he could detect individuals in the crowd who brimmed with skepticism, doubt, even outright hostility. Peter smiled inwardly. It was refreshing to know that his influence was not absolute.

He was also fascinated by the gradual changes in some of his other abilities—or talents, as Daniel continued to call them. He could now tell when someone, or something, was approaching him, even if his back was turned, or if a physical barricade such as a wall or a house was between them. It was like having a personal radar station operating in his head at all times. In addition, he was becoming acutely aware of how people were *feeling*, as if he possessed an internal barometer that measured emotions. When he concentrated on this, his mind would attribute colors and tones to emotional or psychological states of mind.

It was clear to him, although he hadn't shared this with his friends, that he was still becoming.

Becoming *what*?

Peter smiled to himself. Now that was an interesting question, wasn't it?

THIRTY-TWO

Richview, Illinois—Windsor
November 26, 1998

"He does have an effect on people, doesn't he?" asked Marion rhetorically.

She stood at the trailing edge of the crowd, elbow to elbow with Charles Branford, the venerable anchor of CBS News. Flanking her, on the opposite side, stood Mary Chin, the number two on NBC. Marion had just finished interviews with honchos from CNN and ABC, and she was feeling very confident. Her initial video segments on Peter had been extremely well received by all the networks. They all liked her look and her style—and of course the content of her stories was simply sensational.

To be surrounded by some of the biggest media personalities in the world was a testament to what Peter had already done for her. And the most beautiful part, she thought to herself, was that going public benefited everybody—her career, his welfare, the people who obviously needed him so desperately.

"It's an incredible situation," said Charles Branford as he walked down a gentle slope to his limo, followed by an entourage of aides and sycophants. "We'll be following the whole story closely from here on out."

"As long as Peter is willing to cooperate," she said, smiling her best smile at him.

Branford paused, ran a hand through his perfectly cut, silvering hair. He had the classically American angular features of a New England fisherman. Marion could not help being impressed with his sheer presence. His clothes were expertly tailored, his manners impeccable. His baritone voice accented by the slightly flat, midwestern, broadcast-standard English, he was the embodiment of everything identified with style in America. A television critic once said of Charles Branford: "When he frowns, you know things are damned serious; when he smiles, you feel like your grandfather's about to reach in his pocket and hand you a ten-dollar gold piece."

Marion agreed. Charles Branford was the Walter Cronkite of his age. He commanded the respect of just about everybody and he'd earned the reputation of being fair and honest in a business that was anything but.

"Yes ... if Peter continues to cooperate," said Branford knowingly. "And I'm sure you have some influence over him in that regard, Ms. Windsor."

· She smiled. "I hope so, Charles."

He reached his limousine, started to climb in, then stopped and looked back at her. "You're very shrewd, Marion. I imagine you're looking for a spot at one of the networks ... ?"

Marion knew this was no time to be shy. She looked him straight in the eye and stopped smiling. "If you were in my position, wouldn't you?"

Branford nodded. He looked away for a moment, then pulled a business card from his breast pocket and gave it to her. "Good answer," he said. "Let's keep in touch."

"I'll be talking to you soon," she said.

"Good afternoon, Ms. Windsor." Branford and his companions slipped into the car and the door sealed them in behind opaqued windows. She smiled at the blackness, knowing he was still looking at her.

As the limo pulled away, Marion thought about Branford. Usually she could tell when a man was leching after her, but lately, her early warning system was fritzing out on her. She could get absolutely no reading on Peter Carenza, and Charles Branford was so cool, so unflappable, she had the feeling she could dance naked in front of him and his expression wouldn't vary.

Well, it hardly mattered. As far as Marion was concerned, she was definitely in the driver's seat on this one. If she wasn't in line for a network gig after blowing the lid off this whole dog-and-pony show, Marion would be extremely surprised. All of them—Branford included—could cover Peter's *public* appearances. But if they wanted the inside story, if they wanted the man behind the miracles, they would have to come to her.

And what about *her* . . . ? Did she want Peter Carenza, the man?

She felt herself grinning as she walked back toward the Winnebago. Good question, that. Well, journalists were supposed to ask penetrating questions . . .

She almost laughed out loud at her little private pun. Peter was still speaking. The word *preach* had always carried pejorative connotations for her; she had a difficult time thinking of Peter as a *preacher*. Something about his style, his rapport with his audience, elevated what he did to an art form. The chemistry he generated between himself and his listeners was special indeed. You didn't need to be a student of sociology or religion to sense the profound effect Peter had on his audiences. He seemed to be converting them to his way of perceiving the world, and Marion was certain most of them would remain converted.

The sun's light and warmth were less than a memory by the time things settled down at Affholter's farm. The crowds, though thinner and less vociferous at night, were still persistent. Peter had ordered everyone back to their homes, but even more tents and campsites had materialized in a nearby pasture. Like Billy and Laureen, many wanted to join Peter's convoy.

Marion had never witnessed such an outpouring of love

and devotion. Peter handled it as well as any politician she'd ever seen, and better than most movie and rock stars.

It was close to midnight as Marion sat at the kitchen table organizing her notes on a laptop. She'd begun to think her daily journal might form the basis of a book someday. Of course, the idea of writing something long enough to be a whole book daunted her. Still, she kept her notes up to date. She could always hire a ghost-writer.

After an evening spent reading, Daniel Ellington had finally turned out his bunk light and fallen asleep. Peter had been outside, by their campfire, since they'd finished their late dinner. It had been such a busy day, Marion had hardly spoken to him. Maybe now would be a good time, she thought as she folded up her laptop and replaced it in her leather attaché.

Exiting the vehicle, she found him sitting by the fire in a lawn chair. The intensity of his stare, though directed at the flames, was almost frightening.

"Good evening, Father Carenza," Marion said softly. She pulled up a chair.

He looked up at her after a moment's hesitation, as if she'd snapped him out of a trance. His complexion was a deep tan in the warm firelight. Dressed in jeans, flannel plaid shirt, and an L. L. Bean fishing vest, he looked fashionably rugged.

"Funny," he said, looking back at the fire as he spoke, "but I feel very comfortable being called 'Father' by everyone but you."

"Really?"

"Yes. From you it sounds . . . awkward." Peter flashed her a quick glance. His eyes were dark as chestnuts.

"I'm sorry; I was just kidding," she said. "I won't do it anymore."

"No need to be sorry. I wasn't offended—it's just that hearing you call me 'Father' puts a barrier between us. An artificial barrier. And I don't like that."

She smiled, reached for his hand, as if to break down any barrier that might have been growing up between them. He flinched slightly at her touch, more a galvanic response than anything muscular, but didn't withdraw his hand.

They sat without speaking for a moment. Marion looked up at the autumn sky, thrilled by the splendor of the stars. Living in New York, she tended to forget how *bright* the sky was. Sometimes, with the smog and the ambient ground-light, she felt lucky to see the moon.

"So many stars . . ." she said softly.

"And every one a sun, possibly with worlds around each one. Some scientists say there could be a million places just like this one," he said. "Hard to imagine, isn't it?"

She sighed. "Sure is—especially when life is so complicated you barely have a chance to think."

"I know what you mean." Peter left his chair to hunker down by the fire. Picking up a stick, he pushed some of the coals under the remaining logs. "I hope I'm doing my part to make things a little easier for most people."

"They love to hear you talk," she said.

"They seem to . . ." He looked at her; his eyes seemed so wet and deep, they were like wells drilled into the earth.

Marion had never known a man as striking as Peter. He was like a stylized hero-type from the cover of a historical-romance novel. He was just too damned good to be true, but there he was, kneeling at her feet, playing with the fire like a twelve-year-old kid.

"They love you. And I don't blame them," she said, the words slipping out before she thought to stop them.

He looked at her with an expression that was quite unreadable. "Marion, what are you trying to say?"

She flushed; her pulse jumped. It was time to jump—or back off forever.

"I guess I'm saying that I love you too . . . that I've fallen in love with you."

Her words echoed in her mind, and the longer he remained silent, staring at her, the more embarrassed she became. For an instant she felt a schoolgirl urge to jump up and run away from him.

His gaze remained unwavering as he searched her eyes, her soul. "Do you really mean that?" he asked finally.

She nodded, throat tight.

He looked away, into the flames. "What you're telling me isn't really a surprise, you know."

"Has it been that obvious?" She smiled, absently rearranged her hair.

He shrugged. "Maybe not to anyone else, but I sensed it pretty strongly."

"I'm sorry," she said hurriedly.

"Don't be sorry," he said, suddenly taking her hand in his, holding it tightly.

Marion didn't know how to read his expression or his words. How could a man who seemed so open suddenly become so opaque, so inscrutable?

He continued to look into her eyes, to hold her hand. A whisper of memory passed through her and for a single frame of time she was fifteen, sitting with Jamie Falcone in his father's Oldsmobile. Jamie had looked at her, held her hand—just as Peter was doing. There was an innocence in his actions, a *sweetness* so rare . . . Marion could feel her heart soaring.

It was crazy. Unreal. She couldn't fight the sensation.

"Peter," she said after what seemed a very long time, "what are we going to do?"

"I don't know," he said, smiling gently. "I'm not exactly an expert on this sort of thing. I haven't even held a girl's hand since I was in high school."

"Oh Peter . . ."

Before she could reconsider her actions, she pulled him close and kissed him. It was an awkward moment; he fumbled to embrace her, bringing her down to the ground with him. She teased him with her tongue, lightly licking his lower lip, but he didn't respond.

"I don't know what to do!" His words were rushed, his shock and excitement clear.

"Just love me," she said. He held her close. She could feel

waves of heat radiating from him. His scent, his pheromones . . . she'd never wanted a man like she wanted him now.

"Marion," he said, pulling back to look into her face. His lips moved again, but he could not speak.

She said nothing, just kissed him, more languidly now, more confident. This time, he responded. His tongue touched hers, producing an almost electrical shock. Desire churned in her. She wanted him to rip her clothes away, to press her bare skin to his. She just plain *wanted* him.

Moving closer to him, drawing strength from his heat, she could feel his penis growing rigid beneath his jeans. His hands were pressed to her back.

"What are we going to do?" he asked in an urgent whisper.

"Stay here!" she said, gently pulling away from him. "I'll be right back."

Before he could respond, she ran across the field to her Mazda, digging the keys from her pocket, and opened the trunk. Pulling a down sleeping bag from the array of outdoor gear, she closed the lid and returned to the campfire.

"Come," she said, taking his hand, pulling him to his feet.

They moved beyond the fire's light and she unrolled the down bag. He watched her with a doubtful expression.

"Here?" he asked.

"Why not? Nobody's around. It's a beautiful night . . ."

He sat on the inner surface of the bag, pulled off his hiking boots. Marion did the same and moved close to him. This time, their embrace was more graceful—not practiced, but light-years beyond their earlier attempt. He was a quick study, but of course, she'd expected that.

Another early autumn breeze capered across the farmscape. But as she kissed him, ran her hands over his shoulders, down his back, and along his thighs, she could have been on a tropical beach, so strong was the heat of their mutual desire.

Slowly, as though following a carefully observed ritual, she undressed him. She savored each new revelation of his body. Peter's skin gleamed in the dim firelight—warmly tanned, unblemished. His body was sinewy, lean, subtly muscled. There were no extremes in him. Everything in proportion, the geometry and symmetry of his body was simply beautiful.

Marion helped him remove her clothes. There was a boyish quality to his actions, a fumbling uncertainty which she found utterly charming. He seemed grateful for her help, her understanding—making her want him all the more. She kept thinking how new and wild all this must be for him. For Marion, the common fantasy of schooling an adolescent boy in the arts of the flesh had become a reality.

He explored her, slowly, carefully, with his hands, tongue, and body, so choked with sensation and emotion, he could not speak, other than the few times he managed her name. There was a breathless, endless joy to his explorations, and she tried to return each pleasure he gave her so unselfishly.

She could have stayed with him, like that, forever. If she had died in his arms, it would have been perfectly all right.

He was completely without control himself, coming too fast, then coming again. He seemed to be limitless in energy and enthusiasm, and she feared she couldn't keep pace with him.

Finally, they sank into the softness of the downy bag. The white light of the stars burned down on their nakedness. They seemed to float in each other's arms, not speaking, barely breathing.

Then, without warning, he collapsed, trembling, buried his face in her hair and neck, and began to cry.

She wanted to ask him what was wrong, but she already knew the answer.

Nothing was wrong.

And that was the problem.

THIRTY-THREE

St. Louis, Missouri—Targeno
November 29, 1998

He drove his rental car, a functional but ugly Ford, west on Interstate 64. The onboard stereo was tuned to a classical music station; the Baltimore Symphony Orchestra with Claudio Abbado worked its way majestically through the final movement of Rachmaninoff's Third Piano Concerto. Targeno felt the luxury of being able to relax for a brief moment.

He watched the horizon, where the shining arch of St. Louis gradually grew brighter and more prominent. The arch furnished that city's otherwise undistinguished skyline with a touch of class. It was yet another example of the outlandish vision of Americans—there simply was not another nation on earth that would trouble to erect such a structure.

Traffic was relatively light; rush hour had ended two hours previous. The Rachmaninoff piece ended and the low-key announcer introduced an hourly segment of news presented by the unashamedly left-wing National Public Radio.

Targeno reached out to punch in a different station, then paused as the lead story opened with the continuing phenomenon of Catholic priest Peter Carenza. Targeno leaned back in his seat and laughed aloud. It was truly absurd. His bosses had him running surveillance on a subject who was getting worldwide blanket media coverage. Francesco probably needed his reports as much as he needed a terminal case of lung cancer. Shit, journalists could stay closer to the scene, and their material was fresher and cleaner than anything Targeno could gather at his discreet distances.

But he might provide the Vatican crowd something otherwise unavailable: interpretations, inferences, and projections of Carenza's next moves. Targeno's years of experience in studying and modifying human behavior qualified him as an expert on the subject of people under pressure.

The question remained, however: for how long would Francesco and the others feel the need for his input?

The news program continued, detailing the latest developments in the Carenza story—some of which Targeno already knew. Peter and his coterie had arrived in St. Louis to a new outpouring of support from the citizenry. The mayor greeted him and there was a semi-spontaneous parade in his honor. Wherever he appeared, the people loved him. He had received invitations to speak from every large city in the country, and thousands of small towns.

One of St. Louis's wealthiest land developers offered Peter a chunk of real estate and the funds to construct his own church. Peter declined. He believed it was his mission to keep traveling, to help people. He repeatedly disavowed any connection with organized religion, despite his identity as a Catholic priest. The Vatican had remained silent; attempts to question either the Pope or representatives of the College of Cardinals resulted in the standard "no comment" reply.

Targeno smiled as he drove along. What the fuck were those fools doing in Rome? Their little boy was running all over America playing God, and all they could say was "no comment"? Targeno smiled as he drove along. If he were a journalist, the closed-mouth posture of the Vatican would make him very suspicious. And yet, Targeno had noted as he'd scanned the newspaper reports, the magazine articles, and the television coverage, little attention was being paid to the curious silence coming out of Rome.

Exiting the interstate, he worked his way through the city streets until he came to a Holiday Inn. He checked in, ignoring the unrelenting sameness of chain hotel rooms in America. The designers obviously made a conscious effort to strip away any trace of originality, character, and charm from their rooms. What would they think if they traveled the hostelries and inns of Europe? The variety of the experience might prove fatal.

Targeno picked up the phone, keyed in the necessary codes, and finally dialed the unhappy Jesuit in Rome. The phone rang many times before the wiry old bastard picked up.

"Targeno, what do you want?"

He laughed. "How did you know it was me?"

"Who else would call at such an uncivilized hour?" Francesco's voice was harsh, raspy.

Targeno chuckled. "I thought it was appropriate for such an uncivilized man."

"All right, what do you want?"

"What do I want? You who hired me to get your information!"

"You have a report to make—then make it." Francesco cleared his throat, coughed. "And let me get back to bed."

"Flattery will get you everywhere—as usual," Targeno said, "so let's stop fucking around. Carenza's in St. Louis, getting the keys to the city. Everybody loves him. There are more people following him around than the Pied Piper. I believe he and Marion Windsor are sleeping together."

"Why do you say so?" Francesco tried to sound impassive, but Targeno knew the thought of Peter Carenza screwing some redhead was a consummate outrage to Giovanni Francesco.

"From watching the way they act around each other. I stay alive by observing other people, by knowing what they're thinking and doing."

"And . . . ?" Francesco sounded more awake now.

"And there's something about the way they look at each other, the way they move when near each other. It's a manner unconsciously exhibited by people who are intimate." Targeno paused to light a cigarette. "Take my word for it."

Francesco coughed dryly. "We have been wondering whether or not to remove you from the mission."

"I figured as much. With all the media attention why do you need me?"

"If I trusted the integrity of the American media, I would dump you in an instant. But I am of two minds. The others feel you should remain on the mission."

"So? What do I do?"

"If you want out, you can come home immediately. Bring me a full report and pick up your fee. We have decided we don't want him back in Rome—at least not for now."

"That's obvious—but why?"

"There is a prophecy that says the last Pope will come from across a great sea."

"Oh, yes," said Targeno, grinning. "Then it all fits, doesn't it?"

"Yes, it all fits." Francesco sounded pleased with himself. Targeno decided to take advantage of his good mood. His research had left him with a few questions.

"If Peter Carenza was cloned from the blood of the *Sindone*—the Shroud—then how do you account for the findings of the independent tests back in 1988?"

"You mean the Papal Authorization?"

"Whatever you want to call it. 'Vanni, they had seven independent agencies carbon-date the linen. They announced—with the Pope's imprimatur—that the cloth only dated back to the fourteenth century. The Shroud is a hoax."

Giovanni Francesco chuckled softly. "I'm surprised at you. You, who supposedly prides himself in catching the smallest details."

"Go on. Educate me. Make me feel foolish—if you can."

Francesco cleared his throat, segueing into a rolling, greasy cough. Targeno could hear him hawking up phlegm. Stylish indeed.

"All right. Listen," said the priest. "The scientists were correct—the linen is only seven hundred years old. But they assumed the image impressed upon the substance is the same age."

"But it is not," said Targeno.

The priest laughed softly. An overly dramatic and evil-sounding *heh-heh.* "The original Holy Shroud was more than a relic, you see. It was a physical manifestation of Christ's Body and Blood. It was the symbol of the Holy Sacrament of the Eucharist made real! The Holy Shroud was and is the Body and Blood of Christ. The linen contains the molecular elements of both."

"But if the linen only dates from the fourteenth century, then the image had to have been transferred from the original shroud to the current one . . ."

"Ah, Targeno, you are so bright. It is no wonder you've survived so long."

"But how and by whom? The idea of transferring such a delicate image sounds challenging—even for today's technology."

Francesco laughed openly. "Is today's technology any better than the engineering feats or the mummification skills of the Egyptians? The astronomy of the Druids or the Aztecs?"

"I see your point. Go on."

"There is not much to explain, really. The first Pope created *Il Ordine della Sindone*—The Order of the Shroud—a secret society of priests committed to the preservation of the Holy Shroud. By early in the fourteenth century, the original linen was beginning to seriously deteriorate. The friars at the Belle Castro Monastery in Padua, who were well known for their successful alchemies, had studied the secrets of the ancient Egyptians and devised a technique for transferring the substance and the image of the Shroud to a new piece of linen."

"That simple, eh?"

"Indeed. Although 'simple' is not exactly the correct word."

"And you and your old cronies are members of *L'Ordine*, no doubt?"

"Targeno, how could you have ever guessed such a thing?" The priest laughed softly again.

What the old Jesuit had revealed was not surprising when Targeno thought about it. The Vatican and the Catholic

Church in general had been thick with secret orders and organizations.

"One more thing—why did the Pope authorize the 1988 announcement about the fourteenth century dating of the Shroud? Why would the Church do anything that would discredit such a well-known relic?"

"Why?" echoed Francesco.

"It is like an affidavit, that Shroud; it is physical proof of Christ's existence. Why would the Church allow such seeming proof to be debunked?"

"Because *L'Ordine* advised His Grace to do so . . ."

"Oh, that explains everything," Targeno said sarcastically. "I suppose you had good reasons."

"Of course," said Francesco. "In case anyone traced Peter to Krieger, they would not make the final connection to the Shroud—because it had been 'proven' to be a fake. Our secret would still be safe. Besides, prior to 1988, the Church had never officially stated the Shroud was authentic."

"But it was being cared for by the priests at St. John the Baptist's Cathedral at Turin," said Targeno. "That looks pretty official to me."

"Officially, that was done as a favor to the family of Umberto II of Savoy—he is still the actual owner of the Shroud. The important thing is this—our secret remains secure."

Targeno said, "I think you and your friends are more than a little insane."

"It is the world which makes us us."

"Oh yes, this 'vale of tears,' right. If this world is such a terrible place, how come you don't seem to be in such a rush to be rid of it? I have the angel of your deliverance in my pocket, 'Vanni. She's only nine millimeters wide, but you say the word, and she is yours."

"I still have work to be done. That is why God has granted me these many years."

"Yes, of course. Sorry. I forgot."

"Come home and collect your blood money, Targeno. Or

continue your reports. It is your choice. As for me, I am going back to sleep."

Before he could reply, the old man hung up. Suddenly, Targeno felt very much alone in the bland hotel room. The knew knowledge of the Shroud had left him feeling strangely empty. Collapsing on the much too soft bed, he realized he was thoroughly exhausted. Perhaps he was finally getting too old for his craft. In the past, he had banished such thoughts immediately, but maybe now there was some truth to his fears. No doubt he was not as strong or as quick as when he wore a younger man's clothes, but he was infinitely wiser than those earlier years. Was there not a balance?

Yes. For a while. But then the scales would inevitably shift.

For a moment he allowed himself to wonder if the balance might be shifting now. But there was no percentage, no edge, and certainly no pleasure in such thoughts. He turned his mind to other things. What was his next move to be?

He was tired of chasing Carenza across the States, and he had a decision to make. The whole Peter Carenza phenomenon intrigued him. To be so close to the unfolding events could turn out to be a very special privilege. Would it be wise to turn his back on everything and descend once again into the tarpit of international espionage?

Spy versus spy. Steal or be stolen from. Kill or be killed.

It was a weary game he'd played out so many, many times; surely there was room for something more in his life. Looking for distraction, Targeno turned on the television. Absently he punched through the ration of cable channels—a collage of new and old cinema, sports, news, children's pabulum, talking heads, and religious *strunge*. American television contained, without doubt, the most diverse, silly, yet fascinating mix of entertainment and information in the entire world.

At this time of year, Targeno knew, he could find an abundance of American football—played primarily by incredibly agile, large-proportioned, black men. Although he did not really understand the finer points of the game, he could watch football for long stretches of time because it was such a highly structured game. He liked the high level of organization required by all members of each squad; and he enjoyed the choreographed spectacle of its ballet-like violence. In terms of pure ferocity, in an endlessly changing display of combinations and permutations, American football had no equal.

Stretched out on the bed, he watched part of a game between teams from Baltimore and Chicago until the halftime break. Bored with the blather of the announcers and the rash of commercials, he scanned the other channels, pausing on one of the televangelist satellite channels. These programs were basically the same the world over—a richly appointed set with lots of drapery and gold trim, a choir of well-scrubbed, youthful faithful, and a sweeping audience of mostly older people. The star preachers were usually extremely square-looking despite the obvious expense and tailoring of their clothes. Targeno often watched snippets of such broadcasts because they contained some of the most genuine and untainted humor in all of television.

But there was definitely a different look to this show. The set was full of high-tech appurtenances—everything decorated with burnished metal surfaces, laser-lighting, postmodern optical art. There was a glitzy, full-energy, ultra-power gestalt about the show which, Targeno was forced to admit, was somehow attractive and tasteful.

He lay back on the hammock like bed and watched.

The centerpiece of the broadcast was a man whose name Targeno recognized, but whom he had never before seen—Freemason Cooper. He was a tall, broad-shouldered man with a thick head of silvering hair, cut according to the latest fashion. He wore stylish eyeglasses and an elegantly tailored suit. Savoir-faire literally radiated from the man. His demeanor was confident, polished, supremely professional. There was none of the snake-oil salesman about Reverend Cooper. He had a way of staring boldly into the camera that almost challenged the viewer not to believe every word he was saying.

Targeno smiled as Cooper ran through a standard reading and interpretation of some chapter and verse from the Bible.

To the religious, it was probably quite stirring. To Targeno, it was the usual sanctimonious drivel.

What he found far more interesting was the unique way Freemason Cooper integrated his sermon into a fantastic video and audio display. Three large screens semi-enclosed him and his podium, surrounding him in a triptych of ever-changing images. Whoever was orchestrating the three images was a video virtuoso. Not only did the pictures coincide with the Reverend's comments, but they flashed and changed in perfect synchronization with the cadence of Cooper's voice.

The result was a fascinating, almost hypnotic, assault on the visual and auditory senses. Targeno admired the man's skill at using so many current events to illustrate biblical scenes and lessons. It was as skillful a use of high-tech propaganda equipment as he'd ever seen. It was no surprise this Cooper fellow was popular. Lesser minds than Targeno, would have little choice other than to watch their glass teat screens, sucking up its message like helpless infants.

Targeno watched the show for another few minutes, finally growing bored with the unceasing hard-line delivery of Christian dogma. But just as he prepared to switch back to the football game, the image of Peter Carenza filled the screen. Suddenly, Reverend Freemason Cooper stood surrounded by triplicate effigies of Peter Carenza. The familiar newsvideo footage had been carefully edited and reassembled to march to the beat of Cooper's speech.

Targeno leaned forward, taking in the presentation carefully. Reverend Cooper was very careful not to openly denounce the obvious good works of Peter Carenza, but he was equally careful not to praise the man either. Rather, Cooper tried to assume the role of an impartial observer, merely letting his followers know he was aware of the newcomer to the religious scene.

But there was another message being preached—one of which Cooper was probably unaware. Targeno smiled as he watched and listened.

Reverend Freemason Cooper was desperately scared of Peter Carenza. And Targeno had always been wise enough to be scared of desperate men.

Thank you, Reverend Cooper, he thought. You have just helped me make my decision.

THIRTY-FOUR

Richview, Illinois—Carenza
November 29, 1998

It was the best of times, it was the worst of times.

The familiar opening lines of *A Tale of Two Cities* had assumed a new meaning for him. He had never imagined that such a skyrocket of pure elation could be coupled with an ultimate crack-in-the-earth desperation.

Peter Carenza leaned against the railing of a pasture fence and looked up at the awesome magic of the night sky. The power and beauty of the galaxy's rim stars fell upon him as he wrestled with his dilemma. From moment to moment, emotion and rational thought brawled for dominance. How could he have broken his vow of celibacy? Could God ever grant him forgiveness, find enough mercy to absolve him of such a terrible sin? Was it a sin at all? He'd long wondered if some of the more radical theologians who argued against celibacy might be on to something.

Total, unending sexual abstinence was unnatural, he knew, but he'd always accepted it as one of the demands of his faith. The power of the spirit was supposed to hold sway over the flesh.

And yet, when he thought of Marion, of her raw power, her *femaleness*, her sexual energy, the idea of remaining chaste became laughable. How could anyone share the kind of intimacy he'd experienced with her, and ever feel the same way about something as intangible as a *vow*? Some men might be able to withstand the emotional floods released by such an encounter, but Peter could not.

And for this, he should be damned? It seemed an unjust fate, yet if he truly believed in the laws of his Church and the dogma of his religion, then he must believe in damnation.

Damnation. Everlasting agony, and worse—the metaphysical pain of knowing you would never see God's face.

Never. The word repeated in his thoughts until it lost all sense and became only an endless roll of linked syllables.

With a start, Peter's mind returned to the clear night and the farm in Illinois. The real question remained: did he believe, in his heart, that he'd committed a mortal sin against God? Examining his motives at the time of his union with Marion, he could not sincerely believe he was a debased sinner. The idea of sin had never occurred to him.

Even if he hadn't been thinking about sin, there was still the fact that he was a priest, chosen by God—and the greater question of who Peter Carenza really was. Since learning the details of his birth, Peter had carefully avoided serious consideration of his identity and origins. But everything that had happened since he'd returned to America forced him to acknowledge that he might be more than just God's tool or His agent. Perhaps he did possess a spark of something truly Divine.

These were dangerous thoughts, he knew. Upon that path lay madness.

Looking up at the stars, Peter wondered if he was staring into God's face. He sighed and almost spoke aloud as though in prayer.

If I could only know what all this means ... If You would only tell me ...

The universe stared back at him with starry indifference.

THIRTY-FIVE

St. Louis, Missouri—Ellington
April 14, 1999 ·

It had been many months since Peter and his entourage had vacated the Affholter farm. Things had gotten so complicated so quickly that Daniel had no choice but to suggest they set up more spacious, more formal headquarters in St. Louis. Though nothing official had been said, Dan had become the de facto "manager" of their touring operation. It was a geometric progression—the media pressure, the money, the stress from Peter's followers, everything—all seemed to become twice as difficult to manage with each passing day.

They'd accepted the invitation of a St. Louis real estate mogul to use one of his office properties to house the ever-growing organization. Daniel's windowed office overlooked a bullpen area of twelve workstations, almost all occupied. It could have been the workplace of any small business or corporation.

His desk intercom buzzed and the newly hired receptionist told him there was another job applicant on the line.

"Put it through, thank you." Dan sighed and stared at the phone. It finally rang and he picked up the receiver. "Carenza Foundation of Caring," he said softly.

"Oh my gosh," said a female voice, "is this Father Peter?!"

"Well, no, actually, it's not," said Dan, smiling despite his fatigue. "Father Peter" was the media-tag bestowed by a journalist, and the name had unfortunately caught on. "But I work for Father Carenza, and the Foundation uses his name."

"Oh, I see," said the young woman, her voice colored by disappointment. "Kind of like Calvin Klein, I guess."

"Yes, that's it."

There was a pause at the other end of the line.

"Ma'am?" asked Dan. "Can I help you?"

"Oh yes, I'm sorry. I was calling about the ad you had in the paper for an office manager. Have you filled it yet?"

"We're interviewing today and tomorrow."

"I've got five years' experience doing that kind of work for Mayflower Van Lines."

"Well, you'll have to come down to our offices and fill out an application." Dan gave her the address.

"All right," she said. "I'll be down this afternoon. But listen, can you tell me something?"

"I'll certainly try . . ."

"Will this job get me close to Father Peter? Will I ever see him? Talk to him?"

"To be honest, I don't know. We're still setting up, and I have no idea how much time Father Carenza will spend here."

"But he might be there once in a while?"

"I would think so."

"Oh, that's wonderful. All right, I'll be down before noon. Thank you so much!"

Daniel thanked her and hung up. Shaking his head, he looked out onto the office floor where employees were answering phones and keying information into terminals. Mail sacks were being unloaded onto sorting tables. Letters, testimonies, requests, and lots of donations were cascading into the new headquarters at an incredible rate. Despite Peter's frequent requests not to send money, millions of people continued to do so. The Carenza Foundation of Caring was quickly becoming a not-so-little company. It was hard to imagine how it had all happened in such a short time.

Part of this turmoil, Dan knew, was his own fault. He had suggested the need for more organization, had advised Peter to find some headquarters more permanent than a recreational vehicle, to find people other than Billy and Laureen to handle the influx and disbursement of the ever-enlarging cash flow. Now he wondered if it had been the right thing to do.

The right thing to do.

He almost laughed aloud as he considered the phrase. After all the bizarre and wonderful things he'd witnessed in recent months, starting with his own healing at Peter's hands, and running right up to the most recent miracles, Dan had no idea what might be right anymore.

He suddenly realized he'd been staring off into space and he blinked himself back to full cognizance. Woolgathering, his mother used to call it.

He looked beyond the bullpen to where the flock of new employees moved about uncertainly, learning their appointed tasks. Marion Windsor entered the room, escorting a thin, fragile-looking woman who could have been the model for Norman Rockwell's stereotypical librarian. Marion guided her to a desk near the window.

Even from a distance, Marion stood out from the others like a beacon in the night. Wearing a stylish skirt and blouse, she looked like a fashion model. Her long auburn hair fell carelessly to her shoulders. The way she smiled, the expression in her eyes, her gestures . . . every damned thing about her was so distinctive and appealing.

Dan rocked back in his chair, still watching Marion give instructions to Miss Librarian. What was going on here? he asked himself. He hadn't had thoughts like that in years.

Dan had always felt the celibacy issue was more psychological than physical. One of his Jesuit professors used to say your greatest sexual organ was the one between your ears, not your legs, and Dan had agreed. Still, he was certain that young boys who vaulted into the seminary still virgins had an easier time of it than kids who'd had a few sweaty, passion-filled nights. The airy expanse of the office faded away and Dan fell down a rabbit hole of memory . . .

He was seventeen, stretched out on a chaise lounge with Judy Bournewell. Her parents were out at a political fundraiser; her younger brother was asleep; and Judy had decided this would be the night she became a woman.

The memory crystallized, its edges so hard and real, it could have happened only minutes before.

She took his hand, placed it on her knee and slowly traced a line up her inner thigh, up to the soft mound beneath her white, cotton panties. Despite his raging hormones and his lead-pipe erection, another part of his mind had remained cool, rational, etching the scene on a mental plate that would not be diminished by the passing years.

At the moment his fingers touched her inner softness, Judy emitted a sound half purr and half groan. The grown man remembered how he'd thought how much control women had over men, and how utterly different the genders were.

Dan also remembered feeling resentment toward Judy— because she had the power, dammit, to choose when the time would be right. But that hadn't stopped him from plunging ahead. How fast it happened—the fumbling, awkward entry, the rush of heat. Dan's reaction, other than the expected guilt, was embarrassment that he hadn't done it the way it happened in books and movies. Judy's, however, had been one of relief and good humor. She smiled, even laughed, and told him not to worry, that everything was fine.

That night he'd been confused by her cheeriness, but ensuing weeks proved her right. They soon got the knack of screwing and were going at it like they'd invented it.

Judy Bournewell.

His one and only love. His only lover. Dan often wondered what sex would be like with a woman instead of a girl . . .

"Dan, are you okay?"

Her musical voice so startled him, his whole body tensed and his chair pitched forward. Grabbing the edge of the desk, he looked up at Marion as though seeing her for the first time.

"Sorry," he said, feeling his face reddening. "I was just daydreaming, I guess . . ."

Marion smiled and moved to one side to admit the thin,

prim-looking woman. "Dan, this is Mrs. Keating. She's been Harrison-Lloyd's bookkeeper for as long as they've been in business."

"Oh, right," he said, standing up courteously to shake the woman's hand. "Mr. Lloyd volunteered your services to help us grow."

Mrs. Keating nodded, smiled widely. "Believe me, Father, it's a pleasure to help you folks out. I worked all my life to send my boys to parochial schools. Seeing you and Father Peter out there makes it all worthwhile!"

"Well, thank you . . ."

"And Mr. Lloyd donating one of his office buildings like this! Don't you just know the Lord's going to secure his place in heaven for this!"

"Oh, yes," said Dan. "I'm sure of it."

"Well, I guess I should get to work. I'll be out there if you need me, Father."

Dan nodded, smiled perfunctorily. Mrs. Keating departed and Marion sat down in the chair in front of his desk.

"Getting pretty crazy, isn't it?"

"You betcha." Why was he feeling so damned embarrassed? She couldn't read his mind.

"If six months ago someone told me we'd be running a company, with accountants and bookkeepers and secretaries, I would have laughed in his face." Marion pushed her hair away from her face, grinned self-consciously.

"We didn't have much choice. It got so big . . ." Dan's eyes met hers and, in an instant, he broke the contact. He suddenly felt as nervous as a schoolboy around her.

"I know it was necessary, but it never ends! This morning, Peter gets a call from a booking agency in L.A. Can you believe this? They want to help him schedule his 'appearances.' "

"Oh, man, this is insane." Dan stood up, walked to the glass window and looked out at the hivelike activity.

Why was he feeling so edgy? Was it Marion? Was it his guilt, his embarrassment because of the memories he'd been enjoying? Was it wrong to have such thoughts?

"Well, we can't stop now. Us and the South African civil war. We continue to be news 'staples.' Incredible, huh?"

"Incredible. Yeah."

Marion shifted her position in the chair, stretched out a bit. Relaxed, she looked so damned beautiful. For an instant the lunatic thought passed through his mind that he would tell her how she was affecting him, tell her he wanted her.

No. He couldn't. He wasn't even sure of his feelings. Maybe it was just her proximity, their daily contact, that made him feel like this.

Marion continued talking about the employees and Peter's plans for the next week or so. Dan was half listening, and was only vaguely aware she'd asked him a question.

"Well, Dan, what do you think?"

He felt himself flush. "I'm sorry, Marion. I haven't been getting enough sleep lately. I guess I wasn't all there just now."

She laughed, stood up, and moved close to him. Reaching out, she tweaked his cheek as if he were a little boy. "You know, you can be really cute sometimes," she said.

Her words impacted on him like bullets. How did she mean that? He smiled helplessly.

"I just wanted to know if we should tell that writer from *The New Yorker* to call back in a month or two?"

"Yeah. Things might be a little less hectic then."

"Okay, I'll tell Peter your feelings." She turned to go and, with a sudden flash of anger, Dan reached out, touched her arm to stop her. The feel of her flesh beneath her blouse, under his fingers was extremely sensual, exciting.

"You're very close to him, aren't you?" he asked softly, forcing himself to look into her green eyes. "You're a buffer between him and the rest of the world. Everything passes through you before it gets to him."

Marion smiled uneasily, as though seriously considering his words. "Is it really getting like that?"

He nodded. "You're very protective of him, Marion."

"Yes, I guess I am."

"I mean, I've been his friend for a long, long time. I'm capable of telling him myself what I think of a damned magazine writer."

"I know you are, Dan. I'm sorry." She touched his hand.

The effect was galvanic. No woman had ever done such things to him. "Don't be sorry," he said quickly, pulling away. "I didn't mean it like that. I just thought I should point it out to you. Some people might start resenting you."

She smiled. "You're right. I keep forgetting how smart you are, Daniel."

He smiled, sat down behind the desk. As he put some distance between himself and Marion, he began to think more clearly. "Where *is* Peter, anyway? I haven't seen him all morning."

"He's upstairs in the suite—talking to the editors from Simon and Schuster. You know, the book deal."

Dan nodded. Eight months ago, Peter was a complete unknown. Now he was getting the star treatment. Wonder when *Playboy*'s going to want to interview him? "Okay, I'll try to get up there and talk to him later this afternoon."

"See you later," she said as she exited the office.

Yes, they'd see each other again—but Dan would never see her the way he had one night many weeks ago.

He had no idea why he'd peered out through the slats of the closed blinds of the Winnebago that night. Had his unconscious figured out what was going on? The firelight had been dim, but he'd seen more than enough of the scene.

His intercom buzzed again.

"Yes?"

"Father Ellington, there's a Mr. Bevins here to see you."

"Who?"

"Frederick Bevins. He says he has an appointment . . ."

Dan raked his fingers through his long blond hair. Bevins. Right. He was the guy with high-octane credentials who'd applied for a security job. Dan rifled through the stacks of folders on his desk, pulling out the one tabbed with Bevins' name.

"All right," he said. "Send him up, please."

"Yes, Father."

The intercom snapped off. Out in the bullpen, Marion had camped at a vacant desk and was talking on the phone. Dan stared at her, studying her every movement, her every facial expression. Marion Windsor affected everyone. Women respected her, though they didn't often seem to like her. Most men openly leered at her, lusting after her like dogs chasing a bitch in heat. Others tried to be cool, unaffected. Like Branford, the network news anchor. But Dan was a fairly good study of body language, and he could see the tension and the desire twisting behind the flat-screen broadcaster's facade.

He closed his eyes, gently massaged the lids with his fingertips. A part of him wished that when he opened his eyes she would be gone. Well, at least he was facing his growing obsession instead of pretending it wasn't there.

He wished he could talk to Peter about his feelings. How could he? Knowing how intimate Marion and Peter had become, what could Dan say?

There was a tap on the frame of his open office door.

Looking up from the folder he'd been holding but not reading, Dan saw the receptionist and a short, stocky man who wore a plain, gray suit. He looked like he could have been a catcher on his high school baseball team. A trimmed mustache presided over his thin mouth and his nose looked like it had been broken at least once. His eyes were small and wide apart, emphasized by bushy eyebrows that would have made Groucho proud. Although he didn't look much past forty, he was losing his hair fast. That he kept it cut short and combed straight back showed he didn't really give a damn. Although his appearance was not intimidating, the guy sent out a message that he was not to be messed with.

"Father Ellington," said the young woman with him, "this is Mr. Bevins."

Dan stood up and shook the man's hand. It was a strong grip. Calluses indicated the guy wasn't afraid of hard work. "Have a seat, Mr. Bevins."

"Thanks, Father," he said, giving the office a quick once-over.

Dan looked down at the folder again, reacquainting himself with Bevins' background. Associate's degree in Forensic Psychology from University of Missouri; two years in the Army; Deputy in nearby Washington County's Sheriff's Office for three years; and ten years with Wells Fargo—as a security officer, ending up as a sergeant. Three more years as vice president of Secure Systems Ltd.

"Can you tell me about this last credential, Mr. Bevins?"

"You can call me Fred, if you want."

"All right," said Dan. "What is Secure Systems Ltd.?"

"My brother-in-law's company. Always wanted to be my own boss, right? So I talked my wife's brother, Harry, into backing the whole deal. I wanted in on security for the high-tech end of business. You know—uplink and downlink, information transfer, storage and retrieval, the whole computer thing."

Although he knew very little about the "whole computer thing," Dan nodded. "What happened? Why are you applying for this position?"

Fred Bevins smiled and put up his hands in a half shrug. "Well, it's like this—the business took off, and my brother-in-law got greedy. He got some people to do my job—payin' half what I was gettin'—and bought me out. Sent me packin'."

"I see," said Dan, always amazed at how money changed folks. "So you're looking for another security job . . ."

"Well, it's almost the only thing I know. I don't need the money, but it's important for me to be *doin'* somethin' with my life."

Dan smiled. Despite his appearance and his somewhat rough edges, Frederick Bevins had an entertaining, engaging personality. "I see . . . So you want to have something to do with your free time."

"Yeah, but it ain't what you think—I would do a good, serious job. This ain't no lark for me. Plus, I'm a Catholic, and I guess I've been kind of slack in my . . . my church attendance over the years. I figure this job might be a good way for me to get back in God's graces."

Dan nodded. It was a familiar explanation. He'd been interviewing people for months, and it was surprising how many of them espoused similar reasons for wanting to work for Father Peter.

"This boss of yours—Father Peter—I mean, he's doing so many good works for everybody. It's kinda made me think. Like maybe I owe some of the people who ain't had it as good as me."

"Yes," said Dan. "I understand that."

"Have you had many people applying for the security officer positions?"

Dan nodded. "Oh, yes—but not too many with such solid backgrounds as yours. Would you like to hear what we have in mind for the job, Mr. Bevins?"

"Sure! But please, call me Fred, okay?" He leaned back in the chair.

Dan spent the next few minutes outlining the demands and duties of the position as best he could. Peter Carenza needed personal security as he traveled about the country. Crowd control had become a growing concern, and he was attracting the attention of more and more fringe crazies and would-be assassin types. The headquarters building also needed a standard security staff and some technical safeguards against hackers and other kinds of business espionage. Dan listed his concerns and listened as Bevins amplified every one of them with cogent comments and suggested additions. As the conversation wore on, it was obvious Fred Bevins knew enough to be a help in the new security division. A retired St. Louis Police captain had volunteered to run things, but Bevins might make a good sergeant, even a second-in-command. Dan would pass him on to the head of security.

Dan wanted to meet all new employees personally. He never forgot that any applicant might be a Vatican plant looking to sabotage the organization or get close to Peter.

"Hey, you okay, Father?" Fred was staring at him quizzically.

Damn. Woolgathering again . . .

"Oh yes, everything's fine, Fred," he said smiling. "Just thinking over a few things."

"Well, do I get the job?" Fred Bevins laughed at his own joke.

"I have several more interviews to finish up today. We'll let you know tomorrow."

Bevins stood up. "Hey, I'll be waitin' by the phone. Thanks, Father. It's been real nice."

He shook the man's thick hand and ushered him out of the office, through the bullpen area. Marion was nowhere to be seen. Just as well. He didn't need the distraction.

As Dan returned to the security of his desk and chair, he absently flipped through Fred Bevins's personnel folder. The guy was friendly and knowledgeable enough. His credentials were great—far better than anybody else in the stack. Dan sighed audibly. Did he really need to talk to the others? He wasn't cut out to be a corporate type, and didn't really enjoy playing executive, even if it was for a good cause.

He wished Peter would choose to have more to do with the management of the business-face he would present to the world.

"You guys can handle it," Peter had said. "I have to worry about other things."

Dan looked up at the ceiling. Other things. Yes, his friend Peter was certainly right about that.

An image burned in the center of Dan's mind. An image that would not fade in shadows of memory. Silhouetted against the blue-black wash of midnight, a darker shape against the darkness, Marion's perfect body arched and swayed to the most ancient of rhythms.

In those instants when the image burned in him like a new-born star, nothing else mattered. He wanted her.

He wanted her.

THIRTY-SIX

Bessemet, Alabama—Cooper
April 16, 1999

The warm, womb-like embrace of the water calmed him. Reverend Freemason Cooper pulled a final free-style stroke, then coasted the rest of the distance to the pool's edge.

Twenty laps. Every morning. Before breakfast.

Yessiree.

No wonder his doctors told him he had the body of a man fifteen years younger. He felt healthier now than he had at any time in his life. No wonder the women found him attractive—especially since he could still keep his crank hard for hours at a time.

Freemason smiled as he measured his breathing at poolside. Looking up through the glass roof of his indoor pool, he searched for the sun in the gray morning mist. This sort of thin, early spring sky, he knew, presaged a seasonal outpouring of grief, guilt, and heavy donations. Cooper's church was entering into its busiest, most profitable quarter, culminating in Easter. While the prospect no longer thrilled him like it once did, Cooper was pleased to know the cash flow would be turned up a few notches in the coming weeks.

He lifted himself from the water, and before he had settled comfortably on the pool's edge, Lindstrom, his Swedish valet and masseur, had reached his side, a fluffy white, monogrammed towel at the ready.

"Thank you, Linnie," said Freemason, rubbing down his nude body, then wrapping himself in downy softness.

"Shall I tell Frieda you're ready?"

"Yeah, but tell her to hold those phony sausages—I'm gettin' sick of that soybean shit all the time."

"Yes, Reverend."

"As a matter of fact, tell her I want some Jimmy Dean sausage this morning!" Yessiree, he had a feelin' it was gonna be a Jimmy Dean kinda day.

Lindstrom nodded and retreated toward the kitchen. Freemason watched the tall, muscular blond man enter the house and disappear. He figured the guy for a faggot, but he'd never been able to nail him on it. Lindstrom was very quiet, very private.

Probably hates my guts, thought Freemason with a wry smile.

Standing up, he stretched his arms high above his head, enjoying the lassitude of the cool-down after a vigorous workout. Birds' morning-songs filtered down to him from tropical trees, the banyan, the coconut, and the eucalyptus that flourished in the climate-controlled environment of the spacious enclosure of the pool. He liked listening to the birds singing. It was such an innocent, beautiful sound.

The world could always use a little more innocence, a little more beauty, he thought satirically.

A door opened and Lindstrom reappeared. "Breakfast will be served directly, sir. And you have a call on line four."

Freemason nodded, waved him off, and walked over to a set of cabana chairs and table where an elaborate telephone console awaited him. He punched the correct line—his private security line—and lifted the handset.

"Speak to me."

"Reverend Cooper, it's Freddie Bevins . . ."

Freemason's pulse jumped a few points as his P.I. identified himself.

"I'm waiting, Freddie."

"Just wanted you to know everything went just like you said it would. They jumped on that list of credentials like a bass on a bullfrog!" Bevins sounded ebullient, pleased with himself.

Freemason smiled. "The Reverend knows his stuff, Freddie. I told you that."

Bevins chuckled. "I snowed 'em so bad, I bet they don't even check a one!"

"No matter. I have people who will substantiate anything they want. I took care of everything, Freddie—you're perfectly safe."

"Hell, I even told 'em I was Catholic, can you believe it?"

"From you? Certainly." Freemason cleared his throat. He had a sudden craving for some prune juice. "All right—what can you tell me?"

"Not much, yet, Reverend. I don't officially start work until Monday morning. But I've been keepin' my eyes open, you know. I figure I'm going to have open 'n' free access to practically every damned thing in this place—they won't suspect a thing."

"What about their phones? Can you get me taps?"

Bevins chuckled. "Probably. The building already had its own network in place. I'll have to see how secure it was for the previous client. Odds are Ellington won't bother to change it, or even check it out."

"Ellington?"

"Carenza's right-hand man. They were buddies all the way back to the seminary."

"All right, Freddie, you know your job. I'm payin' you well; do it well. Until you get settled in, try to sepnd your time diggin' up everything you can on Carenza. And I mean *everything*."

"Gotcha, Reverend. I'll have plenty of dirt for you. Guaranteed."

"I'm counting on you, Freddie."

"Okey-doke, Reverend. I'll be callin' in real regular-like."

"You do that."

"Oh, one more thing. Here's a coupla numbers where you can reach me if you hafta. Office right here, and the hotel." Bevins dictated the numbers and Freemason scribbled on the pad next to the console.

"Thank you, Freddie. Good-bye."

Hanging up before his hireling could say anything else, Freemason shook his head slowly. Bevins was an unctuous ass, but he was good at his job. The P.I. worked cases better than a mutt with a ham-bone.

Lindstrom returned, pushing a serving cart carrying a silver platter covered by a crystal dome. The valet proffered to his boss the terry-cloth robe draped over his left arm. While Freemason slipped into the robe, Lindstrom uncovered the country breakfast platter and arranged a place at the table. When everything was prepared he departed without being told.

As Freemason savored each mouthful of his decidedly unhealthy breakfast, he began thinking ahead, planning his strategies. Whether he admitted it to himself or not, the facts were simple: this fella Carenza was going to be a major concern in his life till things got resolved.

He was glad Daddy was around to counsel him. The old man might be getting goofy about some things, but he still had his common sense and he could still hold his pee and his liquor.

You gotta deal with this guy, son, the old man had said. *Ain't no makin' believe he ain't there.*

First thing was: know your enemy. Freemason had always believed that gave you an advantage. If, indeed, Carenza was his enemy . . .

Sipping freshly ground and brewed Jambala coffee, Freemason remembered the news tapes and the miracles. If it was trickery, no one had figured out how Carenza'd pulled it off. Hell, probably wasn't anybody *tryin'* to figure it out.

Except maybe Reverend Freemason Cooper.

When he thought about it as directly as he'd allow himself, Freemason just didn't know what to make of it. Not when you had these magicians on TV making the Statue of Liberty disappear and floating elephants across canyons and other bullshit like that.

Even though you couldn't always believe what you saw on television.

THIRTY-SEVEN

Colorado Springs, Colorado—Carenza
October 20, 1999

He was changing.

Every day, he felt himself growing more different. More in touch with himself, but also more aloof, more detached—at least from the self he had been before his curious awakening.

Sometimes when he lay in bed at night, and he couldn't sleep, he would try to pray, but it was like speaking into a dead telephone. Some characteristic of the silence in his mind told him no one was really listening.

Why?

Was no one listening because he wasn't really *talking*? Because he couldn't face himself? And when was the last time he'd said Mass?

Then there was the question of his talents.

Sometimes he felt so invigorated, so intoxicated by their use, he felt limitless, as boundless as the energy of the sun. And at other times, he was so drained and weak, he felt he was dying. It was as if some parasite lived inside him, playing with his mind and body, having no pattern or sense, no logic or purpose.

He was constantly driven to test the limits of his powers. The press and his followers called his feats miracles, and Peter was beginning to believe them. When he healed people, when he restored them, he could feel a force surging through him like sweet, fragrant electricity. No, that wasn't quite right—the power wasn't really running through as much as coming *from* him. It was a geyser of staggering energy.

And later, when he felt so close to death, he would ask himself what the hell was really going on. After the first few manifestations, when he'd asked for divine guidance and received nothing from the cold silence in his mind, he had fallen into an abyss of despair and abject fear.

But recently the fear had been replaced by something else, something more impervious to pain and doubt. The way a tumor can become calcified into a hard encysted lump—no longer the devouring cancer, just a stony monument to the horror that once existed there.

A part of him now felt like the fear didn't matter anymore. There was work to be done, and it didn't matter how that was accomplished, or how he felt. The only important thing was getting it done. Peter didn't think he had a new sense of mission, but he did have an unstated sense of being. If he was being directed by some outside presence, he was not aware of it, and what was worse perhaps, he cared not at all about the possibility.

It would be a lie to say he was not enjoying his recent celebrity. An ass-kicking ego boost accompanied the attention and the hype, the utter recognizability by the public. But Peter tried to keep the glitz within the proper perspective. The last thing he wanted was people thinking he'd deteriorated into some kind of rank performer.

Sometimes he dreamed of standing in the midst of an immense crowd—a crowd that pooled out away from him in all directions with no end—and they were all laughing at him.

He awoke to the warm touch of Colorado sunlight basting him through the withdrawn shades of the hotel window. Fluttering his eyelids, he tried to adjust to the light and fight through an instant of total disorientation. What day was it? Where was he?

Rolling over, his knee brushed Marion's naked thigh, and a jolt passed through him. Still asleep, she lay on her back, face tilted away from the uncurtained window. The memory of her coming to his room in the middle of the night flooded back over him like the return of an ebb tide. That, plus the touch of her flesh, gave him the beginnings of an erection. Unlike in prior months, he felt no guilt or need to repress his sexuality. Indeed, when he bothered to think about it at all, he told himself it was a most natural response.

There was no denying Marion's physical beauty, her simple, overpowering ability to attract men. Minutes slipped away as he studied her in repose. Her hair was a splash of red-brown across the pillow, her body a suggestion of round edges beneath the sheet. Long lashes rested on her high cheekbones, the corners of her mouth curved up slightly.

Suddenly her eyelids fluttered, lifted. Two bottomless portals opened upon him, sea-green depths that housed the secrets of her soul.

"Good morning," he said, leaning close to kiss her.

"I could've slept forever."

"Someday you will."

"Oh, and aren't we cheery this morning." Marion sat up, and the sheet fell away from her small, pink-tipped breasts. "What time is it?"

"Time to get in the shower with me."

Ignoring him, she reached over to the night table and picked up her wristwatch. "Oh, Peter, we don't have time to fool around!"

"What? Why?"

"It's already ten o'clock," said Marion, sliding from the bed and pulling on the robe which lay in a pile on the floor on her side of the bed. "You're supposed to meet Larry at eleven at the control-room trailer."

"Is it that late?"

"Would I kid you? C'mon, we've got to put a serious move on—even if we do have a 'copter waiting!"

Reluctantly, Peter sat up, eased himself from the bed. Before his feet touched the carpet, Marion had slipped into the bathroom.

Larry. Larry Melmanik.

The name suggested a short, fat, oleaginous character, the kind of guy who favored ban-rol trousers and sport jackets by Purina. A man who smoked stubby cigars or pastel cigarettes from Nat Sherman's. The truth was far different. At age thirty-five, Larry Melmanik looked like he should be working for IBM or any good Washington, D.C. law firm on K Street. Short, well-barbered sandy hair, sincere puppydog eyes, and a propensity for traditional tweeds and navy blazers gave Peter's booking agent an overall appearance not out of place in the pages of GQ.

Melmanik's credentials were equally impressive. In a short time he'd hooked up with some of the hottest news acts in the entertainment industry. Some called him lucky; others, percipient. Whatever the source of his success, Melmanik had gained the respect of just about everyone powerful or influential. If you were his client, he could get you work just about anywhere. Of course, Peter didn't need someone to hawk his wares; he needed someone to organize and plan and winnow the thousands of requests that ranged from speaking engagements, interviews, photo sessions, videos, television and movie offers, all the way down to bubblegum cards.

Which gets me here, Peter thought as he absently ran his fingers through his hair. Mountain Rock Ninety-Nine, the biggest music-aid concert of the decade, was getting ready to launch west of Colorado Springs on a middle-aged hippie's ranch. In a media-event coup that Larry Melmanik claimed would double the expected 200,000 attendance, Peter was going to make an appearance to open the festivities.

Peter smiled at the thought of standing before such a huge crowd. Nothing he'd done so far had approached those numbers—except in his nightmares. It would be a great experience.

Marion emerged from the bathroom. "Gotta go back to my room and shower. See you in a half hour."

"You could do that here," he said.

"I have to fix my hair and get into some clothes. I'll be faster if I do it alone." She smiled knowingly as she opened the door and made a quick exit.

He silently agreed with her as he entered the shower. While the hot stream invigorated him, he thought about the man who owned the ranch west of "The Springs," Tim Vernon, who had agreed to let the Mountain Rock organizers stage their festival on his property. "He was at Woodstock," Larry had said half-snidely. "He's trying to relive his past."

The old man probably wasn't doing a bad job of it. American culture seemed to undergo cyclic reflections of fashion, economics, and political philosophy. After the super-materialistic eighties, the limits of natural and industrial resources began to become more evident in the early nineties. Several market crashes and border wars later, the younger generation was ready for a change. The first indications of change were, as usual, in the arts. Music, literature, and theater grew increasingly iconoclastic and more movement-oriented. And, as with many art movements through history, they became aligned, either by choice or by accident, with political or economic postures somewhat left of center. Terms like radical and subversive gained usage in the media and the cultural turmoil gradually fomented into something more than a fad. Young people gave it form even if it had little function. For some of the student generation the new awareness, the new consciousness, became a lark, something to have some fun with. For others it became a cause celebre, a way of life, even a meaning for life.

The time was right. Things had remained static for too long. The culture had acquired a staleness; a stagnant cloud hung over its head. This, coupled with the coming millennium and its concomitant mysticism, provided all the elements for a new Age of Aquarius. The recent availability of vaccines against virulent sexual diseases had enabled people to loosen their collars again. You didn't need to be a Toynbee scholar to see that many Americans were trying very hard to reinvent the sixties.

But just as the sixties had been an imperfect reincarnation of the twenties, so were the nineties something similar to, but different from the sixties. Technology had something to do with it. So had changing world economics and politics, plus some very real environmental problems like the hole in the ozone layer and the vanishing rain forest in South America. There were enough new elements to keep history from completely repeating itself.

So, instead of hippies, the media concerned itself with the antics of the "rads," who, while they wore their hair long and favored the nonaddictive perception-enhancing drugs of he turn-of-the-century pharmaceutical labs, had inexorably gained an identity, a look, a fairly coherent ethical system.

And that's who he would be addressing from the monster platform in the middle of the Colorado grazing lands—the offspring and grandchildren of the beatniks and the hippies, those who carried on the American legacy of healthy skepticism and an eye toward change. For the first time, Peter thought, he wouldn't be dealing with the needs and values of the just-plain-folks from middle-America. He considered it a challenge, a necessary test in his level of acceptance and popularity.

He stepped from the shower feeling renewed. Dressing quickly, he joined Marion, who waited outside the Clarion in the chopper.

"Peter, they're going to *love* you out there!" said Larry Melmanik. As was his custom, he was dressed in a blue blazer, blue oxford shirt but no tie, and a pair of casual khaki slacks.

"I hope so," Peter said. Despite months of public appearances Peter felt a little nervous at the thought of facing such a large crowd. But the doubts passed quickly. He would control them.

"Hey, don't worry about it, Father," said Tim Vernon. He looked about sixty, his bearded face weathered like old wood by southwestern sun. "You're going to do just fine."

"Sure," said Sammy Eisenglass, who was one of Mountain Rock's organizers and promoters. "You're gonna knock 'em out, man. Ain't no doubt we got twice as many people out here because of you."

Sammy, a flashy dresser from Los Angeles, had become a fairly famous person because of all the spectacular events he had "created" during the last decade.

In fact, that's what his business card said:

> SAMUEL EISENGLASS
> CREATOR

Rock concerts and championship fights were his specialties, but he had also been successful with religious convocations and self-improvement seminars. And Sammy was no dummy when it came to making a name for himself. Never one to remain in the background, he always arranged to introduce each new event. His trademark, when before the lights and cameras, was to have a beautiful bimbette on each arm and a pair of outrageous mirror-sunglasses over his sparrow's eyes.

He had a reputation for being a merciless businessman who had left many enemies in his wake along the way to outrageous success. But that description fit more than one Hollywood operator whose edges were more than a little sharp.

Funny thing was, Peter thought, he actually liked Sammy. He didn't exactly admire the man, but he understood Eisenglass's motivations. Though he couldn't justify Sammy's methods and his obvious lack of compassion, he accepted the need for predatory types in any cross-section of society. There was, after all, an ecological niche for sharks in the ocean, thought Peter, a niche that had remained stable for millions of years. He was certain there'd always been Sammy Eisenglasses around; and probably always would be.

Tim Vernon clearly felt uncomfortable in Sammy's presence, and the atmosphere in the control-room trailer was of strained cordiality at best. Tim Vernon tolerated Sammy only because of the Event Creator's unending promises to donate all the profits from Mountain Rock to the millions of displaced refugees from the latest of Central America's endless civil wars and the millions of victims in South Africa's strife.

Peter knew Sammy Eisenglass wasn't interested in displaced refugees. Dispassion oozed from his every pore like dirty sweat. But what did that matter when a mover and a shaker of his magnitude ultimately contributed to a greater good—and provided Peter with his biggest exposure yet?

The thought lingered in his mind, and for a moment, Peter wondered why it was so important to him that he gain wider and wider exposure and familiarity in the public's eye. This unspoken goal had begun to permeate all his actions, all his plans. Sooner or later, he knew, he would have to examine his motivations more closely.

But not right now.

The trailer door opened; Marion entered, wearing jeans and a journalist's field-vest over her baggy white blouse. Her hair was tied back with a multicolored scarf and she was already picking up a healthy glow from the wind and sun of Colorado's glorious Indian summer. Everyone turned to watch as she edged past the banks of consoles and technicians.

"It's time to get started," she said. "The crowd's beginning to chant."

"I'd better get out there," said Tim Vernon.

"Me too!" cried Sammy. Heading for the exit, Sammy paused to look over the shoulder of a video-tech whose monitor revealed a copter-shot of the crowd. Like a roiling, colorful sea, hundreds of thousands of people rippled and surged. Their attention was vaguely focused upon a huge, templelike stage. Black towers of speakers, which rose up like ancient monuments to enclose the stage, were in turn flanked by matrices of Diamond-Vision flat monitors, each one the size of a movie-theater screen. The flat monitors formed checkerboard collages, each one capturing a different aspect of the stage, the crowd, the ranchland, a constantly changing mat of video art. The copter-shot rolled and circled and expanded as the airship lifted higher. The crowd kept growing, like an amoeba enlarging by accretion.

"Hey, what'd I tell you?!" yelled Sammy as he pointed to the tech's screen. "If we don't get half a million, I quit this business and become a rabbi!"

Several of Sammy's attendant toadies laughed a little too

loudly. Tim Vernon nodded politely. Everyone else just tried their best to smile.

"So many people," said Marion. "What are you doing about food and water?"

"My wells and irrigation system can handle it," said Vernon. "Plus plenty of porta-pots. And most people knew enough to bring their own food. Most of these kids're pretty experienced concertgoers, you know . . ."

"I hope so," said Marion. "You might break all the records with this one."

"That's what we're counting on, pretty lady," said Sammy.

"Okay," said Vernon. "We'd better get up to the stage. I'll kick things off, then introduce Sammy. Then comes Father Peter's opening benediction, okay?"

Everyone nodded and began filing out of the trailer. Peter had the urge to take Marion's hand, but knew they needed to be very careful in front of others. No one should ever suspect there was anything between them. Strange, but though he had no proof, Peter suspected Dan Ellington knew they were physically involved. When he thought about the feeling, it reminded him of his proximity sense. Maybe, in addition to the strengthening of his other talents, he was becoming something of a psychic too?

The entourage moved toward the rear entrance to the stage. Chanting from the enormous crowd rolled across the grazing land like thunder. The earth itself seemed to resonate from the sound like after-tremors from a quake. The entire backstage area, including parking spaces for the fleet of trailers and buses and other vehicles that belonged to the performing groups, had been cordoned off with temporary chain-link fencing and supplied with a private security force. Sammy Eisenglass was a seasoned producer and left no organizing stone unturned. Standing at the back entrance to the enormous staging area were Fred Bevins and two steroid mountains in security uniforms and dark glasses.

"Been waiting for you, Father," said Bevins, looking like he was withholding a natural urge to salute his boss.

"We're ready," said Peter. Bodyguards and heavy

security—what a life. Peter hadn't made up his mind about Fred Bevins. The man exhibited a gregarious, almost sycophantic manner, but it just didn't ring true. How had that crapola worked on Daniel Ellington? Peter felt there was something subtly wrong about Bevins. Was his growing sixth sense speaking to him, or was this just a clash of personalities? Peter made a mental note to check out Fred Bevins ... when he had some free time.

It wasn't until he began climbing the long flight of steps to the stage that Peter pondered what he would say to the massive audience. He always relied on being extemporaneous, and it always worked. Even back at Saint Sebastian's, when he would speak to the congregation after reading the Gospel, he never knew what words would tumble from his mouth.

Saint Sebastian's.

He hadn't thought of his little Brooklyn parish church in so long. Seemed like lifetimes ago, even though it was barely more than a year. He couldn't help but wonder what Father Sobieski must be thinking. Was the old man going around telling everyone he knew Peter Carenza way back when?

Peter smiled at the thought. Yes, that sounded like Sobieski.

He stood in the wings, watching Sammy sling an arm around the waist of each member of a matched set of long-legged young women wearing little strips of silk that did a bad job of covering their own matched sets. Tim Vernon strode onto the stage alone and went through his humble, I'm-just-a-simple-man-with-simple-wants routine. The crowd ate it up and cheered him on like the Hitler-worshipers in those old black-and-white newsreels. In the wings on the opposite side of the stage, Lingus, the concert's opening act, stirred and smoked nervously. Six guys in purposely offensive costumes trying to look bored but probably freaked out of their skulls to be a part of this whole gig.

Vernon segued real folksy-like into Sammy Eisenglass, whose appearance at such mega-events had become almost self-parody. When he and his trademark bimbettes pranced onstage, the unending plateau of people erupted into "mega-applause." They hooted and jeered and laughed and clapped. They loved him because he was simply too easy to despise. Peter wondered if Sammy understood that elementary truth . . . or if it even mattered. He was only in front of them for a few minutes, but he made the most of it, strutting and mugging like an old vaudevillian, squeezing his girls' asses and letting them slink all over him on cue.

It was a pretty hideous display of human debasement when you got right down to it, and it definitely qualified as the most bizarre and utterly tasteless introduction to an appearance by Father Peter. Peter wondered if Daniel was watching, back in St. Louis. And what about those praying mantises back in Rome? He smiled at the image of that fat pig Lareggia watching a rock concert.

The crowd noise gradually subsided from the last piece of Eisenglass shtick. Stepping into the silence, Sammy said: "And nowwwwww . . . we're going to jump-start this thing with a little benediction from one of the hottest attractions in the country! By special arrangement with God! We brought you! All the way from St. Louis, Missouri! Father Peterrrrr!"

The vast sea of faces erupted into spontaneous cheering. Peter detected a different tonal quality to the sound, a different message being sent. Absent was the slight derisive inflection. The roaring voice of the crowd spoke only of approval and total acceptance. Peter drew in a deep breath, exhaled slowly, and began walking toward stage center. Sammy and his fleshy bookends swung back from the mike stand, all smiles.

Peter nodded to them politely, then, turning to the crowd, dismissed them as if they'd never been there. He smiled, lifted his hands with his palms upturned, and waited for the applause to subside. The audience was so big that its size lost the power to intimidate. He smiled at them and could feel their warmth radiating outward, touching him. Finally, the ranchland was quiet again. The only sound was a soft breeze, rolling down from the Sangre de Cristos and whistling through towering loudspeaker arrays.

"Thank you for such a warm welcome," he said, speaking

slowly, so that his voice did not echo and roll over each pre-
ceding word. "I know I don't look much like a priest these
days . . ." Peter gestured at his cotton chambray shirt and casual jeans. "But maybe that's because I'm *not* much of a
priest anymore."

The entire crowd seemed to gasp at once, as though it
didn't know what he meant, or didn't want to believe such a
thing.

"You see, I used to spend most of my time locked away in
a church or a rectory or a sacristy—cut off from the people.
Sure, the sanctuary was a good place for people to come and
get the help they needed. But it wasn't enough. If God gave
me a special gift, an ability to reach out to people, to really
talk to them when they need it most, then I think God also in-
tended that I leave the sanctuary and go out where the people
are—where you are."

He paused at what seemed like an appropriate moment, and
the crowd cheered again. Now that they understood, they approved. He knew it would be like that.

And once he had them, the rest was easy. The size of his
audience didn't matter at all. They were so receptive that he
knew unconsciously that he would not need to speak for very
long. It would not take long to perform his special magic
upon them.

He spoke foremost of love and its power. He spoke of the
many stratified levels of the spirit and the soul, and how they
survived because of that special power. Everything started
with a healthy love of self, he said, because if we cannot love
ourselves, we can surely have no excess love for others.

He spoke of unity, and how the only path to survival in the
coming new millennium would be through a concerted
effort—all of humankind working toward the same goals,
wanting the same things. It was a simple, efficient message.
No frills, no rococo borders or decorations. This crowd wore
its souls on its shirtsleeves; they didn't need any sugar-
coating or theatrics.

The most interesting aspect of the speech lay within Peter.
For the first time, he was fully aware of how much he de-

rived from his listeners, his followers. What had previously been a wholly subconscious transformation was now so evident it could not be ignored. The essence of their souls, their most primal life-energies nourished him. He knew that now. From the people he drew his power. They radiated; he collected. He was like a satellite dish, an earth station, gathering a signal and refocusing it. It was the perfect symbiosis. He fed their needs, their dreams; they gave energy back to him in a form which he could use and re-process and re-emit. It was like a psychic nitrogen cycle—an unbreakable food chain for the soul.

As he finished speaking, Peter could sense a powerful charge building in the atmosphere above the prairie. The crowd was like a giant battery, storing up current, waiting to be discharged. When he finished with a quiet, humble blessing, they shattered the silence with lusty approval, but he knew that was not the release, the outflow, he sensed within them.

No, he thought, relying on his growing sense of intuition. That would come later.

BOOK FOUR

"And when the thousand years are expired, Satan shall be loosed out of his prison, and shall go out to deceive the nations which are in the four quarters of the earth."

—Revelations 20:7–8

THIRTY-EIGHT

Colorado Springs, Colorado—Windsor
October 24, 1999

Marion sat alone in her hotel room. On the night table a single lamp fought against the darkness, illuminating a bottle of California zinfandel and a hotel glass sanitized for your protection. The door was locked, but she knew *he* could get in if he really wanted to. She wondered still if there was anything beyond his reach . . .

Leaning against the headboard of the queen-sized bed, legs stretched out, she struggled to put into words the events she had witnessed earlier in the day. Her laptop computer tottered on her knees as she forced herself to write. If she was going to get this one on the air, she was going to need a lot of preparation.

No way could she wing this, not after what she'd seen, after all that had happened in the last twenty-four hours. World events, and personal ones, had shaken her to the core of her soul.

She gulped down a mouthful of wine, looked at the empty screen and blinking cursor, and tried to reconstruct everything she had witnessed and experienced.

The Mountain Rock Ninety-Nine Refugee Aid Concert had been tilting around the clock for almost seventy-two hours. One after another, the top names in the music business took the stage and nailed their most famous tunes. The crowd filled the grazing pasture, overflowing to the outer reaches of Tim Vernon's ranch. Pre-concert attendance had been estimated at around 200,000, but once the show was rolling no one doubted that the figure flirted with a half million.

It's said history doesn't really repeat, but comparisons to the phenomenon at Woodstock were inevitable. Despite the heavy media coverage, and the implicit suggestion that something unpleasant was inevitable, there were no incidents. Sure, there was plenty of nudity and sex, but violence and aggression, even political posturing, simply didn't have tickets to the show. It was a beautiful testament to the integrity and purpose of the massive concert. Mountain Rock was a small piece of history in the making. It was the kind of event of which, many years later, millions of people would claim to have been part.

The first signs of trouble appeared late Friday afternoon, when rumors of food shortages worked their way through the crowd like ripples in a still pond. Suppliers simply hadn't prepared for the size of the crowd. That, plus the large percentage of the audience who hadn't thought to provide for themselves, meant tens of thousands of people were growing hungry. All the sharing and goodwill in the world wasn't going to get everybody fed.

Tim Vernon was growing concerned. Going without food for a day or two wouldn't kill the concertgoers, but it might make them irritable and crazy and there might be trouble.

"How about organizing a food run?" Vernon asked Sammy Eisenglass when the two of them met in the office of the control-room trailer. The sun was westering near the horizon, ready to slide behind a range of low mountain peaks.

Sammy chuckled behind his ever-present mirror shades. "A 'food run'? Where to? The local grocery store or the corner Burger King?"

"Well, I—"

"Hey, Timmy-boy! We're talking about chow-time for half-a-mill! As my grandparents used to say: that ain't chopped liver!"

"I was just thinking that maybe we ought to do something." Vernon shook a Marlboro from a crumpled pack, lit it.

"Yeah, right," said Sammy, grinning. "Even if we organize a chopper lift or a convoy or something, who the fuck is gonna pay for it!?"

"Well," said Vernon, "maybe we could just ask people to donate their time, or their—"

"Or their helicopters?! Right, Timmy . . . sure!" Sammy laughed openly. "I mean, think about it—we're running a charity event, for Christ's sake, and we're gonna ask for more fuckin' charity to keep it from turning into the biggest food riot in history! That's ripe, man. That's really ripe."

Tim Vernon exhaled absently. "Well, what'll we do? You have any suggestions?"

Sammy smiled. "Sure I got one—forget about it! One day without croissants and zinfandel ain't gonna kill 'em."

"That's not all, though," Vernon continued, staring out the trailer window into the growing night. He liked the peacefulness of the desert at eventide; sharing it with a paramecium like Sammy Eisenglass scarred the experience like a diamond on glass. "I guess I saved the worst for last . . ."

"What? What else, for Christ's sake?"

"My wells are pushed to their limits, the Arkansas River's a little too far off to help, and the porta-pots are already full."

Sammy shrugged. "So . . ."

"So we're not talking about croissants and zinfandel anymore." A strong, clear, female voice cut through the small room.

Both men turned toward the office threshold, where Marion was standing. Neither of them had heard her enter, and her voice had plainly startled them. Looking at her, Tim Vernon visibly relaxed; Sammy tried to act like he hadn't been spooked at all. But she'd heard most of their conversation.

"Hey, look, pretty lady," said Sammy, "old Rancher Tim here didn't say we're outta water yet."

"Are we?" She looked at Vernon, noticing his graying beard and shoulder-length hair.

"Not yet, but it's just a matter of hours, I figure."

Marion stepped closer to the table. She could feel Sammy's fondling gaze behind his shades; he was such a slug, she didn't take much notice. "Mr. Vernon, why didn't you foresee this sooner?"

It was Vernon's turn to shrug. "We've been through some fair droughts out here, and the water's always been enough for us. I had no idea how many people would show up, and even less how much water they'd be using. Even so, my system's the best—I figured it could handle the demand. But it's been incredible, I can tell you that."

"What's the worst-case scenario?" she asked.

"If the water runs out by midnight? I figure by noon tomorrow, the climate being what it is, people should be getting pretty thirsty."

"Have you warned them to start conserving?"

"Sure. Every act's been telling 'em since early afternoon. Even so, I'm figuring the water to run out tonight—sooner without lots of conservation."

"Great. Just great. How dangerous is this?" Marion glared at Vernon and Eisenglass.

"Dangerous is a relative term," said Vernon, rubbing his beard pensively. "Some people won't be too bad off. Others could get uncomfortable pretty quick—especially the kids. Lotta people brought their kids—just like the hippies used to . . ."

"What about Peter?" asked Marion. "Does he have any suggestions?"

"I told him about everything right off," said Vernon, "but he don't seem too concerned. He said we'll find a way to take care of everything."

"Somebody's got to do something," Marion continued. "It's possible we can get some help from the National Guard or local authorities."

"The good ole 'local authorities,' " said Sammy, still smiling and leering. "I love the language of you journalists."

"It loves you too," said Marion, sarcastically. Then, to Tim Vernon: "Good luck, I'll check back with you in the morning. If anything happens tonight, call me at the hotel."

When Marion stepped out into the crisp, still, Colorado night, the deep blue of the sky comforted her like a familiar blanket. The air shimmered and shook from the waves of music resonating across the pasture land. Music, music, music. Its ghostly echoes would live on for a long time in the memories of the people who heard it—and the audio and video recordings.

Too exhausted to listen any more, Marion climbed into her RX-7 and drove back to the Clarion Hotel in Colorado Springs. She was tired but not sleepy. She needed some relaxation—maybe a drink.

She wondered about Peter. He loved music, and was no doubt still hanging out backstage, absorbing the whole experience like a dreamy kid in a magic shop. She wondered if he was aware of how critical the food and water problem might become, and more importantly, if there was anything he might be able to do to help.

When she got back to her room, her phone's message light was flashing. Punching the right keys patched her into the hotel's digital switchboard. There were the usual calls from various TV affiliates, the networks, Charles Branford, but the final one caught her completely off her guard: *Surprise! It's Daniel. I flew in around six. If you get back before it closes, I'll be in the bar.*

Daniel Ellington had stayed in St. Louis to continue managing the Foundation. What was he doing here?

Marion headed for the atrium bar, where a tired-looking woman in an evening dress played tired old songs on the baby grand. The bar area teemed with patrons; she didn't see Daniel in the crowd until he called her name above the general din.

He was seated at a low table by the window-wall, wearing a light gray suit and an executive's tie. An almost-empty bottle of Whitbread's Ale stood on the table beside a partially-filled pilsner glass. She'd never seen him out of his "religious fatigues," as he called his basic black outfits, and he looked handsome and stylish. Nobody would have nailed him as a priest.

"Dan, you look terrific," she said, slipping into the chair opposite him. "What in the world are you doing here?"

Dan smiled and shrugged. "Seemed like it would be a little more exciting than St. Louis. Never been to Colorado before, so I figured, why not? Besides, I wanted to see how Peter is doing with the big crowd."

Marion shrugged. "He seems okay. He's very caught up in the concert. So are Billy and Laureen."

"How's her pregnancy coming along?" Dan smiled sheepishly, looking very much like a little boy for a moment. She was a real sucker for that kind of look, a weakness that had gotten her in trouble all her life. "It seems like a while since I've seen anybody."

"Laureen's doing great. The last three weeks she's gotten much bigger, but she isn't having any trouble getting around." Marion shook her head. "I don't know much about babies or pregnant women, but I'd say she's right on schedule and doing well."

"Has she been to a doctor lately?"

Marion shook her head. "No. We've been so busy. Peter said she's fine, and Laureen trusts him more than she would a doctor, anyway."

"He's an obstetrician now, too?"

She shrugged. "No, but he says he gets these 'feelings,' you know?"

Daniel nodded. "Yes, and I'm starting to wonder what it all means."

A waitress materialized, asked if Marion wanted anything. After ordering a glass of the house wine, she looked back at Dan and found that he was obviously admiring her. The glow of several beers warmed his cheeks, and he smiled with an easy candor.

She wasn't in the mood to discuss theology. "Why didn't you go out to the concert site?"

"To tell you the truth," Dan said, "and I guess I'd have trouble saying this without a few drinks in me—I really came here because I missed you."

His words had less impact than he might have suspected.

Dan's attraction was something Marion had sensed some time before, something she'd chosen not to acknowledge. It had never become an issue.

Now what did she do?

She said, finally, "I know what you mean. I missed you too."

The waitress reappeared, set down a glass of wine, and once again slipped away into the crowd.

"You have?" Dan leaned forward, unable to hide his surprise.

"Well, the three of us had been together for so many months," she said. "This is the first time we've been apart."

Dan nodded. "Yeah, but that's not what I mean, Marion."

She sipped her wine, looked at him over the rim of the glass. "I know it's not . . ."

Dan leaned closer to her, sincerity building in his handsome features. "Marion, I don't know how to explain what I'm feeling. It's just that, well, I was back there, by myself, and I realized that I was thinking about you more and more. Every day."

Marion said nothing, just nodded when he paused.

". . . and then I realized: being away from you was driving me up the walls. I've really gotten used to being around you."

"Thank you, Dan," she said, wondering if that was an appropriate reply. He was pouring his heart out, and she had no idea how to handle it. She gulped her wine, wishing for a refill.

"That's not all," he said, then finished the last of his Whitbread's.

"I didn't think it would be," she said. She manufactured a fairly good imitation of a natural, comfortable smile, feeling even more nervous.

"I've never felt this way about a woman before," said Dan. He paused to clear his throat and signal the waitress for another round. "I don't even know if this is the way you're supposed to feel."

"Dan . . ." She wanted to tell him it was okay, that she understood what he was trying to say, but he pushed on.

"I know . . . I know what you're going to say, about me being a priest and all that, but I can't help it, Marion, I'm falling in love with you."

Without thinking, she reached out and took his hand. His grip tightened instantly. "Oh Dan, I don't know what to say, really."

He shook his head, tried to smile and did a bad job of it.

The waitress swooped in to replace their drinks, which both of them reached for as though parched. An almost palpable mist of awkwardness surrounded them.

"I don't even know what it's really like to fall in love with someone," he said. "All I know is what I've seen in movies and read in books."

"Falling in love is different for everyone, Dan."

"You're not upset, then?"

"Upset? No, I'm flattered. And more."

"More?" he said with some effort. "What do you mean?"

She squeezed his hand, which had started to tremble slightly. "Don't ever be ashamed of how you feel, Dan. Feelings aren't always things we can control. They're a basic part of us."

"I feel better letting this out. God, I can't believe how much better . . ." He sipped from his glass. "Marion, it was getting so bad, I couldn't stand to be alone in St. Louis. I made up my mind to get on the next plane, get as drunk as I could, and just tell you everything . . ."

She smiled, more genuinely this time. He had no idea how charming he could be, which was in turn, part of his charm.

". . . And you did it very well," she said.

"I did?"

"Definitely." Marion took a more moderate swallow from her glass. Her moment of desperation had passed. She felt calmer. There was a certain freedom between them now that Dan had aired his pent-up emotions. "In fact, Dan, I don't ever remember a man ever telling me such things in such a nice way."

"You're just saying that to make me feel good."

"No, I'm not. You can't imagine how refreshing it is to listen to a man talk without giving you a lot of the bullshit, without all the slyness, the innuendo."

"I . . . I don't know how to do that," he said, sounding like a little boy again.

"No, and thank God for that."

He held her hand tightly. "That's the other thing that's driving me crazy!" he whispered harshly. "My whole identity, my whole place in the world, is dissolving. I know I shouldn't feel like this, but . . ."

"But what?" she prompted him. "It's okay. Just let it out."

"A long time ago I took a vow of celibacy. That's not something you do easily—at least for me it wasn't. Sure, there were plenty of guys in the seminary and later, during our first teaching assignments, who didn't pay it much attention, but dammit, I always did."

Marion could only nod as he rushed to get out what he was feeling and thinking.

"I was taught if you're going to do something worthwhile, you've got to do it right, or don't do it at all. You know what I mean?" He let go of her fingers, nervously rubbed his lower lip with the back of his hand.

"Of course, Dan." The wine coursed through her like a river breaking up at its delta. The blond, muscular man across from her was looking better and better to her.

"Well, I've pretty much always believed I've done the right thing. I've never regretted going into the priesthood, for instance." He paused, finished off his glass of ale. "Being a Jesuit has been a tremendous experience for me. But—"

"But being a man has not, right?" She wanted to reach across the table to take his hand again, but she resisted. Even though she found him ever more desirable, she knew she couldn't let anything happen between them. One priest in any woman's lifetime was enough.

He stared into her eyes, said nothing.

Silence—and a bond—grew between them. Daniel was such a sweet, innocent, loving man. Marion wanted him as much as she'd ever wanted any man before Peter, but some sense of essential wrongness allowed her to remain in control.

"Marion," Dan said finally, a touch of desperation coloring his words. "What are we going to do?"

She smiled, squeezed his hand, withdrew her own. "We learn to live with it, deal with it."

Just then, the waitress appeared, hesitated as though she sensed she was interrupting an important conversation, then said, "Excuse me, folks, but we're getting ready to close up."

Looking around the bar, Marion realized that the piano music had stopped and the patrons had all vanished.

"I'm sorry. We were so busy talking, we hadn't noticed."

"That's okay," said the waitress as she offered them their check.

Marion nodded, signed off on her room number. Standing up, she smiled perfunctorily. "Daniel, I think we'll have to finish this later."

"Marion," he said quickly, as he rose to follow her, "I'm sorry if I've said anything to offend you."

"Daniel, don't apologize. It's okay," she said in a firm whisper.

"I've . . . I've got to get all this worked out, Marion. Don't leave me hanging out to dry like this . . ." He looked uncomfortably around the hotel lobby.

"Daniel, it's pretty late."

"But—"

"But you still need to talk," she said.

Anger and despair mixed in his voice. "Think about it: I've flown halfway across the country, drunk too much, and bared my soul for what I can tell is a lost cause—Marion, I don't know what to do next and I'm scared as hell!"

The image of the little boy lost overwhelmed her. She couldn't just cut him loose.

"All right," she said. "Come on, we can talk in my room."

That seemed to stun him a bit, but he walked silently with her to the elevators and joined her in the car with another couple. He said nothing until she stopped at her room and searched her purse for her key.

"Marion, I don't think—"

Pausing, she looked straight at him. "Dan, I'm tired. I want

to go to sleep, but I can't get through the night without helping you, without listening until you get used to the feelings
you've let out of their boxes."

She unlocked the door and entered the suite. He moved to
the bar and fixed a bourbon and soda, then started talking.

It was impossible for her to listen silently to his ramblings,
but she knew he had to say everything, once and for all. A
few times she interjected opinions or observations, but mainly
she let him roll on. Gradually, as he grew more comfortable
with knowing that they would not consummate any shared
feelings or desires, and that it was all right to bare your feelings to someone you could trust, he grew less panicked, less
terrified.

Finally, he paused to make yet another drink, and she used
the chance to call it a night.

"Dan, I think it's getting too late for much more. I'm exhausted."

"Really?" He sounded surprised and not the least bit tired.
So much for jet lag.

"Plus it just occurred to me that maybe we wouldn't want
anyone to find us like this."

Dan sat down beside her on the couch, glanced at the digital clock on the end table and its 2:33 AM message. "It's so
late," he said. "Who would bother us now?"

Before she could answer him, the door swung open slowly,
silently, to reveal the lean, rigid silhouette of Peter Carenza.

"How about me . . . ?" he said softly.

THIRTY-NINE

Colorado Springs, Colorado—Carenza
October 24, 1999

Marion jumped from the bed, oddly holding her hand in front of her face.

"Peter! What are you doing here?" There was the merest suggestion of distress in her voice.

"Well, speak of the Devil, eh?" Daniel Ellington looked up at Peter with a foggy smile.

Peter's first reaction, when he'd approached the room and heard their voices within, had been rage. He'd entered, wanting to confront them while the sweet, hot rush of blazing hate and anger novaed within him.

But seeing the two of them fully clothed had defused him. And that reaction bothered him, then angered him again. Had he *wanted* to find them in bed? Confusion spiraled through his thoughts, sending off sparks of doubt which did nothing to soothe his rancor.

He raised his right hand, pointed at her, then him. The unconscious power, the taproot of force that ran deep into the core of his being tingled, then throbbed. A few months earlier, he wouldn't have recognized it, wouldn't have been able to harness it, rein it in, and opt to use or not use it. His hand trembled; the fury that quaked in his mind begged for release, *screamed* for an instant of the purest wrath. Like a trigger straining against the invisible fulcrum beyond which it would trip, his will battled itself.

Daniel looked into his eyes, past the finger that pointed

steadily at the center of his chest. Clearly, Ellington instantly recognized the conflict taking place in the core of his friend's soul.

"I could kill you," said Peter. "Both of you . . ." His words tumbled into the dim abyss of the room, their echo leaving a chill in the memories of the listeners.

Shakily, Daniel stood. He weaved slightly and his eyes had trouble focusing. He raised one arm in a parody of Peter's biblical pose and pointed at Peter. He looked silly, and Peter wondered if his own stance appeared as laughable.

"Yeah right, pal!" Daniel said in a loud, slurred voice. "You're gonna kill us—for what? Since when is having a conversation against divine law?"

"Peter," said Marion quickly. "What's the matter with you? Can't you see that there's nothing going on here?"

He realized she was speaking the truth and started to lower his arm. The anger that boiled in him had begun to subside when Daniel spoke again.

"Just a Goddamned second!" He lurched forward, still pointing absurdly at Peter. "What business is it of yours anyway—if there *was* anything going on? God or no God, you don't own either of us!"

"We've had this discussion before, Daniel," said Peter, trying to stay calm.

"Yeah, right. Free will and all that jazz." Daniel spoke in clipped, half-drunk tones flecked with disdain. "Does God run everything on puppet strings—including me and *you*—or do we really make our own choices, in life and love? Who runs the world?"

"That's enough," Peter said. It was all clear to him, suddenly. Daniel was betraying him, plain and simple. He was cutting himself loose from Peter's authority, betraying the trust they'd built up. In one thing Daniel was right—his relationship with Marion, whatever it was, did not matter. It was the *turning away* from Peter which he could not be allowed to do.

" 'Enough'? Oh, has my Lord spoken? Can you command

me whenever you want?" Daniel laughed. "Last time I checked that was bullshit—and you know it as well as I."

Daniel was dismissing him. *Him.*

Dismissal.

Betrayal.

The same thing.

He looked at his friend and his former rage flared into life.

"Maybe you should have checked more recently . . ." he said through semi-clenched teeth.

"Dan, Peter . . . please!" Marion's voice had trembled up at least one notch.

Dan lumbered forward, an uncharacteristic, arrogant snarl on his face, raised arm still pointing at Peter, whose own arm had dropped to his side, fist clenched. Dan's face flushed as he unleashed his own anger.

"I don't know what's happening to you, Peter, but it's not pretty. Just who the *fuck* do you think you are?"

"That's enough, Dan." Peter stood his ground as Dan moved close enough to touch him. He could feel his friend's hot breath as Dan half-screamed his words.

"You don't *own* us, Peter! Do you understand that?"

"Dan! Peter!" Marion's voice seemed to be coming to him from a great distance. All his senses and his emotions were honed to a fine focus on Daniel Ellington.

Rage capered across Peter's mind, doing a war-dance on his reason, and he began to see Dan as an adversary, an enemy. Dan's pale, florid face, puffing and glaring in anger, seemed to pulse like a beacon that propelled Peter to a darker level of hate.

"Dan. Do yourself a favor: get away from me. Right now." He bit off each word.

"No, Peter! Do your*self* a favor and *you* get out of here. Nobody asked you to come waltzing in here in the middle of the damn night, anyway!" He shoved Peter with his outstretched hand.

Peter stumbled backward from the contact. For an instant, he had the strange sensation of falling *forward*, as though being sucked into a maelstrom. To quell the sensation, he hardened his gaze upon Daniel, who loomed over him, clenching and unclenching his fists.

Peter reached out to him, but not with a real, physical hand. Just as an amputee might feel myriad sensations in a severed limb, so did Peter feel power and strength in an invisible, psychically empowered hand that stretched out toward Daniel. The light in the room dimmed as though slowed in its flight and the sound of Marion's and Dan's voices distorted into a basso moan. Peter sucked in a desperate breath. With his invisible hand he reached up and *into* Dan's chest. A cold shock spiked through him as his fingers touched the hot, greasy knot of Dan's heart, pulsing like a piece of wet and slippery machinery.

He could *feel* Dan's heart.

From that first instant of recognition, he stopped thinking about what he was doing. Instead of pushing Dan away from him, it was so much easier to simply *squeeze*, to feel the obscene throbbing lump of his heart go berserk under the sudden pressure, to feel the valves chudder insanely into frantic dysrhythmia.

Daniel Ellington staggered back, his face twisted abruptly into a snarl of torment. He screamed and dropped to his knees. His eyes bulged in their sockets as though air was being pumped into his head and he clutched at his chest, his arm like the spastic flipper of a skull-clubbed seal.

Peter leaned forward and squeezed harder.

Daniel's scream dribbled away until it was nothing more than a pitiful mewling sound. He wrenched about on one knee and reached out to Marion with a stiff, palsied arm. He held the stance for an instant until his eyes rolled deep into his skull and he collapsed to the floor.

The sensation of the invisible arm vanished; even the memory of it seemed less than nothing.

For an immeasurable instant, there was no sound, no movement. The tableau of Marion standing above the twisted corpse of Daniel Ellington burned in Peter's mind like a sepia photograph ready to burst into flame.

The spell was broken by the low-pitched keening sound

which escaped from Marion like the air from a dying balloon. It was a sound of shock and mourning. She dropped down beside Daniel, touched his stilled form, and began to cry. "Help him! Peter, help him! Do something!"

"I can't," he said.

She looked at him and seemed to know he spoke the truth. "Daniel, ohmiGod, Daniel! Daniel ..." She whispered his name, her body rocking back and forth over Daniel's still form. She looked like Peter's idea of a mythic Irish sin-eater preparing to do her dirty job.

Stepping away, Peter realized that he felt *nothing*.

That place within himself where his emotions normally churned was strangely dark and empty. The coldness seeping into him terrified him. He waited expectantly, for what he assumed would be a vile bilge-like wash of remorse and dread.

But he felt nothing ...

After what seemed an eternity Marion looked up at him. "Call for help! Hurry!"

He moved to the phone as though in a trance, dialed the desk and asked for emergency medical assistance. Turning, he looked at Marion with a blank expression.

"Did you do this?" she asked in clipped tones. "Did you kill him, Peter?"

"He must have had a heart attack. He got too excited, too crazy. I can't be held responsible."

"I can't believe this ... I can't believe this." Marion continued to slowly rock back and forth. Peter watched her, all the while searching for his true feelings and marveling at the total *absence* within him.

Had he really killed his best friend? Was it possible he could kill someone so easily?

No, that was absurd. Impossible. The delusion that he'd had ... an invisible, killing arm ...

No.

A ragged knocking at the door chopped off the thought. Peter looked at his watch—ten minutes gone, lost in the aftershock of the event. He opened the door and the paramedic team burst past him, homing in on Daniel's crumpled form.

Without another word, Peter slipped out of the room and down the long hallway to the lobby. The hotel corridor was as quiet and still as Daniel's heart. Even the sound of Peter's footsteps were absorbed in the thick pile of the carpet.

The solitary night clerk at the Clarion's registration desk recognized him immediately and flashed him a surprised but nonetheless solicitous smile.

"Father Peter . . . Is everything all right?"

"Actually, no," he said softly.

"What else can we do to help?"

"Could you please call the trailer at the Vernon Ranch? Have them send the helicopter."

"*Now*, Father? You want the 'copter right now?"

"Yes," he said. "I have to take a little trip. Tell them I'll be on the roof."

Angling down toward the scrubland like a hungry, broken-winged insect, the chopper skipped over the rough terrain of southwestern Colorado. They'd been flying through the purple night, the rising sun chasing their tail rotor, for more than a hour. Peter sat next to the pilot, absorbing the cool, dark turbulence of the flight. He sat back, eyes half closed, allowing his senses and his proximity awareness to merge with the metal body of the aircraft, so that he might encompass the miracle of flying even more completely. The sensation was exhilarating, but more importantly, it kept his mind free of thought.

There would be plenty of time for thinking.

"That was Dove Creek back there," said the pilot, who, now that he was fully awake, could not resist throwing in bits of tour-guide trivia. Like most Colorado natives, he loved his state.

Peter nodded but said nothing.

"Zane Grey used to live there!" the pilot yelled over the syncopated drone of the rotors. "That's where he wrote *Riders of the Purple Sage*."

Peter nodded again, looked down at the terrain that passed

beneath them—an endless puzzle of ravines and basins, buttes and jagged ridges.

"How much farther did'ja wanna go, Father?"

Peter exhaled slowly. "Get me to some desert. I want to see the desert at sunrise."

The pilot shook his head. "Desert? What for?"

"I've never done it before."

The pilot shrugged and yelled above the engine noise. "You know you're payin' me triple-overtime for this middle-a-the-night flyin', don't you?!"

"Just worry about the desert," said Peter. "I'll worry about the money."

"You're the boss, Father!" The pilot leaned on the stick, pulling the chopper into a left turn that yanked it almost due south.

"Any suggestions?" asked Peter.

"Tuba City's about another half-hour to the southwest. That'n Echo Cliffs. From there you can see the Painted Desert and Marble Canyon."

Peter nodded and the pilot chunked the throttle all the way up. The Bell Sky-Breaker jumped up to top speed and Peter settled back in his seat.

He watched the 'copter lift up, hover for a moment like a curious mosquito, then dart upward and tilt toward the north. The pilot had tried to argue against leaving him on the desolate ridge east of Echo Cliffs. Though Peter had instructed him to return in six hours, before the sun grew too brutal, the pilot had forced him to take a canteen full of water.

Down the sloping terrain to the south, the ghostly, moonlit sea of the Painted Desert seemed to beckon to him. To the east, the peaks of the distant Chuska Mountains had already begun to glow with the first fragments of the new day. The western night sky was still a deep, bottomless blue, but that would be changing soon. Peter looked around him, satisfied that he was utterly alone—the first time in a long time that no one was within striking distance of him. No highways, no cars, no lights or other distractions. Nothing to violate the utter quiet of the desert. Not even the chirping of an insect or rustle of a foraging lizard. The solitude cleared his mind like a breath of cold air.

Just who in the world *was* Peter Carenza anymore? As he replayed the scene in the hotel room, he realized how ludicrous it would seem to other clerics. There he was—a priest, enraged, and ready to kill his best friend—also a priest—for wanting to have sex with his ... his what? His lover? His girlfriend? His *whore*?

Did he have any more right to her than Daniel? He smiled ironically. Priests don't have lovers or girlfriends.

So maybe he wasn't much of a priest any longer ... ?

But why? Because he'd grown too powerful for such a simple office?

Part of him didn't care. He didn't need any of them, did he? He didn't need a damned thing. He could do whatever he wanted, so where would all this soul-searching eventually get him? What good was it?

He smiled ironically, bittersweetly, although not really amused that he could think so harshly. And what about Daniel? Had he actually felt Daniel's heart beating in an invisible hand? Or was it the illusion his unconscious insisted it must be? Guilt washed over him like dirty rain. He shivered as though from a fever, looked up into the boundless night. Sometimes, when he was free of all distractions, of all the clamor and attention that surged around him, he could almost feel the changes churning within his soul. He could actually sense the coming together of new elements, new aspects to his very nature.

Sometimes the feeling was exhilarating; and sometimes utterly terrifying.

What was happening to him? A year ago, he was just a simple man, happy in his small simple life. Now the parish, and the people, of Saint Sebastian seemed lifetimes distant.

He had no idea what lay ahead for him, but he knew one thing: he would never return to Saint Sebastian's.

Time lost its trip on him as he stared into the magic window of the universe. Soon his thoughts melted into one another and he sat in a state of quiet reverie. He felt as if he could sit there forever.

Sunrise flooded across the basins and the desert with alarming quickness. Almost instantly, distant rock formations began to shimmer and waver behind thick lenses of heated air. Peter faced the south and stared at a distant point along the edge of the Painted Desert—a black speck that seemed insignificantly small yet which drew his gaze irresistibly.

He had needed to get away. Away from all of them. This time alone would cleanse him, purge him of the stress from their demands, their expectations . . .

The black speck seemed larger.

Peter imagined it was growing closer—closer, but no more distinct. There was something about the object, whatever it was, that kept demanding his attention. It was definitely *moving*, floating just above the rocky terrain. Each time he glanced at it, the thing seemed closer.

But it had no recognizable shape. It seemed amorphous, mutable, like smoke or mist though Peter somehow knew it was actually some kind of solid. At first he'd thought it might be a piece of sagebrush or half-burned tumbleweed, but it was now obviously something far more strange than that.

The desert panorama faded away, losing its pigments and composition like watercolors being bled from a page. Peter could concentrate on nothing other than the darkness, and he began to feel the first windowpane, taps of apprehension. Whatever was gliding smokily across the desert floor was directed squarely at him.

Despite the dry heat, he felt coldness surround him like a Kirlian aura. If the absence of color is blackness, then the cloak that enwrapped the approaching object was indeed black. But as Peter eyed it intently, he felt the thing was *darker* than mere black.

He was beginning to be afraid.

Closer now, and the object finally began to assume some semblance of a configuration. Roundish, or perhaps ellipsoid, it appeared to have delicately interleaved folds or layers, like the fissures in a brain or the petals of a flower. It seemed as though the more directly he stared into its mass, the less distinct it appeared, but when he only glanced at it from the periphery, it assumed hard, crisp edges. The impression that it was a sentient, intelligent entity came to him in an overwhelming instant like an open palm smacking him in the face.

There was no longer any doubt the thing was homing in upon him. A flash of complete irrationality capered through him—he wanted to start running, to never look back.

But he held his position and waited. He stared into the black depths and realized he was not staring at *something* as much as its *absence*. Looking into the object was like looking into a hole in reality. The shapes, folds, and furrows, the suggestions of things moving within the blackness created a sensation in him of the purest loathing, but he continued to stare.

Such good works you have done, Father Peter . . .

The words touched his mind—there was no other way to describe the experience. The coldness no longer just surrounded him; it was seeping into his pores.

"What are you?"

You know what I am, who I am . . .

He stared into the center of the *absence* and concentrated, trying to make sense of the chaos that swirled at the heart of the darkness. Part of him responded to the thing before him in ways he did not like. There was a certain beauty, a *correctness*, about its asymmetry.

And he *did* know to what, or whom, he spoke . . .

"What do you want with me?"

That should be obvious.

"I'm not sure it is." Peter tried to look away from the thing that hung motionless before him. A visual intoxicant, it was dangerous, yet infinitely appealing.

Peter, don't fuck with me . . .

"What?"

Play semantic and philosophical games with others. Please, Peter, don't insult me. You've turned the corner. I just thought I'd tell you, boy: you're mine now . . .

A chill raced through him as the words touched the center of his being. For the first time in his life, Peter believed he felt true fear.

"Nobody owns me," he said, staring hypnotically into the center of the darkness.

He felt the sensation of laughter rather than the actual sound.

Perhaps you're right. It could be that I've been presumptuous.

Yes. You've made me realize the truth in that. Besides there is no fun in merely taking *you, Peter.*

"Better if I joined you willingly, eh?"

More feelings of laughter.

Infinitely so. You see, like that other great mythical figure—Saint Nick—I was watching and listening when you killed Daniel.

"I didn't kill him."

Liar, liar. Catch on fire.

More laughter.

"I didn't kill him—he had a heart attack."

You really believe that, don't you? You stand here before me, staring into the Abyss, and you don't remember what happened.

"I remember thinking I could feel his heart pumping crazy, like it was going to break out of his chest."

Laughter.

Then: *Oh, you could "feel" it, all right.*

"He was my best friend . . ."

And you thought he might be turning away from you. Forgetting to be properly awed. Oh, and let's not forget—he might be fucking your woman, too. How utterly human *of you.*

Peter felt a pang of guilt, a deep sense of regret. With Daniel dead, his concerns about infidelity seemed pale. What difference did it make if Marion and Daniel had made love? It was merely a meeting of two bodies—brief, ultimately harmless. How and why had so many cultures turned such a simple thing into something so cataclysmic?

You're going to need me.

Its insistent voice invaded his thoughts like a not-so-subtle virus.

"I don't need you."

You're going to need more power, and I can give it to you.

"At what price?"

No reply came, but in its stead, Peter was abruptly stunned by a sensation he'd never experienced before. The perception overwhelmed him, threatened to absorb him totally. He could not describe it as other than an undifferentiated impression of human suffering, of pain and death on an unimaginable, global scale. Like an impossible weight, an unfathomable darkness, the sensation tried to engulf him. Peter backed away from the Presence before him, gathered his consciousness about him like a cloak. Shielding himself, he shrugged off the sum total of all human pain. The thought of enduring anything close to that again laced him with cold, damp terror.

That's coming for you, Peter. It's going to get you. You're not strong enough on your own. You can't create anything, and in order to overcome what you just felt, you will need more power. You can be a Creator. You can have that power. And with the power of creation comes the rest of the world. Your thoughts of Marion and her delicate flesh, flesh which will eventually wither and die, will be as those of a child. With the new power, you will have dominion . . . over all.

Peter smiled. "Is this where I'm supposed to tell you to get behind me?"

You can do whatever you want . . . That's the beauty of it, Peter. It's your show. From here on out—just say the word, and you can make it happen.

"Fuck you. I don't need you. I'm in control."

Brave words. You have the ego to do well at this business. I like that.

"Do your stuff, or get out of here. You bore me," said Peter.

Laughter. Unheard, but *felt.*

I'll show you who I am, and if you can deny me or my na-

ture after seeing the truth, I will leave you forever. No titanic struggle, no metaphysical bullshit. Okay?

"Do your worst."

Just to be theatrical, I think I'll preface this with a nice BE-HOLD!

He stared into the center of the Absence which roiled before him, eating a hole in the hot desert air. It was a spinning galactic cluster of all that could ever be, ever was. The spinning center became the All, the heartbeat of the Universe. Antipodal forces flowed and ebbed like dark tides of fear and elation, love and loathing, pride and humility, hope and desperation, dream and nightmare, sainthood and depravity, and every other emotional bolt ever struck in the stormcenter of human passage. The cluster spun wildly, a vortex that pulled him in. Within its dark center, he could see the folds and petals of the blackest rose, the blossom unfolding in a new and terrible heat. Suddenly he saw a face within the folds of nothingness, and the face was his own.

No war raged within or without. Peter knew what he faced and he accepted the anthracite truth of it.

And so it is . . . said Its voice as It began dopplering away from him like the whistle of a passing train. He listened to Its departure like a sad lover at a midnight station, a last-chance depot of the soul.

The Absence contracted, receded, collapsing into itself. Watching it disappear, Peter had the impression that it was also racing away from him, red-shifting through the spectrum to the vanishing point.

A brief burst of intuition told him that It was taking something from him, something precious and irreplaceable.

He found himself staring idly at a black speck in the mirage-shrouded distance, beyond which the desert loomed like the scape of an alien moon.

The sound of an approaching engine cracked the eggshell silence that surrounded him. Turning, he saw the helicopter approach, canting through a wide, arcing turn. It dipped down to alight testily on the rough terrain. As the rotors whoomped down, Larry Melmanik climbed out, started walking toward him.

A whirlpool of conflicting emotions churned in Peter's soul. Memories of Daniel and his ugly death suddenly surfaced in his mind. Peter still didn't know how he should feel, what he should do.

Maybe he never would.

Whatever he'd been doing before the 'copter arrived now eluded him. A chunk of time and memory—*gone*. The notion gave him a chill. He looked up and tried to shake it off as his manager approached.

Wearing a blue oxford shirt and a pair of tan slacks, Larry looked as casual as he would ever allow himself. Tim Vernon remained in the 'copter's cabin with the pilot, watching.

"Wasn't sure where to find you in all the confusion," said Larry.

"Until you checked with the front desk."

"Right. But I gotta tell you I was a little surprised you called in the Air Force."

"Haven't you ever needed some time by yourself, Larry?"

"Sure, I understand," said Melmanik, waving off the question with an impatient gesture that revealed he didn't understand at all.

"So, you're here," said Peter. "You must want something."

"I talked to Marion. She had no idea where you were. Between Daniel's dying and you disappearing, she was half-crazy."

The mention of Marion's name left him oddly cold. "I'm okay, I guess." He wondered what Vernon and Melmanik were doing out here. And what had Marion told them of Daniel's death?

Larry sat down on a rock beside him; touched him gently on the back. "Peter, I know this is going to sound funny, but at this point, we don't know what else to do . . ."

"What're you talking about?"

"The water's run out, and the food's gone."

"Just like you figured," said Peter.

"Well, with that many people out there, the law of averages

says you're going to have problems, and we're getting them. Eisenglass isn't going to help, and the National Guard isn't crazy about the idea either. We've contacted the governor, but it'll take time to get a decision."

"Why are you telling me all this?"

Larry picked up a pebble, tossed it over the ridge. "I don't know. Everybody suggested you. Maybe you can at least get up there and talk to the crowd. They'll listen to you. Maybe you can keep them occupied until we can get some provisions, some water."

"What about the music?"

Larry looked at him with sincerity. "I think they need more than that right now, Peter."

Frankly, he wasn't in the mood to do anything for anybody right now. He was steeped in the business of learning more about the dynamics of his own soul. He wanted some time to be selfishly introspective, but he had this altruistic, sacrificing reputation, and there was no place for him to turn.

Maybe it would always be like this. Maybe there never would be a time or a place for him to be weak, or to need, or to be comforted.

He picked up a stone, tossed it in the direction where the black speck had first appeared, then stood up.

"Okay, let's go." Peter drew in a deep breath, exhaled. The air was warm but dry and scented with unrecognizable blossoms. "I can't promise anything, though."

Larry nodded. "No problem. At this point, anything's better than nothing, right?"

Peter shrugged. "We'll see."

He climbed into the back seat of the chopper, trying desperately to remember . . .

FORTY

Colorado Springs, Colorado—Windsor
October 24, 1999

She had been standing offstage with two of the guitarists from Your Member when Peter arrived with Larry Melmanik and Tim Vernon. Sunrise had kissed the pasture more than an hour ago, and Daniel Ellington's body was probably just getting cold. She couldn't believe he was really dead. She felt numb, dead herself.

Dan dead? Don't be ridiculous.

And Peter storming off in a Goddamned helicopter. It was like they'd left her to clean up their messes and she wasn't sure she could handle it. It was hard to imagine Peter being so . . . so what? Jealous? Angry? Crazy? She wasn't sure what had gotten into him, but his reaction to finding her with Dan had been way out of line. But then, so had Dan's reaction—although she had a hard time accepting his rage as the cause of his heart attack. She kept replaying those few traumatic minutes in her head until she thought it was making her a little crazy. She had to distract herself.

Even though she wasn't sure what Peter was thinking, she'd wanted to be near him for solace. But he was gone, vanished into the night. She'd thought then of the concert, the musicians she'd met and welcomed the distraction they offered. She'd headed back to the ranch.

Things hadn't turned ugly for the half-million-plus crowd, but such incidents were unpredictable. No food, water, or sanitation was going to make its mark eventually—but

Eisenglass and the others had been afraid to try to shut down early. The rock and the hard place. The music continued, but there was an edge to the performances, a barely hidden apprehension that something was going to happen—good or bad, nobody knew.

"Here comes the Main Man now," said Sammy Eisenglass, seemingly oozing up from the backstage shadows. He brushed very close to her, making sure he came in contact with her breasts, then moved to the landing where Peter had just ascended.

"They're waiting for you," yelled Sammy above the high-decibel level of the music.

Peter nodded, forced a smile. His normally placid, seamless features had traces of fault lines, the gray pallor of stress. He looked directly at Marion and the smile somehow became more genuine. Was he trying to tell her everything was going to be okay?

"Peter . . ." she said, forcing herself to not reach out and grab him.

"Not now," he said softly. "My people need me."

She said nothing but her expression must have held him for a moment.

"Later, Marion . . . I promise."

He sounded sincere and his eyes didn't betray him. Marion felt instantly better. She resented that he had so much power over her, but then, he had great influence over everybody, didn't he? *My people*, he'd said. For some reason, the phrase didn't agree with her. There was something odd about the way Peter said it, something not right.

Peter stood in the wings of the stage, hidden behind a two-story stacked array of speakers, until Oracle finished their song. Sammy Eisenglass fidgeted and twitched alongside him until the final chords and less-then-enthusiastic applause faded away. Then he ran out onstage with a remote mike and screamed at the crowd: "Heyyyyyy! Evree . . . bodddeeee! Here's the guy who can make it all behhhhderrrrrr . . . Father Peeeeederrrrr!"

Peter approached the center of the stage, holding his own

remote mike, as the applause gradually grew stronger, more responsive. Despite the stress and the gradual dehydration, the crowd slowly came to their feet and started calling his name. Eventually the cacophonous calls gathered force and synchronization, and soon the entire pasture thundered with a single, giant voice.

"Help us!" They cried. "Help Us! *Help Us!* help Us! HELLP-USS-HELLP-USS-HELLP-USS-HELLP-USS . . ."

The sound became a meaningless chant rolling over him like words from an alien tongue, like the mindless symphony of a million locusts. He held his hands outstretched, gesturing for them to let him speak. For a moment they ignored him, as though to emphasize how much they needed him, and then suddenly, they stopped. The pasture shuddered once from the sudden implosion of silence. Marion could feel the intensity of the crowd's focused attention.

"Okay," said Billy, as he moved up beside her to watch. "Now we're gonna see the power of the Lord at work."

Marion smiled at him, but he did not take his eyes off Peter. Billy's faith in Peter was a beautiful thing, and she wished she could still share such enthusiasm. Now, she could not escape the feeling that things were somehow getting skewed.

"First, I want to apologize for waiting so long to speak to you," he said. "Believe it or not, I've had a few problems of my own."

For a moment Marion wondered if he was going to tell them about Daniel. Then Peter continued, "But compared to yours, they are nothing.

"We need water *now*, my friends. Our host, Mr. Vernon, tells us his water system can't function because Fountain Creek is running low—mainly because of the strain our needs have placed on it.

"But we must do something before anyone starts getting sick. Evacuating, even if we begin immediately, will take some time, and panic or fighting isn't going to make it any easier—I think you all know that."

Isolated voices cried out for help, pleading on behalf of

friends and family. Their words drifted up to the stage on broken butterfly wings. Marion sensed desperation festering in the crowd; they were starting to give off the first traces of the stench of the loss of faith.

"With the Creator's help, we can help ourselves. That has been my message to you for many months, and now we have the chance to prove it, to make it work."

In the wings, Sammy moved close to Marion. "What's happening, honey? What's he gonna do?"

"Sammy, be quiet, okay?"

"Because we can make anything happen in our lives if we really want it bad enough," said Peter. He was standing still, facing the immense ocean of flesh. No posturing or pacing. No dramatics or body language, just some straight talk. Marion wondered if it would be enough.

"All right, my friends, let's get started," continued Peter. Join hands with the people next to you. It might be difficult if you're holding children, but I want everybody to do their best. I want us all *connected*. I want us all to be part of a much larger thing." He clasped his own hands and waited.

"Are we all connected?" he asked.

"Yes," said the crowd, grunting like a tired beast.

"Good. Now I want everyone to close their eyes. I want everyone to think of a river. A raging river, full of white-capped spray and sun-splashed pools. I want you all to imagine that this river is deep. And clear. And cold.

"Can you see it?"

Again the huge mass grunted its assent. The sound, almost frightening to Marion, sounded like some massive, monstrous creature. She looked out at the crowd; their eyes were closed, they all held one another, swaying ever so slightly to some metaphysical rhythm. She was stunned by the sight, by the knowledge that he had such power over them.

"This river is rushing toward us now," Peter continued, his voice a seductive, electronically-modulated whisper. "It is coming together in our lives because it is coming together in our minds. And our minds are thinking as one mind. We share that single image, that single need. Do you feel it?"

"Yesssss," hissed the beast.

"Bring the river to us," said Peter as he raised his arms toward the crowd. "Bring it down from the icy mountaintops. Bring the cold clear river to the banks of the ranch. Bring It Down!"

He paused and the entire crowd-mass seemed to lean forward and then catch itself as though it had been using his words for support. Marion watched as though through an insulated glass bubble. Whatever he was doing to them had not affected her. She felt oddly disconnected from what she knew was a powerful phenomenon that raged about her. Was he doing it consciously? Purposely excluding her from the experience? Punishing her?

No. She was certain it was nothing like that. Maybe she'd gotten so close to him, so intimate with him, that she had become immune to his influence. It was a startling thought.

"Do you feel it coming?" he whispered across the grazing land. The phalanx of speakers gave his hushed voice soft power. And then gradually growing in volume and resonance, he shouted: "Bring it down ... bring it down ... BRING IT DOWN! *BRING DOWN THE RIVER NOW!*"

The air above the pasture seemed to buckle and snap. In the far distance, beyond the peaks of the mountains, a rolling clap of thunder split the sky, shuddered the earth. Looking up, Marion could see nothing but the deep blue, largely indifferent sky. But she could feel a change in the air. Oh yes. Definitely a change.

She sensed a great roaring going on just beyond the range of human hearing. Like the air surrounding columns of high-voltage power lines, the atmosphere felt poised, waiting ...

But for *what*?

The crowd swayed and rippled, still moving as one single being. Joined physically, and probably in some way mentally, like a gigantic hive, the audience slouched closer to its critical mass. The sky lowered and darkened; flashes of heat lightning capered across the horizon. A windstorm rose as if out of the cracks in the earth.

Marion felt the stage begin to tremble. The tiny, febrile vibrations felt at first like the beats of a million, embryonic hearts, in perfect synch with itself.

And then she could hear it.

"Jesus Christ ... what's that?" Sammy Eisenglass moved past her, along with several musicians and stagehands. They were looking north, toward the foothills beyond the river basin.

The faint drum roll of faraway thunder gave way to the approaching gallop of a million horses, the roar of incoming missiles, the descent of a comet through a hole in the air. The sound rose up in an instant, as if with the flick of a wrist, someone had turned up the gain on an amplifier. The superstructure of the stage shuddered violently as the earth slipped and bucked beneath it. The Arkansas River rose up like an awakened, maddened beast. The noise of its escape was the loudest sound she'd ever heard, and the vibrations from its passing threatened to shake everything into powder. The skyscraper-like towers of speakers on each side of the stage fragmented like toy building blocks, falling in upon themselves, sparking and flashing as wire harnesses ruptured and power lines crackled.

Peter moved back from the edge of the stage; the crowd reeled back to escape the lethal collapse. The spell broken, the thousands of people began moving in different directions.

The river's thunderous arrival created a back-pressure in the tributaries and irrigation canals, which suddenly erupted in cold, wet roostertails and geysers. In an instant the entire pasture sparkled under the spray and patter of artificial rain. People began dancing, sending up a cascade of cheers which covered the sound of the river like a blanket.

Marion held onto a piece of scaffolding, unable to stop watching the spectacle. Slowly Peter walked to the edge of the stage again, treading carefully amidst the electronic rubble, raising his hands high. The crowd loved him, screamed his name. Smiling, glowing in the fierce blast of their approval, Peter suddenly turned and stared directly at Marion, as though the maneuver had been rehearsed. The intensity of his eyes, his tight-lipped smile, seemed somehow threatening.

As though he were sending her a special message: Don't cross me. I can do anything.

Maybe she had stopped standing in awe of his "miracles," but what she had just seen defied explanation or belief. There was no belief, only acceptance. A half-million people needed water and he brought them a river.

Incredible.

She wondered if, by luck, anyone had gotten it on tape, and shaken though she was, physically and emotionally, her professional side edged to the fore. Mentally, she began composing the story she would give the networks tonight. It would be a stunner.

"I told you! I told you!" shouted Billy, beaming like a proud father.

"Jesus Christ! Jesus Christ . . . ! Didja see that?" cried Sammy as he ran past her toward Peter, who still stood facing the crowd. Everyone followed Sammy's lead; in an eye-flash, musicians, roadies, stagehands and techs were all running. They surrounded Peter and lifted him up on their shoulders like a quarterback after the Big Game. Peter welcomed it, gloried in it.

She watched him being buoyed about the stage by the crowd, his dark hair falling over his forehead, his even darker eyes burning with the glow of victory. The word charisma had been invented for people like him. Everybody's hero.

At that moment, Peter's gaze met her own and for the instant they remained locked, she *knew*—with an unnatural clarity—the certainty, that he knew *exactly* what she was thinking. She could do nothing but turn away, break the contact, try to escape the knowledge that he'd even invaded her thoughts.

What else could he do to her? What was left?

She felt suddenly disoriented, dizzy. What was going on? Holding on to the nearest piece of pipe scaffolding, Marion tried to steady herself. She'd never been one for swoons or faints, but felt on the edge of some kind of collapse. After holding herself up for another minute or so, she began to feel better. A wave of total weakness had passed through her; she could still feel it dopplering away from her like the sound of a passing train's horn.

Without thinking why, she moved cautiously to the stairs, exiting the heights of the stage. She seemed to be operating in a vacuum. Shaking her head, she tried to clear the feeling. Maybe she should go back to the trailer and rest?

As she reached the bottom step, she became abruptly aware of sound again, the background din of running water, people laughing, shouting. For some reason, the collective voice of the crowd did not sound as jubilant as before.

Slowly, making sure her dizziness had passed, Marion walked around the stage, toward the audience. When she cleared the pile of rubble beyond the proscenium, she could see the problem immediately. Hundreds of thousands of people were pressing away form the tributaries. Pressing away because the water continued to rise and crest the banks of what had been shallow muddy creeks only minutes before. Huge holes appeared in the crowd as the ground became a quagmire from the overflow and everyone tried to back off from the excess. No longer a celebration, the extra water had doused the party and now threatened to initiate a full-scale panic.

Running back to the steps, Marion raced up the flight two at a time.

"Peter! Peter!" Her voice sounded fragile and impotent against the wall of noise.

He couldn't hear her. The backstage crew had lowered him to the stage and he was trying to get the sound system working again. Workers were scurrying around the spilled spaghetti bowl of wires and cables, trying to make a magic connection. Peter paced frantically on the edge of the stage with the dead mike in his hand. Without the megawatts, he would never reach the mob again. If he needed their attention and their cooperation to stop what they'd started, he plainly wasn't going to get it.

From the height of the stage, Marion had a better view of the pasture and the crowd. Despite their efforts, the people could not escape the effects of the river gone crazy. There was no place to run. Thousands of people were beginning to sink into the spongy mud. The outer edges of the crowd had begun to flake off, tatters of people dragging themselves through the mud toward the rear entrance to the ranch and the state highway. Other fragments were spilling past either side of the stage and the trailers toward the higher ground near Vernon's home. The crowd would gradually, but very slowly, disperse. Sucked down by the quag, the movement of more than a half-million people would take a long, long time.

The river itself had exceeded and obliterated its banks, raging over the land like a maddened beast. The pasture was already changing from mudpit to swamp; soon it would be a seafloor. Hundreds of the thousands in the crowd began to sense the impending flood conditions; panic sparked and jetted amongst them like static electricity. They pushed and brawled with one another, guided by the amoeba-like instincts of a mob, casting off their humanity like a soiled bandage. Bodies were forced down into the mud, never again to surface. Water lapped at everyone's knees, eddying and swirling with tidal force. Marion wanted to turn away from the growing hysteria, but was riveted by the grotesque spectacle. Some perverse side of her *wanted* to watch the wretched mass of them gnaw and thrash at one another like rats drowning in storm-washed sewer.

Peter gestured spasmodically at the front of the stage jumping and half-running along the edge of the now-rickety structure. Some roadies jury-rigged the tangle of cables into a fuzzy, feed-backing P.A. Peter's voice jangled and frizzed from the few remaining speakers like bad reception on a cabbie's radio.

Marion listened to his broken words as he tried to calm the mob, to rally them, bring them together once again. If he had reached them, regained their symbiosis, the river's onrush might still become a miracle. But his powers seemed to have deserted him; he couldn't connect. He stood still, body arched, eyes closed in perfect tension, trying to summon up whatever it was that united him with the cosmos, but nothing happened.

For the first time in his public career, Peter Carenza knew failure.

FORTY-ONE

Rome, Italy—Etienne
October 24, 1999

Despite the crispness in the air, she wanted to walk in the convent garden. Wrapping her cloak tightly about her throat kept the wind from violating the warmth beneath her robes. The walls of the quadrangle protected her, gave her a feeling of security. It was so good to be away from the infirmary, from the oversolicitous prying of the nurses.

That she'd not been able to contact the Pope had initially depressed her, even though she knew it seemed absurd for a simple, lowly, cloistered nun to wish to see the Holy Father himself. But she gradually grew to accept her defeat, accepting it as the will of the Lord. What had become more difficult to accept was her treatment by her colleagues. The other nuns had isolated her, made her a pariah. If not scorned, she knew she was at least laughed at when doors were closed and voices hushed.

No matter, she thought as she walked down a brick path, under a shedding dogwood tree. She neared the rosebed, the spot where the first vision had touched her.

I can remain strong as long as I bask in the grace of God's love. I can—

She stopped abruptly, her attention arrested by the sight of a single flower still in bloom despite the weather.

A feeling of déjà vu ripped through her like a gust of arctic air, leaving her knees weak and her spirit shaken. Something compelled her to bend forward and reach for the heavy blossom. As before, it broke loose to fall into her hand. When it touched her palm, she could feel it beating as though it had a heart. In the intricate pattern of the roseate sworl, where she'd once seen beauty and power and the majesty of the Lord, Etienne now saw something more disturbing, unsettling.

Staring into the depths of the flower, she recognized the complex design, the familiar optical illusion. The image shifted and a remembered wave of nausea curled over her—that same hideous sickness burned and clawed in her belly; that same feeling of her skull ballooning up.

Mary! Mother of God!

It was happening again, and she had no power to stop it.

She knew she'd collapsed to her knees; disorientation and the shifting shapes in her vision kept her off balance. A low-pitched, penetrating sound filled her ears, changing into a remembered dull buzz that threatened to mesmerize her. She could do nothing but stare into the center of the flower, watching its color change from a fragile pink to a blood-red stain and then slowly slide into black.

Then the smell of death and corruption returned, the smell of the end of all things, of dread and repulsion. Everything in the garden, in the convent, all that had kept her safe and sane, began expanding, rushing away from her in an eye-blink. Etienne once again twisted on a line above the abyss. Knowing she'd survived this ordeal once before made the experience no less terrifying, no less threatening.

Paralyzed, pinned beneath the force of the coming vision, Etienne had no choice but to surrender to the crushing magma heat and weight of its onslaught.

Gathering force, the images compressed into the darkness and then unfurled like bloodstained banners to slap the face of her consciousness: the waterstorm winds, the white bricks of a bombed hospital, the mountain-strewn wreckage of a jetliner. Like a collage of torn photographs, the pieces of the vision refused to assume order or immediate sense. But the overriding tableau left scorch marks in her memory. The oppressive weight of the pain of others stamped unmalleable marks upon her soul.

All of this flowed from the blackness of the rose. When she stopped fighting it, she could almost see a face within the folds and convolutions of the petals. A face familiar and yet totally foreign.

It was the face of all that was malevolent or ever would be. It was the face of whatever waited for all humanity at the end of time.

FORTY-TWO

Vatican City—Lareggia
October 26, 1999

Paolo Cardinal Lareggia stood at the window of his office. The narthex of Saint Peter's Basilica dominated the view, but he never grew tired of the Vatican skyline, the color and movement of the Via della Fondamenta. It was a high sky for late autumn, and the sunlight, filtered by the leaded-glass window, felt warm upon his moon face. Sometimes, he wished he could simply put away the mantle of his office, his vows, his obligations, and live out the rest of his days alone in dignified tranquility.

Like most old men, he felt trapped in an aging, useless frame. He grew weary of life, despite his responsibilities and duties. And yet, there was a small part of him—perhaps the part which had, long ago, allowed him to kill a Turkish sailor—which would never go easy into that good night. Heedless of his faith's tautologies and the miracles of his protégé, he sometimes caught himself wondering what really lay behind the Final Curtain.

As though to remind him that he would soon gain firsthand knowledge of the answer, a twinge of pain stung the left side of his chest and was gone. Had it traced, for an instant, a lightning-like sliver down his left arm?

Turning from the window, Paolo shook his head. He lumbered against gravity, which wanted to yank his enormous bulk to the carpet. Even though he had gained inordinate weight over the years, his legs had remained thin. Now their musculature was crying out against the torture of carrying his bulk. Every step had become a terrible labor, and sooner or later he knew he would crash to the floor. Could he break a hip like that? Or would his extra padding save him?

So be it, he thought. I probably deserve exactly such a fate. It was said that every cleric who truly denied himself the pleasures of the flesh always jumped into bed with another vice. Paolo smiled bitterly. No doubt—food had been his mistress for a long time now. Slowly, he eased himself into his desk chair, feeling the relief spread instantly up his beleaguered legs. The ornate gold-leaf porcelain clock at the corner of his desk ticked past the top of the hour. Francesco was late.

The buzz of the intercom and his receptionist's announcement made him a liar—the Jesuit brigante pushed open the door and entered.

"We must talk," said the wolfishly thin priest.

"I know," said Paolo, gesturing toward the chair by his desk. "Sit down. Cigarette?"

"Did you start smoking again?" Giovanni looked at him with surprise.

Paolo shrugged. "I should—what do I have to lose at this point, eh?—but no. I had some sent up for you from the commissary."

Francesco opened the box, took a dark-wrapped cigarette, lighted it with his Zippo. "Grazie. Now, let us, as the Americans are so fond of saying, 'cut the bullshit,' yes?"

Paolo smiled. "I love your way with words. It is, no doubt, the company you keep. You know, you really are a thug!"

Giovanni puffed, shrugged. He looked haggard, worn, and

ready to collapse. "Targeno wasn't pulling any punches. You've seen the satellite news?"

"Oh yes." Paolo folded his hands over his stomach, leaned back, away from the acrid, blue smoke.

"What does it mean?" The Jesuit studied his fingernails, trying to contain his pent-up frustration.

"I don't know! Is he capable of such monumental failures? Did he do it on purpose? I don't know, 'Vanni. I have been pondering the implications.

"The reports claim he is very upset by the disaster."

Paolo shook his head, half-closed his eyes. "More than ten thousand dead. Incredible."

"The tip of the iceberg perhaps," said Francesco.

Paolo raised his eyebrows, puckered his lips, nodded. There was no need to respond, he knew to what his colleague referred: in the twenty-four hours following the disaster at Mountain Rock, the globe had been wracked by sympathetic catastrophes—a hurricane in Bermuda, an earthquake in Mongolia, terrorist bombings in Soweto, a plane crash in Buenos Aires. Paolo sensed a cloud of doom gathering over the earth.

"Death and destruction everywhere," said the Jesuit, shaking his head.

"Well ... not yet everywhere," said Lareggia. "You well know that anything can, and often does, happen in South Africa. And plane crashes are a part of modern life."

"But the timing! There has to be a reason for it!" Francesco pounded the corner of the desktop. "How? Why? How could he let it happen?"

"He obviously had no control over it." Paolo waved at the blue cloud drifting toward him.

"Don't you find that strange? I mean—he had enough control to 'summon' the river in the first place. What happened?"

"Marion Windsor's exclusive mentioned that his 'communion' with the crowd was broken by the water's appearance. She said—"

"That is ridiculous!" shouted Giovanni. He stood up, began his predatory pacing.

"Maybe not. Perhaps, even after all these months, he is still learning to use and control his powers on a large scale. Maybe this was too much to attempt. We don't really know." Paolo shook his head. "It is a shame he is not here with us. Krieger could examine him. Test him."

"He is supposed to be the Christ!" shouted the Jesuit. "We're not talking about some comic book superhero. He shouldn't have to learn how to wield the power of God—if he is who we say he is!"

The Cardinal ignored his colleague's doubts. "Ah, but perhaps he does. He is also a man, you know. And was nothing but a man for thirty years."

Franceso waved him off in a gesture of disgust. "Maybe that is the biggest problem—he was, and is, a man. Targeno warned me of such problems."

"Just exactly how much does Targeno know?" Paolo wondered if their secret would remain much of a secret after all.

"Targeno is very intelligent, my fat prelate," said Francesco. "It is his station in life to figure things out, remember?"

"I wish Krieger could work with Father Carenza. I wish he could be here," Paolo said again.

"Peter will be in Rome soon enough. The prophecies call for that. That is why we agreed not to try to coerce him to return, remember?" Francesco crushed out his cigarette, immediately lighted another. "If I have faith, I must have it totally!"

"Ah, yes, but I am wondering: did the prophecies call for this disaster?"

For an answer Francesco only glared at him.

Paolo exhaled slowly, waved away an advancing bank of smoke. "Marion Windsor says he is still loved by his millions of followers. In her official story, she said the incident has somehow strengthened people's belief in Peter. They do not blame him for what happened—especially the ones who were present at the concert. Does that make sense to you?"

The Jesuit nodded. "Yes. He is a very charismatic figure.

I am not surprised to find no decrease in his flock's devotion."

Neither man spoke for several minutes. Paolo reflected upon their conversation. In the final analysis, they were powerless to do anything more than be armchair philosophers. What had they wrought upon the world? Finally, the Cardinal shifted in his chair, looked at his colleague and said: "What about Targeno?"

"Hmmmpph! What about him?" Cigarette smoke fairly exploded from Giovanni Francesco. He had always been protective of his star killer-agent. Even though a part of him despised Targeno, the Jesuit regarded him as the son he'd never had.

"Has he told you anything about the flood—anything we didn't already know?"

"No."

Paolo twiddled his thumbs as they rested atop the sloping mound of his belly. "Well, then, I was wondering how long you want him to keep shadowing Peter. We are getting plenty of information from the news services."

"Targeno gets me information the media doesn't."

"What? You've said nothing!" Paolo lurched forward, leaned his elbows on the desk blotter.

Francesco shrugged. "It is not pretty."

"Please. Tell me." The Cardinal fairly growled as he spoke.

"Very well. Peter Carenza has been having a sexual relationship with Marion Windsor."

The words stung Paolo as no weapon ever could, jolting the very core of his being. *What blasphemy . . . !*

"No. I do not believe it. I cannot believe such a thing."

"Oh, yes. It is definitely true. Targeno has no reason to lie to me."

"But *why*? How?"

Francesco shrugged again. "Who knows? He is, in addition to his divine nature, also a man. The dogma has been made flesh again, and we must deal with the biological realities."

Paolo remained flush and a bit faint. How could the Jesuit

have such a cavalier attitude? "I just can't—It is so difficult to grasp."

"Besides," Francesco continued lightly, "we have no way of knowing what Christ's relationships with women might have been before he began preaching. It is not exactly trail-blazing theology to suggest he was not a virgin, you know."

Paolo felt a sudden craving for something sweet. A sweet bun. A trattare. "You and your radical Jesuit blasphemies! What good does such talk do?"

Francesco chuckled. "There is more . . ."

"What? What could be worse?"

"Father Daniel Ellington is dead. A heart attack."

"He was so young . . . hard to believe," said Lareggia.

"Targeno has some opinions on the incident. He feels Peter may have killed him."

"What!" Lareggia stumbled to his feet, lurched about the room, waving his arms. "Why?"

"Targeno thinks Ellington may also have been sleeping with the Windsor woman."

"Saints in heaven! What kind of sciattona is she?! And Ellington—another Jesuit. Oh, 'Vanni, this is so terrible! I cannot believe what we have wrought!"

"Boccaccio said all things are done for love."

"Love!" Paolo mouthed the word with disgust. It was like a mealy worm upon his tongue. "What is love?"

Francesco shrugged. "It is what Christ preached, I am told."

"Most amusing, 'Vanni. See how much I am laughing."

"It is better than crying." He paused, sighed. "How did we ever think we would be able to manipulate the boy?"

It was true, Paolo thought. They had been so naïve, so in-nocent. Father Francesco had gained an early reputation as a maverick theologian, and his ideas had seduced the young Paolo and Victorianna.

All they wanted to do was make the world a better place—a world with Christ truly back in its midst. Paolo smiled ironically. Such a simple notion! To bring about the Second Coming!

How could they have been so full of pride? So bold and presumptuous as to assume the Hand of God? Who could have foreseen what had happened already? Only God knew what still lay ahead.

"There is something else," said Francesco.

"What? More blasphemy?" Lareggia sagged into his seat.

"No, it concerns Freemason Cooper's 'International Convocation of Prayer.' "

Paolo nodded with resignation. The Convocation, Cooper's personal brainchild, called together all the religious leaders of the world to share a dais and an altar for an entire day and night of celebration and international prayer. It was to be held at the new Sports Palladium in Los Angeles on Christmas Day of 1999. A quarter-million people in the seats, and a worldwide satellite television audience of more than two *billion*, was predicted for what Cooper and the media had billed as the "capstone to the Twentieth Century, the keystone to the new millennium."

"Yes, the Convocation—what about it?"

"Has the Pope accepted the invitation yet?"

Paolo shook his head. "He is still weighing the alternatives. There is plenty of time. I think he is waiting to see what some of the non-Christian leaders plan to do. He has his reputation as a moderate to uphold."

"What is the College of Cardinals' position on the invitation?" Francesco began pacing the office once again, this time more slowly.

"Opinion is mixed. You know how many of the older, more conservative cardinals feel about the 'left-footers'—the Protestants . . ."

Francesco smiled, nodded.

"And, there is no real precedent for the Holy Father's participation in a 'prayer meeting,' " said Paolo, unable to hide his disfavor with such a Protestant-sounding term.

"So what is the verdict."

Paolo shrugged. "Politically, it is seen as a good thing. Imagine how bad it would look to the rest of the world if the

Christian religion with the largest number of followers is not represented."

"How does he feel about Peter being there?"

"Isn't it a bit early to worry about that?" asked Lareggia. "Has he been invited?"

"No, but Targeno feels that Cooper will have no choice but to include 'Father Peter.' " Francesco paused to exhale. "Targeno feels that Cooper is very much threatened by Peter's popularity."

Paolo shrugged. "I don't blame him."

"Your sense of the Pope's feelings?"

"Before this latest incident, I doubt the Holy Father was very interested. His infrequent public recognitions of Peter's good works have always been positive. It looks as if we were right to counsel the Pope not to align the Holy Mother Church too closely with anything Carenza did. I haven't spoken to him since hearing the news about the river in Colorado, but I am certain the Holy Father is glad the Church is not being seen in any way responsible for the tragedy . . ."

Francesco waved his hand in the air in a gesture of nonchalance. "No matter—His Holiness will attend."

"How can you be so sure?"

Francesco smiled. "Because I do not think the Pope can afford to risk Peter Carenza stealing the show."

Paolo was shocked. "How can you even suggest such a thing? They would be working in concert for the good of the people!"

"Certainly, but the people might not see it that way . . . if the Pope did not appear." The Jesuit ran a long-fingered hand through his thinning hair.

Paolo nodded. Giovanni Francesco always had possessed a keen sense of politics and psychology. Once again, his analysis was probably very accurate, but . . .

"Yes, 'Vanni, unless the people are not, as this Windsor bitch contends, still in support of Peter."

"She doesn't lie," said the priest. "But I think the real test of his abilities is yet to come."

Paolo shook his head. "What do you mean?"

Francesco shrugged. "Just a feeling I have. Etienne's had more prophetic visions, you know, and it has occurred to me that perhaps God is trying to reach us through the nun. She still wants to see the Pope."

"Impossible!" said Paolo. "The Holy Father cannot know of our project until Peter is truly prepared. There can be no hint of division in the Holy Mother Church and there is no telling how the Pope would react!"

Francesco nodded. "I know, I know." The Jesuit walked to the window, his back to his colleague. "Did I ever tell you, Paolo, that I never really believed in what we were doing?"

"What?" Paolo was dumbfounded. How many shocks must he endure in one day? "How can you say that? Krieger's work was impeccable!"

Francesco waved him off. "Oh, I believed he was cloning someone—but I never believed, in my heart of hearts, that it was the Nazarene."

"Then why go through with all of it?"

Francesco smiled. "Because I decided it didn't matter whether or not Peter was actually Christ."

"What do you mean?"

"It didn't matter as long as the world came to believe it. As long as the world came together in harmony as the Second Coming promised."

"What about now, 'Vanni? Do you believe now?"

Francesco sighed. "In all my life, I do not feel I've ever feared anything. But examining my beliefs has become like staring into a dark pit. Every time I attempt it, I am terrified."

FORTY-THREE

St. Louis, Missouri—Bevins
October 30, 1999

Freddie leaned back in his office chair, punched in a call to a phone in a rented room in East St. Louis, which was set up on call forwarding to the Reverend's private number. This slightly costly subterfuge kept Cooper's number from being recorded on any of the Carenza Foundation's phone bills. If Carenza or that stuck-up Windsor bitch decided to snoop around, they wouldn't find a damn thing connecting the Reverend to Bevins.

Pretty slick, thought Freddie as he listened to the ring of Cooper's phone.

"Yeah?" said a voice full of timbre and voice training. "Speak to me."

"Good morning, Reverend. It's Bevins."

"Ah yes! Right on time. I like that, Freddie. You're back from the Old West, I take it?"

"We checked in last night. The whole entourage. Everybody was pretty exhausted, includin' me, or I woulda called you last night."

"Our regularly scheduled time is just fine," said the Reverend. The delicate tinkle of silverware on china filled in the background. "I trust you have news?"

"A little." Freddie shook his head, lighted a cigarette. Talking to Cooper was kinda crazy. He always made everything seem like a little game or a freakin' lesson. Always the silly questions, the lilting sarcasm lurking beneath all his words.

The Reverend chuckled lightly. "After his 'multiple baptism,' I can't imagine what else would be news!"

Freddie laughed, out of obligation, then waited for his cue.

"But tell me, Freddie, are the reports true?"

"Which ones, Reverend?"

"That the people still love him? That the accident hasn't tarnished his image among the masses?"

"Reverend, no disrespect, but I think you've seen the same reports I have . . ."

"Don't get smart with me, Freddie!" The Reverend's mood had changed instantly. "You're right in the middle of that pit of vipers! If you can't tell me more than I can get on the evening news, what the hell am I paying you for?!"

"Reverend, listen, I just meant that I can only be in one place at a time. I can only tell you what I seen firsthand. I talked to a buncha people from the audience. People who were out there in that river. *Nobody* blamed him for what happened! That's the facts, Reverend."

"But why, damn it!? That's what I want to know. And *that's* what I'm payin' you for—to get me answers!"

"Reverend, I realize why you're payin' me—and mighty handsomely, I might add—but we've known each other a lotta years, and I done cases for you before. You know I'm not tryin' to be a wiseguy."

Cooper sighed audibly, paused to sip something. Freddie hoped he was remembering that Bevins was one of the few people who'd been around since the beginning, and that all that haughty bullshit wasn't gonna cut no cheese with an old raccoon like Freddie Bevins.

"All right," said Cooper. "I think we certainly do understand each other—but I need answers, Freddie. Now what's going on—why don't they string him up for what he did?"

"Well, I tried to talk to some of the people," he said, pausing to take a drag from his cigarette. "And they all said pretty much the same thing."

"Which was?"

"That it wasn't just Father Peter who made the river come. They all said they could feel somethin' passin' through them—like a trance or a communion or somethin'. They weren't sure what it was, but they knew it was a power comin' from *all* of them. It wasn't just Father Peter—they all told me that."

"Incredible . . ." murmured Cooper.

"They also said the accident just proved that Father Peter was human just like the rest of them. They seemed to like that." Bevins mashed out his cigarette.

"Did you ask any of them about this 'trance' business? What it felt like? How it worked?" The Reverend sipped from a cup, its edge tapping against the phone's mouthpiece.

"Well, I didn't hafta ask them specifically. They told me themselves." Freddie paused. On purpose. Let the bastard twist in the wind a little. "They all said it was just a great feelin', Reverend. Like they were electrified, like they could do anything."

"You mean a euphoria? A Rapture?" The emphasis was clear even through the phone.

"Hey, I'm not sure what those words mean," said Freddie, who always believed it was better to play dumber than you actually might be. "But they all said it was like being high, but together, you know what I mean?"

"I think so." Cooper sighed. "You're *sure* about this shared responsibility thing? The people really believed that?"

"Oh yeah, that was definite."

"They couldn't have been duped into saying it?"

"Duped?"

"They said they felt like they were hypnotized, didn't they?"

"Well, those were kinda my words, Reverend. You see, when the river kept rising, some of the people started to panic. They said they weren't calm enough to let Carenza help them."

"Amazing," said Cooper. "Anything else?"

"Well, I guess you heard the reports that Ellington had a heart attack."

"Certainly. Mean anything special to you?"

Bevins cleared his throat. "I don't know. The doctors were

pretty surprised. He was a young guy. Smells funny to me, but there's no way I'll ever make anything of it."

"How are you getting along with Marion Windsor?"

"Pretty good, I guess. She don't pay me much mind. Carenza, I'm not so sure about."

"Really? Does he suspect anything?"

"I don't think so. I think it's more he just doesn't like me. And that road-punk, Billy—he definitely don't like me."

Cooper chuckled. "Well, Freddie, I don't think I'd be out of line to say you're not the most personable guy I know."

"Yeah, maybe you're right," said Freddie. *Fuck you, Reverend. Fuck you and your thousand-dollar suits and your cosmetic surgery and your Swedish masseur.*

"Very well, Freddie. Now, is there anything else?"

"Just a couple things: have you got anybody else on this case?"

Cooper drew in a breath. It was as close to a gasp as he'd probably allow himself. "What? Of course not. What're you talking about?"

"I don't know. Probably nothin', really. Just a feelin'."

"Go on . . ."

"Well, I seen this guy at the Colorado thing. Tall, kinda lean, but he moves like he's real agile and powerful. He always wears dark glasses. Thick mustache, dark hair. Sound familiar?"

"Not off-hand," said Cooper, his voice hushed. "What bothers you about him?"

"Well, just that I seen him around a lot. At the Doubletree Hotel, too."

"Has he done anything suspicious?"

"Nah. I just had a hunch he was one of us."

" 'Us'?"

"You know, PI's. Undercover guys, you know."

"Oh, I see," said the Reverend. "Yes, well, keep an eye out for him. Let me know if you see him again."

"Okay, no problem."

"You said a *couple* of other things—what else?"

"This is just a hunch too, but on the plane back here, I had the feelin' somethin' was wrong with Carenza."

"What do you mean—'wrong'?"

"I don't rightly know. He was just actin' funny. I mean *nobody* was dancin' in the aisles after the river-thing, but our mark, well, he seemed to be wrapped up in his own thoughts. Didn't talk to anybody."

"Maybe that's the way he dealt with the tragedy. You might be reading more into it than necessary."

"I don't know. You ain't been around these people. There's been this closeness, a trust I guess you'd call it, and I didn't feel it on the plane home."

"Really . . . ?"

"I mean, knowin' em all, I would've figured they would all be comfortin' and supportin' each other, but they weren't."

"Interesting," said Cooper. "So all might not be serene in the fair land of Camelot . . ."

"Huh?"

"Never mind, Freddie. Thank you. A very good report."

"Right, Reverend."

"And by the way—I don't think I commended you on Carenza's background check."

"No problem. Computers make it easy these days."

"Yes, I suppose so. A pity you couldn't find any dirt, though."

"Well, Reverend, he *is* a priest, you know . . ."

"So they tell me," said the Reverend.

FORTY-FOUR

Bessemet, Alabama—Cooper
November 9, 1999

A synthesized bird's mating call—a northeastern loon—trilled throughout his bedroom suite.

"What was that, Reverend?" asked Lorianne, pausing to catch her breath. She was a coltish twenty-three-year-old blonde who worked one of the on-air telephones during Cooper's broadcasts. Freemason always personally selected his telephone girls—they had to look extremely appealing yet wholesome.

Lorianne looked something other than wholesome in the high heels and G-string he'd asked her to wear; but that wasn't to say she didn't look good enough to eat.

Looking down between his legs, where Lorianne knelt with her ass stuck out, giving him some of the most hellaciously major fellatio he could remember, Freemason smiled.

"What's *what*, Lorianne?"

"That noise . . ."

"That's my intercom callin' me, darlin'. Nice, isn't it?"

"Oh, it surely is," she said, smiling, then returned to her appointed task.

Freemason leaned up against the imported marble vanity, watching the action in the mirrored opposite wall. The smell of cedar from the sauna mingled with Lorianne's perfume, lacing the humid air with a weirdly intoxicating scent. If heaven was better than this, he'd be damned surprised.

The plaintive mating call of the loon sounded once again, and he reached out, flicked the intercom switch.

"Yeah," he said, studying the planes and lines of his face. His thick hair framed features waging valiant battle against the years. With the help of a little surgery and the latest dermatological drugs, he was Looking Good.

Lorianne increased the rhythmic movement of her head and he gasped involuntarily.

The intercom squawked unintelligibly. Cooper smacked it. "I said *yeah*! Speak to me!"

"Mason," said the voice of Preston J. Pierce. "I've got Mel Cameron on the line."

"Who?"

"Mel Cameron, sir. The guy from ABC. You know— *NewsNight*."

Christ—*that* Cameron!

For an instant, Freemason felt an additional jolt of excitement, which he quickly quelled. Though Cooper's upcoming appearance on *NewsNight* was not his first, it was still hard to not think of Mel Cameron as a star, a famous, deity-like person who never spoke to mere mortals. His show, broadcast every evening all over the world, was easily one of the most watched programs of the late nineties. Cameron's blond hair and angular face were instantly familiar to billions of the earth's populace.

And here was the host of *NewsNight* on telephone hold, twisting in the wind of electronic oblivion, waiting to talk to Freemason Cooper!

But hell, why not?

Sometimes you just forgot how famous you were in your own right, thought Freemason. And when he thought about it like that, well, maybe it wasn't so unusual that Cameron would want to talk to him.

"Thank you, Press," he said, trying to sound as nonchalant as possible. "Put the boy on, why don't you."

Pierce grunted assent; there was a click as the intercom went dead. The telephone chimed and Freemason tapped the speaker-phone button.

"Hello," he said softly.

"Hello?" asked a female voice that definitely was not Cameron's familiar baritone. The intercom speaker was flawless, enhanced even further by the bathroom's acoustics. "Reverend Cooper?"

"You got the one and only! But who're you, darlin'? I was expectin' to hear ol' Cameron's voice." Lorianne shifted position, caught her breath, and began to flick her tongue about in great earnest.

"I'm sorry, Reverend, my name is Deborah Curtis. I was just calling to give you our schedule tonight. Mr. Cameron never handles these kinds of details. I'm sure you understand . . ."

"Why certainly," said Mason, although he couldn't help feeling snubbed. It wasn't like he and Cameron were strangers, after all.

"Are you ready, Reverend?"

"Fine. Fine. Whatever you have planned will be all right with me," said Mason. "We supposed to crank it up at eleven-thirty, right?"

"That's when we go on-air, yes, that's correct. Mr. Cameron will do the warm-in solo, then we will begin cutting back and forth among the various guests—yourself included."

"Okay, sounds good to me, Debbie." He looked down at the splash of long blond hair rippling rapidly. Lorianne had stepped up the pace another notch.

"Unfortunately, I can't give you a specific time-frame—you'll have to be ready to come on at any time, all right?"

"I think I'm ready *right now*," said Freemason. Bells and whistles were starting to go off in his body. The early warning system in his groin was sending out signals that an explosion was about to happen.

Cameron's production assistant chuckled in a controlled, utterly professional manner. "Well, I can certainly understand your enthusiasm, but we'll all have to wait until tonight, Reverend."

"I understand," said Freemason, gritting his teeth, trying to remain in control. He should tell the bitch to stop, but it felt too damn good.

"All right, then," said Ms. Curtis. "Mr. Cameron looks forward to talking to you tonight."

"You betcha," said Freemason, almost crying out the words. "Tonight!"

Touching the cancel key, he leaned back against the countertop and let go. "Jeeeee*zuzz!*" he cried as he convulsed through a series of outbursts.

Lorianne didn't miss a beat, continuing to oscillate back and forth like a well-oiled machine. Damn, this bitch was *good.* She continued until he began to go soft, the tension and strength leaving him like dishwater down a sink drain.

Lorianne looked at him with a shiny smile. "I guess that means you liked it, huh, Reverend . . . ?"

FORTY-FIVE

St. Louis, Missouri—Windsor
November 9, 1999

Even if it was just for appearances, since returning to their St. Louis headquarters, Peter had acted as though nothing awkward squirmed and writhed between them.

Marion leaned back in her office chair and looked out her window, which overlooked Grand Boulevard and the Missouri Botanical Gardens. Evening prepared to put the city under siege. A gray pallor settled in among the leafless branches of the trees and shrubs, punctuated by the occasional protest of an evergreen. The year was careening past her in a blur of highly charged, emotional incidents; she wondered if she had the strength to endure many more of them.

Her feelings were so screwed up, she had no idea how she really felt about anything. There was something new about

Peter, something so far unidentifiable. After all those people had died in Colorado Springs, he'd retreated from everyone. Without formal authority, she'd suddenly been forced to represent him to the world.

She wondered if this was Peter's way of punishing her for talking to Dan, for panicking when he died.

She smiled bittersweetly. Well, if it was, she certainly deserved it.

All Peter would say was that he needed time to reevaluate his purpose, his "part in the larger scheme." Even days after the group had returned to St. Louis, he continued to avoid everyone, using Marion and Billy as buffers. But his dealings with Marion were cool, distanced, very businesslike. She couldn't really blame him—his ego had suffered two devastating onslaughts in a twenty-four-hour period. That he had consented to the international television interview spoke of his courage, strength, and inner reserves.

Dan's death, the summoning of the river and its violent after math had shocked her into a reality she had forgotten existed, as if she'd been thrown from a warm cabin into the teeth of an icy rainstorm. Did she really love Peter Carenza? Or had she been entranced, like everyone else who met him? Had he made her love him? The questions were unsettling.

Where was the happy-go-lucky, fiercely independent, on-the-rise TV journalist? Her self-image seemed eroded, made coarse by her relationship with Peter. Had she actually become dependent upon him?

Certainly not financially. Technically she was still employed by WPIX, back in New York, though she hadn't touched her local station salary in months. Her WPIX paychecks, and the *beaucoup* bucks she was making as a freelancer to the national networks, were being deposited directly to her St. Louis accounts. With that kind of income, she'd purposely left herself off the Carenza Foundation payroll.

No, he wasn't controlling her with his money. But there were other ways to attach a person's soul, bonds equally as potent, and just as hard to break.

"Excuse me," said Billy, appearing in the doorway. "You have a minute?"

Slowly she turned her chair away from the window, faced him. His hair had been barbered into one of the latest styles. He was wearing one of his *GQ* casual ensembles. Though he'd only recently assumed some of Daniel's old duties, Billy had begun to heed Peter's suggestion that he drop the retired biker look for something more amenable to society at large. It was a good idea, but Marion knew it would take some time to grow accustomed to seeing Billy in worsted wool slacks, oxford button-downs, and penny loafers.

"Of course I do," she said. "Close the door."

Billy nodded, shut out the general din of an office under siege from ringing phones, chuddering printers, and whining copy machines.

"Ever since Daniel died, Peter's been different," said Billy. He might have changed his appearance, but his straight-ahead way of dealing with issues hadn't altered a bit. Billy was not one to dissemble.

"I know . . ." Marion didn't want to talk about it. She couldn't possibly tell Billy she suspected Peter of being the actual agent of Daniel's death. It was just too crazy.

"I mean, Peter's basically not talking to me about anything if it's not business related. I have no idea what he's really thinking."

"I know," said Marion. "But I think he's dealing with his problems in his own way. And I think, when he's had time to analyze what's happened, he's going to understand and come back to us." She ran a hand through her hair, fluffed it absently.

Billy shook his head slowly, gently. "Maybe you're right. I hope you are. I practically worship Peter, but he's also been my friend for a while now. I don't want to lose him."

She reached out, touched his hand. "You won't, trust me. After the *NewsNight* show, he should relax, and I'm going to try to make him talk to me."

The insider-rumors about ABC doing a piece on Peter had finally become fact. Marion had figured that after the river incident in Colorado, Peter would be added to *NewsNight's* "topics of the minute," as Charles Branford referred to ABC's programming tactics.

"That's right," said Billy, checking his watch. "Only six more hours. Do you think Cameron's going to go after him?"

"Probably, but subtly."

"How's that?"

"I think Cameron's attuned to the mood of the general population," she said. "He knows they like Peter. I don't think Cameron will do anything that would jeopardize his own position with the public."

Billy nodded. "Yeah, a real ballsy attack, if he makes it too obvious, would get a lot of people pissed off."

Marion looked up at the ceiling, thinking. "You know, if I was Cameron, I'd probably let my guests do the attacking for me. I've seen him do it before, and it works perfectly."

"Really?"

"The guy's a master of subtle manipulation," said Marion. "Plus he has control of all the cameras, the cuts, everything. If one of his guests starts saying something Mel doesn't like, he can just cut to somebody else. It's instant editing. Cameron's a master at shaping the show in real-time as it's playing to the whole country, to the world."

"Wow," said Billy, his awe echoing something she'd once seen in Dan Ellington's eyes.

Marion backed away. She couldn't keep tears from appearing at the corners of her eyes. "I'm sorry, Billy . . ."

"You were thinking about Dan, weren't you?"

"Yes. How did you know?"

"It happens to me too. All of a sudden, I'll think of him. For no good reason."

"I can't believe he's gone . . ." Marion wiped awkwardly at the tears.

"Laureen says you loved him," he said with his usual directness. "You know, like you were in love with him."

"She did, eh?"

"Well," he said with an impish smile, "were you?"

"Billy, I've had my share of experiences. I've been in love

before, or at least I thought I was. And one of the things you learn when you've been around the horn a few times is that it always feels different."

"Okay," he said, folding his arms, his body language trying to express neutrality.

"What I'm trying to say is I don't know. I'm not sure what was going on with me and Daniel, or with me and Peter."

He nodded. "Yeah, right. 'Triad.' "

"What?"

"An old Jefferson Airplane song. Gracie Slick sang it. 'Why can't we go on as three?' Or something like that. I always thought it was a weird song, you know."

She stood up, wiped a tear from the corner of her eyes. "Yes, Billy, you're right about that—it was a *very* weird song."

The video crews from ABC arrived just after 6:00 PM and began commandeering an entire floor of the building, concentrating their efforts on Peter Carenza's office, the conference room, and the surrounding area. Lots of people in jeans, Banana Republic vests, and Sennheiser headsets hustled about the place like members of an electronic guerrilla army. Marion was familiar with all the pre-broadcast craziness and for once was grateful to not be a part of it.

To avoid the planned chaos, and as a celebration of Peter's appearance on *NewsNight*, she and Billy took the executive office staff out to dinner at a nearby Mandarin Chinese restaurant. Peter declined an invitation to join them, claiming a need to make last-minute preparations on his own.

Maybe the office staff bought it, but Marion felt the snub personally.

The party ordered the house special, "the Emperor's Feast," and the long table of Foundation workers spent several hours working through the endless variety of dishes, tureens, and braziers. The high point of the evening came when the waiter suggested that everyone take a bite from the head of the grouper—a gesture certain to bring good fortune to all the banqueters. No one wanted to be the first to crunch fishhead bones beneath their teeth. At last Billy volunteered, but even though he claimed it tasted like potato chips, nobody followed his lead.

When they returned to headquarters, Marion and Billy retreated to her office to watch the late night news and *NewsNight*. Peter had requested that he be left alone with the ABC crew—no Foundation staffers present. Billy used the remote to mute the sound of the last of the news and the blur of commercials between programs. Finally the ABC logo appeared on the forty-inch screen that hung on her wall like a framed picture.

"Okay," said Billy. "It's zero-hour."

Suddenly there was a lump in Marion's throat and she realized she was nervous for the first time that evening. On the floor above them, she knew, technicians were running about, making last minute checks, the unit director was scanning his consoles, and perhaps the makeup person was dusting a few finishing touches on Peter's classic features.

After the familiar theme music died down, the camera zoomed in on the familiar face of Mel Cameron. He stared straight into the lens, eyes unwavering, his hair perfectly in place, as if it were a helmet of some synthetic material.

CAMERON: Good evening and welcome to *NewsNight*. I'm Mel Cameron. Two days ago, at Mountain Rock Ninety-Nine, Peter Carenza, better known across the country as "Father Peter," appeared as a guest speaker. The Festival was in trouble, having reported sanitation problems, plus food and water shortages. In an effort to help, Father Peter became the centerpiece of a controversial incident. When the Arkansas River inexplicably crested its banks and flooded the festival basin, thousands were killed. However, thousands of eyewitnesses claim to have had a "religious experience."

And that's what we are here to discuss tonight—The Religious Experience In America or, more specifically, Christianity—Organized or Not? Our guests include Doctor Gerard Goodrop, the President and founder of the Church of God-Given Liberties; Father F. X. O'Brian, the president of Notre Dame University; Deacon Bobby Calhoun of the Righteous Television Network; Doctor Jonathan Edwards Smith, Chairman of the United Protestant Churches of America; Reverend Freemason Cooper, president of the Church of the Holy Satellite Tabernacle; and Father Peter Carenza, the peripatetic priest who claims that he is but a simple instrument through which God can perform His miracles.

In light of Father Peter's recent experiences and Reverend Cooper's upcoming International Convocation of Prayer, to be held in Los Angeles on Christmas Day, we thought it might be of interest to examine Christianity's place among the religions of the world—especially as practiced in America.

We'll return in a moment to begin tonight's discussion. But first, these messages . . .

As Cameron spoke, the huge screen behind his head had been illuminated, initially with footage from the rock festival, and then from one remote unit location to another, individually displaying the evening's principals. Marion found them to be an outrageously sundry lot.

"What a bunch . . ." said Billy, turning to look at her.

"I know. I can't imagine what this is going to be like. But watch Cameron. He's the key. He'll set the tone and subtly push his premise."

"You're really a student of the game, aren't you?"

"Student? No, I think I'm a player by now, Billy. But you have to watch the best if you want to play in their league. This guy's slick. No other word for him."

The montage of commercials faded to black and Cameron again filled the screen. Seated in a rigid pose, his impeccable suit looking like it had been pinned to a Fifth Avenue window mannequin, Cameron opened the forum.

CAMERON: As the world careens toward the turn of the century, we face the end of the second thousand years since the coming of Christ. This marks an important moment for the Christians of the world. In order to better understand what is happening among the various religions which fall under the wide mantle of Christianity, we have gathered with us tonight prominent spokesmen from some of the most prominent Christian churches in the United States, and by default, the world.

Cameron turned and faced the huge wall-screen. It blinked like an eye and revealed the image of a slender man wearing a dark suit and horn-rimmed glasses. He looked like a high school principal or perhaps an insurance salesman.

CAMERON: Let's begin with Doctor Jonathan Edwards Smith. Doctor Smith, after several decades of declining attendance and enrollment, the nineties have witnessed huge gains in church affiliation. How or why do you account for this?

SMITH: Well, Mel, it is very gratifying to see so many people rediscovering God and their faith, so to speak. I think there are several factors which have fostered this: one, the baby boomer generation is slipping into old age territory—and it's a well-known fact that people tend to "get religion" as they get older, and two, I think the modern Christian church has learned how to be truly modern—that is, to offer contemporary humanity a viable set of ethics and moral standards.

CAMERON: A very reasoned response, Doctor. Thank you. However, I suspect others among us tonight would champion other reasons. How about that, Reverend Cooper?

The screen blinked and Freemason Cooper appeared in all his sartorial splendor. He looked as stylish as Cameron, but infinitely more virile and handsome. He radiated charisma like gamma rays from plutonium. Marion had caught glimpses of him on and off for years. He was so ubiquitous, like smog or bad poetry, he was virtually unavoidable. And while he and his kind were a subject for snide remarks among the enlightened, it remained a fact he was wealthy and extremely powerful. Beneath his urbane smile, he was as dangerous as a snake in your boot.

COOPER: Thanks, Mr. Cameron. I think we cannot overlook the idea that organized religion has become fun. I am forced to use my own Church and television programming to illustrate this. Surveys and polls have proven a simple fact: when people watch my satellite channel they enjoy themselves. My show makes them feel good! And isn't that the bottom-line function of religion? To make people feel good?

CAMERON: A good question. Let's go to South Bend, Indiana and Father F. X. O'Brian for an answer.

The wall-screen de-rezzed behind Cameron and reformed with the image of an elderly man in a black cassock and roman collar. He wore wire-rimmed spectacles, combed his thinning white hair laterally across his head, and smiled as though someone were forcing him to do it.

O'BRIAN: Well, Mel, as you know, when you talk about the organized religion of Christianity, the Catholic Church is the oldest church of them all. It all started with us, so to speak. As far as Reverend Cooper's comments are concerned—I'm not sure religion should be viewed as "fun"—at least not at the bottom line.

The Catholic Church always relied heavily on ritual and the celebration of the Mass.

COOPER: But the Mass was becoming anachronistic! Latin was a dead, alien tongue, and you were losing members at a fantastic rate during the last half century. Why else would y'all have changed it to English?

The screen blinked to show Cameron facing his wall portrait of Freemason Cooper. As each subject spoke the screen changed images. As the discussion heated up, the video display became a symphony of facial images.

CAMERON: Good point, Reverend. How about that, Father?

O'BRIAN: Ah, yes ... Native languages certainly made the Mass more accessible. But—

CAMERON: But maybe the Mass is out of synch with today's congregations. Witness the popularity of television ministries, both large and small. Reverend Freemason Cooper runs the largest television church in the world; Deacon Bobby Calhoun operates a local cable channel church in Chicago. Is ritual still a viable, if not popular means of satisfying the flocks? What do you have to say about that, Deacon Calhoun?

The screen rezzed into an image of a thin, long-haired black man wearing what looked like a white choir robe trimmed in purple and gold. His face was creased and grooved, and almost polished like old mahogany. The natural composition of his features made him appear eternally angry.

CALHOUN: I don't know what you mean by viable, Mel. All I know is my people do a lot of singin' and prayin' together, and they get satisfaction from doin' it. I think the TV has made it much easier to reach everyone who needs to hear God's word.

CAMERON: Yes, but there are critics of the hi-tech church. They say television allows a handful of individuals to become extremely powerful—both financially and politically. Much negative criticism has fallen upon Gerard Goodrop and his Church of God-Given Liberties. Much has been said about your blatant attempts to have politicians legislate a particular brand of Christian morality, Reverend Goodrop, claiming you are advocating a violation of the principle of separation of church and state. Any comments, Reverend?

GOODROP: Certainly, Mel. If people think the United States is not a Christian country, then how can they explain Christmas being a national holiday!? And what about laws already on the books preventing the spread of sinful practices, such as gambling and prostitution? Politics and religion have *always* been intertwined in America, Mel! My church has only blown the lid off the issue, and let the sun rain down on its shining face! I will always be involved in politics because I refuse to stand idly by and watch my country be handed over to junkies and harlots and gangsters and other godless minions of Satan.

CALHOUN: Amen to that, Brother! A-*Men!*

CAMERON: We have yet to hear from our final guest, Father Peter Carenza, a young Catholic priest who has been making news, in a most spectacular fashion, for over a year. Unless you have been living in a cave or on a desolate mountain-top you must know about "Father Peter," as his followers most affectionately call him.

Cameron's studio screen revealed a very flattering shot of Peter seated in his St. Louis office. He wore a casual flannel shirt and corduroy slacks. His dark brown hair was fashionably long and just this side of unkempt. Artfully lighted bookcases composed a simple but elegant background for the shot. He could have been a young-turk author from New York, a chart-topping rock star, or even a brash, visionary defense lawyer. He looked directly into the camera with a force and confidence that would be obvious to even the most dull-witted viewer.

CARENZA: Thank you, Mel. It's a pleasure to be included among your special guests.

CAMERON: You arrived on the religious scene only re-

cently, Father, but undeniably with great
impact. Your supporters are legion, your
critics few. It's been said, even by your de-
tractors, they remain critical only until
they've actually met you. You seem so accessible, and yet the real Father Peter
Carenza remains largely a mystery.

CARENZA: Why do you say that, Mel?

CAMERON: Well, Father, let's face it. Very little is
known about you. I have a piece of paper
here which tells me you were born thirty
years ago, in Rome, were abandoned as an
infant and raised in a Catholic orphanage.
You were sent to an American seminary
school as a young boy, and have essentially
grown up in the church.

CARENZA: That's all true, Mel. No mystery, really.

CAMERON: Perhaps not. And yet less than a year ago
you began traveling the country, performing
what many have called "miracles," preaching to hundreds of thousands of people. Despite your involvement in the recent
Colorado tragedy, no one can be found to
cast any blame in your direction. Addition-
ally, it's been said you're trying to start a
new religion, or at least a church of your
own.

Peter smiled and leaned forward, growing more intimate
with the camera and his audience. He did it so naturally, only
a trained professional like Marion would notice the gesture,
would notice how effective it was in drawing in viewers.

CARENZA: I have no desire to start a new religion.

There are certainly more than enough religions in the world already—especially among the Christians. Just look at all the groups represented here tonight. It seems—

GOODROP: Wait a second, son!

Cameron's screen shifted to show the plastically-groomed Gerard Goodrop leaning forward on his desk. He was grinning, but it was anything but a benign overture.

GOODROP: Are you trying to make fun of my church?

Cameron's big screen blinked rapidly as a spontaneous dialogue was quickly established. Then in a burst of digitized wizardry, it broke up like a jewel being cut into multi-facets, and became a collage of smaller screens with all the guests' faces looking at Cameron at once. At first, the multiple imaging was distracting, and reminded Marion of the timeless *Hollywood Squares* game, but it was an effective techno-technique to carry on the heated-up dialogue. Just the kind of thing Cameron always hoped for on his show.

CARENZA: Fun? No, not really, but I often wonder if the Jews and Hindus and Buddhists and other non-Christians are secretly laughing at all of us—everybody who calls himself a Christian.

GOODROP: Laughing?! Let me tell you something, son! There is nothing funny about Christianity!

CARENZA: Oh, come on, Doctor Goodrop, do we ever take the time to listen to ourselves? "Our church is the only true church," we say. "Ours is the only true way!" We spend half our time and energy denouncing other faiths because secretly we're all afraid our flocks might stray into someone else's fold. We *all* can't be right, Doctor. All the petty bickering—it's just silly.

GOODROP: Blasphemy!

CALHOUN: Cast out thy tongue, boy!

O'BRIAN: Now, wait a minute, I think we can at least listen to the point he's trying to make.

CARENZA: Thank you, Father.

CALHOUN: I might-a known you Cathlicks would team up! Where's the Pope! Why ain't he on here tonight, too?

CAMERON: Deacon Calhoun, I think you and Doctor Goodrop are only serving to demonstrate what Father Peter tried to point out in the first place.

GOODROP: The Church of God-Given Liberties doesn't even recognize the Catholic Church! So how could I even be accused of bickering with it?

As the pace of the discussion slowed, the television began once again to show the speakers individually. Goodrop looked into the camera and smiled his snake-oil salesman's smile.

CARENZA: That is precisely the kind of silly, divisive, thinking I'm talking about. Right or wrong, the Catholic Church exists, and has almost three quarters of a *billion* members.

Frankly, it doesn't need Doctor Goodrop's recognition to hold its place in the world.

SMITH: Well said, Father. I think the spirit of this program is being lost. If we continue in this vein, I fear we will do more to harm our respective causes than help them.

CAMERON: An interesting observation. I agree, gentlemen.

CARENZA: I don't want to play the devil's advocate here, but—

CALHOUN: How dare you bring Lucifer's name into this?!

CARENZA: Deacon, it's just a figure of speech. What I was trying to say is that it's time for all religions—and not just Christian religions—to stop accusing each other. We're all in this together. And as Jim Morrison said: "No one here gets out alive."

GOODROP: That's very clever. Quoting a rock star who was known for his bacchanalian excesses— who died of a drug overdose, most likely while fornicating in a Paris bathtub!

Peter laughed as he responded.

CARENZA: Yes, you've got to watch out for those Paris bathtubs.

CALHOUN: And you call yourself a Christian! Get down on your knees, boy!

CARENZA: Deacon, have you ever listened to me speak?

CALHOUN: Of course not! Have you ever listened to *me*?

CARENZA: Well, let's see ... last Saturday night, you sang and prayed with LaBelle Washington. Then you gave a sermon on money being the root of all evil. After that, you spent an hour huckstering products.

CALHOUN: Huckstering? What are you talking about?

CARENZA: Let's see if I can remember everything: $19.95 for a "lucky prayer coin"; $49.95 for a boxed set of your choir's gospel music on CDs; $199.95 for a bible autographed by you, and bound in white vinyl. *Vinyl*, Deacon? Just for fun, I located the jobber who supplies you with those bibles. Would you like me to share with our audience how much each one of those "books which shine with the white, glorious light of God" costs?

CALHOUN: I don't know what you're talkin' about, son. What jobber?

CARENZA: The R. D. Dalhousie Cò., located on 3909 West 85th Street in Chicago. The owner, a Mr. James Dalhousie, says he charges you fifteen dollars apiece for those two-hundred-dollar bibles. Now, would you like me to tell the audience how many *thousands* of "lucky prayer coins" you can buy from your distributor for your "special on-air price" of $19.95?

COOPER: I think this has gone far enough. You've made your point, Father Carenza.

Freemason Cooper, had a naturally pleasant timbre. It was a well-trained voice—trained, controlled, appealing, and literally dripping with reason and common sense.

CARENZA: And what point was that?

Cooper hesitated, but only for an instant.

COOPER: That there are churches in operation whose ... priorities have been ... let's say ... juxtaposed.

CARENZA: That's an interesting word for it.

COOPER: But what about you, Father? Isn't it true your "Foundation" receives hundreds of thousands of dollars in donations every day?

CARENZA: Of course it's true. I've mentioned the fact publicly many times. But I have never asked my audiences for a cent. In fact, I tell them *not* to send me anything. Since they continue to do so, I was forced to open a Foundation to see that the money is redistributed to those who need it.

GOODROP: Do you mean to sit there and tell us you are not trying to recruit members to your own ... your own church? Why call it a "Foundation," when you know that's not what it is?

CARENZA: The books of my Foundation are open for public inspection—anyone can come take a look. But please, Doctor, don't tell me what I "know" or how to think. Save it for your followers.

GOODROP: You have nerve, young man. I'll give you that, at least.

CARENZA: Thank you.

GOODROP: But while we're on the subject of followers, I thought I might ask you about yours.

CARENZA: I think "followers" isn't quite the right word. But you can call them whatever you'd like.

GOODROP: How do you feel about being responsible for so many of their deaths?

The screen behind Cameron divided itself like an electronic blastocoel, displaying all the guests as Goodrop's question sparked an outburst from practically everyone.

O'BRIAN: That remark is totally uncalled for!

SMITH: Gentlemen, do we really have to carry on like this?

CAMERON: If I may step in here, gentlemen, I think it's only fair to note that Doctor Goodrop's question has been addressed rather extensively in the media. Whatever happened at Vernon Ranch, eyewitnesses and participants have testified that Father Peter was in no way responsible.

COOPER: How do we know those "witnesses" haven't

been paid by your so-called Foundation to say whatever is most favorable to you?

CARENZA: You know because I can tell you quite plainly—they're not.

COOPER: And because of that, I'm supposed to believe you?

CARENZA: Frankly, Reverend, it isn't important whether or not *you* believe me. Only the members of the audience matter.

Clearly, Cooper hadn't been expecting such a reply. He paused to summon up the right comeback, but the moment was lost and the point had been chalked up for Peter Carenza. Marion smiled as she watched Peter take on the charlatans. That he'd done his homework didn't surprise her at all. Being thorough and dedicated was natural for him.

"Boy, the battle lines have really been drawn haven't they?" asked Billy. "I've never seen anything like this."

"No," she said. "It's beautiful. *He's* beautiful."

Sensing the awkwardness of the moment, Mel Cameron cut in.

CAMERON: Perhaps, Father Peter, you have touched your finger on the single most important aspect of any discussion of religion—and that is *faith*. Gentlemen, it all depends on what the people believe, doesn't it?"

SMITH: I agree, Mr. Cameron. We church leaders can get wrapped up in our own affairs—because we are after all humans and prone to error—and we forget churches are comprised of *people*.

CALHOUN: Maybe you forget, but I never have! I *love* my people! They'll always come first with me.

CARENZA: Well, at least their bank accounts will . . .

GOODROP: This is getting ridiculous, Mr. Cameron. Do we have to put up with this kind of abuse?

CAMERON: Gentlemen, I—

O'BRIAN: Father Peter is only defending himself, Gerry. He was, after all, accused of bribery.

COOPER: Which, reminds me, Father Peter, of something I wanted to ask you. Are you an official representative of the Catholic Church?

CARENZA: No, I am not.

COOPER: Really? Haven't you received a special—what's the word for it?—"imprimatur" from the Vatican to go about delivering sermons of a distinctly non-denominational flavor?

CARENZA: No. As a matter of fact, I have never received any kind of communication from the Vatican.

Freemason Cooper smiled and shook his head.

COOPER: Don't you find that a bit odd?

It was Peter's turn to smile.

CARENZA: Actually, I do.

O'BRIAN: Didn't the Pharisees try to ignore the presence and the influence of Jesus?

Goodrop's face grew red with the force of his anger and shock.

GOODROP: You dare compare this man with the Savior, Our Holy Lord Jeezuz?!

O'BRIAN: Oh come on, now, Gerry . . . I certainly wouldn't be the first! The tabloids and magazines have been full of it! And how can you deny the beauty and the power of what this man has done in the name of God? If there was ever a time in the history of the world when the people needed real proof of a caring God, it is now, gentlemen. I think Father Peter has fulfilled that need better than the rest of us thrown together!

SMITH: Well spoken, Father O'Brian.

As he began speaking, Freemason's image burned fiercely among the six squares behind Cameron.

COOPER: Yes, let's talk about those miracles of yours, Father Peter.

CARENZA: They're not mine, I've said that many times.

COOPER: How so? You raise your arms and things happen, Father.

CARENZA: I am no more responsible for the events than a musical instrument being played by a virtuoso is responsible for the music it makes. God makes the music, not me.

COOPER: How wonderfully metaphoric, Father. Did
            you learn such things during your Jesuit ed-
            ucation? No matter—despite what you say,
            I'm forced to wonder if maybe you don't
            believe your own party line.

CARENZA: What do you mean? That maybe I *am* re-
            sponsible for what happens?

COOPER: *You* said it, Father. Not me.

CARENZA: I detect more fear than sarcasm in your
            voice, Reverend.

COOPER: Fear? Why should I fear you?

CARENZA: Not me. Listen. I'll try to explain what I
            mean.

Peter leaned forward, stared directly into the camera. His
image was so powerful, so handsome, so sincere. He obviously had complete and total control over the situation.

CARENZA: When I first became aware of the . . . the
            power . . . which manifested through me, I
            was terrified. Anybody would be, I think. It
            was only after I learned to use the gift of
            this power, this "talent" as my late friend,
            Father Daniel Ellington called it, that I
            stopped fearing it. So I don't blame you or
            anyone else for feeling suspicion, fear, or
            even loathing. You see, I feel a certain inev-
            itability about my situation—I have no
            choice, Reverend. I must continue along the
            path God has laid out for me.

COOPER: I see . . . And tell me, Father, where does
            that path lead?

CARENZA: I'm not sure. But I do know where it does not lead.

COOPER: And where is that, Father?

CARENZA: To the door of the Church of the Holy Satellite Tabernacle.

Freemason Cooper chuckled very softly as he digested the remark. The screen behind Mel Cameron registered a variety of reactions ranging from merely stunned to Deacon Calhoun's wide-eyed outrage. The only one who stayed calm was the supremely cool Freemason Cooper. In that single instant, Marion recognized him as the archetypal dangerous man. An aura of dark power surrounded him like a dirty halo. He was a man who disliked being screwed with.

The Reverend leaned back in his chair and steepled his hands as though deep in thought. It was a pose he affected so often on his satellite channel, stand-up comedians all over the country could elicit immediate laughter at its mere imitation.

COOPER: You find my church not to your liking?

CARENZA: Frankly, I find your kind of religion offensive.

Cooper smiled.

COOPER: Well, that's a surprise. I would have never suspected such a sentiment.

CARENZA: I'm compelled to be truthful. Millions of people belong to your church—after sending in a variety of fees of course. I'd say you're more interested in saving money than saving souls, Reverend.

COOPER: The funds needed to operate a twenty-four-

hour satellite broadcast are staggering. I
don't need tell you that.

CARENZA: No you don't, Reverend.

Peter turned and retrieved a print-out from his nearby
desktop. He paused for an instant to glance at the sheet.

CARENZA: Your operating expenses last year totaled in
             excess of 456 million dollars—for every-
             thing from launch and orbit fees to paper
             clips. Your income, as close as I've been
             able to ascertain from public records for the
             previous year, comes to more than 503 mil-
             lion dollars. Is that correct, Reverend?

Cooper appeared stunned for an instant. Then he smiled
flatly.

COOPER: Ah, I have no idea. That's why my church
             hires accountants. You'd have to ask them
             that question.

Peter smiled.

CARENZA: Well, then, it must be correct. Because
             that's exactly what I did—I asked the firm
             which did your books.

COOPER: You what?! And they *gave* you this infor-
             mation?!

CARENZA: Yes, they did.

Cooper was obviously angry, but he was doing very well to
control his outrage. Several veins had thickened across his
brow, and his left hand had knotted into a white-knuckled
fist, but that was it.

COOPER: I see . . .

CARENZA: And so, assuming their calculations are even close, we're talking about more than 47 million dollars going into somebody else's pockets. I don't know about the rest of the viewing audience, but the questions which spring immediately to my mind are: whose pockets? And: how much?

COOPER: I really don't pay that close attention to the monetary matters of the church, Father. I'd have to consult the financial officers or the board of directors on such things.

CARENZA: Yes, I'm sure those fellows would have a *very* good idea where all that excess cash is going . . .

COOPER: I don't like your tone of voice, Father. Are you suggesting malfeasance in my church?

CARENZA: I don't know what you would call it. But tell me, Reverend—isn't it true you practically own the towns of Bessemet and Birmingham, Alabama. That you, in fact, have controlling interests in almost all the industries and franchises operating within Shelby County?

COOPER: Several corporations do a lot of business in Shelby . . .

Peter checked the computer printout on his desk for an instant, then looked back at the camera.

CARENZA: Ah, right . . . companies with names such as Lamb of God, Ltd.; Mount Olive, Inc.; and

> The Freecoop Corporation . . . which are in fact, wholly owned by you. Isn't that correct, Reverend?

COOPER: It appears you've done your homework well, Father.

CARENZA: Thank you.

The image changed as Mel Cameron's face suddenly dominated the screen. He appeared as smug and pleased as he would allow himself to look. The show had been as volatile as he'd obviously hoped.

CAMERON: Gentlemen, I'm sorry to interrupt the proceedings, but we have to break for some commercial messages.

The screen behind Cameron flashed from one close-up of each guest to another. Freemason Cooper's image reflected a lot of bottled-up stress and anger.

COOPER: Wait a minute! How dare you stop things now?!

CAMERON: I'm sorry, Reverend, but we must give our affiliate stations a chance to identify themselves. It appears we will extend beyond our allotted time, and our affiliates should stand by for this program to continue.

COOPER: What about the fairness doctrine!? I demand equal time!

CAMERON: You've been afforded equal time, Reverend. Everyone here tonight continues to receive it.

The screen de-rezzed into a computer-generated network logo, which faded quickly into a new round of commercials. Taking the remote from Billy, Marion muted the sound, then turned to Billy.

"I didn't expect Peter to bring out the heavy artillery, did you?"

Billy shook his head. "Nope."

"Incredible," she said, shaking her head slowly. "It's like he's declaring war on them."

Billy nodded. "Did you see Cooper's face at the end?"

"Sure was pissed, wasn't he?"

Billy cleared his throat. "That's not what I meant. Didn't you see his face, Marion? I think Cooper's a snake, man."

"Billy!"

"No, I mean it. Anybody with Cooper's kind of money can get anything he wants. I think Peter is crazy to want to take on a guy like that."

Marion looked at him for a moment before saying anything. "You're serious, aren't you?"

"Serious as cancer," said Billy. "Mark my words. This guy Cooper is nobody to screw around with."

"All right, I believe you," said Marion. "You think maybe we should tighten security around here—especially for Peter?"

"Yeah," said Billy. "I'll talk to the boys about it in the morning."

Marion looked back at the screen. Mel Cameron's emotionless face filled its dimensions. Marion keyed up the sound in time to hear him reintroduce his guests. Then he gave Reverend Cooper a chance to comment on the facts mentioned by Peter. But with a not very surprising tactic, Cooper avoided the issue. The moment having been defused by the long break, Cooper chose to emphasize the need for religion in today's troubled world—citing the recent rash of calamities. He made the obvious links between the coming end of the millennium and the sudden multiple occurrences of floods, tornadoes, volcanic eruptions, the horrors of the South African civil war, and the general breakdown of law and order throughout the world.

Calhoun added undocumented information about the rash of birth defects in Chicago hospitals and the reports by Illinois farmers of many monstrous births among their domestic animals. Marion wanted to discount these generalities but some of the catastrophes mentioned could not be overlooked. The world did seem to be careening toward that singular event which was far more than just the turn-of-the-century, and sometimes she felt civilization was on the brink of true cataclysm.

If signs and portents were in the air, as the preachers were saying, perhaps Peter could mitigate the situation. She watched the wrap of the show, which was admittedly more tame than she would have expected. Peter, remaining quiet, had apparently said all that he wanted to say, and when Cameron sensed the show was losing energy, he made preparations to shut it down.

Marion looked at Billy, who sat silently watching Cameron say goodnight to all the guests. Peter had reached out to a huge audience this evening—reached out, and succeeded. The Colorado disaster faded into insignificance. She could almost *feel* his power growing.

FORTY-SIX

St. Louis, Missouri—Targeno
November 10, 1999

It was after ten the next morning as he sat in an Olive Street corner diner. Since seven-thirty, he'd been drifting in and out of diners, coffee shops, newsstands, and other places where people pause to discuss what they'd seen on the news the previous night. Targeno did nothing—other than watch closely and listen intently.

It was a tactic he'd learned long ago; there was no better way to take the pulse of the average citizen, no better way to know what the great herds of "sheeple" were thinking.

The *NewsNight* broadcast danced upon the lips of everyone but the most numb-brained in the city. Though he'd known of the program's popularity Targeno was surprised at the size of the show's audience. As he sipped his coffee, black with three sugars, he mentally tabulated the results of his totally unscientific, but historically accurate pollstering.

Carenza had scored points with just about everybody. From Indian and Vietnamese shopkeepers to Southern Baptist laborers to agnostic investment brokers, everyone came away feeling good about the roguish priest. They liked his style; they liked his honesty; and they especially liked the way he'd humbled Freemason Cooper.

Targeno couldn't blame them. The broadcast had been truly fascinating. There was something about Carenza that almost, for want of a better word, *charmed* you. You found yourself liking him—unconditionally.

Personally, Targeno found this state of affairs perplexing. He didn't particularly want to like Carenza, or even be sympathetic to the man or what he might represent. Targeno had survived by never letting his guard down, by never, ever, ceasing to suspect everyone, to view everything as a source of danger, treachery, or even that ultimate disappointment—death.

In ways he could not yet articulate, the undercurrent of populist support for Father Peter Carenza was beginning to worry Targeno. He would have to contact Francesco and discuss their options.

Targeno believed Carenza had bested Freemason Cooper, but also that he might have made himself a very powerful enemy. Whether or not Francesco agreed, Targeno decided it might be wise to make a trip to Bessemet, Alabama. Cooper couldn't be trusted—but Targeno had seen the man's face while he squirmed under the probing lights and painful sting of Carenza's video dissection. Behind Cooper's eyes had burned a clear white anger, a refined and purified hate. It was a controlled burning, almost perfectly camouflaged by the Reverend's sardonic smile, hidden to all but the most thoroughly trained professional. Targeno had stared into the eyes of many a desperate, vengeful man, and he knew that look.

The look of death.

FORTY-SEVEN

Bessemet, Alabama—Cooper
December 1, 1999

The man had balls, he'd give him that, thought Freemason. At least until I cut them off . . .

He chuckled as he drained off the last of his Maker's Mark. Lunch had been a spinach salad with sesame and lemon dressing, accented by a smoked salmon paté. He didn't really like the crap, but he had to watch his diet. If he couldn't top it off with a small ration of sour mash, then the whole ordeal wasn't worth much.

As he sat within the cocoon of his glass-domed indoor pool, his mind kept returning to the roasting he'd taken at Carenza's hands. Unbelievable that the man had been able to access so much poop on the whole operation. Heads had started rolling over that mess before the day was out. Then he'd spent weeks tracking down the information leaks and purging his corporations of all the disloyal riffraff. Some of this had actually been fun. He'd almost forgotten what it was like to feel grown men writhe under the lance of their ruined futures. He'd especially enjoyed hearing them beg for the forgiveness he so diligently preached.

Shitfire, didn't they know he was forgiving them? He was only taking away their jobs. He could have done much worse.

The house phone chimed and he picked it up. "Yes?"

"All right, son," said his father. "I've been mullin' over everythin'. Why don't you come on down and lemme give you my thoughts on the subject."

"I'll be right down, Daddy . . ."

Freemason pulled on his robe. As he walked briskly through the opulent rooms of his mansion, he tried to anticipate what his father might have to say. Hard to figure what the old coon-dog might come up with. 'Course he was like that. Never predictable. That's what made him such an interesting character.

"Door's open," his father said in a loud clear voice, after Freemason knocked on the apartment door.

Upon entering, he saw his father seated at an upright secretary's desk, dressed in a fine wool suit of charcoal gray. He'd chosen to accent it with a white shirt and a bright red string tie. Freemason couldn't remember the last time he'd seen his pa looking so dapper.

" 'Lo, Daddy. What's up?"

The old man chuckled. "Well, you know it ain't my dick!"

"Why so dressed up?"

"I think I'll go into Birmingham tonight. Been a long time since I done that. Go see a movie or somethin'."

"Sounds like a good idea." Freemason remained standing near the old man. It was better to not rush or pressure him. His moods these last few years had been damned mercurial— something Freemason chalked up to his daddy's advanced age.

His father gestured at a chair adjacent to the secretarial desk. "Siddown, Mase . . ."

He did, clasping his hands in his lap. "Okay, what're you thinkin'?"

"Bad thoughts, son. Terrible-bad thoughts." His father wiped his mouth with the back of his hand.

It was a mannerism Freemason had associated with his father for as long as he could remember, and it meant two things. He was nervous or upset, and he needed a drink somethin' powerful.

"Tell me, Daddy," said Freemason.

His father looked at him with his tiny, bird-like eyes. "Don't need to be a brain surgeon to figure you got to get rid of 'im, son. If y'all let him go on like he's doin', he's gonna bring down all of yuhs. You see that, don't you?"

"Yes, I do." Freemason swallowed hard. There was a sudden thickness in his head, like the beginning of a major migraine. His hands felt like they wanted to start tremblin'. It wasn't that the idea of killin' a man upset him so much. Desperation sometimes dictated such things, and there were a few times in his life when he'd been this desperate. It was just the idea of killin' a man of God that bothered him so much.

"You don't think there's anything else we can do? Short of killin' 'im?"

The old man cocked an eyebrow. "You mean what're your other options? If any?"

Freemason nodded, swallowed hard.

"Well, you can try'n discredit him. A scandal's always good, but this fella looks like he could handle any of that kinda poop. Or you can just ignore him and hope he'll go away—that seems terrible unlikely, however . . ."

Neither man spoke for what seemed like a very long time.

Pa coughed, wiped at his mouth absently. "Nope, I can't see any way around it . . ."

Freemason shook his head. "Neither do I."

"So's that mean yer gonna do it?" His father continued to look at him as hard as blue coal.

"Yeah, Daddy, I'm gonna do it."

His father smacked his hands together, rubbed them like he was getting them clean. "Okay, that's the boy I raised! Now, look, yer gonna need a plan, so listen up . . ."

FORTY-EIGHT

Vatican City—Francesco
December 11, 1999

It was very late when the phone rang; before he was even fully conscious Giovanni knew who was calling him.

"Yes, Targeno," he said as he placed the receiver to his ear. The urge for a cigarette pierced him and he automatically reached for his packet and lighter on the night table.

"You are getting very good at anticipating my contacts," said Targeno.

Giovanni fingered his Zippo into flame, clanked it shut. The smoke immediately soothed him. "You have news?"

"I think so. Freddie Bevins received a message from our friend, the Most Reverend Cooper. Basically, Cooper ordered his gopher back to the home burrow for a big meeting of some kind. Scheduled for tomorrow evening."

Giovanni nodded. "You know the nature of this meeting?"

"Not yet, but I will. I plan to be there. Besides, even though we do not know the exact nature of the proceedings, we are probably safe putting our favorite miracle-worker at the top of the agenda."

"Ah, Targeno, must you always be so disrespectful?"

"It helps keep me alive, I have always believed."

Giovanni exhaled a thin stream of smoke. "Perhaps. Anything else I should know?"

"Don't you want to know who is coming to the meeting?"

"Yes, of course," he said wearily. "Tell me."

"The guest list contains many familiar names—the leaders

of the televangelist churches and all the larger 'traveling' ministries."

"Hmmm, interesting. A group of rival piranhas like that, sitting down in the same room together. Never thought it could happen."

"Not unless they all faced a common threat . . ." Targeno chuckled softly.

Giovanni crushed out his cigarette, coughed up some dark phlegm. It felt like a piece of slippery rubber in his mouth. Someday it would spring to cancerous life and kill him.

"How are you going to crash the meeting?" he asked.

"Ah, a trade secret. Do not worry about it. Even if something goes wrong, I have some backup bugs on Bevins."

"Any chance he will 'make' them?"

"Doubtful. He is pretty competent—in fact I think he may have 'made' me out in Colorado—but he is not of international calibre."

"He 'made' you? Are you serious?!"

"Relax, my excitable Father. He might have noticed I was more than a participant-observer, but no more. Probably figured me for FBI or some other government agency, just watchdogging. No matter, I have changed my appearance since then. He won't recognize the new look."

"I hope you are right . . ."

Targeno chuckled again. "That I still live proves I usually am."

"This meeting bothers me. It has the sound of something urgent and hastily called."

"I share that view," said Targeno.

"Has everyone responded?"

"All but one. Robert Q. Sutherland is skiing in Switzerland."

"You will contact me as soon as you know something?"

"Of course. As the Americans would say: you write the checks."

"Such loyalty," said Giovanni. "I do not know how I would live without it."

"I must go," said the agent. "Much to do before tomorrow evening. Is there anything you should tell me?"

"Not really. Etienne keeps asking to see the Pope. She still says she has information for His Holiness alone."

"Will the Pope see her?"

Francesco chuckled. "He does not even know of her existence. Perhaps we can arrange something—an impostor, perhaps. It may bring her out of her hysteria."

"Do what you wish," said Targeno. "I am ringing off."

"May God go with you," said Giovanni.

Targeno laughed. "I do not think He would enjoy my company. Good night, 'Vanni."

The line clicked and buzzed in his ear. Replacing the phone to its cradle, Giovanni sighed audibly. It could be nothing more than preliminary preparations for the International Convocation of Prayer.

Yet his instincts told him this was something more. Something much more.

As he turned off his light, returning to the starched emptiness of his bed, Giovanni cursed his predicament. Being so removed from the arena plagued him. He hated relying on Targeno for information, but far worse was the knowledge that he had virtually no control over the situation.

Freemason Cooper.

Giovanni Francesco would give anything to know what the man had in mind.

But the specter of the powerful television preacher palled when compared to the larger shadow lying across his every thought. Something was going wrong with the entire plan. Despite Peter's impact upon the world, the planet was not spinning toward paradise. Instead, disasters and catastrophes seemed to stalk Peter's every triumph. And now, since Peter had thrown his own catastrophe, Giovanni could not banish the notion that perhaps his grand idea had gone terribly wrong.

Perhaps Victorianna was correct? Perhaps God was trying to speak to them through Etienne. Maybe her visions were not hallucinations after all, but rather a batch of celestial telegrams being dispatched by the urgent hand of God the Father.

And they had done nothing but dismiss her.

The thought struck a chord of fear in him which he had never felt before. The terror he had often felt when examining his beliefs seemed puny and pale before this new reckoning. What had they brought into the world? And what would be their accounting for it?

He brushed a spidery hand through his hair as he thought of what it might truly mean to be damned . . .

Damned.

For all time. An endless, timeless, continuous state of pain? Or was it something worse? The knowledge that there is no longer hope. No longer any order or light or comfort. The knowledge that your own squalid end fell upon you by the hand of your own pride and arrogance.

Years earlier he'd read one of the atheist philosophers, who wrote of staring into the Abyss and feeling it stare back at him. Giovanni had never understood what that dead man truly meant.

Until now.

FORTY-NINE

Bessemet, Alabama—Cooper
December 12, 1999

Dominated by a sixteen-foot table fashioned from a single slab of southern California redwood, Freemason Cooper's corporate war-room reflected all the traits Freemason wanted people to perceive in him.

The museum-quality accoutrements, ranging from a full

suit of medieval armor through Civil War firearms to World War II German military paraphernalia and weaponry, lined the walls in box frames, upon massive shelves, and beneath glass-topped, locked display cases. Original oil paintings by Delacroix, El Greco, and Goya loomed from the walls with dark visions of vitality and triumph. Massive, gem-cut chandeliers filled the room with light.

At the head of the table Freemason stood looking at his assembled guests. In addition to Jerry Goodrop and Deacon Calhoun, ten other satellite ministers had elected to join the meeting. Several had been around before the days of widespread TV preaching, not to mention cable and satellite broadcasting. Freemason knew everyone at least as acquaintances, and although he could not claim many of these men as true friends, he could at least consider them allies—at least for the moment.

After getting through the preliminaries—introductions, shop- and small-talk—Freemason asked for their attention. Everyone quieted and turned to regard their host silently.

"I think we can dispense with any bullshit, gentlemen," said Freemason. "Y'all know the reason we're here—we've got to come to a few decisions regarding this fella, Father Peter."

A general murmur of consensus buzzed around the table. There was the expected hand-wringing and head-nodding.

"I have a couple of ideas I'd like to parcel out to everybody," said Freemason. "But I'm willin' to take any comments or suggestions y'all might have first. Anybody?"

None of them gave any indication they had any concrete ideas—as he'd figured it might be. They all just sat there, staring at him like a family of 'possums looking up from the riverbank. Well, boys, if the cat's got your tongue, you can bet your collective's asses she ain't got mine."

Freemason poured himself three fingers of Maker's Mark, neat, from an Italian crystal decanter. He took a sip, drew a breath, and started in on them.

"Okay, boys, listen up. I know we're all men of God here, but we're also businessmen. I don't mind tellin' you: my income's been droppin' faster'n owl-poop from a pine tree. And we all know why."

Bobby Lee Masters from Knoxville raised his hand, spoke softly. "But Mason, don't you have to figure some of that's 'cause of the dressin'-down he gave you on *NewsNight*?"

Cooper didn't like being reminded of that goddamned show, but facts were facts, and he conceded it was a right fair question.

"Surely," said Freemason. "That should have caused a bump in the road, but not the danged *beatin'* my accountants are squawkin' about. Now, come on! I need you to come clean! I'm not ashamed to admit I'm losin' money. I need to know how it is with the rest of y'all."

Everybody looked at each other, as though afraid to be the first one to speak. Freemason prodded a few of them.

"Sam? What about you? And Jimmy, come on, now, I know you've felt the pinch . . . ?"

"Yeah, okay—I'm gettin' stuck like a pig's chops in a bar-becue pit," said Samson J. Giddings.

"Me too," said Reverend James Lakerby. "And it's been a steady decline. I don't see no signs of it turnin' around."

That seemed to open up the gates.

"Me too," said another. "I'm going down fast."

"Same here, Mase."

"Yeah, what the hell—I ain't kiddin' anybody but myself, I guess."

"Count me in too, Reverend."

"Okay, it's like I suspected. So the questions are: one, *why* is this happenin'? And two, *what* can be done about it? Any-body?"

Samson J. Giddings leaned forward, pulled out one of the fat, nasty cigars he'd never let his congregation see him suck-ing on. As he carefully trimmed the end with his pocket knife, he looked around the table. "Well," he said, "it seems pretty obvious to me—he looks a damn sight better'n we do, And I ain't talkin' about his pretty face."

"Yes," said John Goodenough, a stout man with a poorly

fitted toupe and practically no neck. "He makes us all look bad. He performs good works and asks for nothing."

"Good works, hell! They look like miracles to me!" said Giddings.

"Amen, brother," said someone.

"People are looking at us in a different light," said John Goodenough. "Myself, I've tried to ignore the man. I never even mentioned him, and I think it makes me look like I've got my head in the sand."

"Or up your ass . . ." said Samson J. Giddings with a half-kidding grin. ". . . 'Course some of us've been sayin' that for years!"

A soft, rippling chuckle pattered through the room.

"And I don't think it's doing us any good to bad-mouth the boy, either," said James Lakerby. "Makes us look like we figured the grapes were sour."

"Worse'n that," said Bobby Lee Masters. "We look like fools! Like Philistines! People are wonderin' how we can ignore a man who's appeared almost exactly at the end of the millennium and might be—and I say just might be—the one we've all been talkin' about."

Someone had finally suggested what they all must be thinking. It was time to face a few facts and nobody was really in the mood.

"I don't know about you," said Freemason, "but I'm not prepared to believe that."

"Some of the stuff he's done don't require much 'belief,' Mase," said Giddings.

"So what's the point of all this?" asked someone else. "I don't figure you asked us here to have a theological discussion."

"Hell no, boys. I'm here to ask you what we're gonna do about this fella Carenza."

"Ain't nothing we can do, Reverend, except prove to him we can also be a force for what's good in the world."

"No," said Freemason, flatly. "Has it ever occurred to you nitwits that maybe he's *not* who we all think he might be?"

"No!" said Goodenough. "Right in our midst! Impossible!"

A chorus of shocked denials encircled the table. Freemason should have expected this from such a flock of quail, but he was surprised. There was no sense playing games with them. Better to get it over with.

"Gentlemen, I have reason to think we've been selected to perform a Divine Act ..."

Jerry Goodrop stood and faced him. "Cooper, I think you've lost your mind ..."

That single comment touched off an eruption from everyone at once. Their fears and desires and outrage poured forth like a foul-smelling stew. He tried to infect the debate with the notion they'd been picked by God to smote down the impostor, but they were buying none of it. Freemason soon knew he would not gain their seal of approval, and recognized that if he took his father's plan any further, he would do so on his own.

Although everyone shied away from Cooper's suggestion that Peter Carenza be "removed," the group found itself divided on whether he was at fault for even espousing such a "solution" to their problems. Some chalked up his plan to simple religious zeal. The others' feelings ranged from bemusement to fear to absolute outrage. That he'd overstepped the boundaries of what was proper, even for a band of thieves such as the current assembly, was evident, however.

He acceded to their veto, and wrapped things up as quickly as possible.

When the meeting ended, Freemason led most of the men down to poolside to join a platoon of young Christian women he'd invited just for this occasion. All those long legs and high breasts gave them a chance to forget their troubles for a couple of hours. But some of the more outraged members of the group had politely declined Cooper's hospitality and took their limos out to their private jets. If he'd lost their favor, too bad. He stood to lose a lot more if he didn't take a stand. And if they were too weak to back him, then he had no choice, really.

If the thought was really as good as the deed, then fuck it—it was as good as fuckin' done.

He sat off to one side, watching the proceedings, and buzzed Bevins on his private intercom. The man had flown in from St. Louis for this meeting.

"You got the Fred-man, Reverend . . ."

"Mr. Bevins," Freemason said softly. "You will come by for a private discussion this evening. I have a new job for you."

FIFTY

St. Louis, Missouri—Windsor
December 13, 1999

Cold, December winds whipped up from the icy riverbanks and into the crowded streets of the city. Marion looked out her office window at the slate-colored sky and wondered if spring would ever come again. Winters in the Midwest, like the summers, were unforgiving and relentless—but that wasn't why she was so depressed. When she was honest with herself, she knew it was Peter, and not the winter, turning her heart into stone.

It had been more than four weeks since his *NewsNight* appearance, and he'd spoke few words to her. Peter had been spending more and more time completely alone—either in his office in the Foundation building, or in his penthouse apartment down by River Park. By overscheduling appointments and appearances, Peter effectively insulated himself from everyone—but especially, pointedly, from Marion.

It's my punishment, she thought calmly, turning back to a desk full of paperwork she'd been trying to ignore. The network had begun to register some displeasure with her recent work. Since her contact with "Father Peter" was now almost nonexistent, Marion had very little to tell anyone that any other reporter could not find out.

She shook her head slowly. Some super-correspondent she had turned out to be ... If things didn't improve soon, Network Chief Branford might start making real trouble, even though Marion had no contract with CBS. Well, fuck him.

No, he'd probably like that ...

There was a light tap at the door; she welcomed the interruption.

"It's open ..."

"Hello," said Billy, stepping inside. "You'll never guess who wants to see us."

"He does? When?"

"Right now," said Billy.

Marion pushed back from her desk, stood up and smoothed her skirt. The demands of Billy's position in the Foundation and his responsibilities as a soon-to-be father had changed him so much. People who recently encountered him would never have believed he'd been a road-punk, a Harley-head. She'd grown to respect his ability and willingness to change, and allowed herself to become his friend. Recently, if she hadn't had Billy to talk to, she would have started to fall apart.

"All right," she said. "Is he upstairs?"

"His office, yeah." Billy waited by the door. He looked nervous, and she felt uncomfortable too, but she also was curious to find out what Peter wanted.

"Have any idea what this is all about?" she asked as they passed through the office to the elevator bay.

Billy shook his head. "No. I was hoping maybe you would."

Marion grinned. "Maybe he's going to fire us ..."

Billy laughed. "Hey, that's weird. Really weird. I had the same thought!"

The elevator opened and they stepped in. Billy selected the next floor up.

"Well," she said, "at least we can always get our old jobs back."

He looked directly into her eyes, then shook his head. "Not me, Marion. I think I'd even be afraid of my motorcycle now."

Taking his hand in hers, she squeezed lightly. "I know what you mean, Billy. We've all been changed by him, haven't we?"

The doors chuddered open. They stepped out into a hallway, and Billy led the way to a large two-room suite. In the main room Peter sat behind a large desk littered with papers. A PC flanked one end; several phones the other. He wore his familiar casual clothes—a blue chambray shirt under a khaki photojournalist's vest, faded jeans, and a pair of Reeboks. He looked up from his work as though he hadn't been expecting them, then nodded simply without altering the totally neutral expression on his face.

"Sit down, please. I need to talk about something."

Marion slipped into one of the two chairs in front of the monolithic desk, Billy into the other.

There was a tone in Peter's voice she couldn't identify. She worried that the distance which had grown between them had destroyed her understanding of him.

"What's up?" asked Billy, trying to sound casual and doing a very bad job of it.

"Just got this off the E-Mail," said Peter, handing them each copies of a document.

Scanning it quickly, Marion realized it was a formal invitation to the International Convocation of Prayer in Los Angeles.

"Isn't Freemason Cooper the driving force behind this thing?" asked Marion.

"Yes, he is," said Peter.

"Are you going to accept?"

"That's what I wanted to talk to you about. Do you think it's a good idea?"

"I don't know," said Billy. "It sounded like some kind of

a scam from the first I heard of it. Like a big huckstering job for Cooper and all his TV-buddies . . ."

"Yes, I thought so too. But now—it's possible we could use the event for some essential good, don't you think?"

"Do you *want* to go, Peter?" Marion looked at him intensely.

"Yes and no. The Pope has decided to come," he said, handing them copies of another letter.

Marion read the letter. From a Father Giovanni Francesco, it expressed the Pope's intentions to attend the Convocation and Francesco's urging that Peter also be there. She could not help notice the personal and yet strangely respectful style of the letter.

"It sounds like you don't have much choice," said Billy.

"No, not really. But I always have some options."

"I'm assuming this is *the* Father Francesco?" asked Marion, tapping her copy of the letter.

Peter flushed for an instant. "Oh yes, that's him."

"So, are you going to go?" Billy's voice sounded stronger now.

"Despite what either of you may think, I still value your judgments and opinions," said Peter. "What do you two think?"

"Are you planning to pull off another spectacle?" she asked.

He almost let himself grin. "What kind of spectacle? I think I'm capable of several kinds, don't you?"

"I mean like *NewsNight*," said Marion.

He shook his head. "No, not at all. Believe it or not, I didn't really plan what happened that night. I did my homework just to be on the safe side, and then when they started to gang up on me, I guess I just let it all go."

"What's the connection with the Pope?" she asked.

"I think the Pope believes it is important that we present a kind of united front to the rest of the world—especially the Catholics around the globe. I mean, let's face it, even though I am, or was, a priest, there's never been anything said by ei-

ther me or the Pope to suggest I represent the Catholic
Church."

"Do you think the Pope would want the world to perceive
that as the case?" asked Marion.

"At this point, when you consider my popularity, he might.

"At any rate, I think I'll attend. Tie it in with the Washington and Oregon tour." Despite his earlier reassurances Peter
spoke as though Marion and Billy were just a couple of
working stooges. "You can put out a story detailing the itin-
erary if you want," he continued, "but I'd like to keep this
low-key."

"Sure," she said, trying to establish a friendly, informal
tone. "When was anything you ever did 'low-key'?"

Instead of laughing, or even offering a small grin, he chose
to take her remark seriously. "Well, let's see . . . I think *our*
relationship was pretty 'low-key,' wouldn't you say?"

Her mind snagged on the word "was"; she lost the rest of
whatever he was saying. *"Was?"* Was it truly over between
them?

Peter looked at her with virtually no expression; his dark
features were a mask of perfect placidity, as though he could
wait forever for her reply.

"I don't know," she said finally. "I guess it is, or was . . ."

He nodded.

Billy cleared his throat as tension filled the room like a
sudden draft. "Hey, listen, guys, is this really necessary?"

Peter glanced at him and almost smiled. "No, you're right.
I suppose it's not. I'm sorry, Marion."

He shifted his attention to the papers on his desk, shuffling
through them. Billy and Marion were dismissed; it was that
simple.

You bastard! Marion thought, glaring at him. Why are you
treating me like this? Can't you see what I'm going through?

She stood up, continuing to look at him with all the wrath
and indignation she could muster. Peter didn't even look up.

"See you guys later," he said casually, swiveling his chair
to face his computer station and picking up his wireless

mouse. "And let me know how that story comes along, okay, Marion?"

"Sure, Peter. I'll let you know."

She walked from the office as briskly as she could without actually stomping. She wanted him to know how pissed she was, but he didn't seem to give a damn.

Billy followed her, silently until they reached the elevator bay.

"You shouldn't let him upset you so much," he said.

Marion felt a single tear burning its way down her cheek. She was hurting so bad and no one could ever know how much.

"Things will work themselves out," Billy was saying.

Marion began to weep in earnest, her self-control fragmenting. "I'm sorry, Billy, I'm really sorry," she said, feeling angry and frustrated and ashamed.

"It's okay," he said. "It's okay."

"No, it's not," she said. "Billy, he's turning into something scary. He's turning into a fucking monster."

The moon burned a hard yellow light through the lens of her bedroom window. Marion lay in bed alone. She and Peter hadn't made love since before Daniel's death. Marion's feelings about Peter were so confused that she couldn't yet even begin to think about closing the books on that relationship and looking for another. Even masturbation didn't bring total release from the sexual tension that seemed to increase in her with every passing day.

Tonight a new desperation added urgency to her movements. She needed to escape, even for a little while, from her memories of Daniel. From her attachment to Peter. From her worries about the changes she saw in a man she thought she loved. From her guilt and her desires. But though small spikes of pleasure had begun to radiate from her core, her vagina remained dry, the touch of her own fingers harsh and stimulating at the same time.

Each caress, each stroke pushed her a little closer to the

cresting edge, but sluggishly. It was like a wave that never breaks, a beach that never runs out of sand.

Sometimes this exquisite balance point made sex exhilarating, an exercise in maintaining a perfect pitch of tension, but tonight she wanted to push through it, to tip the balance and reach the heights.

Abruptly she tripped through the relays and whited-out her thoughts for an instant of clean pure joy.

But even that moment was tainted. A presence loomed in her mind. It was tall and faceless, yet she knew it was Peter.

The moonlight darkened as clouds occluded the orb, and for the first time, Marion believed she could fear him.

FIFTY-ONE

St. Louis, Missouri—Clemmons
December 14, 1999

Clear winter sunlight poured through the window of the second bedroom, the one she and Billy had fixed up as a nursery for the baby. Laureen sat in a rocker, hands resting on her distended abdomen, looking at the new crib and the diaper-changing table both trimmed with ruffles. The tabletop was littered with brightly colored accessories. Billy had bought all the stuff with his first paycheck as Father Peter's new assistant.

Laureen smiled when she thought about Billy. He'd become so much closer to Father Peter since Father Dan had died—it made Laureen real proud of him. Not that she was glad Father Dan was dead or anything like that, but what the hey, it was good to see her Billy doing so well and dressing in fine suits and turning into a regular gentleman.

A gentleman. The idea of *Billy* being talked about like that almost made her giggle out loud. So much had happened to them in the last year or so—all of it good, and most of it because of Father Peter. What a great guy he was. She and Billy used to sit up late, talking about whether or not he was really the Lord. And that was really funny, because before they met Father Peter, neither one of them gave a snot for religion. But now they were deep into God's work and Peter's work.

When she thought about it, it seemed like her and Billy running away on a motorcycle was a dumb, bad dream. Had they really tried to rob that grocery store? She giggled thinking about that day . . . suddenly she got a really funny feeling at the bottom of her belly.

Standing up, she took a step toward the bathroom; she felt a soft *pop*! and then there was water all down her legs and feet. Laureen started giggling again as understanding flooded her. It was time! It was finally time! She didn't know what to do first—pack some clothes for the hospital, change into something dry, call the doctor, call Billy . . .

Twenty hours.

That's what one of the nurses told her. Twenty hours since she'd dilated completely. The contractions felt like they were coming every ten seconds.

"Billy, this is *killing* me!" she screamed.

"Just hang on, babe," he said, squeezing her hand. Though he was clearly worried, he tried to smile reassuringly. He was so handsome he could have been a doctor, especially since he was wearing green surgical scrubs.

"Did you . . . call . . . Father Peter?!" she grunted.

"Long time ago. He's on his way."

"Good." A while back, Laureen had decided that Father Peter should be there when the baby came, but when she'd asked Billy, he'd tried to talk her out of it. But she'd kept at him and pouted, and like always, it worked. He'd finally given in and called Peter. Well, why not? she thought between bursts of pain. Billy was his right-hand man now. And he and Laureen were going to name the baby after Peter if it turned out to be a boy.

A spike of pain shot through her. Her skin felt like it couldn't stretch another inch. She was gonna bust open like a piece of rotten fruit. Suddenly her bed was moving. Ceiling lights flicked by overhead as they wheeled her gurney down a long hall and into a brightly-lit blue-tiled room crowded with people wearing pale green scrubs. Billy was gliding alongside her, still holding her hand.

"Okay, babe, it's gonna be fine now. Pretty soon we'll have our baby."

The gurney stopped. Laureen turned away from Billy to look straight up at the ceiling and saw, bending over her, a doctor with thick eyeglasses. Several sets of hands touched her on each side and lifted her gently onto another bed, one with stirrups.

"Okay, Laureen," the doctor muttered through his mask, "let's have this baby, all right?"

"I'm tryin'!" she screamed and then, as though on cue, another series of contractions wrung through her body. "Oh God, I don't care what you do—just get it the hell outta me!"

"You've got to help us, honey," said a nurse. "You've got to start pushing again."

"Don't forget to breathe, babe." Billy's voice sounded so far away.

"It hurts too much! I can't push no more or I'm gonna die!"

"Yes you can," said the doctor. "You know you can do this. I know it's hard, but the baby's almost here and you just have to do a little more work."

"Where's Father Peter!" Laureen heard herself screaming, but it sounded distant, not really her.

"Here I am, Laureen," said a deep, familiar voice. In an instant she felt a warm glow spreading through her. He was there.

"Oh, Father!" she said between gasps for air. "Please! Help me! Take away the pain! Oh God, take it away!"

Something *huge* was coming through her bottom, gouging

her out as if she was an apple being cored. She could feel herself being ripped apart.

"I can try," said Father Peter. She felt the heat of his hand as he laid it on her belly. His touch was like a sponge; she could feel it soaking up the hurt and the pain like dirty water.

"One more push, Laureen," said the doctor.

Oh God, she couldn't believe it! As fast as Father Peter could absorb her pain, a new torture rushed in to take its place! Push?! How could she push when it already felt like something was pulling her whole skeleton out through her bottom?!

"Is that the head?" asked one of the nurses.

"Yeah, here we go," said the doctor. "Okay, Laureen, another push. Let's go."

Oh God, something was yanking at her insides. She was going to get turned inside out. She'd never let another man near her! Oh God, no!

"Okay, here it comes . . . That's it." The doctor's voice was so calm. "A little more and—"

It was like passing a bowling ball with spikes.

She heard a woman screaming nearby. For an instant she wondered how she could be screaming when she couldn't breathe . . . then she realized they were not her screams . . . Her vision was glazed, foggy, but she could see vague shapes all around her. Staggering back, slack-jawed, the doctor had put his hand back against his masked mouth. The nurses were still screaming.

Something exploded from between her legs. She could hear a heavy plopping sound as it landed on the cold tile. She felt a great gush of hot liquid and the release of pressure but the pain didn't go away.

The lights above Laureen's head began to spin and everything started to turn gray. People were moving around her quickly and talking in hushed, mumbled tones that sounded frantic. One of the nurses was whimpering, gagging.

But she didn't hear a baby crying . . .

"Billy! Billy! What's the matter?! Where's my baby!?"

"Hang on, babe, you're gonna be okay!" Billy's voice

came to her weakly. He sounded strained, upset. "Oh God . . ."

"Father Peter! Where's my baby! I want my baby!"

"I'm here, Laureen," said Father Peter. She felt the firmness of his grip on her hand.

"Father, what happened?" Someone was mopping up between her legs, applying compresses. She didn't care; she just wanted her baby.

Father Peter leaned forward so she could see him more clearly. He had a weird expression on his face—like he might suddenly burst into either tears or laughter.

"Laureen, the baby's . . . dead."

Somehow she'd known what he was going to say. The words did not sting as much as confirm. The pain of her delivery was suddenly a distant memory, it was as though it had never happened. Knowing that her baby was dead became a blackness at the center of her soul, a cancerous knot that would eat her away.

Someone was holding her hand, squeezing. She looked over to see Billy's tear-streaked face. "It's better this way, hon . . . It couldn't have lived anyway . . ."

"Was it a boy or a girl, Billy? I've gotta know . . . Can't I at least *see* my baby?"

"Laureen . . ." Father Peter's voice wavered, cracked with pain.

"I wouldn't advise it," said the doctor.

"Why can't I see the baby? Billy, was it a boy or a girl?"

Billy started crying, shaking his head. "We don't know, Laureen."

She'd started crying too. Wracked with sobs, she tried to sit up. Hands tried to contain her as she strained to see what was going on in the room.

"I wanta see my baby!" she screamed over and over. A motion caught her eye: a green-gowned nurse covered something on a gurney as she wheeled it quickly from the room.

Laureen saw what lay on that gurney for an instant, but the single eyeblink-framed image burned into her memory. Small and glistening red. A bulbous, misshapen head too large for its body. The thing's limbs lay twisted up like the branches of a diseased tree. It wore its organs on the outside of its body as though it had been turned inside-out.

The sheet fell into place and it was wheeled away forever—to be bottled and pickled in a lab jar, or maybe dissected and gawked at by medical students, or perhaps just tossed into a plastic bag and crated off to the crematorium. It didn't matter, she thought as the shadows of unconsciousness closed in.

Even if it was a monster, they hadn't stopped her from seeing her baby . . .

FIFTY-TWO

United Airlines Flight 1104—Bevins
December 15, 1999

The takeoff out of Birmingham had been as rough as Freddie could ever remember. A rare snowstorm had rolled down from the northeast and socked the shit out of the top-end of the state. High winds had rocketed across the tarmac, jerking the jetliner around while it taxied to the beginning of the runway. Freddie hated to fly even when the sun was shining, but on a night like this he was always ready to bet his left nut the plane was going down like an over-the-hill heavyweight.

As the "unusual turbulence" (the pilot's words) buffeted the plane's western approach to Lambert Field in St. Louis, Freddie watched the left wing light through his cabin window. The blizzard swirled and danced in the rhythmic flashes of the red beacon; the effect was almost hypnotic. One good thing about the damn storm, though . . . it kept him from thinking too much about his latest assignment.

Christ, he'd pulled some real pranks for Cooper, but never anything like this . . .

What the fuck was he thinking about when he said yes?

The money, of course.

When you get offered enough jing to guarantee you never have to work for the rest of your life, you don't turn down the job—no matter what it is.

No matter what.

The problem, though, was whether or not he could pull it off. Not that he couldn't figure out a way to make it happen. We're talking about some logistics and timing problems, which were *always* solvable. No, something more basic was bugging him, burrowing up into his gut to have a meal.

The big question here, Freddie-boy, was if you plain-and-simple have the stones to pull if off. Yourself. Alone. Naked and alone under the hard-edged gaze of whatever was Out There watching all of us. Despite all the kowtowing to Cooper and "the Reverend"-this and "the Reverend"-that, Freddie wasn't sure what he believed about God and the here-after, and good and evil, and all that shit.

To put it bluntly, he never really wanted to be bothered by questions which might be labelled "ethical" or "moral." Freddie was the kind of guy who figured he wasn't really doing anything worse or better than the next simp. Most people grafted a little if they got the chance; cheated, noodged the numbers in their favor; lied when they could get away with it; bullshitted when it seemed to be needed. Most people, yeah.

But most people never agreed to—

"Can I get you anything to drink, sir?" The female voice entered his thoughts like a ballet dancer—smooth, effortless.

Looking up, Freddie only half noticed the forty-ish attendant's plastered-on smile. Either the rough flight really had her worried, or she was just burned out on acting nice to a bunch of assholes who rode planes.

"Uh, yeah, that sounds like a good idea. You have any Wild Turkey?"

"No sir, but I have Old Grandad."

"That'll be fine," said Freddie. "Give me a double. Neat. And a little Coke and ice on the side."

The flight attendant continued to smile as she mixed his order at the drink cart. The pitching and yawing of the plane made her splash everything around and by the time she had his Grandad poured, it was closer to a triple. Which was just fine with Freddie.

Freddie grinned sardonically. Cooper might sound like a good ol' boy, but he was nobody's fool. Though his latest idea—well, it just seemed crazy.

Freddie slurp-sipped his whiskey, followed it with a little sweetness from the Coke. The first few gulps were already leaching some of the flight-tension out of him. He wondered what it would be like to be falling out of the sky and be so drunk you didn't care, didn't even know the plane was going down.

Yeah, he thought, calmly, taking another gulp, and raising his hand to get another drink: maybe if he was completely wasted by the time they reached St. Louis, he wouldn't worry about catching Father Peter in the crosshairs of the weapon of his choice.

FIFTY-THREE

Los Angeles, California—Targeno
December 25, 1999

Sunrise.

Christmas morning was warm and sunny with a breeze more than subtle, less than brisk. Californians knew this as sweater weather. Golfers loved it; so did surfers, as long as they had a wetsuit. People from other parts of the country could never get used to bright sunshine and warm temperatures at Christmastime, and even if they didn't like blizzards, many seemed to require some gray sides or nasty winds to get into the mood of the season.

But this particular Christmas morning in Los Angeles was special. Hundreds of thousands of people had migrated to New Gomorrah; pilgrims from across the continent and a hundred other countries gathered at the city's newest architectural shrine, the Los Angeles Palladium.

The Palladium: big enough to hold six Houston Astrodomes, it could easily accommodate more than a quarter million people. Sky-boxes, suites, restaurants, bars, and even nightclubs accented the gigantic, concrete torus like gems in a tiara. At night, seen from Mulholland Drive, it looked like the mothership from Spielberg's *Close Encounters*, ready for lift-off. The envy of every other city in America, the Palladium had become the Mount Olympus of urban coliseums. The mayors of most of America's major cities were jealous. They knew that their constituents couldn't see the effects of better public education, or programs to help the aged or the homeless, but they could undoubtedly see a stadium as big as Rhode Island, lit up like a Georgian's birthday cake.

Rock concerts, ballgames, the NFL, and the Goodwill games had already called their worshipers to the Palladium's altars, but the International Convocation of Prayer was the first truly "religious" event to take place there. Radio and television crews from more than 140 countries had wired up the place until it looked like the world's biggest bowl of spaghetti. Satellite uplinks sprouted along the stadium's rim like mushrooms after a night of hard rain. The Convocation would be witnessed simultaneously by billions of people. Technicians swarmed about like worker bees readying the hive for their queen's coming-out party.

If Francesco had seen his agent at that moment, it was doubtful the old wolf would recognize him. Long, blond hair had replaced his close-cut black; his dashing mustache had been sacrificed to absolute deep cover. Wearing the white coveralls of the Church of the Holy Satellite Tabernacle technical crew, he scrambled around the upper levels of the Palladium and pretended to be part of the army of drones making the final connections for the big broadcast. There were dozens of crews from scores of networks, individual stations, syndicates, and satellites around the world; many different languages were being spoken. Targeno was surprised no one had yet been electrocuted. Confusion ruled the hour and he had the freedom to go anywhere he pleased.

Later, he imagined, the various security agencies would give the screws a few good turns and start setting up procedures for the event. But now, there were virtually no security goons about. Targeno stood still for a moment in the early morning shadows of the light towers which soared up and over the rim of the giant doughnut like great curving horns. Like strands of endless webbing, catwalks and ladders interleaved the superstructure. The beauty and the terror of such a design were that everything was either camouflaged or hidden by architectural trickery. The Palladium offered plenty of places for an assassin to hide.

Targeno smiled as sunlight tickled the back of his neck. Finding such a place was, in fact, his first priority. He planned to locate several sites, so any contingency might be covered. As he strode briskly through the mass of coveralled technicians, each displaying the colors and logos of myriad countries and broadcast systems, Targeno carried a clipboard and pretended to be speaking into a remote headset. To the average observer, he was probably just another foreman or shop steward trying to honcho an assignment to completion.

Up on the rim, he had a clear view of the dais far below. Located in the exact center of the Palladium, mounted on a complicated set of gears and electric motors, the huge, circular platform had been designed to perform one rotation per hour. Used often for concerts and other performances, the revolving stage had proved a big hit with the audiences, and made the arena's publicity hype—"Not a Bad Seat in the House!"—true.

The clockwork movement would also afford any possible assassins an ever-changing panorama of potential targets. And the rotation was slow enough to have no serious effect on a killer's aim. Targeno shook his head as he surveyed a crew connecting their KU band uplink dish to a small platform out on the rim. There were literally hundreds of these mounting platforms encircling the arena, a mark of the foresight of the architect, who had anticipated worldwide coverage of Palladium events. He had fairly well ruled out the mounting platforms and the dishes themselves as possible hiding places—too open, and too vulnerable to infrared scanners, which might pick up the body heat of a lone figure in an unexpected location.

No, he thought, he'd have to find a site that was accessible, and perfectly camouflaged. Perhaps a less obvious spot . . .

To anyone using a sniper-scope, the rim of the arena would be no obstacle to a clean kill. At this distance, Targeno could use one of his own weapons to delicately snick a fly off the Pope's nose. And Targeno was not an exceptional shot; there were plenty of men who could shoot as well or better than he. But being a good marksman was not the only requirement for a great assassin. There was also the matter of perfect timing, that knack of selecting the precisely correct moment when no one was looking, when your prey was most vulnerable, when your avenue of escape lay the widest, and of course when your kill quotient was the highest.

Targeno was constantly aware of this rough-edged equation. The closer one could get to the rotating dais, the higher the odds that even a botched job would be successful. And so he would have to be thorough; he would have to slowly work his way down through the labyrinth of seats, checking everything.

It also meant he would have to consider alternative methods—the most obvious being a bomb. Time-honored methods of searching for an explosive device would take weeks in the Palladium. Impossible. Pointless. But thanks to the microelectronics of the very late twentieth century, Targeno had some very reliable help in snooping out the distinctive electrochemical atmospheric signatures of portable bombs. Other weapons or devices, such as equipment using laser or microwave technology, were more difficult to detect, but there were ways of coping with that sort of thing too. No one had a better bag of tricks than Targeno. If there was anything out there, he would know about it.

He looked at his watch and noted the time—just after six AM. The Convocation's opening ceremony would begin at noon.

He smiled as he pretended to make a note on his clipboard.

Six hours.

He'd been left with a lot less on many occasions.

FIFTY-FOUR

Los Angeles, California—Windsor
December 25, 1999

Peter had flown out the day before, disguised and alone. Marion was no longer personally offended by his aloofness, but that didn't keep her from worrying about it, about him. As her jetliner taxied to a stop at LAX, she tried to stop thinking about the way he'd changed, and still seemed to be changing. He was no longer—

The pilot's standard deplaning message and the instant rustle of surrounding passengers distracted her and she lost the thought. Billy and Laureen had already moved out into the aisle to pull down their carry-on luggage. She followed them out of the plane and into the cattle-herd environs of the terminal itself. The crowds were, as usual, thick and pushy and slightly hostile.

Having shipped the majority of their luggage ahead to the Westwood Hotel, Marion was glad to be able to avoid the baggage-pickup circus. "Let's see if we can find the limo we ordered," she said. "I feel like I need a shower already."

"The guilt of an unclean spirit," said Billy, smiling at her. "Praise the Lord and, shower or no shower, your soul will be clean!"

Despite the loss of the baby, Billy seemed to retain his strength and his resolve. If his faith in Peter had been shaken, it didn't show—at least not yet. He remained loyal and utterly dependable. Laureen still suffered. The anguish, the pain and the loss were etched in her pale face. Marion watched her move listlessly through the crowded airport, apparently oblivious to all the noise and color around her.

"There it is!" Billy said, pointing to a long egg-white car. The driver, standing beside his vehicle, held a sign that said "Windsor." The car was flanked by other stretch limos and a massive phalanx of taxis. The driver was efficient and respectful as he helped them get comfortable before entering the fray that was driving in Los Angeles. As they drove along, Marion noticed Billy gawking at everything.

"See anything familiar?" she asked, putting on her sunglasses. The harsh glare of Southern California sun gave the whole vista a calcified, silvery edge. Despite the visible layers of smog hanging over the horizon like layers in a cake, things seemed uncommonly bright.

"Kind of . . ." he said, "but don't forget—I haven't been here since I was a kid. The only thing I remember is the Hollywood sign and those stars in the sidewalk."

"A regular tourist you were! That's Culver City coming up over there," she said, pointing off to the right. "The famous Venice beach is that way."

"So many cars. How do people stand it?" Laureen shook her head, leaned down and kissed Billy's neck.

"Money has a way of making things bearable," said Marion. "You don't see a lot of Porsches and Lamborghinis in this town by accident."

They continued to head north, past Santa Monica and Century City, exiting the Freeway on Wilshire. Their hotel was south of UCLA's main campus, surrounded by giant desert palms and lush shade trees. As they checked in, under the aegis of her television network, Marion felt the tension layering away from her.

"Yes, ma'am, Miz Windsor," said the clerk, handing them magnetic cards instead of keys. "Suite seven-eighty."

"Thank you," said Marion.

She wanted nothing more than a shower and a few hours to relax before spending the rest of the day and night at the Palladium. She kept telling herself she didn't really care anymore who or what Father Peter Carenza might or should be. Having decided everything was way beyond her sphere of influence and control, she would let the forces that swirled around her continue to do so without her concern.

"Excuse me," said the desk clerk, looking at Billy. "Are you Mr. Clemmons? William Clemmons?"

Billy nodded. "Yes, why?"

"I've got a message for you, sir." The man handed him a sealed envelope with the Foundation logo in the left corner.

"What is it?" asked Marion. She wanted to move close enough to read it over his shoulder, but forced herself to wait.

Tearing open the envelope, Billy read the message quickly. "It's from one of the security guys—Bevins. He wants to meet with me."

Marion said, "Bevins? Does he say what the problem is?"

Billy shrugged, showed her the note: *Urgent that I see you as soon as you arrive. Alone. The lobby of the Beverly Hills Hotel. This morning. F. Bevins.*

"How far is the hotel?"

"Not too far. East on Wilshire, then north on Beverly up to Sunset."

Billy turned to Laureen. "Gotta go see what this is all about, babe," he said. "Be back in a little while."

"Okay, Billy. Be careful . . ."

He nodded, turned to Marion. "Can you help her get settled in? I'll be back as soon as I can."

"We'll be fine."

"Okay. See you guys soon," he said, turning toward the lobby doors.

Marion watched him leave before picking up her carry-on suitcase and walking to the elevators. A bellhop appeared out of the ether to help her and Laureen. As the elevator doors closed, Marion had a sudden flash of insight, a fleeting impression that something was wrong. Please, God . . . please make everything all right.

The prayer skipped across her mind like a stone on a still pond. Please, God, whoever you are . . .

Beverly Hills—Clemmons

Freddie Bevins was sitting in the lobby reading the *Los Angeles Times*. He wore a gray tweed jacket and a dull tie, which marked him so blatantly as an out-of-towner, Billy wondered if he dressed like that on purpose. His whole "look" clashed perfectly with the ultra-chic trappings of the hotel.

"Mr. Clemmons," said Freddie, standing up to shake his hand. He dropped the newspaper to the couch to reveal a large, white tyvek envelope still in his grasp. "Have a good trip?"

Billy shrugged. He didn't feel like he had time for small talk. "The plane was crowded. It was okay, I guess. And you can call me 'Billy'—everybody else does."

Bevins smiled, said nothing. He just stood there staring at him.

"What's the problem, Mr. Bevins?"

Bevins drew in a breath, exhaled slowly, dramatically, even arched his eyebrows. "I was told to get to you on this, since you're always around Father Carenza. Let's go to the bar. I'll buy you a drink and explain what I need you to do."

"I thought you were staying at the Westwood with the rest of the security people . . ."

Bevins nodded. "I am. I have some friends staying here, so I figured I'd kill a couple birds with one stone. You know how that goes."

Bevins grinned and Billy reciprocated uneasily. Bevins seemed like a nice enough guy, but there was something oily just beneath the surface.

The security man led the way to the bar through the lush gardens and walkways, past the pool where nearly naked women posed and pranced and sunbathed to get the attention of anybody important who might be looking for a walk-on bimbette in his next flick.

Bevins smiled as he caught Billy stealing a look here and there. "Nice, huh, Billy?

"You know, they say more cock gets sucked in this town

than any other spot on the face of the earth! I sure wouldn't bet against it, eh?" Bevins laughed. He and Billy seated themselves on a pair of plush stools at the bar. *Au courant* fixtures surrounded them. The room screamed of trendiness.

The bartender materialized in front of them; Bevins took a Wild Turkey, Billy a Corona.

"So what's up, Mr. Bevins?"

"Call me Fred."

"Fred." Billy just stared at him, waiting.

Bevins exhaled slowly. "Your boss might've made some powerful enemies, Billy. Do you realize that?"

"I figured it was bound to happen. He's become very . . . outspoken lately."

Bevins chuckled. "Yeah, I'd say."

The bartender appeared with their drink order, then did a discreet fade.

Billy threw the lime slice in the nearest ashtray, then sipped his sweet Mexican beer. "So what're you getting at, Mr. Bevins?"

"Security's my concern, Billy." Bevins knocked back his drink, slowly opened the tyvek envelope. He pulled out a small square of white plastic.

"Here . . ." He handed it to Billy, who recognized it as an ID badge—one with Peter Carenza's photo on it.

"What's this for?"

"It's a Palladium ID," said Bevins. "Their internal security is issuing them to everyone who's going to be up on the dais and anybody else on the floor—media, techs, you know—all the gofers."

"Okay," said Billy. "So what's this all have to do with me?"

Bevins looked at him with a buddy-buddy conspiratorial expression. "I want you to make sure Father Peter wears his badge today—*this* badge."

"Why, what's so special about this one?" Billy looked at it closely.

Bevins chuckled. "It's a solar-powered microchip scanner and transmitter."

"What's it for?" Billy swallowed hard. He had no idea what the answer might be, but he was certain it was something weird.

Bevins smiled. "It's beautiful, kid. This little sucker will let us know if anybody is using ultrasonics or laser/maser aiming devices . . ."

Billy nodded. "You mean like on sniper-scopes?"

"Right. But even more sophisticated stuff too." Bevins ran a hand through his slicked-down hair. "Get this—if this thing does pick up anything, it sends a signal to us security guys immediately."

Billy sipped his beer. "Sounds like a good idea."

"It is," said Bevins. "But I need you to make sure Carenza doesn't take it off, okay?"

"Why don't you give it to him?" asked Billy.

Bevins chuckled. "Because he's like anybody else I've tried to protect. He thinks everybody loves him, and that he's invincible."

"So why'd he listen to me any better?"

"You don't understand," said Bevins. "Don't explain all this security stuff to him. Use reverse psychology. Don't even bring it up unless it becomes an issue—like if he takes it off at some point."

"Oh, I see." Billy took a longer pull on the clear-glass bottle.

"You got it," said Bevins. "Just make sure he keeps the friggin' thing on, okay?"

"Yeah, I think I can do that."

Bevins took the badge, replaced it in the envelope and handed the package to Billy. "Thanks, son . . . You're making my job a hell of a lot easier."

"No problem."

Bevins slipped off his stool, patted him on the shoulder. "Well, I better be getting to work. Lot to do before it's showtime, huh?"

"Okay, Fred. Don't worry about the badge—I'll take care of it."

Bevins smiled. "I know you will, son. I know you will."

FIFTY-FIVE

Rome, Italy—Etienne
December 25, 1999

Though she lay upon a bed in a white room, the sensation of drifting upon a small raft was overpowering. It was as if gentle waves rock-a-byed her toward an arctic place where white sky met white glacier. Where nothing but the purified expanse of whiteness covered the world.

What did the whiteness mean?

Was it the state of her soul? Unsoiled by sin, either in thought or deed? Or was it the world itself, somehow wiped clean and new, unsoiled, pristine?

No. That was not the world she'd always known about. Especially now.

Slowly, as she forced herself to keep her eyes open, her vision began to focus. The whiteness resolved itself into the prosaic trappings of a hospital room. A gray form gathered substance, assumed the shape of a human figure dressed in dark blue.

"Good morning, Sister," said the figure.

Etienne blinked. A name floated to the surface of her thoughts.

"Abbess . . ." she whispered. "Victorianna."

"Very good," said her Superior. "The doctors said you were doing much better today. You had a relapse. Do you remember coming back here? They said you wished to speak to me."

"Yes. I can see ... the world. I understand things better now."

"What do you mean?" asked Victorianna.

"I must speak to His Holiness the Pope about this."

Victorianna smiled. She was a pretty woman despite her age. "Yes, you have said this before. But you must realize he is a very busy man. He is rarely in the Vatican these days."

"Yes, I know. He will travel soon again. I must see him before he does this thing."

Victorianna leaned over the bed. Her face was very close now, her breath sweet and fresh. "Etienne, you must speak to me first. You have been very ill. We feared you had lost your mind."

"Perhaps I have. Madness might be better than my dreams."

"What dreams?"

Etienne turned away from the Abbess. "No . . ."

"Etienne, tell me!"

Etienne looked at the whiteness of the ceiling. It had an odd but pleasant calming effect on her. She could use it to blot away all distractions most of the time.

"I am sorry," she heard herself saying, as though listening to another. "I cannot tell anyone but the Holy Father."

"It is about the child, isn't it?"

The whiteness hardened, chilled her. How could Victorianna know?

"Yes," said the Abbess. "Your eyes betray you. You think I could not guess what all this has been about. We have all known. You may as well speak of it."

"He is no longer a child," Etienne said flatly.

"No."

"He is a man, but he is also more than a man. I think he is a monster."

"Yes," said Victorianna. "And your visions have told you this."

"It was not right what you had me do. It was a terrible sin, and only the Holy Father can forgive me."

"No," said the Abbess. "You are wrong. You have no sin, my child."

Etienne allowed herself to glare at the old nun. "We all do, Mother Superior. Do not think otherwise. The world writhes in pain, in change. Each night I live through the dying! I feel millions of lives being winked out like stars at morning. Their pain is my pain. And there will be more. Much more."

She rolled away from the nun and would speak no longer. They would not let her see the Pope. The knowledge was as certain and final as a door being slammed shut and bolted against the coming night. It was as though she could feel God's hand withdrawing from her, giving up, finally seeking to touch the soul and the ear of another.

If only she could face Him and ask forgiveness . . .

FIFTY-SIX

Los Angeles—The Palladium
December 25, 1999

Windsor

Marion could sense the presence of the crowd beyond the entrance gate as though it were the heaving, sweaty body of a great beast lying in wait for the huddled group of participants and media types who would be soon dumped into the giant caldron of the Palladium.

She stood with Billy, Peter, and the small video crew who would be waiting to serve her every broadcast need. Each guest and his immediate entourage were encircled by Palladium security personnel, plus undercover and uniform cops from the LAPD.

An amplified voice relayed last-minute instructions to everyone as the entrance procession began. Marion wasn't really listening. Billy had already told her about their seat assignments in the first few rows in front of the rotating dais.

He seemed overly concerned about the crowds at the Palladium. After he'd made several references to the number of people jamming the place, Marion had asked him what was really bothering him.

"I don't know," he said abashedly. "It's just that I have this feeling that things are going to screw up. That something bad is going to happen."

She nodded, recognizing what he meant. The high-octane rush of Peter's rise to popularity and the excitement of bringing the world to a new level of understanding had been slowly eroding, gradually being replaced by something darker, something undefinably wrong. Maybe she was too close to the whole phenomenon to see what was really going on. Maybe Billy was too, but he'd said something to the effect that things would be better once they got through the ordeal of the Convocation and the coming turn of the century.

Ordeal.

An accurate word choice.

Targeno

For the last two hours, the crowd had been filtering into the massive bowl. Outside, traffic twisted and curved in upon itself like non-Euclidian math, creating jams and gridlocks of classic beauty. People streamed through every access to the Palladium, wearing the robes and garments of their various faiths and occupations. The sheer spectacle was impressive even for someone jaded by the pageantry of the Vatican. The crowd eddied in vast whorls of color and motion, and the air crackled with the languages of a hundred different countries.

Wearing the invisibility cloak of a technicians' coveralls, Targeno shifted through the crowds with impunity. His forged security badge and the way he moved confidently past the checkpoints provided him with unlimited access to every inch of the gigantic arena.

So far, though, it had done him little good.

He had placed portable scanning devices at strategic points throughout the Palladium, multiplexing them to detect a variety of transmission/reception modes, but there was no way to adequately cover the entire space. It was simply too big. He could only hope for a little luck and trust in the intuitive abilities which had kept him alive for more than twenty years in the business.

The opening ceremonies had finally begun, only fifteen minutes behind schedule. Too bad, actually—it gave him less time to scope out the operation. Bevins might look the part of the workaday sap, but he was a very competent covert operations man. Targeno had uncovered enough dirt on Frederick G. Bevins to know he was a careful, thorough operator—and therefore very dangerous.

Stationed on the platform by one of Cooper's church uplink dishes, Targeno slipped on a pair of sunglasses that were actually hi-rez binoculars. His view of the entrance gangway was unimpeded, and he could clearly see the mini-processionals of each guest entering the vast space and navigating toward the huge central dais. The PA boomed the names of sundry dignitaries across the artificial canyon and the crowd cheered perfunctorily, like dogs salivating to a gigantic bell. The list ranged from the mayor and his fellow politicos to the seemingly endless roster of religious pundits and churchly demagogues.

Only a dunderhead would not recognize the precise order in which the guests made their appearances—a gradually ascending order of importance, or more pointedly, of internationally visibility. But Targeno could anticipate problems as the procession reached the upper end of the spectrum. Idly, he tracked the audience responses. The pathetic, doddering Bishop Tutu was met with polite applause, but Gerard Goodrop and several of his political cronies, following the bishop, were greeted by a thunderous ovation.

A stroke of true inventiveness saved face for the most exalted guests in a subtly brilliant tactic, an en masse appearance of all guests with the highest profiles. And so, when a virtual tsunami of cheers and screams rocked the foundation of the Palladium, it was impossible to know if the audience was losing its collective mind over Freemason Cooper, or Amahl Sulamein, or Bandi Mansammatman, or Father Peter Carenza, or even the Pope himself.

The processional music of the opening ceremonies reached a majestic crescendo, and the thousand-member choir voices peaked at just the right moment. If Targeno had been a particularly religious man, he would have thought that a typical day in heaven might start like this. In the gulf of silence that followed the break in the music, he could feel the entire arena seeming to catch its breath. As all the dignitaries, some sixty strong, took their seats, the huge round platform began its almost imperceptible rotation.

Freemason Cooper, the nominal host of the proceedings, stood up and approached the central podium. Flanked by monolithic towers of speakers, he looked like a high priest standing among the pillars of a great, ancient temple.

Windsor

The noise of the crowd set up vibrations in the concrete beneath their feet. The glare of the midday California sun was nothing compared to the stare of a half-million eyes. Even though Marion's rational mind told her the mass gaze was trained upon the dais, she could feel the power of that baleful, burning stare. Everyone was watching and waiting for something uncharacteristic to happen.

As she took her seat, the music died and a vacuum of expectant silence rushed into her head. Peter had been seated between the Archbishop of the Lutheran Church and Father Peterakis from the Turkish Archdiocese of the Greek Orthodox Church. Freemason Cooper, she noted, was seated at the antipodal point of the great circle of seats, which all faced a central podium-cum-altar. Cooper stood, smoothed out his designer apparel, and strode toward the center of the dais.

Marion's mind seemed frozen on a single thought:

If Billy's right, and something is wrong, then what is going to happen?

And when?

Targeno

It might be a very long day.

Unable to simply sit and listen to the endless droning, he had left his original perch and begun a systematic, patterned movement around the rim of the stadium. He paused at various points to check his scanning equipment, but found nothing. This was pretty much as he'd expected. In addition to the normal problems with picking up the kinds of electromagnetic disturbance which might indicate weaponry or surveillance, he had to contend with an electronic stew cooked up by the gigawatts of power generated and broadcast from the mixing bowl of the Palladium.

One thing in his favor—the area was aswarm with security types. Plainclothes, uniforms, private organizations, and even the hapless rent-a-cops had blanketed the Palladium with a net of support and protection that would be tough to penetrate and even tougher to strike from.

Targeno's trained eye told him that, all around him, others were watching. Watching for the odd move, the strange lump in a jacket, the inappropriate piece of luggage or shoulder bag. Not to mention the metal detectors at every access point.

And because of this, Targeno had almost ruled out a single man with a gun. The possibility of a bomb was also remote because of security's extreme awareness of terrorist tactics.

He figured Bevins would wait until Carenza's turn at the podium. The most logical and most dramatic times were the entrance ceremony and spotlight time. Carenza's moment in the sun was drawing near.

So what would it be?

He was hedging his bets toward something extremely sophisticated: microwaves, ultrasonics, maser or laser technology. All these remained definite threat modes.

He moved to his next checkpoint. As he climbed to the uplink platform, he knew the security types were watching him. Pausing next to an uplink dish, he pretended to plug his diagnostic black box into the array's base coupler. He opened his toolbox and acted as though trying to decide which instrument might best suit his current task. As long as he appeared to be performing normal activities, they wouldn't bother him. He calmly assessed his equipment, nodding as he silently approved his selections. What appeared to be innocuous instruments and light power-tools could be snapped together to create weapons of extreme accuracy and lethality.

Targeno smiled. Now there was a great agency buzz-word for you: *lethality*.

He wondered where governments found those guys who sat around thinking up all the snappy phrases like *with extreme prejudice* and *conciliatory invasion*.

But for now, he thought, let's try the KA band . . .

Windsor

God, this was getting boring!

She almost smiled as she realized the prayerful aspect to her last thought. Her video crew had been dutifully recording everything and she had been making some notes on what might prove useful when she sat down to do the edits, but in general, Freemason Cooper's Convocation was a thundering bore.

Marion had been carefully watching the various participants, almost more than she'd been listening to the prayers and speeches. After a while, everybody started to sound alike, and it was more interesting to read the diverse facial expressions. She saw a mixture of ennui, anticipation, and a little enjoyment.

Until she studied the face of the Pope.

The old man's attention seemed fixed upon Peter. In fact, Marion noticed, the Holy Father's gaze never strayed from

Peter's position on the dais. He did not seem fascinated or admiring, but Marion couldn't accurately identify his emotions. The Pope seemed to be simultaneously puzzled, suspicious, and at times philosophical.

Why was he so wrapped up in Peter? Jealousy? Fear? Wonderment as to the true nature of this man who brought miracles to the modern world? She kept checking on Peter, to see if he was aware of the Pope's obsession, but Peter gave no indication he noticed or cared.

Freemason Cooper moved again to the podium. It was time to announce the next speaker. Marion didn't need to check her schedule—she knew it was Peter Carenza.

Bevins

All right, this was it.

Freddie moved slowly from his post near the entrance to the base of the elevated section of VIP seats. He'd activated the laser's A'n'A (aiming and arming) buss just as Freemason Cooper announced Carenza. The only trouble was the goddamned rotating platform. As the target reached the podium to shake hands with the plasticly smiling Reverend, he was a little less than 180 degrees opposite the weapon.

That meant it would not lock onto the target—Carenza's ID badge, with the built-in homing beacon—until the rotation of the platform brought Father Peter around to face the disguised uplink dish. Half an hour max, depending on the angles. Carenza had been allotted forty-five minutes to speak; even though the scheduling was tight, there was still plenty of time for him to catch a good burn.

Bevins stood up, pretending to scan the faces in the crowd, pretending to be doing his job. In the center of B-Section, he caught the eye of Billy Clemmons and nodded. He was thankful the boy had been so conscientious with that badge.

Bevins checked his watch. Pretty soon, now, this place would be jumpin'.

Windsor

The funny thing was, bored as she was by the general tenor of the ceremonies, she found herself captivated by Peter's words. In spite of the months she'd spent listening to his messages and observations, she found his speech inspiring, trenchant, and insightful.

So, apparently, did the other quarter million attendees.

For the first time since the ceremonies had begun, Marion was aware of an almost total absence of noise. Turning in her seat, but trying not to be obvious, she studied the crowd. They were silent, attentive, focused on Peter. She wanted to get their reaction on tape, but was aware of the need to remain unobtrusive.

"Phil . . . ?" she whispered into her lapel-mike. "Can you and Gary get some reaction shots and sound-bites?"

"Of what?" asked her cameraman.

"That's just it," she said softly. "I want to catch the silence, the total attention of this place."

"Okay, I gotcha . . ."

She watched her crew mobilize but keep a low profile as they taped the rapt faces and consummate silence of the crowd. It seemed like everyone in the Palladium had become as quiet as stone. No one stirred, and Marion thought she could hear everyone breathing simultaneously, as though the crowd were one great living thing.

It was eerie. She could feel goosebumps freckling her arms and the back of her neck.

Peter's words soared like a flock of doves. He was soothing and disturbing, beautiful yet fearful. His fertile, deep voice rippled outward through the crowd in concentric, echo-free rings of wisdom. Even skeptics and the outright enemies of his position could not keep from being carried aloft by his message. His theme was the universality of belief, the need for a single, coherent faith in the power and purpose of God. He downplayed the differences between the great number of religions represented; he called for a commingling of spirits so that the prayer which rose up from the Palladium would truly be a single voice. A strong voice. A voice united in faith and power and love.

Despite her role as a journalist, Marion kept being drawn into the mystical experience. She'd been with him from the beginning, had believed he couldn't top the majesty or the failure of Colorado, but he was leaving all past appearances far behind.

A quarter of a million people sat still, beguiled by the young, handsome man. Marion quickly scanned the dais, surprised to see Freemason Cooper and Gerard Goodrop unconsciously nodding their heads. *Everyone* felt the enchantment.

No, not quite everyone, she thought, as her gaze rested upon the Pope.

The look in the old prelate's eyes reminded her of a rabbit's black fear as it stared into the eyes of its predator. But there was a glaze of defiance there too, intense suspicion and suppressed rage. This was not jealousy. Marion recognized the Pope's bottomless gaze for what it was—a perception of true horror.

There was understanding in the old man's eyes, a knife-edge clarity honed by a sudden and single revelation. She had no idea what the Pope saw. She didn't *want* to know.

Targeno

His instrument spoke.

He had been telling himself he had to get up, to change positions, but had found himself listening to Carenza speak. Almost against his will, he allowed the man's words to touch him. Between glances at his equipment, Targeno had studied the others on the dais. Everyone seemed enraptured, except perhaps the Pope. Targeno raised his binoculars to study the Pope's face.

Then the scanner registered a transmission and shattered the spell. The signal was weak but steady and rhythmic. Highly directional, it was an ultrasonic beacon, pulsing regularly at 112,000 cycles per second.

The signature was unmistakable to any high-tech weapons

expert. The beacon operated at a high frequency to ensure great reflectivity over large distances, which would ensure accurate target-locking. Targeno recalibrated his instrument, which automatically triangulated the position of the beacon.

Targeno swallowed with difficulty. The device confirmed what he already suspected. The beacon had been planted on Carenza's body. The signal grew progressively stronger—which meant the dais was slowly bringing the directional beam into line with Targeno's position.

All right, he thought, as he keyed in a new command-set for the scanner, we've found the transmitter. Find the receiver, and we've got the weapon. His mind ticked off the possibilities, trying to eliminate anything that would not fit the pattern for a sophisticated ultrasonic receiver/reflector. That would rule out anyone moving about in the crowd, or even a single man with a hand weapon. The best kill-method employed a stationary receiver . . .

Of course. The uplinks.

The configuration of a satellite dish was the perfect disguise for the sound receiver and the parabolic focusing characteristics of a laser or microwave weapon.

The setup was as elegant as a mathematical proof. Elusive, yet simple and effective. He had to find a receiver attuned to 112,000 cycles, and he had to do it quickly. The arc of the Palladium's rim he needed to cover was roughly fifty degrees of the entire circle. In that space loomed at least twenty uplink dishes, all canted at various angles, homed in upon distant orbiting birds.

And all would remain so, save for one.

The problem, he mused, was finding the one that would react to the ultrasonic beacon. And finding it in time.

Scrambling down from his perch, Targeno ran along the uppermost concourse to the uplink platform at the farthest degree of the rim's arc. Losing precious minutes as he ran, he knew the weapon dish could activate at any moment.

Try not to think about it. Just get the job done.

Despite being in crisp athletic condition, he was breathing hard as he reached the base of the farthest dish and cabled his equipment into the diagnostic serial port at its base. A few seconds of electronic analysis told him all he needed to know—no ultrasonic receiving chip.

Down over the edge of the platform; up and over to the next one. Keep checking. Keep repeating the procedure until either he found the weapon, or until it burned Carenza like a steak on a grill.

Bevins

Checking his watch. Checking his watch. The mannerism was driving him nuts. He was doing it automatically now, and the minutes dragged by with glacial slowness. Carenza was trying to hypnotize him or something like that, but it wouldn't matter. It wasn't gonna work because everything was automated.

Not too much longer. Time was running out. It didn't matter what that guy was saying. Just hurry up and get this crazy fuckin' show done with. Yeah. All over soon.

Clemmons

It was hard to describe the sensation that had suddenly come over him. No way to deal with it, other than just accept it. Ever since the . . . the baby died, Billy seemed to be overly sensitive to everything.

Like right now. Here he was listening to Peter and this ugly notion, like a thorn puncturing his thoughts, kept sticking him. That something was wrong. That something was going to happen and that maybe Peter was in danger.

He had absolutely no reason to feel or think this way, but no matter what he did to suppress it, it just kept coming back . . .

Targeno

Six dishes checked and he was running out of time. The dais continued to rotate Peter Carenza into a direct line with the section of the arena where he worked. The weapon was somewhere in this section, he was sure of it.

Time was running out. Failure had always been life's most bitter pill to him. I don't swallow it easily, Targeno thought as he approached the base of the seventh dish.

"Hey, buddy, what do you think you're doin'?"

The gruff voice broke his thoughts like a hammerblow. Turning, he saw a broad-chested, broad-bellied, black man approaching him. He wore a pair of technician's coveralls, like Targeno's, which identified him as an employee of the Church of the Holy Satellite Tabernacle. The man was very large. Larger than most professional footballers or wrestlers.

Where had he come from? The rim of the Palladium and maintenance catwalks had been totally deserted only seconds ago. Targeno watched the man move closer.

"Hey buddy! I'm talkin' to you!"

"I must adjust the gain on this dish," said Targeno, gesturing upwards. "The guys in the NorthStar 7 booth said they're getting a fuzzy signal . . ."

"Uh-huh. Sorry . . . but I got to keep everybody away from this one."

This was it!

The thought danced madly in his head as the big man reached out to grab Targeno's shoulder with a large, ham-like hand.

"You do not understand," Targeno said calmly in his best American accent. "It's broken. If I don't fix it, it won't run."

"Then it ain' gonna run. I don' care, man. My orders are to keep everybody off that platform, and that includes you."

Targeno looked up at the dish, sighed, added a resigned, slightly overdramatic shrug. Seconds tripped by in his head. Below, the dais continued to rotate. Carenza was practically facing their position. If he turned his body, just faced this way for an instant, it might be enough. The device could trigger any time now.

"All right," he said. "You're the boss."

He started to amble away and sensed the man's neck muscles begin to relax.

"But what am I going to do with this?" Targeno turned back and asked as dumbly as he could muster.

"With what, man?"

The man took a step closer. It was a simple stride forward, but it was the instant Targeno needed. His target was off-balance, even if only for the briefest moment.

"This!" he cried as he stepped into the man's unguarded middle with a swift uppercut. Catching his lower jaw half-open, Targeno's blow clacked the target's teeth together with such force that chips of enamel exploded from his mouth. In a quick follow-up, a short knee-kick to his testicles doubled him over for a stunning chop to the back of the neck.

This series of blows, memorized over a lifetime of dispatching larger, unexpectant adversaries, was usually enough to put a man down and out. But the guardian was so huge, so full of meat and impact-absorbing bulk, that he did not go down, didn't even take his eyes off Targeno.

"Hey, you fucked now, man . . ." The black man forced out the words as he fought to draw his breath, gaining strength and confidence with every second. He even smiled through his chipped teeth and bleeding lower lip. "Now it's my turn."

With the speed of a heavyweight boxer, the man lashed out with a right jab that would have poleaxed Targeno like a slaughterhouse calf had it connected. He dodged the attack, blocking the second half of the combination with a perpendicular forearm.

He simply did not have the time to let the fight continue. He shoved away his opponent and readied himself for a killing blow. The enemy raised his right arm and strode toward Targeno.

Seizing the moment, Targeno spun into the man with a neck-level reverse-kick. The flat of his foot struck the man's larynx squarely, crushing the cartilage and collapsing the target's throat. Despite the great size of his bull neck, the man's head flopped forward as his eyes bulged out like a frog's. He gasped for air with a sound like gas leaking from a balloon. He fell to his knees, thick-fingered hands clawing at his throat, as though to rip away the occluding flesh. His huge chest heaved like a bellows.

It was not a pretty way to die. But then, few are . . .

Stepping over him, Targeno clambered up to the satellite dish. No time to check for the U-sonic chip. This had to be the right dish. With a power-driver, he unscrewed the plate at the base of the dish. As it fell away, it revealed all the confirmation he needed—instead of the videocipher motherboard, he saw the glass-boxed amplifier of a high-intensity military laser. In his long career, he'd sabotaged many a similar device. Grabbing a pair of needle-nose snips, he cut the jumpers that connected the amp to the digital temperature gradient regulator. When the laser was triggered it would either melt down or blow up. In either case, it would not be able to focus its light into a lethal beam.

Leaning back against the metal railing behind him, Targeno drew in what seemed like his full first breath in a long time. His limbs tingled from the sudden drop in adrenaline levels; a wave of dizziness rippled through him.

But there was no time to rest. He forced himself to his feet and climbed down to the maintenance concourse, then dragged the dead man's body as far under the platform as possible. Unless someone was looking for him, he would not be discovered for some time.

Now, thought Targeno, it was time to go down for a closer view of the proceedings.

Bevins

What the hell was taking so long?

The dais rotated with agonizing slowness like a carousel in a dream. The more he tried to detect its movement, the more frustrated and crazy he was getting.

The goddamned weapon should have fired by now.

Looking up at Carenza, Bevins had no doubt his prey was in the right position for a kill. He even chanced looking around to check on the disguised laser. Yeah, it looked good. No problem there.

So what was going on?

He wondered if the microtransmitter in Carenza's badge had failed. No—what was the chance of that? More likely, Billy Clemmons had fucked up. Gotten the badges mixed up? Had some other poor bastard gotten the death-badge?

Questions rattled off his mind like hailstones on a tin roof. He wished now that he had enlisted a couple of accomplices. Every good security operation always had proper backup systems in place. In this case, Fred Bevins was primary and backup. He was it.

Well, he would do what needed doing. For what Cooper was paying him, he could retire for the rest of his life and not give a shit about any of these religious phonies ...

Detecting movement out of the corner of his eye, he turned to the VIP section, where Billy had jumped up from his seat.

What the fuck—?

Clemmons

If he kept listening to Peter's impassioned presentation, he risked being swept away by the sheer power of the words and the almost mesmeric cadence of the delivery. A part of his mind kept fighting to stay alert. The sensation that something was about to happen ... it just wouldn't leave him.

He glanced at Marion. The sun, high above the Palladium's rim, diffused its light through the auburn nimbus of her hair. Her green eyes were so bright they seemed electrified; her milky complexion seemed to glow. He'd never bothered to imagine what a saint like Teresa or even Mary herself might have looked like, but seeing Marion at that instant, he knew. She seemed charged with a special energy.

Was *she* the one in danger, not Peter?

Confused, Billy scanned the crowd. Behind the rows of seats, he saw Bevins, the guy who'd made a big deal about Peter wearing his security badge. Bevins stood out from the crowd like he was wearing neon. He had a completely *weird* look on his face and kept looking at his watch and then turning to look at something up near the rim of the stadium. Then the watch, the rim, then Peter, then back again.

Bevin's face seemed to change, then, as if he'd made a decision. He took a step forward; Billy watched as the man reached into his jacket where a shoulder holster bulged under his arm like a growing tumor.

Got to do something . . . !

Billy heard his own voice, breaking the solemn silence of the crowd, cutting into the spaces between Peter's words. He jumped to his feet and the radioactive gaze of half a million people seared him.

"Peter! Stop! Stop! Get away!" His voice sounded far away, distant, threatened to be absorbed by the monstrous hush of the crowd.

Billy struggled toward the dais, toward the man he had served faithfully for so long. It felt like he was moving through the gelatinous haze of a dream. He moved, but he did not move.

Bevins reacted immediately, moving forward and loosing a dark, ugly handgun from its case, but keeping it concealed. Anger and frustration flickered over his face as he looked from Peter to Billy and back again. Billy watched him break into a jog as he shouldered past confused people in the crowd.

"They're going to *kill* you!" Billy screamed as hands reached out for him. "For Christ's sake, Peter! Move!"

Other VIP's were already clearing out, making a path for the sudden madman, and ducking for cover. The Pope, however, sat rigid in his seat, watching events as though he had expected them. Security types of every flavor began converging on the dais. Billy knew he had very little time—he headed straight for Bevins.

Cooper

Holy Christ-a-mighty, what was that bastard doin'?

Peter Carenza had fallen silent at the first sign of disturbance, though he still stood at the podium. Stunned, Cooper

watched plainclothes and uniform cops materialize all around
the dais as some of the religious leaders began to stir. There
was a sudden swirl of movement and color and noise. It was
hard to see what was happening.

One thing for sure. Freemason knew his plan was shot to
hell.

Clemmons

"Bevins! He's the one!"

Billy leaped over the railing around the box seats, hurling
himself at the stocky man. Bevins turned clumsily to face
him, swinging the portable cannon out like a tank rotating its
turret.

A brilliant muzzle-flash was followed instantly by a hot
sledgehammer just below Billy's rib cage. He was flipped
sideways into the air from the force of the slug, landing at the
base of the dais. Shock waves of recognition and panic rang
outward through the crowd as he got to his feet and stumbled
along the edge of the cinder track.

People were swarming all over him as hands reached down
for him. He heard a feminine voice call out his name.
Laureen? No, it couldn't be. Marion, of course. She sounded
crazy, panicked. He felt lightheaded; his pain seemed to skip
away like a ping pong ball across a tiled floor. He could almost see Time itself stretched out before him like an enormous length of taffy. Everything was slowing down except
the downhill schuss of his thoughts. All around him boiled
the noises of fear and outrage—shouts, screams. Terror. Confusion. Then an explosion—far off, but full of crackling energy. Billy heard it all as though from down the length of a
great tunnel. The bright sky was turning strangely dark. Was
there a storm coming? He wondered idly how that could be.
Laureen . . .

He saw Peter moving toward him.

"Billy . . . hold on," said the voice. A deep, resonant,
soothing voice. He wanted to feel Peter's hands touching his
wounded belly. He knew, somehow, that they would be im-

possibly cool, that they would reach right *into* him ... He wanted to just close his eyes and rest for a while. It would be best. So easy ...

"I'll get you, Billy," said the familiar voice.

Why was it getting so dark?

Targeno

He was halfway through the lower level, wading through the labyrinth of box seats and VIP sections, when the disturbance began. Billy lurched up out of his seat like some puppet with half its strings cut; Bevins blew him away, and all the VIPs scrambled for cover. Then the laser dish kicked in and blew itself into tiny pieces of junk. As hot chunks of metal rained down on the people in the upper deck, they began to stampede.

The crowd surged all around him like whitecaps in a choppy sea. If he didn't move instantly, he was going to be caught up in the current of the mob and held helpless. Leaping over the railings and sluicing down the aisles, pushing errant bodies aside, Targeno reached the cinder track in the midst of ascendant chaos.

He watched security people swarm about, watched Carenza leap down to help his fallen friend. Bevins wheeled about, backhanding with his handgun a uniform who tried to disarm him. The air grew clotted with screams and orders. Clearly no one knew what anyone else was doing.

In that moment of total chaos, when no single track of events had yet assumed control, in that solitary instant—Targeno could act.

Bevins

His whole hand and forearm vibrated from the vicious contact with the rent-a-cop. The mob-panic was rising like a rainy creek. Fuck it, he thought. Got to finish. He'd already decided to use Clemmons as the fall guy. He would say he thought the kid was a secret assassin, and when he tried to take him out an errant slug caught Father Peter as well. It was a hastily cut plan, but just crazy enough to work.

Climbing up to the dais, where he could get a clear shot, Bevins aimed into the center of the circle of bodies which had converged around Billy and Carenza. Billy was still staggering forward, reaching out. Bevins extended his arms, holding the 9mm automatic with both hands.

Carenza suddenly looked up at him as though alerted by some strange sixth sense. There was something about the cold, utter emptiness in the man's eyes that stunned Freddie, kept him from squeezing the trigger.

Carenza turned away from Clemmons, defiantly facing Bevins.

The crazy bastard!

The volley of slugs from the machine pistol ripped through him with such surgical efficiency, Freddie was taken instantly from the realm of thought. Bone-shivering impacts danced up the length of his torso. The last seconds of his life were hastily-sketched sheets of awareness. Pain from the first explosive shell ripping out his crotch in a bloody fireball of soft tissue. Even more exquisite pain as the wet center of his bowels and stomach exploded like a ruptured water balloon. Then dull, black shock as the last two bullets shattered his rib cage and shredded his neck and lower jaw into a fine pink mist. He spun downward into dead dark calm of infinity.

Carenza

He hadn't wanted it like this. His ascendance should not spring from panic, from chaos. But he had been propelled into a reality far beyond the petty concerns of human emotion and rational thought. If he did not take control *now*, he would lose the reins of the crowd's energy and enormous will.

Dispassionately, he watched the already-lifeless corpse of Freddie Bevins dance and shudder from the hail of bullets. Turning, Peter faced the assassin's killer. Long blond hair, and wide-eyed. Dressed all in white, weapon still braced for firing, he looked like an avenging archangel.

Suddenly everyone was pulling out weapons, pointing them at each other. The man in white lowered his gun, and for the first time stared into Peter's eyes . . .

Targeno

There was no sound as the half-million held its collective breath. No sound but the caress of the steel being slipped from shoulder holsters.

Had to be careful now, he thought as he slowly lowered his weapon. Best to ignore everybody but Carenza. He was the focus of everything. He exhaled and looked, as though for the first time, into Carenza's eyes.

Utter coldness filled him in that instant, reaming him, obscenely probing the deepest parts of him. Targeno wanted to vomit. His mind was flooded with the smell of death, the taste of blood, the essence of fear. His thoughts hissed with recognition of abomination like water splashed upon hot coals. Carenza's eyes were endlessly dark. For an instant they reflected no light at all, as though they were two perfect black holes in Carenza's skull—holes into the obsidian reaches of infinity, which drew in all things. A soul-gravity so powerful that even the light of hope could never escape.

Evil in all its myriad forms was no stranger to Targeno. Indeed, he'd courted it, wallowed in it, and had even, at times, *enjoyed* its seductive influence. But as he stared at Peter Carenza, he knew he had just met something that transcended mere evil.

The image of a black rose, unfolding like a dark galaxy, appeared inexplicably in his mind's eye as he stared into the face of the rough beast which slouched toward all the new Bethlehems.

He knew now what had been bothering the Pope.

And even as the nerve-impulse left his brain to move his arm, to raise and fire his weapon, he knew he would fail.

Targeno had long wondered what it would be like to die. He had pondered over this in the abstract for many years.

Now he felt himself withering under the foul breath of its reality, come round at last.

Windsor

Stunned, she tried to hold up Billy's head. As soon as Peter had turned away from him, Billy's eyes had rolled toward the top of his head. So much blood everywhere. So much.

Marion tried to stop the bleeding but kept her gaze locked on Peter. He stood staring calmly at the stranger in white who'd saved his life. The atmosphere danced with pent-up emotion. She could feel a sense of expectancy, of brittle, glass-edged anticipation holding the crowd in its slick grip.

The stranger stared directly into Peter's eyes for an instant, and then, assuming a classic dueler's pose, the man in white began to raise his gun—the gun which had literally shredded Freddie Bevins into something unrecognizable.

Peter raised one hand, as though in warning or denial, but Marion was not fooled. Light burst from his palm like a miniature sun, and the collective voice of the Palladium gasped and screamed like a sudden storm. A tongue of blue-white fire arced from Peter's hand to touch the stranger. Time seemed to slow. Marion could see the lash of force reach across the space between the two men. The flash burned the image into her retinas. The gunman erupted into the purest, whitest flame she'd ever seen. So bright, so hard and clean, she could not look into its core.

And then it was gone.

Like the man in white. In his place tottered an obscene column of charcoal. Greasy smoke wafted upward as it fell, shattering into shining crystals of anthracite.

Not one person in the giant arena spoke or moved. Marion knew they were waiting for a sign from Peter. His power was full-grown now. She could feel it emanating from him in thick, hot waves. She was repelled by its overwhelming aura, and yet irresistibly attracted at the same time. The crowd could feel it too—the same way.

Looking down at Billy, she was surprised to see his lips trembling.

"I need help. I could almost see back there . . ." he said, his voice cracking like a dry twig.

"Billy, please, don't talk now. It's going to be all right," she lied. She wasn't sure what he was talking about, but it didn't seem to matter anymore. Nothing seemed to matter.

His left eye remained fixed on her while the right orb rolled back whitely. He coughed up a wad of blood and his chest spasmed, then froze and went still.

In the confusion which boiled around them, no one noticed that the light that Billy had been was now out.

Marion felt nothing. Nothing at all. This numbness should have bothered her, but she felt so spent, so totally used up, she could feel nothing. She just sat there, with her dead friend's head in her lap, her soul full of emptiness.

The silence in the Palladium became oppressive, choking with foulness. Still no one uttered a sound. No one moved.

Until . . .

On the dais, where knots of stunned security personnel surrounded amazed dignitaries and religious world leaders, one man stirred to his feet.

Resplendent in his ceremonial robes, sparking with a kind of pure, brilliant whiteness, the Pope glared at Peter and stepped forward.

"Io ti conosco," he said. *I know you* . . .

Peter looked at the old man in the tall, mitred hat and grinned lopsidedly. Marion had never seen such an expression on his face, but she knew instantly she didn't like it.

The Pope jerked to a halt in mid-stride. As he grabbed his left arm with his right hand, Marion could see his jeweled ring sparkle in the midday sunlight. The old man pressed both liver-spotted hands to his chest as his eyes widened and his round little mouth popped open. He collapsed into the arms of his onrushing entourage, but Marion knew he was dying.

She'd seen another man stagger and fall under the cold

stare of Peter Carenza. The first time, she hadn't comprehended what was really happening.

But this time, as the Holy Father's body bucked in its final, fatal contractions, she knew who, or *what*, had dealt the death blow.

The signal had been given. The sign had been proffered, and the crowd sprang to life. A huge roaring rose up from the assembly. The great hive of people attuned itself to the overmind of its new ruler.

A figure loomed over Marion.

Looking up at the dark silhouette framed by bright light, she saw Peter extending his hand to her.

"It is time to go," he said.

She did not want to be with him any longer, to go anywhere with him. But she knew she'd given up the right to choose months ago.

"Come," he said.

"Where are we going?" She touched his hand and shivered.

He grinned again. The lopsided smile she didn't like.

"To Rome, of course."

EPILOGUE

Vatican City—Lareggia
December 25, 1999

Turning away from the large television monitor, he dared look at his colleagues. Like pieces of rough stone, Francesco and Victorianna still stared at the screen, as though unable to comprehend what they had witnessed. In all the years he had known the rogue priest, Paolo Cardinal Lareggia had never seen fear in Francesco's face.

Until now.

"What have we done?" asked Victorianna. Tears grooved her cheeks; her thin, white fingers trembled.

Francesco stood quickly, stalked away from them. He stopped at the window, pretended to be looking at something in the street below.

"Who gives a damn at this point!?"

Lareggia pulled his great bulk from the chair, forced himself to move forward. At this moment, he felt extremely ancient. Defeated and drained. Useless.

"Perhaps it was all meant to be like this?" he asked semi-rhetorically. "Perhaps we were merely the instruments of prophecy . . ."

Francesco wheeled on him, his lean face flush. "Yes, Cardinal, but the question remains: *which prophecy are we talking about?*"

They would soon know.

THE BEST IN SUSPENSE
FROM TOR